THE WATER OF LIGHT

Christopher Lewis-Smith

THE WATER OF LIGHT

Typeset in Times New Roman

ISBN-10 1 898368 04 x
ISBN-13 978 1 898368 04 5

Pre-press and production by
Richard d'Alton of 147design

Printed and bound by MWL Group,
Pontypool, South Wales

TRAETH PUBLICATIONS

visit the author's website at: http://web.mac.com/turnedoutnice

THE WATER OF LIGHT

This story is for Arabella, Molly and Louis.

THE WATER OF LIGHT

Contents

Book 1
THE EEL CATCHER

Book 2
DARKWATER

Book 3
LIGHTWATER

THE WATER OF LIGHT

PROLOGUE

Imagine This

You are deep underground. No matter where you turn, no matter if you put your hand right in front of your face, you can see nothing. You are standing on rock, that much you can tell, you can feel it, hard beneath your feet. You reach down and touch it, smooth and cool as a pebble. The damp air stinks of rotten fish.

Above the soft murmur of slowly running water, you hear the faint padding of an animal's paws somewhere ahead of you. Each pad has with it a faint click, the sound of claws on rock, and they are getting louder. Then you hear footsteps followed by a flicker of soft light in the blackness.

The light grows and a wide low cavern takes shape before you. The rock you are standing on is beside an area of dark mud. Across the middle of it a small river flows. Between you and the river the smooth mud is cut with lines of twisting tributaries where small rivulets run. There are other lines too, snaking up from the water where something has slithered across the ground. Some of them run up to where the mud meets the rock at your feet.

From a wooden post, set at the edge of the water, the mud is pocked with a line of deep footprints that lead to a narrow cave opening in the far rock wall. It is from this narrow cave that the light is shining. It is getting brighter and the footsteps are getting louder. You hear a throat clearing cough and the sound of someone sniffing and then spitting. Silhouetted by the light from behind and sending a long shadow over the mud, a huge black dog lopes into the cavern. It stops and looks back. A figure appears, a man carrying a hurricane lamp. He is so tall and thin that it looks as if he might be wearing stilts beneath his trousers. Matted hair hangs from beneath a black cloth wound round his head. His eyes are shadows set deep in wrinkly skin and his mouth is hidden beneath a dark beard that bushes out from beneath his nose and is flecked with slime. There are lines of stitches, faintly visible in the lamplight, on his long leathery black jacket and trousers, as if the material is made from a patchwork of long strips. Over his shoulder hangs a large black bag.

The dog lies down on the rock at the cave mouth, resting its long muzzle on one front paw, and the man walks straight on into the mud. His feet sink almost to his knees, squelching and sucking with each step until he reaches the wooden stake. He hangs his lantern on the stake, crouches down and pulls at a slim rope that trails into the river. A fine meshed metal cage, the size of a small suitcase, breaks the surface of the water and the man hauls it on to the mud. He undoes a catch, opens the top and, thrusting his arm inside, pulls out a long writhing black eel, gripping it by the neck with his powerful bony hand. It coils its body around his wrist leaving glistening slime on his skin. With its white teeth snapping, the creature tries to twist round to bite him. He holds the eel's face up to his own and begins talking to it in a language you don't understand. With his other hand he pulls a long knife from a sheath on the back of his belt. He brings the blade up to the eel's neck and holds it there for a moment. Then in one swift movement he slices the eel's head off, twisting the neck away as a spurt of dark blood jets out. The head falls onto the mud among other decaying eel heads. Small flies rise from the decomposing flesh and settle again one by one.

The eel's body continues to grip the man's forearm and he flicks his wrist several times until the headless creature hangs from his hand, still twisting and lashing, glistening in the lamp-light. He lifts the flap of his bag and pushes it inside. Turning back to the cage he pulls out a second eel and does the same thing again except, this time, he drops the severed head back into the cage. He closes its door and throws it back out into the river where it sinks from sight.

You make a slight movement and the man looks up. He remains still for a moment, looking across at you. He removes his headgear and puts it on top of the post. Then he drops his head and shoulders forward and slides head first into the water, disappearing, leaving the river flowing quietly on as if nothing had happened. Then the water breaks on your side of the river and, silhouetted by the lamp behind him, he reappears and strides on his great long legs through the mud towards you. He is the Eel Catcher, and if the rumors are true, he'll grab your wrists in one hand and your hair in the other and, talking to you in his strange language, he'll drag you, screaming, struggling, and slithering across the mud, down to the river. He'll push your head beneath the freezing water and you'll struggle and hold your breath for as long as possible. Your shoes will brush against the bottom but it will be impossible to get a foothold however much you twist and turn. You will be bursting to breathe, bursting, bursting, until water floods into your lungs. You'll struggle for a few more moments until you lose consciousness.

Pulling your lifeless body from the river, he'll cut pieces from you to feed his dog, though he'll keep the best bits for himself. It is possible, so they say, that he might not have even bothered drowning you first

THE WATER OF LIGHT

THE WATER OF LIGHT

Book 1

THE EEL CATCHER

7

THE WATER OF LIGHT

1
The Side Tunnel

The old plastic football rolled and skittered ahead of the five boys as they chased it along the neon lit Main Tunnel. The slapping of their shoes on the concrete beside the narrow gauge rail tracks, echoed from the walls. Wesley, his ragged jacket flapping behind him, reached it first and kicked it sideways. The ball bounced off the wall, flew over his head and shot straight into a small brick arched tunnel opening half way up the wall on the other side.

The boys came to a halt breathing hard. They could faintly hear the last bounces of the ball from inside the opening.

"Oh no!" Wesley put both hands on his head and gripped his mop of curly hair.

"Exactly," said Martin. "That was our only ball, idiot. And that guy from Stores, what's his name?.."

"Max?"

"Yeah Max, said there weren't any more."

Wesley was looking up to the opening. It was completely forbidden to go down any tunnel unless it was part of work or you had permission. He drew a deep breath. Although it always made him nervous, Wesley was a risk taker.

"Where's that one go to?" he said.

"Dunno," said Martin. "The grid's probably only a few yards in."

Wesley looked up and down the Main Tunnel. There were no supervisors in sight. He unclipped his lamp from his belt.

"Someone give us a leg up, I'm going in."

The other boys looked at each other. Martin, who was the tallest of all the Tunnel Children, linked his fingers together into a step. "Go on then," he said, and then added with a snaky wiggle of his arms and a grin. "Watch out for you know who!"

Wesley fastened the lamp strap around his head, stepped onto Martin's hands and hauled his wiry thin body up into the tunnel mouth.

The battery needed replacing and the beam from his lamp glowed yellowy and dim on the damp walls and uneven floor that sloped gently downwards. The brick arched ceiling was just high enough to walk under, though in places some of the bricks hung dangerously out of place or had fallen completely and lay among the dust and rubble. Wesley made his way carefully forward. He started at a soft scrabbling sound ahead. A rat scuttled across the lamplight and disappeared into a hole in the wall. He breathed slowly out. He'd never got used to the rats.

He edged past the hole and on down the tunnel. After a short distance he saw light shining on the wall ahead where the tunnel curved out of sight. He stopped. If he were caught here he would certainly be in trouble, and for a moment he considered returning quietly back. But he was curious and, cautiously, he edged around the bend. Ahead, silhouetted by an electric light set in the ceiling further along, were the criss-cross metal bars of a grid, held closed with a heavy combination lock. At the base of the grid was the ball but behind it stood a girl, looking down, her long dark hair falling in front of her.

Wesley stayed still for a moment, not sure if the girl was aware of him. Her skirt and jumper, though old like all the children's clothes, were clean and carefully patched. Wesley never thought much about his own appearance but she made him aware of his un-brushed hair and the rip across one knee of his trousers. She suddenly lifted her head and looked at him. The light from his lamp caught her wide face and blue eyes. She looked quickly back down and Wesley turned off his lamp.

"Hello," he said, moving a little closer to the bars. The girl remained silent.

"Hello?" he repeated. "How did you get there, on that side of the grid?"

The girl didn't reply or look up. She remained quite still except for her fingers, which she wiggled stiffly backwards and forwards at her sides.

"My name's Wesley," he went on. "From the work gang."

"Wesley…Wesley…Wesley

"Wesley…Wesley…Wesley…Wesley."

The girl softly repeated his name, looking at the ground to one side. She pulled back both sleeves of her jumper to reveal a watch on each wrist and looked from one to the other.

"Eleven twenty-eight, going back in two minutes. I only listen for ten minutes. Go back at eleven thirty." She kept looking from watch to watch, "sixteen twenty-four now. Going in one minute."

"Going back where?" he asked hurriedly.

He wanted to know how she'd got on the other side of the grid and it was clear that she was about to leave.

The girl lifted her head and stared straight at him.

"Live in the Care Halls. Come here Sundays eleven twenty. Go back eleven thirty." She looked back at her watches; her fingers were still wiggling as if they had a life of their own.

"But how did you get on that side of the grid?"

"I know the little tunnel Wesley. I go through the little tunnel. Go back at eleven thirty."

"Why are you here?"

"I listen to your voices," she said, looking again from one watch to the other. "Going now Wesley."

With that she pushed her hair back over her shoulders, turned and walked away. As she disappeared round the curve in the tunnel, he could hear her repeating, "Wesley… Wesley… Wesley…Wesley," until her voice faded away and he was left standing alone by the grid.

"Wesley!" Dan's voice called down from the main tunnel, "Wesley, you've got to come out."

"Yeah, I'm coming." Wesley picked up the ball and made his way back. He didn't much like the sound of 'you've got to come out', and when he dropped back into the Main Tunnel it was worse than he thought. The four boys were standing together, looking nervous, and in front of them, facing Wesley with his arms folded, stood the grey uniformed Supervisor Pearson.

None of the children liked the supervisors, but Pearson, whom they nicknamed Spider, was one of the meanest. He had narrow shoulders and a long thin neck. He walked like a hanging puppet made of sticks and liked to pull at his bony fingers until they clicked. Everything about him looked brittle but he was as tough as wire.

He had been a teacher, before the meteorites had driven everyone underground, and now he was a supervisor for The Order. If the young tunnel workers didn't do their duty, in his opinion, and work hard enough to deserve their keep, then he issued them with mathematic calculations to *'make their brains work instead'* as he put it. Most of the children had only ever had a few years at school and struggled with the simplest of calculations. Incorrect answers meant working on the weekly maintenance day, the only day off. Being forced to work for six long days a week, mostly unloading the heavy ore rocks, was exhausting enough without anything extra. Pearson was quick to crook his long bony finger at a worker, scribble a calculation into his notebook as they approached and then tear out the page. 'By tomorrow', or 'three days', would be all he'd say, handing the paper to his victim. Wesley was hopeless with numbers and Pearson knew it.

There was a slight smile at one corner of his mouth as he beckoned Wesley over with the long bony finger. He narrowed his eyes to read the number badge sewn onto Wesley's jacket.

"Collecting the ball, eh number twenty one?" He lifted and lowered his heels. "You know very well, that you're not allowed into any side tunnels without permission, don't you...well?

"Yes sir, sorry sir."

"Yes sir, sorry sir," Pearson mimicked. He pulled the notebook from inside his jacket and began writing a column of numbers. "We try to protect you boy. How many times do we have to tell you? These old tunnels can be very dangerous. The least that can happen to you is that you'd get lost, and you know very well that just the sound of your stupid feet can cause a collapse. Furthermore, there's the danger of gas leaking in from outside. And we know...," Pearson looked up and fixed his narrow eyes on Wesley, "...that some of you like to do a bit of *exploring*. If it wasn't for the grids keeping you children in to protect you, you for one, *Wesley,* would have died the slow choking gas death a long time ago, if the Eel Catcher hadn't got you first".

He stepped forward and leaned close to Wesley's face. There were yellow stains in the corners of his eyes and his chin sprouted grey stubble. Wesley smelt his stale breath as Pearson said quietly; "Not that I'd miss you much." He tore the page from the book, folded it in half and pushed it into the outside pocket on the front of Wesley's worn jacket. "One week."

Pearson stepped back and looked at all of the boys. "No more kicking this football around for the next two maintenance days and this tunnel is out of bounds until then.

And, if I catch any of you *exploring* again, you'll spend a week in The Pit. Now get back to The Centre."

The five boys started back towards their quarters. No one dared say a word.

"Wesley!" Pearson called after them. "Give me that ball, you won't be needing it for two weeks."

Wesley walked back and handed him the ball.

"Just how far *did* your ball go down that tunnel number twenty-one?" said Pearson quietly.

"Not far sir. It rolled against a grid."

"Against a grid," Pearson mocked. He looked at Wesley for a moment longer through his narrow eyes and then seemed satisfied. "Go," he said.

Wesley, not daring to run in case he was breaking some unknown rule of Spider Pearson's, walked quickly away. He hated Spider Pearson, and was frightened of him too. As he closed the distance between himself and the others, he remembered the girl behind the grid. He knew that the Care Halls were only for adults who had gone mad from breathing the meteorite gas. Perhaps she'd been poisoned too, but they said children always died from it and besides, she didn't behave like the adults there. He had been to the Care Halls. Everyone had looked half asleep, and besides, he hadn't seen any children.

The girl knew a way past the grids and Wesley was intrigued. He knew the old tunnels were dangerous, but Pearson was right, he did like to explore. It was rumoured that there were air shafts, big enough to crawl through, that ran above the guard's quarters and through the vents you could overhear them talking. What a prize it would be to be to report back to the others what they talked about.

Perhaps the girl would be there on the next maintenance

day, but quite how would he get there, now they were banned from the Main Tunnel, he wasn't sure.

It occurred to him then that he hadn't even asked her name.

2
Katie

"My name's Katie, Wesley," she replied. "No children playing today. S'all quiet today, Wesley."

She stood on the same spot behind the grid looking down at the floor with her arms held straight at her sides and her fingers wiggling stiffly like little running legs. She looked agitated.

Wesley had risked it. He had sneaked down the Main Tunnel, running as quietly as he could in the shadows and stopping at each bend to listen out for supervisors or guards. With a leap, he had managed to get a grip on the edge of the side tunnel floor and haul himself in. He still had Spider Pearson's paper in his pocket. No one had been able to help him with more than a guess at the answers. There were seven calculations. Wesley couldn't answer one.

Katie suddenly looked up at him. "My birthday Wesley, my birthday."

"Oh, happy birthday."

"Got a watch," said Katie. She pulled back a sleeve of her jumper to reveal two watches on the same wrist. Wesley wasn't sure which of the two was the new one.

"That's nice," he said. "Who gave you that?"

"Grandpa," she said, still looking at the watches. "Eleven twenty-four, go back at eleven thirty, go back in six minutes Wesley."

Wesley was keen to find out about the little door that Katie used to get to the other side of the grid, but he sensed that he needed to be friendly first.

"It's my birthday soon, on the sixth of May. I'll be thirteen," he said.

"Tuesday, Wesley."

"What? What's on Tuesday?"

"Your birthday Wesley, it's on Tuesday."

Wesley was intrigued. "How do you know that?"

Katie dropped her hands to her sides again and looked back down to the floor.

"I know numbers Wesley, I know numbers."

He knew she was right because he had worked it out weeks ago. He couldn't help asking her another date. He tried Martin's birthday. "What about the twentieth of September?"

Katie replied without hesitation, "Friday, Wesley."

Wesley had no idea if that was correct. Last year his own birthday had been on a Monday. He tried it, "What about the sixth of May last year?"

"Monday, Wesley," she replied.

He couldn't understand how anyone could work out something like that so quickly? He lifted his hand to the front pocket of his jacket.

"Can you do maths, Katie?"

"I know numbers, Wesley. I can do all the numbers," she replied, still looking down at the ground, her long hair falling forward and almost closing together over her face.

Wesley pulled the paper from his pocket, unfolded it and held it up to the grid. "Can you do these?" he said.

Katie straightened up in one quick movement and looked through at the page. "Sum one is four hundred and eight Wesley. Sum two is eighty-one. Sum three is…"

"Hold on, hold on," said Wesley, "This is fantastic, I have to write it down." He reached into his pocket again and drew out a stubby pencil with his fingertips. "Can you start again Katie? I'm ready now."

He could hardly write fast enough. In less than a minute he

had all the answers. He couldn't tell if they were right but *he* wouldn't get them right anyway.

"Thanks Katie, old Spider Pearson's going to…"

"Eleven twenty-nine," Katie interrupted, she was looking at the watches on both wrists, "going back in one minute. Go back at eleven thirty, eleven thirty Wesley."

"Katie, you know the little door you go through', said Wesley. "Is it in the Care Halls?"

Katie was looking at the ground again. Her fingers were flicking and wiggling. She said nothing.

"Katie," repeated Wesley, "you know…"

"My birthday today, Wesley. My birthday today," Katie looked up and smiled. "I'm fourteen." She looked back at one of the watches and rubbed the glass against her other sleeve. It had been a long time since Wesley had received a present and for a moment he remembered the feeling, the excitement, of getting one. He wished he had something to give Katie, now. He guessed that she didn't know what it meant to him if the calculations were right, and he had the feeling that they were.

"Go back at eleven thirty. Go back then." Katie pulled her sleeves back over the watches.

"Katie, the little tunnel, where is it? Can I go through it? Is it in the Care Halls?"

"Yes, and Katie can fit through the tunnel. Wesley can fit through the tunnel. Adults can't fit through the tunnel. Adults are too big, Wesley." Katie had lifted her head and was speaking straight at him. "I know other tunnels, Wesley. I watch the trucks come in and out. I watch birds. *And* I listen to the children playing here. It's all quiet today. It's all quiet"

He gave a little shake of his head. Birds? He knew there were no birds left. She was obviously making it up.

Katie looked back at her watch and then at the ground.

"Going now," she said, turning. As she walked briskly away she spoke to herself, "four hundred and eight, eighty-one, three hundred and seventy, fifty-four and a half, two, ninety-five and three quarters…" Wesley could still faintly hear her after she'd rounded the bend in the passage ahead. He realized that she was repeating all the answers to his calculations.

As he moved back into the darkness, he found that the his lamp battery had completely given out. He carefully picked his way back through the small tunnel, running his hand along the cold bricks. He had just got to the point where light from the Main Tunnel ahead glistened on the damp walls of the last bend when he froze, hearing the voices of two men, talking at the entrance. One was unmistakably Spider Pearson.

"This is the one he went down. I've checked the maps and the grid is only a short way in. It was the old route to the Care Halls before the Main Tunnel was finished."

Wesley felt dread filling his stomach. It was some relief to hear what Pearson said next.

"Said he'd been to collect a football, and there were a bunch of the little beggars outside waiting. Maybe he had, but that number twenty-one, he's a bit of an explorer. We need to keep an eye on that one."

"Mmm…never know what he might discover" The other voice was nasal and thin. "The Tunnellers recently found two exits that hadn't been gridded. There could be more, and it would be our heads on the block if our little orphans started finding things out."

Wesley remained completely still. Other than his own breathing, there was silence for what seemed like ages. What were they talking about? What might he *find out?* He heard the two men's footsteps begin walking away.

"Might not be too much longer." Pearson's voice was

fainter but still clear. "If the rumours are true, then we won't have to deal with these kids anymore."

"Sooner the better," replied the other man. "A nice little house, that's what I want. There's plenty of 'em still out there." Standing in the dim light, Wesley let out a long slow breath. Like the twenty-six other children, Wesley had never had any reason to doubt what he'd been told by The Order. That because of the meteorite storm and the poisoned atmosphere above ground, he and the other orphans had no choice but to work to help everyone left alive to survive in the shelter of the tunnels. So how could the man be talking about getting a house? And what exactly did he mean by 'not having to deal with these kids anymore'? Something was going on, something that was clearly being kept from the Tunnel Children. Whatever it was, he wanted to find out about it.

He moved quietly to the end of the tunnel. The train tracks beside the road shone where they swept round the bends in each direction. There was no sign of Pearson or the other man.

Keeping to the shadows, Wesley set off at a run back to The Centre, the underground quarters where he and the other children slept and ate. He had lived there since his parents died in the virus that had swept through the tunnels years ago. Wesley was one of the children who had survived and wandered through the tunnels in gangs, starving and dazed, until they were rescued by the grey uniformed members of The Order. Some children were too weak from hunger and grief and within a few days had perished. He, like many others, had recovered under the strict but adequate care then had been put to work by the Supervisors, crushing the rocks of ore that were bought into the tunnels by the train. He was alive, and though the work bruised and blistered, it was bearable. But like all the orphans, he suffered in another way. A feeling of loss lived inside him. An emptiness that no food could fill. And, although the children were a comfort to each other, at night in the dark dormitories Wesley's dreams were beyond comfort and left shadowy memories on waking. He tried to forget them by working until his hands hurt and his fingers bled. Anything to stop them gnawing away at his spirit.

Breathing hard, he reached the small concrete-lined passage that led through to the Common Room of The Centre. He stepped in and walked softly to the steel doorway at the far end. Through the door he could hear the young voices of the others. There was a burst of laughter, a sign that there was unlikely to be a supervisor present. He pushed the door open just enough to peer into the large room. The neon lights in the ceiling were all on, reflecting brightly from the monotonous white tiled walls. At a row of tables and benches, boys and girls chatted, their lamps and water-flasks on the table. Some played cards or board games from the battered selection of cardboard boxes that were given out on maintenance days. Mixed with the sound of quiet conversation, and occasional laughter, was the steady whirr and soft rush of air from the ventilation grills in the walls.

In a half-full wicker clothesbasket with its lid leaning back against the wall, sat Christmas. She was reading a book, one of the precious few that they were allowed from the stores. She held a teddy bear against her. When she was rescued, she had been unable to remember anything except that she had been born on Christmas day. She was the shortest and youngest of all the children.

Beneath the large wall-clock, Martin stood at the work schedule board, just a few paces into the room from the door. Seeing there were no supervisors, Wesley slipped round the door, closed it quietly behind him and walked over.

"Hi Wes," said Martin. "Where you 'bin?"

"Went back to that grid," said Wesley quietly. "Where that girl was I told you about."

"You did?"

"Yeah, and when I was coming out, I heard Pearson and another man talking."

"You overheard them? What were they talking about?"

The twins, Charlie and Bobby, and three other children came over from one of the tables. Wesley wasn't sure he wanted to tell everyone what he'd heard. Not just yet. He needed to make some sense of it himself first.

"Tell you later," he said softly to Martin.

"Hi Wesley," said Charlie. "What've you been up to?"

"Been… Getting Spider's work done."

"You done 'em?"

"Hopefully."

"Work schedule's up for next week." Martin tipped his head at the board. "We've got a cleaning day, look." He ran his finger down a printed list. "Saturday, Cleaning Duties – Care Halls. It'll be like a day off!"

"Martin?" said Wesley suddenly. "What day's your birthday going to be on?"

"Twentieth of September."

"No, I mean what day of the week?"

"Dunno, why?"

"Just wondering."

"Didn't know you cared! Let's have a look."

Martin moved to the end of the board and examined the work calendar that was pinned there.

"Friday. And yours is going to be on a…"

"Tuesday," said Wesley.

"Yeah, that's right."

"When's ours?" The twins squeezed in front of Martin to see the calendar but turned, together with Wesley and Martin, at the sound of Pearson's voice behind them.

"Birthday talk. How sweet." Pearson's hands were clasped beneath his chin, fingers folding and unfolding like crab legs.

"How sad that we won't be able to provide nice cakes for you all." He turned to Wesley. "Do you have something for me, number twenty-one?"

"Yes Sir." Wesley pulled the paper from his pocket and held it out. Pearson pinched it between his finger and thumb.

"Well now, let's see what we have." He opened the paper, took a ballpoint pen from the inside pocket of his jacket and clicked the button on the end repeatedly as he examined Wesley's answers. He looked back at Wesley. His eyes were narrow and angry.

"Who helped you?"

Wesley felt his legs begin to tremble. He tried to stiffen his body so that it wouldn't show, folding his arms tightly in front of himself.

"I.. I did them Sir. No one helped me."

Pearson waved the paper at Wesley's face.

"Oh no. I don't think so boy. You've cheated, haven't you? And if there's one thing I hate, it's a little cheat. And cheats get punished, just like lazy workers. Who helped you, eh?"

"No one sir, no one." Wesley replied. "I just…"

"You just cheated, and I shall find out who helped you."

Pearson turned on Martin and the twins. "Well, perhaps one of you was so kind as to help your little friend here. Which one of you eh?"

The boys looked at one another and shook their heads.

"Wesley did do them Sir." Martin's voice wavered a little as he spoke. "I saw him Sir. He's been working at them all week."

"Liar," Pearson shouted and wagged his finger at Martin. " And liars are as bad as cheats. They also get punished." He glared at the boys, then turned and strode to the nearest table and thumped his fist several times hard on the surface, scattering the dice and counters of a game. The room fell silent and all faces turned towards Pearson.

"Who," Pearson's voice boomed, "has been helping this boy," he swung and pointed at Wesley and turned back, "to do his punishment calculations?"

No one spoke or moved.

"Well?"

There was complete silence for a moment as Pearson scanned the nervous faces. Martin took a step forward.

"I did Sir."

Pearson turned and with two steps he stood glowering down at Martin with his fists clenched at his sides.

"You!" He sneered. "So you're the little helper are you? Being involved in cheating makes you a cheat yourself, wouldn't you agree? Eh?"

"Yes Sir."

"So now we have two liars and cheats," Pearson continued.

"Tell me, *Martin*, the first sum. What was it?"

"I can't remember sir." Martin glanced sideways at Wesley.

"Oh! We can't remember. Well there's no point looking at him. He probably doesn't even know himself. But tell me this boy. Is the big single number that I wrote right here at the top of the page", he poked the paper with a finger, "a two, or a three?"

"I think it was two Sir, though I'm not quite sure, it could have been a three."

"Oh," Pearson's voice went soft. "A two, or maybe a three. Well, let me remind you." He held the page up in front of

Martin's face. There was no number at the top.

"Mmm? Two or a three?" His voice changed back to the harsh sneer and he snapped the page away from Martin. "Liars and cheats. Add those together and the answer is a day in The Pit next maintenance day. I hear that it is particularly cold and muddy down there at the moment." And, you can be quite sure that you will be joined by whatever little bright brain *did* these calculations. I shall find out."

From the corners of his eyes, Wesley could see that the other boys, like himself, were trembling. Pearson put on a sickly smile and looked from one to the other. He turned back to the room. No one had moved or said a word. He bought his hands together in front him and cracked each finger in turn as he spoke.

"Number twenty-one has decided not to reveal his kind little helper, yet. If he doesn't before the end of the week, or if that kind little helper does not reveal his or her self to me, then you will *all* be spending next maintenance day in the Pit." He gave one last crack of a finger and smiled once again. "Carry on," he said, and strode out of the room.

3
The Dead Horse Caverns

Wesley lagged behind the cleaning party as they were led through the poorly lit Care Halls. The guests, as they were called, sat in worn old armchairs and sofas. A few were reading but many just stared into the space ahead of them. Nobody talked. There were no children. Most people seemed roughly middle aged. They hardly registered the scruffy group of children, with their buckets and mops, as they passed through.

In the corner of one of the rooms was a television and DVD player. An old film was playing. The children slowed and hung back watching, unwilling to take their eyes away from the screen. Max Cotton, wearing his worn brown stores coat, was in charge of the party. He paused for a minute before hurrying them on.

For a fleeting moment, Wesley was absorbed by a memory. He is sitting in front of a television with a group of other children, friends from school. But he is not watching it. He is looking out of the window at a black and white cat that is crouched on the top of a thin wooden fence in the sun. It is looking down at something on the other side, its tail flicking one way... and then the other. He wants to go outside but he doesn't want to leave his friends.

"Come on," said Max. "No watching, sorry. There's work to be done, let's get on with it."

The children moved on, craning back their heads to catch a last glimpse of the film. Wesley looked in the opposite direction, and there was Katie, sitting on a large wooden trunk in the opposite corner of the room. He stepped sideways and crouched down behind an armchair. No one noticed. Cotton and the rest of the group moved on into the next hall and Wesley walked quickly over to Katie.

As he approached, she stood up and smiled.

"Katie," he whispered. "The little door. Could you show me?"

She appeared not to be paying attention to what he'd said. She opened the box. It was filled with blankets which she began taking out and putting neatly on the floor. Wesley looked back at the guests. No one seemed to be paying him the slightest bit of attention. Katie removed the last blanket and lifted a wooden board from the bottom of the box.

"Katie," Wesley persisted. "Where's the…"

In the bottom of the box was a hole leading into a round vertical shaft going down through the floor. A metal pipe, roughly cut off flush with the floor, fixed to the side of the shaft with brackets, dropped down into it. He leaned forward and looked down. There was a faint light at the bottom, no more than six feet down.

"Can I go down?" he whispered.

Katie nodded.

"How will I get up if you close the box after me?"

"Knock on the pipe Wesley."

Wesley looked behind him once more and then quickly climbed into the box, squeezed through the hole, and climbed down the shaft, using the steel clamps on the pipe as rungs. He looked back up at Katie.

"Thanks," he whispered. "I won't be long."

Katie smiled down at him and then replaced the wooden board softly over the hole, leaving Wesley alone in the shaft. He climbed down. At the bottom he stepped out onto a pile of rubble in a musty smelling tunnel.

He scrambled down the pile and found that he could just

stand upright. Caged bulbs were set at regular intervals in the brick arched ceiling. Only a few of them were working but enough light remained for him to be able to pick his way along the dusty, rubble strewn floor. It sloped gently downwards, past a narrow wooden door set in the wall on his right, then leveled out and turned a corner. Ahead of him was the grid where he had first met Katie. Only now he was on the side Katie had been. He returned back up the tunnel to the wooden door. It was completely rotten along the bottom edge. With a creak, it pushed inwards on its rusty hinges. Ahead lay a narrow unlit tunnel. Turning on his lamp and brushing aside thick old cob-webs that stretched across the low curved roof, Wesley made his way in. After a short distance, it opened into the side of a natural cave of undulating grey rock, streaked with bands of black. The floor sloped downwards in each direction. Not knowing which direction to explore, he put his lamp on the floor and gave it a little spin. The beam flashed round and ended pointing left. He picked it up and set off to the left.

Everything looked as if it had been smoothed by water. In places, his lamplight reflected off water that ran down the walls, and make the floor wet and slippery. Other than the occasional drip, the only sound was the crunch of small stones under his worn boots, and his own breathing.

After several minutes walking, the ceiling of the cave became lower and Wesley was forced to drop to his hands and knees to continue. His lamp dimmed, the first sign of the battery beginning to die, and he knew that to be safe, it was time to return. A few feet ahead, the floor dropped away, almost vertically downwards, and Wesley lowered to a crouch, curious to see what lay beyond before retracing his steps. In front of him lay a wide chamber, in places only a little higher than his head and in others, three to four times that height.

From the ceiling, white stalactites hung down into fine points and directly below them, growing upwards from the smooth rock floor, stalagmites reached up to them like piles of knobbly candle wax that gleamed wetly in Wesley's dying torchlight.

From the far left hand wall of the chamber a small river flowed out of a cave mouth. It ran silently and smoothly across to where it disappeared into a low opening on the other side. In the centre of the river, moving gently from side to side in the current and tied with a rope to a stalagmite, was a wooden rowing boat.

The ceiling directly above where he stood was higher than the low passage behind him. He stood up on the edge of the slope and reached up to tap his lamp in the hope of brightening up the beam. As he did, the smooth soles of his boots lost their grip on the wet stone. He sat down hard and skated down the slope, unable to stop himself, and landed heavily on the ground below. He gasped at a sharp twinge of pain in his ankle. His lamp slipped sideways from his head and landed on the floor. With the sound of the lens glass breaking, Wesley was thrown into complete blackness.

Sunshine streamed across the room through the tall window in Hillside House. Beyond the glass, the view stretched for miles across the green April countryside. The old hedgerows, now grown into lines of tall bushy willows and hazel, stood out above the overgrown fields where reeds and saplings thrived in the abandoned landscape. The rocky rim of a small meteorite crater pocked the landscape between the house and the distant skyline where the decaying city rose up like dark broken teeth. Above it a band of thin herringbone cloud stretched away westwards across the wide estuary to the mountains.

Colonel William Dove, wearing a neatly pressed camouflaged jacket, stood with his hands behind his back looking out. A bird darted across the window and he flinched slightly. Birds made him nervous. As a child, he had lured a crow into a box and had listened fascinated by the scratching of the trapped creature. But it had escaped, brushing past his face with its stiff bone black wings, flapping wildly to get airborne. It pecked at his right eye as it passed. The eye was not blinded but his eyeball remained permanently bloodshot and his lower eyelid twitched at times, especially when there were birds close by. The disturbance of the weather, caused by the clouds of ash and dust thrown up by the meteorites, had decimated the bird population, but now that the air was clear again, they were starting to get more numerous.

He lifted a pair of small silver binoculars to his eyes and panned slowly across a wide stretch of tarmac less than a mile from the bottom of the hill.

The old airship port had remained mostly free from damage, though one of the giant hangers, the closest to the meteorite hit, had collapsed. Gorse and weeds now grew between the rusting steel uprights and, when the wind blew, the twisted roofing sheets that remained flapped and banged against one another.

Dove followed the course of a lorry returning from the long tubular gas tanks that bordered the port. It passed the bright flickering pinpoint of a welder where men from the ground-crew were working. He blinked and panned away, across to the centre of the port, to where a huge steel framed tower held the nose of the Titus, The Order's airship. Its long grey flanks, twisting gently in the breeze, filled the lenses of the binoculars. As it did, The Order's emblem, a black eagle with its wings outspread against a red circle, emblazoned on the side of the airship, dipped and rose in the sunlight.

A buzzer sounded on the desk and Dove turned back into the room. He pressed a small button on the intercom and leaned towards it.

"Yes?"

"Chief Supervisor Pearson here to see you, Colonel," replied a cheery woman's voice.

"Ah yes, send him in. Thank you Janis".

Dove tugged at the cuffs of his jacket and, flicking a speck of dust from the lapel, dropped into his leather swivel chair. He glanced at the small metal model of the Titus that stood on the side of his desk and then began examining some papers before him. Two knocks sounded on the door.

"Enter."

Dove continued to leaf through the papers as Pearson carefully closed the door behind him, approached the desk and stood waiting.

"Pearson". Dove shuffled the papers into a neat pile and then looked up.

"Yes Colonel".

"You've lost one of them".

"Yes Colonel, number twenty-one. Wesley Pike."

"How?"

"From the Care Halls, Colonel. From a cleaning party. We've not been able to find any…"

"Who was in charge of his party?"

"Cotton Sir, Head of Stores".

"Cotton. Mmm. But you have overall responsibility for these work parties. Is that not so?"

"Yes Sir".

"Pearson." Dove leaned back in his chair. "We've achieved a great deal. However, many challenges still lie ahead of us if we are to build a secure future. I rely on Supervisors like yourself to run a tight ship. Escapees are loose cannons. If they reach the outside, and the message gets back that, you know, all is not quite so bad after all out there, then it would obviously become very difficult to maintain the smooth running of power production. Ultimately, everything we are doing, tough though it is for some, is for the benefit of all of us. I'm sure you understand."

"Yes Colonel, completely."

"I assume the boy is tagged."

"Yes Colonel, they all are."

"Then it shouldn't be too difficult to find him, should it?"

"No Colonel. I've already sent out a tracking party."

"Good. What will you do when you catch him?"

"Brick him up Sir, with your permission."

"Brick him up." Dove sighed and shook his head. "Always seems so… cruel. But if he's been out, then I just don't know what else to do."

He rose from his chair and walked over to a leather armchair in the corner of the room. A well-fed white cat lay curled up on the seat. He picked the animal up, crooked it comfortably in one arm against his chest and stroked it. It began to purr softly. Pearson remained standing beside the desk.

"Now that you're here Pearson, I'd like to talk to you briefly about schools."

"Schools Sir?"

"Yes, schools. I know that your background is in education and I would like you to consider founding The Order's first school."

"For the orphans Sir?"

"Sadly no. I don't think we can afford to do that. I'm looking ahead Pearson, to the new world, to the futures of children of The Order. You are aware of Saint Terresas, the settlement over the estuary?"

"Yes of course Sir. The Horse People."

"Indeed. The Horse People. Rather a fine name for a bunch of hippies turned horse breeders I always think. However, in terms of their skills and assets, they have much offer. An undamaged, and might I add a rather picturesque, town, plus fertile agricultural land and the knowledge of how to farm it. You are probably aware of this. However, simply put, they are squatters, moving in when the original population fled underground. I can only imagine that they must have weathered it out in cellars and suchlike. Quite how they avoided the virus I don't know. Luck we can only assume." The cat continued to purr. It stretched out a front leg and hooked its sharp white claws into Dove's shirt. He carefully unhooked it and brushed at the fabric with his hand.

"Up until now, I have been reluctant to take the town by force. Not that we would have any trouble doing so, but because I had no wish to inflict casualties. The Horse People are a part our future workforce. We need them."

"And the orphans Colonel?"

"With a new home for The Order in Saint Terresas, I will scale down our operations here. The tunnels beneath us will become no more than a garrison, like the North Garrison close to the bridge. The orphans will no longer be needed."

"And the school Sir. That would be at Saint Terresas?"

"Indeed it would Pearson. And I'm sure you will make a wonderful job of it."

"And may I ask, Sir, is all this in the long or the short term future?"

Pearson put the cat carefully down, unhitching its claws

from his sleeve again and returned to his chair.

"Short term, Pearson. Let me put you in the picture. Doctor Thornberry and I have been trying to obtain a certain form of water. Lightwater, you may have heard talk of it."

"I have heard the Doctor mention it Sir."

"Indeed. Lightwater was discovered, or should I say re-discovered, by a certain Mikhail Kuroski shortly before the meteorites."

"The gentleman in the Care Halls Colonel? The one that has his granddaughter with him?"

"That's correct. Doctor Thornberry worked with him on the project and I went to great lengths to ensure his safety here with us. The water has huge medicinal potential, so we understand. As part of their research, Kuroski and Thornberry also looked at another potential of Lightwater. The reversing of its polarity into its opposite, Darkwater. Darkwater has the potential to subdue, to make people completely docile and subservient. In effect, it's the perfect weapon for our needs. Thornberry knows that Kuroski has a supply of Lightwater somewhere, but the old man has gone senile and we can't get the information out of him. I want it. And if this supply still exists, then we shall find it sooner or later. However, we can't wait any longer. Our stores are dangerously low, as you are no doubt aware, and so I have decided to take Saint Terresas by force. There you have it Pearson.

"So, I am looking ahead. Good homes for our people. A good supply of food. The establishment of new territory for The Order, and of course, amongst other things, a school."

"I shall do my best for The Order Colonel," said Pearson.

"Good. I'm sure you will Pearson. In the meantime catch the boy and send me your report. Oh, and do include his escape route. I'm sure you'll be able to persuade him to tell you. I'll leave it all in your capable hands."

"Thank you Colonel."

Dove looked back down to the papers on his desk. Pearson continued to stand.

"Was there anything else Pearson?" Dove asked without looking up.

"Er, no Sir."

"Then that'll be all, thank you."

Pearson left the room, closing the door carefully behind him. Dove reached forward and closed his fingers around the model airship. Slowly, he lifted it vertically upwards from the desktop and, tipping it slightly sideways, flew it slowly away as far as his arm would reach.

A drip landed on Wesley's head and the cold water ran down through his hair. The blackness was so complete that he couldn't even see his own hand inches from his face. He guessed he had been in the chamber for an hour, or could it be two? He had tried again and again climbing back up the slippery slope in the darkness, but each time he had slithered back down onto the gravel. It was impossible to get a grip. Even if the supervisors did send out a rescue party, how would they know where he'd gone?

Somewhere in front of him the river gurgled quietly in the darkness. His ankle ached from the fall. He wished he'd just stayed in the Care Halls. He wanted to be found now. Whatever punishment awaited him, he would take it, if someone could just find him.

He had began to shake, partly from cold and partly from the thought that no one would find him. It might be only a matter of time before he became, like all the others, and like his parents, just another pile of bones and rotting cloth left forever in the darkness.

Like the other tunnel children, the memory of the terrible fate that befell his family was buried away deep in his mind. To forget was to survive. But now the memory of them wormed itself back into his thoughts. He remembered their haggard faces when the sickness took hold of them and how they'd asked him to find water for them. And he remembered how when he returned they lay motionless and how he had desperately wanted to believe that they were only sleeping. He knew that somewhere in the labyrinth of tunnels and caves their bones probably still lay in the silent darkness. Perhaps it was near here, he didn't know. The utter despair that he had felt then, began to creep back into him. It was as if the blackness that surrounded him in the cavern was seeping into his mind. He wondered if it would hurt if he died, and how long it would take. And afterwards? What would happen then? He shivered violently and blew out a long breath, willing his thoughts to blow out of his head. He didn't want to die. If he shouted loudly enough, perhaps, just perhaps, someone might hear him and he would be rescued.

He filled his lungs to shout and just as he opened his mouth he heard a splash… He held his breath and listened. There came more splashes and then a faint light appeared shining on the river from upstream. Its reflection skittered about on the rocks above. The shout that he had been about to give was still a lungful of air and without meaning it too, a short squeak escaped from his mouth.

The whole cave filled with a deep-throated growl. The light was extinguished and all that Wesley was aware of was growl after growl echoing around the chamber. Shaking with terror, he pushed himself to standing against the rock wall, ready to kick and punch into the darkness.

The growling stopped and for a moment its echo hung in

the rocky corners of the cavern.

Silence.

Then a breathy whisper came from the river tunnel.

"Who there?"

The growling, low this time, started again.

"Shhhh, dolce", the voice came again. The growling stopped.

"Who there?"

As much as the shaking in his body would allow, Wesley held himself ready, fists clenched tightly in front of him.

The dim light returned and, accompanied by more splashes, began to grow from the mouth of the river tunnel.

4
THE EEL CATCHER

Anguillaro Ferrarazi could see in the dark like a cat. He needed only the faintest light to see in the underground caves that had been his home since the virus.

He had been a water engineer, an expert in dams, sluices and pumps. He was an exceptionally tall man, who had always kept himself to himself, preferring to live quietly with his wife, away from attention. His skills, however, had been well known, and those that needed them sought him out knowing that he was not just an expert, but that he was generous with his time and advice. He'd been doing consultancy work far from home, free of charge, advising on the digging of the tunnel shelters, when the meteorites struck before they were expected. He witnessed the impact of one of the first small hits. When he had regained consciousness, dazed and half deafened from the blast, he saw that what had been a railway station and its surrounding buildings, had become a huge deep smoldering hole. The departing train blown off the track like a shoelace.

He could find no survivors in the immediate area. The nearby riverbank was broken and water poured into the gaping crater. Fish that were not swept into the huge swirling pond were left to die, floundering in the mud along miles of empty riverbed. Only the eels survived, snaking across the sodden ground in the rainstorms that followed, to find new pools and streams. The rain washed the airborne dust down, turning everything to a slippery stinking mess.

Along with the rest of the population, Anguillaro had moved down into the unfinished tunnels. But when the virus came, killing his wife, he took to living alone in the Dead Horse Caverns, avoiding the newly formed Order and melting into familiar shadows if ever people passed. For food he learned to catch eels and frogs from the underground river and when his clothes wore out he sewed himself a suit from eel skins. The smooth black leather turned slimy when wet, allowing him to slither through narrow places in the underground labyrinth of caves.

On occasions, parties of tunnel workers had caught glimpses of him, and once, a search party looking for a lost worker disturbed him whilst he was emptying his eel trap cages. He melted away into the shadows, leaving them to examine the traps in the powerful flashing beams of their lamps. When tunnel workers became lost and never returned, stories grew about how they had been murdered and eaten by the wild underground man. He became known as The Eel Catcher and the supervisors spread rumours about him among the orphans. They described how he skinned and ate eels while they were still alive and how, if he caught you, he would do the same to you and feed the leftovers to his huge black dog. Even the supervisors themselves had begun to believe the stories.

And so, when Anguillaro stepped out of the water into the cavern and walked towards him, Wesley was terrified. After the hours of darkness, even the dim light of the tall man's old hurricane lamp left Wesley in no doubt that this was The Eel Catcher. Beside him walked the great black dog.

Wesley scrabbled on the ground for a stone and hurled it at him. The Eel Catcher ducked and it hit the rock behind him, splashing down into the water and sending reflections from the lamplight rippling across the stone ceiling. The dog barked and the man reached forward and gripped his collar. Wesley, trembling, stooped down again, desperately searching for another stone.

"Ey ey ey, woa. No stones." The Eel Catcher's voice was deep, as if it came from the back of his throat. "No stones. Ey... you just a boy. No stones boy, no stones".

Wesley backed across the rock wall to the place where he had slid into the cavern. He turned and desperately began trying to climb the slippery surface once more. The light from behind him grew stronger as he clawed for finger holds to haul himself up the slope. Somehow, he managed to climb a few feet up the slope. But his worn old shoes could not grip. He slipped and slid downwards, face to the rock, landing hard on the rock floor. He felt a stab of pain in his ankle. He knew before he turned that the man was right behind him. He shielded his head with his arms.

"Ey ey ey...easy, easy you boy, easy".

Shaking, he turned slowly round.

The man stood holding the lamp in front of him. His fingernails were long and curved. He was the tallest, thinnest man Wesley had ever seen and was dressed from neck to foot in a rough suit of strange black material. It looked wet and slimy and glistened in the light. He carried a bag of the same material over his shoulder and Wesley thought he saw it moving, as if there was something alive inside. The man wore a thick turban-like hat, in which Wesley thought he could see the glint of glass, and his hair and beard, which also glistened with slime, was matted and long. His face was as thin as the rest of him and his nostrils sprouted dark hair. Perched on his big arched nose, were a pair of round spectacles through which his eyes bulged beneath thick wild tufts of eyebrows. He smelled strongly of fish. The man looked aside to the great black dog whose long body swayed from side to side. It was wagging its tail. It stepped forward and with its enormous raspy tongue, licked Wesley's hand. Wesley pulled his hand back quickly.

"Ey, Sargazzo is please to see you". The Eel Catcher put his hands on his hips. "What you doing down here eh? Explore or escape?"

Wesley's heart was still beating fast. He wasn't sure what story would be best. It was a gut reaction to tell the truth.

"Escape," he blurted out in a shaky voice. "I found a way to the other side of the grids and…and, I found this tunnel and I got lost".

"Lost eh?"

The Eel Catcher's knees began to bend forward and he sank straight downwards and sat on his heels. The dog sat beside him while he put the lantern carefully on the floor before him. Wesley's voice was unsteady.

"I'm stuck. I can't get out. My lamp's broken".

"Lamp broken. Mmm…But they find you, oh yes, they find you. I know them, Supervisor eh? Oh yes, oh no, they don't want children finding out and oh yes," his gaze fell on Wesley's number badge, "they can find you no problem".

"You're The Eel Catcher aren't you?" said Wesley, trembling uncontrollably.

"Ha yes, The Eel Catcher, is me". He leaned towards Wesley bringing the fishy smell with him. "My real name? Anguillaro Ferrarazi and this," he rubbed the dog's head with his hand, " is Sargazzo. Who are you?"

The dog lifted its ears and cocked its head quickly to one side.

"My name's…"

"Ssh…" The man held his finger up to his lips.

Wesley held his breath and listened. A drip landed on the rock behind him but he could hear nothing else. The Eel Catcher whispered quickly.

"You want them to find you?"

"No".

"Then come with me...number twenty one".

He rose in exactly the same way as he had sat down, his great long legs scissoring him straight up from the floor. He turned, and with the dog at his heels, strode across the rocky floor to the boat was moored in river. Wesley took a deep breath and remained with his back to the wall. The Eel Catcher stopped and turned back to him.

"Eh," He hissed. "You wanna me help you? Or you wanna them get you?"

Wesley didn't move. Sargazzo left the Eel Catcher's side and trotted back with his head down and his long tail wagging. He pushed the side of his head against Wesley's leg and Wesley cautiously put his hand down and stroked the dog's ear. The fur was warm and smooth against his hand. The Eel Catcher turned and continued towards the river. Sargazzo padded a few steps away then stopped and looked back. He tipped his head to one side and lifted his ears a little. To Wesley, in that moment, it was the friendliest look in the world. He took a deep breath, pushed himself off from the rock, and limped quickly after him.

The Eel Catcher untied the rope from the stalagmite and pulled the boat towards them, holding it steady as Sargazzo jumped in and settled himself in the stern.

He turned to Wesley and cocked his head to the boat.

"In, quickly".

Wesley clambered in and sat on the seat in the middle.

"No no, here, here". The man hissed, pointing to the bows, and Wesley climbed forward into the narrow prow.

Pushing the boat away from the bank, The Eel Catcher climbed aboard with the lamp and folding his great long limbs beneath him, sat on the floor.

"Down, down," he whispered, "head down boy".

Crouching down in the bow of the small boat, Wesley could just see above the gunnels. The awkward position made his ankle hurt but he held still. The Eel Catcher adjusted the wick of the lantern leaving no more than a faint glow. The boat rocked gently as the current began to carry them downstream.

Then came voices and footsteps echoing in the cavern. Beams of light flashed across the ceiling, casting moving shadows from the stalactites. It grew lighter and the voices louder. The beams lit the river where moments before they had boarded the boat. Flashing this way and that, they moved rapidly across the water towards them.

A great darkness rushed above Wesley's head and the voices and footsteps cut to a faint murmur against the sound of water slapping the hull. The boat had entered the low tunnel, and as the entrance receded, Wesley could see that the chamber behind them was flooded with light from the powerful lamps of the tracking party.

5
Anguillaro's Restaurant

"Head right down now," hissed The Eel Catcher.

Wesley squeezed down as low as he could in the cramped prow of the boat. He was breathing fast and he could feel his heart thumping beneath his ribs. In the dim lamplight he could see the rock ceiling passing fast only inches from his head. Several times the wooden prow ground against the roof, shaking and twisting the small boat as the current carried it along.

Then the ceiling rose a little higher and the current eased. The Eel Catcher sat up onto the seat and rubbed his knees.

"Is ok now, you can be up", he said in a low voice. "But quietly, quietly. Sound can travel very well for those who have the ears to listen. Now, there is something important to do".
The Eel Catcher turned the wick of the lamp higher and Wesley saw that they were floating on an underground lake. The ceiling was low; he could have reached it by standing. Ahead the water spread out into the dark distance and in places, thick pillars of rock rose up like tree trunks from the surface, curving outwards at the top where they joined the roof. To one side there appeared what looked like a muddy beach in front of a cave mouth. The Eel Catcher pointed to it.

"That cave. It joins up with the one you came down. The beach is where they'll come to find you. You are tagged, tagged. I know these things. They can follow you wherever you go", he pulled a dull bladed knife from a sheath on his belt, "but I can stop them finding you, oh yes".

Wesley quickly stood up, rocking the boat. The sight of the knife in man's hand made him realize what a stupid decision he'd made. He should have stayed in the cave. He'd been tricked. He'd been warned about The Eel Catcher and now he'd let a dog lead him to this. His legs were shaking so much that the boat was sending jittery little ripples out across the surface. The water looked dark and deep but he readied himself to jump.

"Don't come any closer Eel Catcher... I'll jump".

"Shhh. Keep your voice down. I swim better than you anyway".

"Keep away from me," Wesley's voice trembled. He prepared to jump from the side of the boat. The muddy beach was not far away. Though he wasn't much of a swimmer, this was the only chance he had.

"Ey, stupid," The Eel Catcher whispered, "the tag is behind your number badge. Here, take the knife, unpick it yourself". He offered the knife handle to Wesley, "get on with it, number twenty-one".

With a shaky hand, Wesley took the knife and managed to unpicked a few stitches at the side of the badge with the sharp point. He slid his finger and thumb in and pulled out a small metal disc, no thicker than a piece of paper.

"That's the one, yes yes. They used to put them into your shoes, ha, but they kept wearing away. Then they stitched them in there. I know these things, oh yes".

The Eel Catcher held on to the side of the boat and stepped straight out into the water. It only came up to his knees. He reached down beneath the surface, lifted out two large flat stones and held one out to Wesley.

"On here, put it on here".

Wesley placed the disc on the wet stone and The Eel Catcher put the other stone on top of it. He reached into the boat and pulled out a length of cord with which he lashed the stones together. He put them into the boat and climbed back in.

"Now we need deep, deep water; that's where they will think you will be".

He lifted the lamp onto the seat and shuffled himself down until he lay on his back in the bottom of the boat and, lifting his long legs into the air, he placed both feet on the rock ceiling above and started to walk. Sargazzo's friendly face, watching Wesley through The Eel Catcher's legs, remained perfectly still in the stern as the boat travelled out into the lake.

"Tracking party will locate your tag. They will think that you were taken by the river and drowned, but, they will be wrong, ha!"

The water was completely black and Wesley had no way of knowing how deep it was. The Eel Catcher kept walking but still the far side of the lake was lost in the gloomy darkness. Ripples caught the lamplight and threw it onto the ceiling, surrounding them in dancing zigzag waves of light. The smooth rock passed slowly on above his head and Wesley's fear began to recede. He wondered if this all might be a dream, and that he would wake up at any moment in the dormitory with the other tunnel children.

"Here", the Eel Catcher said quietly. "Is very, very deep. Throw in the stones".

Wesley lifted the rocks, leaned over the side of the boat and released them. With a splosh, they disappeared instantly into the inky blackness.

The Eel Catcher continued to walk the boat across the water. "What is your name?" he said quietly.

"Wesley. Wesley Pike. Tunnel boy twenty one."

The Eel Catcher chuckled.

"Pike, ha. Good name. Well, Wesley Pike, Anguillaro at your service".

"Angua…Angualer..rado?"

"Just call me Laro if it's easier, or The Eel Catcher, ha, I don't mind!"

46

Wesley's breathing settled. Although he had no idea if he could trust this strange man, there was something reassuring as well as frightening about him He hadn't forced him to get in the boat, and anyway, how could a dog like Sargazzo belong to a murderer?

"Laro?"

"Yes Wesley Pike".

"Where are we going?"

After a silence the man replied:

"You hungry?"

"Yes".

"You need a new lamp?"

"Yes".

"Ok… then we go and find you a lamp, maybe we find you a few other useful things. But, ha, first we go to my restaurant."

"Restaurant?"

"A place, Wesley Pike, where they serve the best eels in the world."

Anguillaro lowered his legs and pushed himself back up to sitting. He held up the lantern and Wesley saw that the roof was lifting and they were drifting towards a grey stony beach in what looked like the mouth of a jagged vertical cave. The bow of the boat rode up as it grounded on the stones and Wesley climbed out. Anguillaro shook the base of the lamp beside his ear then handed it to Wesley.

"Enough oil. You take this now, I have other lights."

He reached up and fiddled with his hat. Two beams shone out, one from each side, illuminating everything except what was directly in front of him. He tapped his fingers to the front of the hat and a third beam flickered and then shone out ahead of him. He turned to Sargazzo:

"Come on boy".

In spite of the extra lights from Anguillaro's hat, Wesley could see little of the high roof of the vertical cave. It was, however, so narrow in places, that he had to pass with his shoulders twisted sideways. Rough gravel crunched under his feet as they made their way on. For every stride of Anguillaro's, Wesley took two, and there were times, where the cave was wide enough, and despite the fact that his ankle still hurt, when he had to run a few steps to catch up. However near or far he was behind The Eel Catcher , the smell of fish that wafted behind the tall man was almost overwhelming.

After what seemed to Wesley like miles, the floor changed to solid rock and began to slope upwards. They reached a place where the cave widened out. To the left, part of the roof appeared to have collapsed leaving a pile of rough boulders against the side of the cavern. The ceiling above them rose away into darkness and water dripped down and splashed off the rocks. Anguillaro stopped beside the tumble of boulders and scissored down to his knees beside a small dark hole between two of the rocks. He looked back at Wesley.

"Go in backwards and mind your head." He said, and feet-first he disappeared into the hole. The light from his turban shone brightly from inside, but the cave around Wesley dimmed to the soft light of the hurricane lamp that he held. Sargazzo hunched his back down and scrambled in after Anguillaro, blocking the light from inside. For a moment Wesley was alone again and other than the soft scrabbling of stones from the hole and drips landing on the stones, the cave fell quiet. He looked back at the narrow cave from where they had come and then back to the hole in between the boulders. Anguillaro's light was just a dim flicker from inside.

He could turn and run now, get back to the boat and escape. He had a lamp. The oars were in the boat. He could find the muddy beach across the lake. He turned, began walking back, and then stopped again. He felt frightened but also excited at the same time. If the Eel Catcher had intended to get him then he wouldn't have gone through the hole first. He had no idea what he was letting himself in for but, it was precisely because he had the chance to run back, Wesley decided not to take it.

He returned to the hole, crouched down and crawled feet first into it. The floor was wet and sloped sharply downwards and, lying on his front, he slithered backwards, holding the lamp as best he could to stop it banging on the stone. His feet met with level ground again. He carefully turned and found that the ceiling was once more high enough for him to stand. Anguillaro and Sargazzo were waiting for him. They were in the entrance to what appeared to be a man made tunnel cut from solid rock. The sides and arched ceiling were criss-crossed with chisel marks and the smooth floor was littered with little stones. The tunnel ran level for a short distance and then rose steeply upwards. Narrow steps had been chipped out of the stone and pitted iron railings, held fast in iron pegs driven deep into holes in the stone, ran up the sides.

Anguillaro strode on ahead, his long legs taking the steps two at a time and his glistening black bag swaying at his side. Once again Wesley was sure he noticed the bag moving as if it contained some living animal. But he could not look at it for more than a glance at a time, it took all his concentration not to fall behind and to keep his footing on the steps as they climbed higher and higher.

Without warning, Anguillaro and Sargazzo stopped and Wesley stepped up beside them. They had reached the top of the steps. Not six feet ahead, the floor ended abruptly at the edge of a vertical ravine. Above their heads, the ravine continued upwards, the sides narrowing together. Peering up into the gloom between the closing rock faces, Wesley could see huge boulders lodged between the rock faces. They looked as if they might fall at any moment. Drips of water sailed silently down past them into the dark depths below.

In front of them, spanning the ravine, was an old iron bridge. The railings on each side were corroded and a section on the left side was missing altogether. The wooden decking looked sound, and, in places, as if it might have been renewed. The bridge ran straight across to the same man-made tunnel continuing on the other side.

"Only one at a time," Anguillaro held his finger up. "One at a time, Sargazzo, go."

The dog obediently set out across the bridge. The decking tipped a little to the left as he passed the middle then straightened as he reached the far side.

"You now Wesley Pike. Careful now".

Wesley set out across the wooden planks. At the point where the railings were missing the bridge creaked and suddenly tipped sideways as it had with Sargazzo, but much further. He held tight to the remaining railing.

"Ey. Go on boy", Anguillaro called, "hurry up".

Wesley walked on to the other side and the bridge leveled itself with another creak.

Anguillaro walked fast but softly. The bridge tipped sharply but he strode confidently over and on into the tunnel opening beyond. Wesley fell in behind him. Sargazzo ran on ahead.

After another flight of steps, the cave floor leveled and opened into a chamber with a wide flat gravelly floor. A narrow chimney-like tunnel twisted up overhead into darkness. The place smelt of smoke, mixed with an odor of fish that was even stronger than that of following behind Anguillaro. In the centre of the floor was a plinth of carefully laid grey stones on top of which ash and charred wood spilled to the edges. A pile of fire-wood was stacked neatly close by.

Against one wall of the chamber, wooden boxes, large and small, were stacked high against the rock. Beside them was a large metal trunk. Beyond the raised fire, beside a table, a framework of sticks held up a long wooden rack. From the rack there hung dozens of gutted black eels of different sizes. Bunches of dried skins hung from one end.

Anguillaro slipped the bag from his shoulder and lowered it to the ground. "Tonight's special dish is Anguilla Fuoca." He tossed a box of matches to Wesley. "Now Wesley Pike, fire please".

Wesley is holding a matchbox in one hand and a match in the other, watching his father set small twigs over crumpled paper. He strikes the match but it doesn't light and the stick breaks. He is holding it too close to the end, his father says. He tries another match and it flares into life. He puts it to the edge of the paper, which catches alight. The flame spreads, eating the paper with a brown edge, and then grows into bright yellow flickering fire.

Caught unexpectedly by the memory, Wesley remained still for a moment. Then he shook his head briskly and looked around for some paper. He found twigs and pieces of bark but nothing to put beneath them. As if he had read Wesley's thoughts, Anguillaro handed him a scrunched up bunch of dried grass and then walked away over to the rack.

He soon had a small fire going. Showers of tiny sparks leaped into the air as he added more sticks to the blaze, lighting up the cavern. He looked over at Anguillaro. The man had turned off all but the front lamp on his turban and was facing away, busying himself with something at the table, silhouetted against another hurricane lamp on the wall in front of him. His shoulders and long arms were moving smoothly and gracefully as he worked. His body tipped and swayed from one side to the other, and he quietly talked to himself.

The flames of the fire grew, lighting up more of the cave. The black bag, lying at arm's reach on the stony floor, caught Wesley's attention again. In the firelight, he saw that the sides were moving. It was as if hands were slowly washing themselves beneath the strange black fabric. He reached over and took the corner of the flap between his fingers. It felt cold and slimy. He opened it. Immediately, a curve of wet black piping, as thick as his wrist, pushed out of the open bag and began to move as if being pulled at one end. Then the head of an enormous eel snaked out towards his hand, its black eyes reflecting the yellow flames of the fire and its open mouth showing rows of white needle teeth. Wesley scrambled backwards, unable to hold back a cry of fright.

"Ah ha. You so hungry you can't wait eh?" Anguillaro strode over from the rack. "Let me tell you, Mr. Pike, is much better cooked, yes, much much better. Ha!" With that, he reached down and grabbed the eel by the neck and pulled its long writhing body from the bag. It twisted and knotted itself around his arm but Anguillaro's grip was so strong that with all the snaking power of the slimy creature, it could not escape. Then in one quick movement, he opened his mouth, thrust the eel's head between his teeth and bit hard. He spat the black head out onto the floor and twisted the severed neck away from his face. Dark blood squirted onto the floor. Wesley scrambled backwards and got to his feet. To add to his horror, the body of the eel continued to writhe and twist. With a powerful flick of his arm, Anguillaro dislodged the headless creature and it fell to the ground where it carried on coiling itself into knots, its blood darkening the stones beneath it.

Close by, the severed head was still slowly opening and closing its mouth. Anguillaro took a stick and pushed it between its teeth. The jaws closed and he held it up to the flames.

"Mmm... A little snack while we wait?" He glanced back at Wesley. "Hey! Did they tell you that I eat them alive? Eh? Ha! Alive, who do they think I am? They tast'a disgusting alive!"

The eel's head hissed and charred in the hot flames. Anguillaro withdrew it and offered it to Wesley.

"You sure you don't want? Just a little bite? No?"

Wesley clamped his mouth closed and shook his head. Anguillaro lifted the eel's head to his own mouth, looked at Wesley, winked and then threw it into the fire.

"Me neither. Who would ever eat the head? Eh? Disgusting! Ha ha ha, disgusting!"

Wesley drew back from the fire and sat on the gravel floor, hugging his knees to his chest. He watched Anguillaro pick up the body of the eel and carefully cut it into slices. These he laid carefully, one by one, hissing and sizzling into a blackened pan that he balanced on the fire. From glass jars that he kept at the base of the hearth, he added pinches of herbs and salt and the savory smell of cooking joined with the other smells of the cavern.

When Anguillaro handed him a fork and a plate heaped with small strips of the cooked black flesh, Wesley poked at them suspiciously. He picked off a tiny piece and chewed it. It tasted muddy, but also savory and rich. He ate, pulling tiny bones from between his teeth with each mouthful. Anguillaro pulled up one of the wooden boxes and sat on it. He ate with his fingers, pushing each mouthful through his bushy beard. When he had finished he turned to Wesley and smacked his lips.

"Mmm...Anguilla Fuoca, Just like'a my mother used to make. Ha!"

He reached down and rubbed his oily hands on his boots, working his fingers carefully over the stitching. On the other side of the fire, Sargazzo lay on a bed of old blankets, his front paws crossed and his muzzle resting on them, eyes open, watching Anguillaro and Wesley in the firelight.

Wesley knew that the supervisors would make a thorough search for him. If they found the hole beneath the box, Katie might be blamed for helping him escape. Would she lie if they asked her about it? He wasn't sure that she would. They would put her in The Pit. He had already got some of the others into it over the calculations from Pearson. He had left a wake of trouble behind him. He wondered if the Eel Catcher would take him back over the lake so that he could warn her. Tomorrow was maintenance day; she'd be at the grid. And what then? Should he give himself up? What else could he do? Thoughts bubbled through his head in quick succession. He felt tired. The dying fire glowed on the stones, warming his face. He yawned.

"Tired eh?" Anguillaro sat up and rubbed his hands together. "We have a lot to talk about, but it can wait until tomorrow. Now is time for sleeping."

He stood up and circled the fire. As he passed Sargazzo, the dog raised his head and Anguillaro stooped and ruffled his ears.

"You are safe here Mr. Pike. Sargazzo is a better guard than twenty trackers put together. He can hear a fly fart. Ha! Can't you boy, eh?"

He crunched over the gravel to the metal chest, took from it an armful of blankets and made a bed beside it on the floor. He waved Wesley over.

"You are our first visitor here. But I must apologize; we do not have a nice bed for you. You must sleep with plenty of blankets beneath you. Plenty more in the chest. If you get cold you can always sleep with Sargazzo. He likes you."

He strode back over to Sargazzo and spoke quietly in his ear. The dog watched Anguillaro walk towards the entrance of the cavern.

"I am going on a little visit, Mr. Pike. I shall see you for breakfast." He paused for a moment and adjusted the lens on the front of his turban. "Buona notte, Sleep well."

And with that, he strode on into the cave and was gone, leaving Wesley in the flickering firelight and silence of the Eel Catcher's cavern.

6
Boots and Shoes

Mikhail Kuroski sat with his granddaughter, Katie, on the wooden trunk. His hair was completely white and waved back over his head like a white sea. He had a broad mouth in a wrinkled wide face and blue eyes set generously apart. He was gently braiding her hair. He knew that for as long as he remained doing this, Katie would stay silent. She never spoke when anyone played with her hair.

The tracking party, blue uniformed men and women, were returning through the room. The search of the Care Halls was over. Mikhail and Katie had been ignored.

Pearson marched into the room. He wore a shabby tweed coat over his uniform and with quick turns of his head he searched the white cement walls and ceiling for clues of an escape route. Mikhail swayed slightly from side to side and continued with Katie's hair.

A tracker marched up to Pearson and stopped.

"Chief Supervisor Pearson, Sir".

"Well?"

"We've located the boy Sir".

"Ah, good", Pearson's mouth twitched into a smile. "Now we can find out how the little blighter got out of here".

"Sir?"

"Yes tracker".

"He's dead Sir. His tag registered at the bottom of one of the lakes in Dead Horse Caverns. We think he must have got washed there by the river. We were never far behind him Sir".

"Dead eh! Well, that's his own fault".

"Yes Sir".

"But how...?" Pearson looked back over the room. "How

56

did he get out of here?"

He fixed his gaze on Mikhail and Katie then strode over to them.

"You two, what about you? Did you see a boy in here recently? Eh! Well?

Mikhail continued working at Katie's hair while he lifted his gaze up to Pearson. His eyes were watery and pale and he swayed a little from side to side.

"S'cold".

"What?"

"S'freezing. Never seen so much snow…have you Billy? Ever seen so much?"

"What?" Pearson shook his head in frustration at the senile old man, "I'm not Billy. I am Chief Supervisor Pearson. What's in that box? Eh? Let's have a look."

Without letting go of Katie's hair. Mikhail slowly stood up. Katie rose up with him. Pearson flipped open the lid with his boot, pulled out one of the blankets and dropped it back in again.

"Blankets!"

He turned sharply and strode quickly away followed by the tracker.

When they were alone, Mikhail closed the lid of the box.

"Katie?"

"Yes Grandpa?"

" Did he go through the box?"

"Katie can fit through, Granddad. Wesley can fit through". Katie started fidgeting with her fingers. "Wesley's my friend Grandpa."

"I know that Katie."

Mikhail sighed and put his arm around his granddaughter. They sat together back on the box.

"Katie. Wesley might not be there when you next go to meet him. I think he's…gone away for a while".

"No Grandpa, no." Katie's fingers started up again. "I meet Wesley at eleven twenty. Wednesday Grandpa, eleven twenty. I did his sums".

Pearson found a bicycle at the entrance to the Care Halls and he helped himself to it. He pedaled off, coat tails flapping behind him, through one of the well-lit Connector Tunnels towards the stores.

The wide store gates were slightly open. Pearson rode the bike through the gap and into the delivery area, beyond which stretched the chambers of the long subterranean warehouse. A man and woman in brown storekeeper's uniforms were prizing the lid from a large packing case.

Pearson pulled up beside them.

"Cotton at home?"

"Spades and shovels", the woman replied, "aisle number seven, chamber three, 'bout half way along… Sir."

Pearson nodded briefly and rode away between the rows of neatly packed high steel shelving.

Head Store Keeper Max Cotton kept careful account of all that came and went from the underground warehouse. Some areas were still well stocked, but others, like food and medicine, were dangerously low and soldiers of The Order were constantly out looking for supplies. The deserted supermarket stores of the city had been stripped of canned and other preserved food even before the virus came and it was hard to find any supplies that had been missed. Max was careful to ration things that were in short supply. Pearson had heard rumours that he slipped a little extra to the orphans when they were sent to collect supplies for the kitchens.

Pearson's bicycle wheels chattered over the steel grating at the entrance to chamber three and at aisle seven he leant the bike against a store rack. Max Cotton was standing beside a rack of shovels, jotting down figures in a small notebook. He slid it into his top pocket and ran a big hand over his shaved head as Pearson walked over.

"Losing a child in your charge is rather serious, Cotton. I hope you'll be able to come up with a good excuse for my report."

"I'll give you the details in the normal way, in writing. If you want something from the stores I need a request sheet. Or have you come to gloat?"

"Didn't you notice that he'd gone, Cotton? Eh? Unlike you to lose count. Still I'm sure that you'll be pleased to hear that he's been found".

Pearson was watching Cotton carefully. "Got any chewing gum in store?"

"Request sheet only." Max was expressionless. He pushed his hands into the pockets of his brown store coat and faced Pearson. "Where was he hiding then?"

"In water. In The Dead Horse Cave Complex to be precise. As a matter of fact, he's still there".

"Still there? Why haven't …..?" Max's body tensed slightly. "He's drowned, hasn't he? He's drowned".

"That's correct. It's a shame, because he's unable to tell us now, just how he got there. You're quite sure you didn't see him sneak off somewhere, eh Max?

Max held Pearson's stare.

"You'll have my report, Chief Supervisor Pearson".

"I do believe, Cotton," Pearson scrutinized Max through narrowed eyes, "that if The Order were not going to lead the way into a secure future, then you might not necessarily *be on our side*, as it were."

Max shifted uncomfortably. He turned aside to a rack of steel shovels and began counting under his breath. "Two, four, six…"

"How lucky we are," said Pearson, "to have someone in charge here with such a mathematical mind."

Max continued, "fourteen, sixteen, eighteen…"

"I'm sure there are many among us who could benefit from your skills, Cotton. You're not, by any chance, in the habit of helping some of the children with their own numerical tasks? Eh?"

"What?"

"You know, helping them with their mathematics, from time to time."

"Mathematics is your department Supervisor Pearson. I leave that to you."

"Correct. My department," said Pearson. "I just wondered if I needed to remind you of that. Please give me your report by tomorrow Cotton. Good day."

Pearson turned and walked back.

"thirty four, thirty six, thirty eight…"

He mounted the bicycle and rode away, his coat flip-flapping behind him.

Max leaned against the shelving and blew out a long breath. He ran his hand from neck to forehead and back. For a moment he remained there, stroking his chin. Then he strode purposefully to the end of the aisle and looked both ways. There were no other workers in the main alleyway. He walked on, a little softer than before, down the aisle on the other side to a metal ventilation grille in the wall, the size of a small door. The fresh air that it was supposed to feed into The Store had not been blowing for over a year and dusty cobwebs hung from the grating. He put both hands on his head and with small casual steps, turned a complete circle, checking that there was no one around. He pulled a stubby pencil from behind his ear and a scrap of paper from his notebook. Holding it against the wall he wrote:

'NEWS?'

He folded the paper several times until it was just a small wad between his fingers and started to slip it between the bars at the base of the grille. Then he noticed a similar piece of tightly folded paper on the other side. Max withdrew his note and squeezing his hand through, retrieved the other and unfolded it. On it was written:

'STRONG BOOT SIZE 8. LAMP AND BATTERIES. SMALL PACK FOR BACK. THANK YOU FRIEND, LARO. P.S. CHEWER GUM PLEASE.

Max unfolded his own message and added;

'Pike? Number 21?'

Refolding his note, he pushed it through base of the grid and, stuffing Anguillaro's into his top pocket, walked away towards aisle number sixteen, Boots and Shoes.

7
AQUA DI LUCE

Wesley opened his eyes. Above him was a ceiling of grey rock. For a moment, he had no idea where he was. He sat up, remembering everything, and quickly pulled the old woolen blanket up over his mouth and nose. Like everything else, it stank of fish, but he held it there tightly. The soft light that filtered down from the chimney of the cavern had his full attention. Unmistakably, it was daylight, and with that, surely, came the gas.

Slowly, he drew the blanket away. He drew in a small breath. There was no pain, no choking, and he'd been sleeping there, perhaps for hours, breathing unfiltered air from outside without knowing. He pushed aside the blanket and stood up. Sargazzo still lay on his bed, one eye open, watching.

"Laro?" Wesley called softly.

There was no reply.

The ashes of the fire were grey and cold. He looked up through the narrow smoke blackened cut in the ceiling. Stepping one way and then another, he found the point at which he could see furthest up the rock chimney and there, thirty feet or so above him, was a small bright slice of brilliant blue. For the first time in years, he was looking at the sky.

He quickly set about looking for another way out of The Eel Catcher's cave, convinced that there would be some way to get to the outside, to be able to look up at the whole of the blue sky. Beside the eel drying rack, he noticed a low tunnel that he'd not seen by the lamp or firelight. The same soft light that came from above also dimly came from its entrance. He walked quickly over, crawled in a few yards and then sat back on his heels and stared.

In front of him, gently moving in a light breeze, green leaves glowed with morning sunlight, casting moving patterns of shadows into the cave mouth. Small birds perched on branches, quick and busy, chattering and flitting between branches that bounced and bobbed under their weight. For a time he stayed perfectly still, entranced. He breathed in deeply. The air was fresh and carried the scent of plants and flowers and he knew now that everything that he had been told, about the poisoned air outside, was a lie.

Wesley stood and the birds scattered. Pushing his way through the branches he found himself on the side of a narrow valley. Everything was bright and rich with colour. Tall trees grew up from a tangle of brambly undergrowth on the steep sides where blue and white flowers pushed through like patches of coloured mist. At the bottom of the valley, adding to the sound of the birds, a small river splashed and chased its way downwards between rocks overhung with ferns and wild roses. A pair of woodpigeons took flight from a tree beside him and swooped across to the far side where others cooed out their lilting call. Everything was bathed in spring sunlight and Wesley felt the warmth of it on his face.

He smelled fish again, and there was a polite cough behind him. He started with fright and turned. It was Anguillaro.

"First time you see this eh? For long time."

Wesley took a deep breath and nodded. Anguillaro looked down at him through his round spectacles. He was chewing.

"Is good you see this. Now you know. Everything is ok outside now, just a lot of big holes. Here? No holes, is beautiful here. This place? '*Mia Porta Altro*', my *Side Door*".

Wesley breathed in the fresh air as they stood quietly looking out at the valley in the sun. Sargazzo pushed through the leaves at the cave entrance and stood between them. He pushed his muzzle against Wesley's arm and Wesley stroked his warm black head.

"Mr. Pike," said Anguillaro. "There are things I want to know and there are things I wish to tell you. Important things. But first... breakfast. Come!"

Wesley followed him back into the cave where Anguillaro pointed to a small green backpack on the floor. "Is for you," he said.

While Anguillaro busied himself over by the table, Wesley opened the pack. Inside was a pair of stout boots with good treads and a lamp with fresh batteries. He pulled off his old shoes and tried the boots on. They fitted perfectly.

Anguillaro would light no fire during daylight hours, so breakfast was cold, salted eels and tough barley flour biscuits. They sat on wooden boxes in the soft light from the chimney.

"Your mother and father? Die from the virus?"

Wesley looked down to the floor and nodded. For a moment they remained quiet. The reminder bought the familiar ache of loss rising into his chest.

"You were there? You watch them, die?"

"Yeah."

"They return in your dreams?"

"Yeah. Sometimes."

Wesley looked up. Anguillaro sniffed and put his arm across Sargazzo. With the fingers of his other hand he twisted a strand of his beard thoughtfully.

"Everyone has suffered. The people from The Order too, but their hearts have gone hard. Children for slaves. Pah! And the grids, they are your prison bars. Did you know that? Eh? They don't tell you what is really happening. Oh no." He stood up, still twiddling his beard, and began to pace around the chamber. "I have been finding out some things about The Order. Oh yes. I have a friend there these days, and now," he stopped, turned towards Wesley and winked, "I believe I may have two. Ha!" He paced off again. "Wesley, I am angry for what is happening to you and your friends." He clenched his fists. "And the more I find out, the more angry I feel, here…" He put his hand on his heart. "In here. You, lost boy Wesley, are, how do I say… a '*catalizzatore*', a catalyst. There is someone from The Order that I am very angry with, oh yes. Someone I would like to squeeze very hard… around the neck. Now, I am going to do something about all this. And," he turned and faced Wesley. "You are here and you do not know what to do. Eh?"

"I don't want to go back," said Wesley. "Not after what I know now. But how can I survive on my own, I don't know how to, I've never had to, you know, fend for myself." He looked at Anguillaro. "So I feel… stuck really. But I know what I would like to do."

"What would you like to do?"
"I'd like to get all the others out, the tunnel children." Wesley took a deep breath.

"I don't really know who you are, but I don't believe what they say about you, about you eating people and all that". He paused for a moment and then continued quietly. "It isn't true, is it?"

"A good story, eating people, I like that one. I can tell you, when I bump into any of these *Order* people, I like them to believe it. Oh yes. Sargazzo and me, we make them shit their pants. Ha! Anyway," he winked at Wesley. "I prefer fish. Ha, ha!"

"Would you help me Laro?"
Anguillaro nodded slowly. "I will help you Mr Wesley

Pike. But you cannot just let everybody run away. Oh no. Everybody has to have something to eat, somewhere to go, you know? And besides, children running away from the tunnels? The soldiers will get them, easy. You must have a very good plan, oh yes, a very good one. But yes, Anguillaro The Eel Catcher will help. Helping you will be helping me. Ha! Here, shake on it."

Anguillaro stretched out his long hand and Wesley shook it. It felt leathery and damp. Sargazzo padded across to him with his big tail swishing from side to side and pushed at Wesley's arm with his nose. Anguillaro patted the dog's flank.

"This dog, he can read a person's heart. He don't push his nose on the arms of people who are no good. He prefer to bite their legs."

Wesley sniffed a laugh. He rubbed a finger and thumb together. They were slightly slimy.

"Eh! The boots fit?"

"Yeah, just right. Thanks."

"Good. Look after them. Use eel fat. Is very good for the leather."

Anguillaro crunched across the gravel to the stack of boxes and bought one back to the center of the room where the light was strongest. With his knife he sliced through the tape that held the lid down and opened it. It was packed with wide metal tubes. He lifted one out and ran the point of his knife around the edge of the lid at one end. Sargazzo sat with his full attention on the tin. He dipped his nose slightly and swallowed.

"Mmm.. They pack things very well at the stores. So kind of them to share with us." He popped off the lid and slid out a packet of biscuits. "As good as the day it was taken from the shop." He handed it to Wesley. "Put in your pack."

He opened another can, tore off the end of the packet and

66

offered one to Wesley. A thread of saliva lowered slowly from Sargazzo's mouth.

Wesley took a biscuit and bit into it. The taste of the sweet oatmeal reminded him of the packed lunches his mother used to make him for school. *He is with Martin, eating outside by the railings; they throw the crusts of their sandwiches through the bars, across the canal path and into the river for the ducks. The ducks race each other to get them. A girl is walking on the path.* He suddenly thought of Katie.

"Laro? Do you have a watch?"

"Watch? Oh yes." He rolled up the leathery sleeve of his jacket and tapped his finger on a large old-fashioned looking wristwatch. "Clockwork. Was my Grandfather's. Swiss make. Waterproof. The best. Very hard to find batteries for the more new ones. I have two more. Always good to have three, if two stay the same, they are probably right. Why?"

"There's a girl who helped me escape. Katie. I'm worried that if they question her she might say something. She's… a bit strange. Brilliant with numbers but, well, if they asked her anything she might just tell. Then they'll punish her, and it would be my fault. She'll be at a place this side of the grids, the place I meet her, she'll be there today at eleven twenty. She always goes there. If I got there I could warn her. She said she'd been outside too. I didn't believe her, but maybe she has, maybe she knows another way out. Everyone might be able to escape…"

"Ey. Steady. If was so easy, we would go now. But, we have to be very very careful." Anguillaro closed the lid of the box and sat on it. Sargazzo swallowed again, still looking at the biscuits.

"Said she lived in The Care Halls," said Wesley. "With her grandfather. Maybe he could help."

Anguillaro turned quickly and starred at Wesley. "Grand-father? Katie? Good with numbers? Does she do little fingers? Like this?" Anguillaro held up his hands and flicked his fingers from side to side, exactly as Katie had done.

"Yes, just like that."

"Katie." Anguillaro stood, clapped his hands together and looked up at the ceiling. "And Mikhail. Yes, it must be them. Alive, they are alive." He turned back to Wesley, grinning. "Wesley Pike, you bring me very good news. These people I know from before. Very good people." He turned to Sargazzo who was still sitting looking at the biscuits. "Mikhail and Katie. Remember? You remember, I know you do. Ey? But you, hah hah," he ruffled the dog's head, "have something else on your mind at this moment I believe. Eh? Here." He tossed a biscuit up and Sargazzo snapped it out of the air. "I don't usually give him biscuits, bad for his teeth, but he never gives up hope. Ha!"

Anguillaro began to pace slowly back and forth, twiddling the end of his beard with the fingers of one hand, the other thrust into a pocket of his long black jacket. Sargazzo, clearly sensing that there were no more biscuits to come, settled down on the ground and watched.

"The Care Halls eh?" He stopped and looked over to Wesley. "You met Mikhail? You seen him? The grandfather?"

"No. I don't know what he looks like."

"Don't know what he look like. Mmm." He continued walking again, occasionally muttering to himself in his strange language. The packet of biscuits stood on the unopened box. Wesley could still taste the deliciously sweet flavour and, with his tongue, searched around his teeth for bits. He was about to ask if he could have another when Anguillaro strode over and looked down at him, his eyes wide behind his spectacles, his arms folded.

"Mikhail is a very important man. A scientist. The Order will be looking after him, oh yes, they will be." He looked aside and continued, as if talking to himself once again. "But why in The Care Halls? I wonder?" He shook his head and was silent for a moment before turning back to look down at Wesley.

"Young Mr. Pike. This is very interesting. If The Order are *keeping* Mikhail, and it must be him, then they will be doing this for a reason. The Order, they wish for the power. Mikhail will know what is going on and I do not believe he will be, how do you say, '*collaboratore*', '*helping them*'. He will be able to help us, both." Anguillaro dropped vertically down and sat on his heels. "What time you say Katie goes to this place? Eh?"

"Eleven twenty."

Anguillaro glanced at his watch. "One hour and a half. Just enough time. I will take you over the lake to the beach." With his left hand, he gripped the base of a finger on his right hand and began to twist one way and then the other. He slipped the finger away and handed Wesley a silver ring. It was shaped as a tiny eel biting its own tail.

"Tell Katie to give this to her grandfather. You don't say my name. Sometimes she repeat names, maybe at a bad time. Like you think, she don't always understand. She needs the special water to help her mind. The Order, they will be wanting this water also. This water is very powerful medicine, and also, is very powerful weapon. Mikhail, he knows where to find it. It is *Aqua di Luce*, The Water of Light."

8
The Titus

Beyond the open doors of the old airship port lounge, thick mist obscured everything beyond a few yards out onto the tarmac. The early morning sun, unseen but shining above, illuminated the tiny droplets of water as they moved slowly past, giving the appearance of a glowing white veil, shifting and sparkling in the air.

Inside, the colours of the once bright walls and check-in desks, were muted by layers of dust. Paint peeled from the ceiling and pieces of glass from a smashed section of the panoramic window lay swept in a jagged pile. The faint drone of a generator could be heard through the wall from the back of the building.

A little way into the room, a bank of strip lights shone above a large table. "Where's that driver?" Dove lent on the table, each hand holding down a corner of a large aerial photograph. The pilot looked up towards the door

"I could send someone out to look for him Sir."

"No no. He'll arrive. Look," Dove drew a small circle with his finger on the photograph. "This is the other corral. See how close they both are? Two bombs in each one will do the job. Pretty well all their horses will be in there between eight and nine o'clock, and a few of the Horse People, it's feeding time, or saddling up or something they do. Who's your bomb aimer?"

"Stover, Sir."

"Well tell Stover not to miss. Bombs primed?"

"Fitting them into the cradles now, as we speak Sir."

A man in the white overalls of a Ground-handler entered the lounge and hurried over to the table. "Sorry to take so long Colonel. Bit misty out."

"Bit misty out, *sir*."

"Sir. Yes Sir."

Dove pulled a camouflaged cap on by the peak and picked up a pair of leather gloves from the table. "Right, let's get this mission underway." He slapped the gloves together and marched briskly towards the door, followed by the two other men.

The car was one of the few non-military vehicles that The Order maintained. Fuel was precious and the dwindling reserves were carefully rationed. The first thing that a soldier had to do when finding any abandoned vehicle was to check its tank. Even small amounts were siphoned off and stored.

"Damn fog." Dove peered through the windscreen as they drove slowly across the tarmac.

"It's just an early morning mist Colonel." The pilot leaned forward from the back. "It's already beginning to clear. We don't expect much wind. A Westerly. Three knots, four at the most. Should be over Saint Terresas in four hours."

A light breeze ghosted the mist across the ground ahead of them. A tractor appeared and passed by in the opposite direction, towing an empty bomb trolley. A group of men, dark shapes at first, materialized at one side of the car, coiling thick rope onto a large wooden drum. On the other side, two men dragged thick fuel lines across the ground, holding them over their shoulders, the black ribbed pipes snaking away behind them.

Petrol fumes from outside blew through the ventilators as the driver bought the car to a halt. Dove and the pilot got out. For a moment the mist thinned ahead of them to reveal one of the leg girders of the mooring mast, anchored into a huge block of concrete. Voices shouted instructions from somewhere ahead and a lorry engine started, the sound receding as it drove away. The two men had taken a few steps towards the mast when a light gust of wind lifted the mantle of mist and pushed it swirling away above the ground to reveal the huge under-belly of The Titus flexing gently in the breeze. The four fins of the tail were still lost in the mist beyond.

Ground-handlers were stationed in twos at the ends of dozens of ropes that hung from high on the flanks of the great airship. The ropes passed through steel shackles fixed into the tarmac at their feet and the men held a simple twist in the rope, restraining the giant craft above them. In the centre of the great belly, where it curved down closest to the ground, hung the gondola, its shiny metal sides reflecting the first rays of the morning sun that pierced through the disappearing mist.

Held fast in steel cradles attached to the side of the gondola were four bombs, two to each side. Set further out from these, supported by long struts, were the engines, blackened along the sides from their exhausts and shifting slightly with the movement of the airship.

The gondola bounced as three soldiers stepped into it, ducking through the low door. Outside, a man and woman in khaki flying suits stood talking. They looked up as Dove and the pilot approached, then moved a little to one side as one of the engines started to whine, its red tipped propeller beginning to turn slowly. With a roar, the engine burst into life sending clouds of blue smoke belching from the stubby exhaust pipes and the propeller became a blurred disc with a pink rim. Dove held his hat to his head as he and the pilot strode over to the man and woman.

"Everything ready?" Dove shouted.

"Just waiting for the technicians to start the other engine Sir and we'll be away," said the woman.

"Good. Remember. Do *not* risk The Titus by flying low.

Three thousand feet, minimum. They have nothing more than shotguns and a few old rifles, you'll be quite safe at that height."

On the other side of the gondola the second engine started and more blue smoke tore away behind it in the blast from the propeller. Still holding his hat, Dove stepped back and gestured impatiently for the aircrew to board. He turned and walked back to the car.

The last of the mist blew away beyond the airship, which began to buck softly in the growing breeze. High above on the mast, where the long seams of the ship's fabric came together, the black nose cone was held fast by a hefty steel pin. The Pin Man knelt on a small platform beside it. He gazed down and readied himself as the engines settled into a steady beat. The Ground-handlers held fast to their ropes and waited, leaning back against the twist in the shackle, while the massive body of the airship above them flexed and twisted as if impatient to get away.

A loud horn sounded from the gondola and all at once the ropes were released and the pin was heaved from its socket. The nose lifted slowly upwards, swinging a little to one side as the engines roared. The huge craft began to drive upwards into the air, its mooring ropes dangling beneath it. As it rose, it turned and climbed up into the morning sunlight, heading for the hills in the west and the territory of the Horse People.

9
MIKHAIL

"Laro, There's something on the beach."

The boat rocked from side to side as Anguillaro swung his feet down from the roof of the underground lake and turned to look. In the dim light of the hurricane lamp, a white object showed at the water's edge. Reaching up, Anguillaro twisted the lens on the front of his turban and tapped it sharply with his finger until it flashed into life, illuminating the beach ahead of them. Drawn up on the mud was an inflatable dingy, its taut tubular sides tailing into points at the stern where it still touched the water. The handles of two paddles jutted out from inside.

"Zodiac. Tracker boat." Anguillaro spoke softly. "They have followed the signal from your tag. Mmm.. Be very careful my friend. Always stop to listen, and tread like a cat. Eh, Sargazzo." He turned halfway to the stern of the boat, the beam of his head torch dashing across the lake surface. The dog sat in the stern with his ears alert and his head cocked a little to one side. "*Gatto*, yes. Ha. Not even you can hear them!"

Anguillaro lifted an oar from the bottom of the boat and, fitting it into a little half round notch in the stern, moved it from side to side, propelling them forward to the beach. The front of the boat slid into the mud and Wesley climbed out. There were boot prints around the Zodiac and the white fabric was smeared with more mud, still soft and wet.

"Two hours." Anguillaro whispered. "You sure you can guess that?"

"Yeah. We're used to counting every minute until the end of work shifts."

"Ok. See you back here." He pushed the boat back out onto

the lake with the oar and then lay back and started to walk himself silently away, the masts of his great long legs moving smoothly backwards and forwards in the dim light from the hurricane lamp.

Wesley tightened the straps of his new lamp around his head and, hitching the pack further onto his shoulders, made his way up the beach and into the cave entrance beyond it. The rock of the walls and roof was smooth and rounded and his own muddy boot prints added to those of the Trackers. As Anguillaro had told him, the cave was the other end of the one that led down to the cavern with the river, and Wesley soon found himself at the entrance to the short passage that led to the tunnel where he hoped Katie would be waiting. The old wooden door at the far end creaked as he pulled it open and stepped out.

Several new bulbs had been set into the cages in the ceiling and he turned off his lamp and walked quietly down the curving tunnel to the grid. Katie was not there. Leaning against the wall, a few paces up from the grid, was another Zodiac boat. It was black. Beside it on the floor was a partly dismantled outboard motor. The upturned engine casing lay to one side and in it were a screwdriver, a hammer, and a piece of the engine. The grid, with its combination lock hanging undone, was slightly open.

He pulled it open a few inches further, the hinges groaning loudly in the silence, and slipped through. The tunnel was bright from the new bulbs. He walked towards the end where, less than twenty-four hours earlier, Martin had helped him climb up from the Main Tunnel. He was just few paces away when the top of a wooden ladder appeared, waving in the air ahead. He jolted back a step. The ladder top came to a rest against the lip of the opening and there was a rough cough from below. The ladder began to wiggle slightly and Wesley heard the sound of boots climbing the rungs.

He turned and walked as fast as he dared, not knowing if the sound of his feet would be heard or not, back to the grid.

"Wesley."

It was Katie's voice, from close by. He stopped and looked from one side to the other but she wasn't there.

"Where are you?" Wesley whispered.

"Up."

Wesley looked upwards. behind the grid, Katie's hand was hanging down from an opening in the concrete ceiling that he had not noticed before. Her fingers were wiggling and he could just see her face in the darkness above.

"You can climb up here Wesley."

As fast as he could, Wesley climbed the metal latticework of the grid and reached up through the hole. Gripping the top edges, he heaved himself up onto his elbows and pulled himself through the hole.

"Gate open today Wesley. Gridkeeper in the…"

"Shhh…" Wesley put his finger to his lips and leant towards Katie who was sitting on the other side of the hole. She continued, but whispering now.

"Horrible man. He tried to kiss me. I saw him coming Wesley."

"Katie," Wesley whispered. "Shhh… Or he might find us."

From the tunnel below came the sound of heavy footsteps and the mumbling voice of a man talking to himself.

"Lazy bastards. Why can't they close 'em themselves?" He coughed. "Didn't even pull the boat through."

Wesley and Katie leaned forward on their hands and looked down. The man was fat and long strands of greasy hair were combed back over a bald patch on the top of his head. The hinges of the grid squealed and groaned as he pulled it closed and hooked the lock back into its metal ring. He tried twice to snap it closed but the lock would not click into itself.

"Gawd!" He carried on to himself. "They've even jumbled the bleedin' numbers up. Let's see now." He pulled a notebook from his back pocket and leafed through the pages. "Here we are. One, three, one," he turned the numbered wheels on the lock and then looked back at his book. "four, one, five." He adjusted the remaining wheels and snapped the lock into place, rotating the barrel of wheels several times in each direction. With that, he cleared his throat, spat, and walked away back down the tunnel.

Wesley let out a long breath. "Thanks Katie."

"Next three birthdays Wesley."

"What? What birthdays?"

"Your birthdays Wesley. Thirteen, fourteen, fifteen. The lock numbers. One, three, one, four, one, five."

"Was it?" Wesley smiled and gave a little shake of his head. "I never even noticed."

"No playing. You not playing today Wesley?"

"Not today Katie." He stood up and turned on his lamp. Katie shielded her eyes from the light. She was wearing yellow trousers. The hole in the floor was at one end of a long thin room. Along one wall were several large pumps connected to thick pipes that disappeared into the wall behind them. One appeared to be partly dismantled and sections of its dull green metal casing lay on the floor beside it. The others were covered in a layer of dust so thick that it was only on the undersides of the pipes and cover plates that he could see that they were also green. Wesley looked behind him. In the concrete wall was a metal door. He stepped across and tried the handle. It was locked. He turned back to Katie and crouched down beside her.

"Katie. I've escaped, run away… and I'm not going back, and I don't want any of the supervisors or trackers to know that you've seen me. Please don't tell anyone."

"Grandpa said you wouldn't be here."

"Did you tell him you'd met me?"

"Told him I did your numbers."

"Katie, is Grandpa's name Mikhail?"

"Mikhail Kuroski, that's Grandpa. Katia Kuroski, that's me." Katie looked at her watches. "Eleven forty five. Too long. Going back now Wesley."

"Can I come with you? Can I talk to Grandpa?"

"Yes." She replied with a smile. She lowered herself through the hole and climbed easily down the grid. Wesley climbed down after her and followed her back up the tunnel, past the wooden door, to the pile of rubble beneath the narrow shaft with the pipe in it. Katie climbed the pile and squeezed into the shaft, leaving just the bottom of her yellow trousers and her shoes standing on top of the rubble. Then she climbed out of sight and Wesley made his way up the shaft behind her.

Mikhail was sitting in an old armchair set against a white-washed wall in the Care Halls. In front of him, on a low table was a large completed jigsaw.

"Who's this, Katie?" he said.

"Wesley, Grandpa. Wesley."

"Wesley?" He looked at Katie, puzzled, and turned to Wesley. "You're Wesley?"

"Yes."

Mikhail blew out from his mouth and smiled. "Very good to meet you young man. Last news I heard, or overheard, was that you had, well, drowned. I am pleased that, by the looks of things, this is untrue. Unless you're a ghost!" His smile turned to a look of concern. "Are you on the run?"

"Yes. And I met a friend of yours." Wesley fished in his pocket. "He asked me to give you this."

Mikhail took the ring and gasped. "Laro." A smile spread back across his broad face. "Well, well. My dear friend," he spoke to himself. "I had always wondered." He looked up at Wesley. "Where did you meet him? Can you...? Wait," he said looking around. "Get behind my chair. A Supervisor could walk through here, or the Matron. Katie, come sit beside me on the arm."

Wesley crouched down behind the chair and Mikhail continued quietly, as if he were talking to himself. "Can you get a message to Laro?"

"Yes." Wesley replied, as if talking to the back of the chair, "I'll be meeting him in about an hour and a half."

"Tell him I am a prisoner here in the Halls. That everyone here is given sedative drugs except me because they believe I am senile. Tell him that I must escape with Katie, soon, to get to my old laboratory, if it's still there, he will know what I am talking about. Have you been out Wesley? Outside?"

"Yes."

"Then you know. Good. Listen, there cannot come a day soon enough when this slavery, because that's what it has become with the tunnel children, comes to an end. I have been helpless, kept in here. If Laro will help then there is hope, for us all. Tell him that knowing that he is alive and nearby is the best news I have heard for a very long time." He glanced at Katie. "Remember Laro?"

She nodded and they smiled at each other. She slipped off the arm of the chair and wandered off between the other chairs in the room, tapping the back of every one of them twice in a solitary game of her own making. Mikhail watched her.

"My granddaughter is very precious," he said. "She has a brilliant mind and much to offer a new world, if that can ever be achieved. But her mind is partly blocked off, locked away. She had... an accident, in my laboratory. I was researching a special form of water. Water that holds the key to bringing her back to how she should be. I managed a partial cure, she was... what shall I say? Without joy, dark in the mind, and that much has lifted. But when the meteorites came, we had to seek safety like everyone else and the water got left behind. I believe she just needed to drink it once more. Tell Laro that I have to return, to my laboratory, in the city. If it is left too long, Katie's condition may not respond to the water. Now, you must go. Do not stay here for any longer that you must. Get back to Laro. Tell him he must help. And you Wesley, you will have a role to play in this also. Running away puts a weight of responsibility on your young shoulders. You have a task, a challenge, set for you by the very fact that you are free."

Katie had completed her round of the chairs and returned to sit beside Mikhail.

"There's one more thing I going to do before I go back to meet Laro," Wesley spoke from the back of the chair. "I'm going to find my friend Martin, tell him what I've discovered and that I'm going to do something... something to get everyone out of here."

"Where?" Mikhail had his head half turned as he spoke quietly to Wesley behind him. "Where is he? In the Orphan's Quarters?"

"Yes, it's a maintenance day, he should be there."

Mikhail was silent for a while and Wesley looked round the side of the chair. The old man had his eyes closed and he and Katie were holding hands. He opened his eyes and looked sideways at Wesley.

"That's a great risk. You must be very careful. If they catch you, they will make you tell them everything. They have ways of doing that. I have told you a great deal, and it is Katie who helped you escape, they would find that out also."

A large woman wearing a white skirt and jacket strode into the room on clumpy shoes. Her red hair was pulled back from her chubby face into a bun at the back of her head. A watch hanging from the front lapel of her jacket bounced on her bosom with each step. She scanned the room from one side to the other. Wesley shrunk back behind the chair and Mikhail raised his hand and stroked Katie's hair. The woman stopped and waved at Mikhail.

"Jigsaw finished Mikhail?" she said loudly, smiling. "What a clever man you are. Let's get you another one shall we?" She clumped her way between chairs and tables and stood in front of Katie and Mikhail with her hands on her hips. She glanced down at the watch on her bosom, several extra chins appearing round her throat.

"Twelve o'clock. You are getting fast at this aren't you." She leaned forward and began lifting and crumbling the jigsaw into pieces. Mikhail began to sway gently backwards and forwards. Wesley tucked himself tight in at the back of the chair.

"There." The woman stood back with her arms held behind her. All the jigsaw pieces were now piled into a loose heap.

"Another one for you. Off you go."

She turned and clumped away between the furniture and disappeared into the next hall.

"Wesley," Mikhail said softly. "You must go now. The Matron will be coming back through when she has finished her rounds. You have a few minutes. Katie and I will be at the box when you return."

Wesley came round from the back of the chair and, unconsciously, gave a little bow. The old man smiled and closed one creased eyelid into a wink. "Be careful," he said.

"Bye Wesley." Katie wiggled her fingers in a wave.

"Bye Katie." Wesley said softly then turned and left. He glanced through the door into the next hall. At the far end two guards sat at a table by the main entrance, one of them had a shaved head. Wesley began to walk briskly, as if running an errand, towards them.

He was aware of them watching him as he approached and noticed that the shaved head was tattooed with a blue pattern. The other guard was chewing. A worn paperback lay open, upside down, in front of him. Wesley walked past them and stepped into the Connector tunnel beyond, one of many that linked the various underground centers like the Care Halls. A line of bulbs, set in the rounded concrete ceiling, curved away in both directions, left to The Stores, and right towards The Main Tunnel and the children's quarters. He had taken a few steps to the right when one of the guards clapped his hands fast, three times.

"Hey, Where're you going lad?" Tattoo Head sat up and put his hands on the table.

"Just running an errand Sir."

"Who for?"

"For… For The Matron."

"For Matron. Ok."

A telephone, fixed to the concrete wall behind the table rang and the other guard answered it.

"Halls, Jarvis speaking".

Wesley began to walk on.

"Eh." Tattoo Head shouted. "I never said you could go yet. Did I?"

"Er no, I thought…"

The other guard put his hand over the receiver and mouthed, "For you. The Colonel." He passed the receiver to Tattoo Head.

"Yes Colonel Dove. Drummer speaking Sir."

He waved Wesley back to the table with his free hand.

"Yes Sir. The old man. Kuroski, yes Sir."

Wesley could hear the voice on the other end of the line squeaking from the earpiece.

"Very good Colonel. I'll tell Matron. Twelve o'clock, tomorrow, up top in your office Sir."

The voice in the earpiece spoke again and Tattoo Head looked up at Wesley.

"Yes Sir, that was *me* shouting. Just talking to one of the young workers here, on an errand for Matron apparently."

"All just leaving The Pit? Well there's one of 'em here Sir."

"Number and name? I'll ask him." He held the receiver against his shirt. "What's your number? Come here so's I can read it."

Wesley stood completely still.

"Well come on. Name then?"

Wesley spun round and sprinted away down the tunnel.

"Oi you. Come back here," Tattoo Head shouted. "Get after him Jarvis."

Wesley glanced over his shoulder. Jarvis leaped from behind the table, knocking his chair over, and ran into the tunnel. Tattoo Head, holding the telephone with the wire at full stretch, said a final word, dropped the receiver and ran after him. Wesley clenched his fists, punching ahead of himself as he ran, forcing his legs to keep up the pace. The sound of running boots and the shouts of the guards echoed around him. Ahead, the tunnel curved to the left. He pushed himself on, breathing hard. At the bend he glanced again behind him. He was losing them. With a little more distance they would not be able to see him around the curve. A little further on was the main junction of the Connector Tunnels where five tunnels merged. If there were no guards there...

The Junction came into sight. It was deserted. Behind him the guards could not be seen. He sprinted in beneath the domed ceiling of the junction and, his feet skidding on the gritty concrete, turned right and ran over to an alcove in the wall. The floor of the alcove gave way to a dark shaft. A deep humming sound came from below. Gasping for breath, he leaned over the hole and grasped the rungs of a steel ladder and began to descend.

10
Janis

Beneath The Junction and the network of Connector Tunnels that The Order had taken for their base, was the huge chamber of the Generator Hall, where ore that was extracted from meteorite stone was processed and fed into the generators. The main entrance tunnel to the complex sloped directly down into the Generator Hall from beneath Hillside House and it was here that the ore train was offloaded and the rocks crushed with hammers by the tunnel children. The train engine was electric, and whilst the children worked it was plugged directly into a generator and recharged for its next journey.

From The Junction above, a Connector Tunnel had been cut through the rock in a wide downward sweeping curve to the Hall. Wesley and Martin had discovered the shortcut down the shaft whilst running an errand from the stores. They had climbed down and stood for a while, unnoticed in the shadows, on a raised steel walkway that ran along the edge of the Hall. They had to talk loudly into each other's ears to make themselves heard above the loud noise of machines. Concrete pillars rose up to the high rock ceiling and below them, six generators, looking like a row of crouching metal animals, filled the air with a deep hum.

Behind these, over the rail tracks, was the processor. The machine rose high above the level of the walkway and, lifted on a conveyor belt, a thin dribble of crushed rock fell into a wide funnel at its top. Above it, the flared end of a giant pipe hung down from the rock ceiling. A mist of dust, illuminated by the lights behind it, rose steadily up from the funnel and was sucked away into the pipe. The machine roared and occasionally juddered, shaking the network of ladders and platforms that criss-crossed its metal coverings. Technicians clambered over it, checking the machinery through small windows in the side. They made hand signs to each other and shouted, though the boys, standing in the shadows on the walkway, had heard nothing of their voices over the din of the machines.

Now, Wesley climbed down the shaft as fast as he dared. The noise grew louder as he descended. On the last rung, he looked back up. There was no sign of the two guards above. He stepped onto the walkway. Less than a stone's throw to the left, two technicians leant on the railings, looking down over the generators. With the noise, there was no fear of his footsteps being heard on the steel decking and Wesley walked away fast and purposefully in the opposite direction. Ahead, a flight of steps led down to the main floor of the Generator Hall. It was only a short walk from the bottom of the stairs to the entrance of the Main Tunnel. From there he could run up to the children's quarters and then return back through the grid, now that he knew the combination, to meet Laro.

He was a few paces from the top of the stairs when a door in the wall ahead of him swung open and a strip of light flooded out onto the decking. A technician in brown overalls stepped out and Wesley almost bumped into him.

"Hey kid." The man shouted. "What you doing here?"

Wesley took a step back. "Er, running an errand."

"Running an errand for who?"

"For, er, for… Jarvis and Drummer, Sir."

"Drummer. Don't know why he's sent you this way? This ain't a kid's route. But here, hold this for me for a minute." The man handed Wesley a heavy wrench and turned to a hole in the wall from which two thick pipes emerged and dropped down through the decking of the walkway. He pushed both arms and half his head into the hole and, screwing his face up, appeared to try turning something that was jammed. Wesley stood holding the wrench, back to the wall, looking back at the two technicians who still leant on the railings. He felt a faint shaking of the walkway beneath his feet and turning, saw a group of guards running up the stairs. He turned back and tucked his head into the hole beside the man. He could hear him grunting and swearing and saw that he was trying to loosen a tap on one of the pipes. He smelt of stale sweat. The walkway beneath him began to shake more and, looking back under his arm, Wesley saw the boots of the guards run past behind him. The shaking began to subside and he was about to withdraw his head when the man's elbow jerked sideways and caught him hard on the side of his face.

"Got it. Sorry kid. Shouldn't have your head in here anyway."

Wesley had hardly heard him. Pain shot through his head and he dropped the wrench, staggering backwards until he felt the railings against his back. Holding the side of his face he dropped down onto his knees. He heard shouting. It was the man's voice. Wesley looked up at him, his vision was slightly blurred but he could see him waving, waving someone over. The man shouted again. This time Wesley heard the words over the noise.

"Hey! Guards. This kid here. Needs help. I 'aven't got time. Not my responsibility."

Wesley felt the decking shake once more as the guards ran back.

"It's him," one of them shouted. "We got him."

He was hauled to his feet and, head throbbing with pain, his vision still fuzzy, was marched away by the guards.

"Mikhail, remember me? Your old friend?" Doctor Thornberry sat on the edge of Dove's office table. His grey hair was neatly cut and the nails of his large hands were carefully manicured. He lit a cigarette and slid his silver lighter back into his suit jacket pocket.

"Mikhail, it's me. Thornberry, Edward Thornberry. Mikhail?"

"Billy?" Mikhail rocked a little on his chair. "A suit. You're looking very smart, very smart. Are Mum and Dad back yet Billy?"

"Mikhail. I'm not Billy. It's me, Doctor Thornberry. Mikhail." The Doctor leaned forward. "Where's The Water? Where does it come from? Mikhail? The Water?"

Pearson, standing by the desk, took a deep breath and turned to where Dove sat behind his desk. "Colonel Sir, this is a waste of our time. He's completely senile. The Matron's always said so. I mean, look at him."

Mikhail was looking around the room, smiling. A small dribble of saliva hung below his lip. "Such a wonderful library Billy," he said.

"Ok." Dove pushed the intercom button on his desk. "Janis?"

"*Yes Colonel?*" Janis's voice came through.

"Come and take Mr Kuroski out please. Get someone up here to take him back."

"Pearson," Dove sat back in his chair. "Back to the subject of the boy. He had biscuits from the stores in his pack, I believe."

"Yes Sir."

"New boots also?"

"That's right Sir. Cotton's in a cell Sir."

The door opened and Janis stepped into the room. She hooked an escaping strand of fair hair behind her ear and walked softly over to Mikhail.

"Time to go Mr. Kuroski." She gently took his arm and

helped him to his feet. The doctor followed her with his eyes, taking in her cotton shirt and jeans, as she escorted Mikhail to the door.

Dove stood up and stepped around to the back of his chair.

"And the boy came out from the Care Halls."

"Yes Sir."

"Have the place searched again. There must be a way out." Janis closed the door behind her and led Mikhail to a chair. On her desk, the intercom machine was still turned on and Dove's voice continued from within his office.

"Where's the boy now?"

"Also in a cell Sir."

"Has he talked yet?"

"No Sir, not yet. But I believe I could persuade him to."

"Good. Well if you'd like to get on with it. The sooner we know the better."

"Yes Colonel. I'll go down and visit him now."

Janis looked at Mikhail. His head was bent forward and his eyes flickered up briefly to hers. The door swung open and she clicked the intercom off, pulling her arm back quickly. Pearson walked through the room, glanced at Janis and Mikhail, and left. Mikhail looked up as Pearson's footsteps faded outside.

"I know you're acting," Janis said quietly.

Mikhail remained completely still, looking at her.

She reached forward, and clicked the intercom back on.

"Damn. Isn't there some way you can get something out of the old man Edward?" Came Dove's voice. *"Surely there must be some drugs or something?"*

"I've tried before, William. I never thought he was all there anyway. He definitely knew where it was though, back then, but he never actually told me. Said he would when he'd done more experiments. I was just biding my time. But now, he's just

a senile old fool, mind's gone."

"Try again. It's in his head somewhere. We must have that water Edward. There has to be a way. What about the girl, Katie, his granddaughter, do you think she'll know anything?"

"She's a complete simpleton. He was trying to find a cure for her, though quite frankly I don't believe he would have succeeded. She has the mentality of a little child."

"Aren't there other drugs you can try?"

"There's Lysergic Acid. I've not used it on him. It's unpredictable. Could make him even more of a vegetable."

"Time's running out Edward. The raid on the Horse People was a joke. There wasn't a horse in sight. They knew we were coming. There's a leak, a spy, there has to be... and I shall find him you can be quite sure of that. Someone at the airship port probably. A Ground-handler perhaps. There aren't many people who knew the details of that mission in advance."

"What about Cotton and this boy? You think they have anything to do with it?"

"Cotton, no. He's trustworthy, even if it's just the sense to be on the winning side. And the boy can't have."

"Want me to help the boy remember his way out?"

"You work on the old man, Pearson will get the boy to talk. I'll deal with Cotton."

Janis clicked the intercom off. Mikhail was still looking at her.

"I know you're not senile," she said, "and I know you don't know anything about me, but I need to get out of here and so do you. I need you to trust me."

Mikhail held her stare. After a long pause he said, "how do I know I can?"

"Because I haven't told those two," she nodded her head towards the office door, "that you're faking it."

Mikhail took a deep breath. "Ok," he said. "I'll have to trust you. I have no choice. And, I have to get the boy out."

Janis nodded once. She pulled a black sweatshirt quickly on over her head, freeing her hair from the collar. "We need to go right now." She reached over to the wall behind her and lifted a set of keys from a hook. "The cells are beneath us."

As they reached the door, the buzzer sounded on Janis's desk. She moved quickly back to the table.

"Yes Colonel?"

"*The Doctor and I would like coffee please Janis.*"

"Yes Colonel."

She clicked off the intercom and quickly poured two cups of coffee from a heated glass jug. Pushing the door handle down with her knee, she carried them in to the office, one in each hand. She was aware of the Doctor watching her.

"Enjoy working for The Colonel, Janis?" he said.

"Yes Sir." She avoided eye contact, putting his coffee down on the desk top beside him.

"He's a lucky man." The Doctor winked at Dove. "Bright attractive girl like you."

"Thank you Janis," Dove interrupted. "That'll be all."

Keeping her eyes down she left the room and rejoined Mikhail, closing the door quietly behind her. She took a deep breath. "Let's get out of here," she whispered.

Together they hurried out of Janis' office and across the wood paneled hallway of Hillside House. The walls were hung with large dark oil paintings. Landscapes, hunting scenes with dogs, and dark portraits. On one wall hung a stag's head mounted on a wooden shield. Its antlers forking and re-forking above it, its brown glass eyes reflecting red light from a stained glass window above the main entrance door. Beneath the stairs, Janis unlocked an old oak door and pulled it open. A flight of stone stairs spiraled downwards. A cold iron handrail ran down the curving brick wall and the air was damp and musty. In places the steps were worn and Janis and Mikhail kept close to the wall where they were widest.

"How do you know I was acting?" said Mikhail quietly.

"Amongst other things, I am a trained psychotherapist." She glanced back and smiled. "Your acting isn't good enough for me. Did they really use drugs on you?"

"Yes."

"What happened to you? What did they do?"

"Most of it I cannot remember. But at least now I know that I never told them anything."

At the bottom of the stairs was a metal door. Janis tried three keys before the lock turned and the door opened away from them. The cellar smelt of damp brick and sour wine. A low vaulted ceiling was supported by two rows of brick pillars that ran the length of the long room. Bulbs hung down on their wires and beneath them, set here and there on the flagstone floor, were long tables laid with grubby white cloths. On the tables were empty bottles and glasses. Unwashed plates were stacked on one table; one lay broken on the floor. At the far end of the room was a large black metal winch. A heavy chain hung from its oily drum into a dark hole beneath it and the long handle that turned it lay detached on the floor. Beside the winch, metal stairs with a handrail wound down into a second vertical shaft.

To the left side of the cellar, a section of brickwork had been removed where a neon lit Connector Tunnel had been dug, its concrete floor sloped downwards and away. To the right, two low wooden doors were set into the wall. They each had small barred windows and from between the bars of one of them a face appeared. Janis ran softly to the door. It was Max. He glanced at Mikhail, then back to Janis, and raised a finger to his lips.

"I always knew you weren't one of them." He whispered, grinning. "The boy, Wesley," he continued, "he's in the next cell. Pearson's in there."

Mikhail moved quickly to the other door. A set of keys hung in the lock. There was a loud crack from inside the cell and a cry from Wesley. Mikhail pulled the door open. Janis ran over and looked in from behind him. Wesley stood against the far wall, one hand holding his leg and the other held up to protect himself. Pearson stood before him with a long thick stick, held up ready to strike again. He turned and a puzzled look crossed his face.

"Mikhail, Jan…"

"Leave him alone." Mikhail glared at Pearson.

Pearson looked beyond him. "Janis? What's he doing here? And how come," he looked back at Mikhail, "how come you're speaking like…" His question was cut short as Wesley crashed into him from behind, sending him sprawling forward. The stick clattered onto floor and Wesley grabbed it. Pearson quickly shuffled backwards to the edge of the cell. "Stupid," he sneered. "Think you're going to escape, do you? You won't last ten minutes." He pointed at Wesley. "And I haven't finished with you."

Wesley gripped the stick tightly and shook it at him. "You want to know what this feels like, Spider?"

"Leave him. Let's get out of here," said Janis. "The creep can spend a little time in here on his own."

Pearson shrank back against the wall as Wesley jabbed the stick in the air towards him before turning and limping after the others back through the cell door. Janis locked the door and unlocked the next cell. Max stepped out into the cellar. He winked at Janis.

"I'd never have believed it Janis, and I'm not quite sure

what's going on but boy, am I pleased to be out of there. Wesley, you all right lad?"

"I'll be ok."

"Janis," Max continued, nodding towards Wesley's leg. "You're a nurse or something aren't you?"

"I'll be ok," Wesley repeated.

"Not a nurse," said Janis, "a psychotherapist. Afraid you'll have to just grin and bear it Wesley." She turned to Mikhail. "Mikhail, this is Max. Max, Mikhail Kuroski."

Max leaned forward and shook Mikhail's hand. "Seen you in the Care Halls. Pleased to meet you Sir."

"We need to get out of here," said Janis. "Fast. Back up the stairs. We must get out and away from the house before the alarm's raised."

They ran back towards the stairway door, but before they reached it, it was clear that it was too late. Voices and footsteps, growing louder, came from beyond the door.

Max changed directions and ran towards the nearest table. It still had glasses on it. "Quick Wesley, grab that end. We'll block the door."

Janis was by the lock, looking through the keys. The voices from behind the door were louder still.

"I don't know," one of them said. "Orders from the Colonel. His secretary and some old man."

Wesley and Max lifted one end of the table each and carried it as fast as they could. A glass toppled from it and smashed onto the stone floor.

"What the hell's going on in there?" called a voice from behind the door.

Janis pushed a key into the lock and turned. The lock clicked smoothly into place, and as it did, the handle of the door turned from the other side.

"S'locked," the voice came again. "Give us your keys Dunster."

Janis turned to Wesley and Max and waved her arm downwards. They put the table down. She gave the key half a turn more and a moment later a key could be heard poking into the lock from the other side.

"Can't get the key in."

"Here, let me try."

"The hole's blocked, there's a key in the other side. Hey, you in there, what's going on? Open this door."

"Trapped like rats eh?" Pearson's voice came from the cell window behind them. His face was visible behind the bars. "Shoe's on the other…"

Limping, Wesley ran towards the cell brandishing Pearson's stick. The face shrank back from the window moments before Wesley angrily smashed the stick against the bars. Max sprinted to a table by the wall and dragged it towards the cell door, the wooden legs screeching over the flagstones. Together, Max and Wesley heaved the table up onto its end and let it fall against Pearson's door, blocking the window completely.

Janis, followed by Mikhail, ran over to them. "Down the tunnel, run," she said urgently. "If we can get to The Junction we might be able to hide somewhere."

"We'll never make it," said Max. "It's nearly quarter of a mile. Once that lot get back upstairs, they'll put out an alert. Guards will be on their way up here before we're round the first few bends."

"There are some side tunnels," said Janis. "Bit less than half way. If we can make it that far…"

"Ok." Max shrugged. "We've no choice anyway. Let's go."

At Mikhail's speed, as he was the slowest, the four set off into the tunnel. Bright strip lights were set at long intervals in the ceiling and they ran, as quietly as possible, from shade to light, shade to light, down the gentle slope. Short stretches of the tunnel were straight and here the patches of light dotted ahead of them. In other places, it curved slightly to the left or right, making it impossible to see far ahead. Mikhail was already breathing hard.

"I'm sure it can't be far now to the side tunnels." Janis spoke softly.

"Katie," said Mikhail between breaths. "I need... to get her."

"Stop," said Wesley urgently.

As soon as the sound of their feet was silenced, they heard the sound of running feet echoing up the tunnel towards them.

"Guards," hissed Max. "The echoes carry a long way but they'll be fast. Back to the cellar."

Once again they had to keep to Mikhail's speed and he soon slowed down further now that the slope went upwards. It was not long before the sound of the guards could be heard over their own footfalls.

"That winch thing." Wesley spoke as he jogged alongside Mikhail, still holding the stick. "There were railings. Looked like a stair. Might go somewhere."

"It's the well," Janis replied. "Stairs go down to the water. Never been down."

"It could go further. Couldn't it? Maybe?"

"We could take Pearson hostage," said Max.

"Never work." Mikhail was breathing hard, forcing himself on. "We'd have to threaten... his life. Wesley's right... if there's a chance... then we must... try the well."

As they neared the cellar, Max turned to each of the others with his finger to his lips, warning them to keep as quiet as possible. The sound of the guards behind them was growing louder but they were still out of sight. Mikhail had slowed down to a fast walk and Max and Wesley walked beside him, supporting him by his elbows. They stepped back into the cellar and Max pointed his finger at the table leaning against the cell door, and once again bought his finger to his lips. They tiptoed across the flagstones to the railings beside the winch.

A rusty metal staircase twisted down the sides of a brick lined shaft. Wesley leaned out and looked down the gap in the middle. He felt a gentle breeze of air against his face. All he could see was the edge of the stairs spiraling down into darkness. With Max leading, they made their way quietly down. Above them, boots and voices filled the cellar as the guards ran up the last straight of the Connector Tunnel. Max urged everyone to descend faster, using the noise of the guards to cover their own.

"Keep to the sides," he whispered loudly. "Freeze if we see shadows from above."

The light grew dimmer as they descended and Wesley put his hand onto Mikhail's shoulder in front of him. With his other hand, still holding the stick, he steadied himself against the damp brickwork beside him, feeling for the edge of the stair-treads with his heel at each step. Janis's hand rested on his own shoulder from behind and, in the dim light, he could see that Mikhail had done the same to Max. The sounds from above had become muted, though it was clear that the guards were now in the cellar and Pearson's voice could be faintly heard, shouting from the cell.

What light remained suddenly dimmed and voices, loud and clear, came down the shaft. Everyone froze against the wall.

"Well if the keys are in the door, and it's locked, this is the only other place they could go."

"Can't see nothin'. Here…" A guard's voice dropped volume as he shouted away from the shaft. "Bring a lamp. They must be down here."

Moments later, a powerful beam of light flashed down the shaft, lighting the edges of the stairs only inches from their feet. The metal was heavily corroded, more than it had been at the top. It looked paper-thin in places. Wesley flattened himself against the brickwork.

"Ain't no one down there," the voice continued from above, "unless they've gone through to the well. Let's 'ave a look down past the winch."

The light disappeared and for a few moments they could see nothing after the brightness. Then a faint light appeared below them. Wesley leaned forward and looked down. The light shone from a small opening at the bottom that appeared to lead into the well shaft. The voices, a little muffled, continued.

"Well if they were down there, we'd see 'em. They'd be trapped."

"Dunno. There's little tunnels all over. Ventilation and all that. They used to burrow in to anything. I ain't never 'bin down this one. State of them stairs! Too rusted for my liking."

With the back of his hand still touching the wall, breathing as quietly as possible and trying not to move a muscle, Wesley had not been aware of how lightly he had been gripping the top of the stick until he felt it slide downwards. He clamped his hand closed too late, and the stick clattered noisily down the stairs, past Mikhail and Max, rolling and then falling over the edge, silent for a moment before it landed on stone with a loud knock and a clatter that echoed back up the shaft.

"Down", hissed Max. "let's just hope there's a way out at the bottom".

11
The Horse People

Owen dismounted and walked carefully down the slope to the dead horse. Flies rose in a buzzing cloud from the gaping wound where the back leg of the animal had been hacked off and the grass was sticky with thick dark blood. The air smelt of raw meat. A lone buzzard glided in a wide circle high in the clear blue sky and crows strutted on the grass, cawing, at a safe distance from the group of five riders waiting at the top of the slope.

The horses dipped and lifted their heads with uneasiness and the riders, men and women of the Horse People, wearing thick jumpers and worn old jackets, held them on tight reins. The riders leaned forward and spoke to the animals reassuringly, stroking their necks to calm them. Sarah held the reins of Owen's bay mare, and she spoke quietly into the creature's ear.

This was high ground, and although the early morning sun shone, and the fresh green of spring showed itself in the grass and in the thickets of bramble and hawthorn, there had been a frost and the breath of the horses steamed in the chilly air. Owen wore a thick coat, gloves and a woolen hat pulled tightly down over his ears. Across his back he carried an old rifle.

Close to the riders, a patch of ground lay jumbled with fallen tree trunks where a spinney of mountain ash had been ripped from the ground by the windblast of a meteorite hit. Most were dead but a few still remained joined to their roots and from these new leaves were appearing on branches that grew up from the fallen timber. Elsewhere, the ground was mostly open grassland dotted with outcrops of pale grey rock from which tufts of grass and wild thyme grew, rooting into crevices in the stone.

Below the riders, to the east, the land sloped away into the deep sheltered Afen valley. Here the trees still stood and behind them streaks of foam could be seen where the river dashed between boulders. To the west, behind the riders, a wide tract of land lay wasted from the meteorite hit. At its centre a deep hole, now half filled with water, had been blasted into the earth. Jagged pieces of shattered rock littered the ground for miles around it and little vegetation had taken root there. The Horse People avoided such areas, it was difficult terrain to cross on foot and for their horses it was almost impossible, the sharp stones cutting at the animals' hocks and causing them to stumble.

Other than the sound of the crows, the buzz of flies, and the shifting hooves and blowing breath of the horses, the distant rushing of the water was all that could be heard.

The eye of the dead horse was wide open. Its pupil, glazed over, was looking backwards. In its neck, two dark bullet holes were surrounded with congealed blood. Owen crouched down, lifting the hem of his coat clear of the blood and examined the harness briefly. He pulled his hat off into his fist, passed his hand over his forehead and down over his unshaved cheeks, then stood, scanning the ground ahead where it fell away down the slope. He turned and made his way back up to the other riders.

"It's Marco, Joe's horse." He took the reins of his horse from Sarah and swung easily into the saddle. "Unless they've taken him, he'll not be far away. He may be injured. Fan out and search the hillside."

The riders split into pairs and began to descend into the valley, the horses edging down sideways where the ground was steep. Owen and Sarah rode over to the flattened spinney. Sarah rode straight-backed, rising and sitting in the saddle, her grey hair falling loosely. She was the oldest rider among them and known for her skill with horses. Long rides such as this, far from the pastures and corrals of Saint Terresas, were tiring to her, but Owen was glad she was with them. He respected her clear thinking and insight into situations like this, and she wasn't easily frightened.

"What do you think Sarah?"

"Soldiers, from the North Garrison by the estuary bridge. A small party I imagine, otherwise they'd have taken more than one leg. Could be just another of their sorties out here. Spying on us, scavenging for food, and the rest. But Joe could have been seen returning across the estuary after his rendezvous with Janis. If that's what happened, then we must hope that she wasn't seen with him. The Order's short wave radios have enough range to contact a roving group over here. If he was seen, then one of their patrols may have lain in wait. Was he armed?"

"Yes, he was."

"At least then he may have had a chance to defend himself, but if he was ambushed…" Sarah pulled her horse to a sudden stop. They had almost reached the edge of the fallen trees. She was leaning sideways, looking at the ground.

"What is it Sarah?"

"Look."

There were gouges in the grass and a set of hoof marks facing both forward and backwards.

"This has to have been Joe's horse," said Owen. "Looks as if he skidded to a stop here, turned round and headed…" he looked and then pointed in the direction of the slope where the dead animal lay, "there."

They dismounted and picked their way in among the fallen trees. Beside one of the trunks, Sarah stooped and picked something from the ground.

"Owen, here. Shells." She held up two shiny brass bullet casings.

Owen took one and examined it. "Not Joe's. This is from a military weapon. We have nothing as powerful as this."

A little further along the trunk Owen found three more shell cases. He sat on his heels and carefully examined the ground around them. Boot prints, in a patch of loose soil, led towards the tangle of roots and soil uplifted at the base of the tree. Stepping cautiously round it, he saw the body of a man, lying face down on the ground. The back of his uniform, that of The Order, was darkened with a patch of blood. One arm was crumpled awkwardly beneath him and his head was twisted towards Owen, mouth open, eyes shut, skin grey and wax-like. Flies buzzed around him.

"Sarah," he called. Sarah arrived at his shoulder and drew in a sharp breath. For a moment neither of them spoke. Owen shook his head. "I never did get used to this. Death. Though we've seen enough of it." He turned to Sarah, "but I'm glad it's not Joe, there's still a chance…"

A shrill whistle came up from the valley.

"They've found something," said Sarah.

They were the last to arrive at the edge of the wood, close to the bottom of the valley. A man, in the clothes of the Horse People, was sitting with his back against a tree, hands resting on the ground. His head was leaned back against the bark, his face ashen and pale, and a rider was carefully unbuttoning his coat. Owen dismounted quickly and ran over. The man was breathing in shallow gasps. His lungs made a bubbling sound and he winced with each out-breath. Beneath his coat his shirt was covered with blood. Without moving his head he looked sideways as Owen arrived and crouched beside him. Owen lifted his hand gently from the ground and held it in his own.

"Can you speak Joe? Tell us what happened?"

"Four soldiers." Joe's voice was barely louder than a whisper.

"I fired back. Hit one I believe but… they shot Marco. Don't think they realized they got me too. Think they thought I'd run off. How bad d'you think I am Owen? I've… lost lot of blood. Hurts like hell."

"I don't know."

"Listen, that's my lungs bubbling." He gripped Owen's hand slightly. "I might die. Owen? Do you think I might? Oh my God."

"Joe. Did you rendezvous with Janis?"

"Yes… saw her." Joe winced and closed his eyes. "Lightwater," he continued with his eyes closed, his voice still quieter. "More talk of this Lightwater. They want it, but… can't find it. Janis doesn't know… what it is. But it's… powerful. A medicine and a weapon. They say that whoever has it… the future's theirs. Something about us becoming… docile slaves. She's taking a huge risk… being there." Joe opened his eyes once more and looked at Owen. "They must have seen me… in the boat, from the bridge. Ambushed me here. Marco, have you… found him?"

Owen nodded. "We found him. I'm afraid he's dead Joe."

Joe closed his eyes once more and Owen felt a slight tightening of the man's grip on his hand. The man opened his mouth to speak again but no words or breath came. Slowly his mouth closed. Owen felt the hand relax until he felt only the weight of it in his own. As Joe's lips joined, the branches in the tree above him stirred in a light breeze. Owen reached forward and touched the man's neck with his fingers. He turned and looked up at Sarah. "He's dead."

12
A Speck of Light

At the bottom of the well Wesley, Janis, Max and Mikhail found the entrance to a tall thin tunnel. With his arm, Wesley brushed aside a veil of dusty cobwebs. Inside was completely dark. Shouted orders came from the guards above and a clatter of boots sounded on the metal stairs.

"In," said Max. "Fast."

The torch beam was flashing down on them again and more boots could be heard stepping onto the stairs. Wesley grabbed his stick. The stairs shook and thick flakes of rust showered down onto him.

"Wesley go! Use the stick," said Janis.

Wesley ducked into the tunnel and started walking. What faint light crept in from behind him was immediately blocked off by Janis, holding Mikhail's hand, then Max, following him. He tapped the stick from side to side on the walls, feeling his way forward. Janis clutched at the back of his jacket. Behind them the stairs rang with the boots of more and more guards hurrying down. Then a new sound, a loud groaning creak of twisting metal, followed by frantic shouting, came from the well shaft.

"The stairs," said Janis. "Too many…"

A crash and a rumble of bricks drowned her voice and a billow of dust blew in behind them. Max coughed hard and spat.

"Collapsed." He coughed again. "Brickwork too. I can only see a thin gap of light behind us."

"Luck's on our side," said Janis, "for now. Keep going Wesley."

The labyrinth of tunnels and chambers, that The Order now occupied, had been dug when the first warnings of the meteorite storms had been broadcast. When the storms began and the atmosphere swirled with clouds of dust and eye stinging gas, air was filtered and pumped into the tunnels. It caused a gentle wind to blow outwards from all the exits that had not been sealed, keeping the dust and gas from entering. Extra shafts were dug between the existing tunnels to circulate the filtered air through the miles of underground passages. In some of these, fans had been installed to blow the air through. To allow them to be accessible for repair, the tunnels were built as tall as a man, though no wider, and at intervals alcoves were set into the walls to allow people to pass.

Though the atmosphere had now cleared, the ventilation system continued to be used, though less than half the fans still worked. In places the brickwork had become unsafe and some of the tunnels that had been hastily built had collapsed altogether, but the air still slowly circulated, and with far fewer people after the virus, it was adequate.

It was the breeze of this ventilation system that Wesley now felt against the skin of his face. With one hand stretched ahead of himself into the blackness, he swung the stick from side to side, hitting the wall, walking as fast as he dared. In places there were stones or bricks on the floor and he lifted his feet high with each step to avoid tripping. The sound of the commotion back in the well was muffled and faint now and the sounds that surrounded the four of them were their own feet stepping uncertainly forward, their breathing and the tap tapping of Wesley's stick. Wesley could feel his heart beating in his chest. He closed and opened his eyes, but there was no difference. He walked blindly on as fast as he dared.

It was hard to judge how far they had travelled, feeling their way forward, hands touching the unseen brick walls. The tiny gap of light from the blocked entrance was lost by a curve in the tunnel behind them. If the blockage was being cleared, they couldn't hear it. Wesley blinked his eyes, open and closed, and strained to see ahead into the darkness.

"I think I can see something," he called back softly. "A speck of light."

Janis craned her head and peered past his shoulder. "Yes. Yes, I can see it."

The speck grew as they walked. It was round, and as they got closer they saw that it was a soft light showing between the still blades of a fan. It was as wide as the tunnel, set at chest height. Beneath it was dark, blocked off in some way. The pale thin light bought the sides of the tunnel into vision and Wesley no longer needed the stick as they covered the last few yards. Janis squeezed in beside him and they peered through the bars that caged the blades. A little way ahead light shone up through a grille in the floor. From there on, the tunnel continued on into darkness. Wesley pulled at a bar of the fan. It was gritty with rust but was firmly fixed to its steel framework. He tried each of the bars in turn. None of them moved. He kicked the filled in area beneath. Metal!

"Well?" Max called from the back. "What can you see?"

"Light's coming up through a ventilation grille of some kind," said Janis.

"This lot's all metal." Wesley called back. "Can't even make it bend. Max. Do you think you could squeeze up here and have a go?"

"No way! I'm fourteen stone! If everyone backed up a bit, and knelt down, I could try..."

Two things then happened at once. A low rumbling sound came from beyond the fan, getting louder, and a flash of faint light from behind dashed along the wall beside them.

"Guard torches, they've got through, "said Max. "Down everyone, I'm coming over."

"Wait," said Mikhail. "There must be an easier way. It would make no sense for this to have been made without a way through. Wesley. Feel around under the fan. Look for a catch or something, they must have built some kind of hatch in there."

The rumbling sound was louder now and Wesley could feel a slight vibration as he ran his hands over the rusted metal. He found a handle on one side. He tried it, lifting and pushing down. It wiggled a little but was too stiff to move far. With more effort, he managed to get the handle to move a little further, up and down, but still it would not travel far. More light flecked onto the wall beside them from the torches and with it came voices from round the curve in the tunnel behind them.

"Can't budge it," said Wesley.

"Can't budge what?" called Max.

"A handle. It moves a bit, up and down. That's all."

"Step on it."

Wesley pushed down hard onto it with his boot. It moved further then jammed again. He stamped on it and with a crunch of rust the latch sprang open and a low hatch creaked open a few inches, away from him. He kicked at the metal and it swung aside with a groan. Dropping to his knees he crawled through and the others followed. More light from behind them, direct torch beams this time, flashed through the fan blades. Max pushed the hatch closed behind them. The rumbling was louder now and as they approached the grille in the floor it became clear that it was coming from below, through the grille. Wesley reached it and looked down. Through a mess of old cobwebs he saw slowly passing lumps of ore, then, the gap between trucks, then more ore.

"We're over the Main Tunnel. It's a train."

Janis looked down beside him. "Step back off the grille. Try to lift it. If we can drop into the trucks…"

Wesley moved back and dug his fingers into the grit and dust around the edge of the grille. Several trucks passed by, but he could find no edge to prize up. He took the stick, poked it through one of the holes and levered it backwards. The far end of the grille sprang up. The stick broke and the grille crashed down again. Wesley threw his half of the stick onto the ground ahead, leaned forward, gripped the bars and heaved. The grille rose again and he managed to push it forward a little, enough to make a small gap in front of him. The trucks continued to rumble past below. He sat back, knocking into Janis who steadied herself against the wall, and put his heels against the edge of the grille. He pushed. It moved back a few more inches but he himself slid back on the floor. He hitched himself forward again. Janis turned, dropped to her heels and pushed her back into his. He pushed again. This time the grille slid all the way back, leaving the hole open with the lumpy rocks of ore passing steadily a few feet below.

"Quickly," Janis called above the noise. "There can't be many more trucks to go."

Wesley swung his legs out of the hole. A gap between two trucks passed slowly beneath him and he dropped the short distance onto the next truck, landing on his hands and feet among the lumpy rock. The ceiling passed above him. He looked back and saw Janis's feet dangling down from the hole. A whole truck had already passed. Janis dropped into the next. She turned briefly to Wesley and nodded. He counted the trucks to the end of the train. Four. Two each for Mikhail and Max. Mikhail's legs were now coming down, but it was clearly more difficult for him than the others and two trucks passed before he landed awkwardly on top of the rocks of the third. Only one truck remained. Over the rumble and squeaking of the wheels on the tracks, Mikhail yelled back. "Last truck Max."

Max's legs had not appeared and it looked impossible that he could make it. Then, in one jump, he came through, landing as they all had, on his hands and knees, onto the very back of the last truck. He sat up and waved a thumbs-up forward to the others, then clambered over the gap to Mikhail and waved Janis and Wesley to join them.

Wesley looked forward towards the engine twenty or so trucks ahead. The small cab was hinged back onto the top of the batteries behind it and the heads of two drivers, squashed together side by side on the narrow seat, poked up. He guessed, by their movements, that they were talking to each other. It was evident that they were completely unaware of what was happening behind them. Wesley clambered back to the others with Janis.

"Tried to lift the grid to see if I could make it fall down behind me." Max was explaining, talking loudly to be heard above the noise. "Don't think it worked though. I heard Mikhail, saw the end of the truck coming and jumped for it." He looked quickly from one person to another. "Anyone have a ticket for this train?"

The ticket collector has punched a small triangular hole in his ticket. He is playing I spy with his father. Out of the window the countryside rushes by. There is a lake beyond a field of mown grass. There are five white swans on the water… The wheels of the train started squealing as it rounded a bend.

"Ticket?" said Mikhail, a little out of breath. "Must have dropped mine,"

Max chuckled.

"Anyway," he continued. "Which way is this train going? In or out?"

"In," said Wesley. "The door to the children's quarters is just a bit further on from here."

"Is this the way we want to be going?" said Max.

"Yes." said Mikhail, holding one hand to his chest. "I must get Katie." He looked quickly from person to person. "I need to get her out. They may question her, they may…"

Janis was looking back past Max. "Here they come," she said. "Get down."

A black uniformed guard hung briefly by his hands from the hole in the ceiling behind them and dropped down onto the track. He looked straight at the train. Mikhail was slow to crouch down and the guard saw him. A second guard dropped heavily down onto the track. The first guard pointed and the two men began sprinting after the train. As they ran, more guards came down and began running behind them. The entrance to the corridor that led to the children's quarters passed beside them and as the guards drew level with it, one of them stopped and lifted the telephone from its cradle beside the door. The running guards were slackening their pace. Little by little they fell behind. The trucks rumbled on. The drivers in the engine were still talking, oblivious to what was going on behind them.

"The tunnel where I meet Katie," said Wesley quickly. "If we stay on the train we'll go right past it. I can get into the Care Halls from there. I can get Katie. Then there's a tunnel to the underground lake… except…" he shook his head, "except that there's no light in it."

"I have a lamp in the Care Halls, Katie knows where it is," said Mikhail.

Wesley continued eagerly. "Well there's a boat there, and

Anguillaro," he looked at Max and Janis. "He's a friend of Mikhail's… and mine… he's got a secret place there."

"Who?" said Janis.

"Anguillaro, "said Max. "The Eel Catcher. The best person we could possibly be with."

"The Eel Catcher!" said Janis. "He really exists?"

"Yes. And he has a way out," Wesley added.

"Well, if you think we have a chance, Wesley," said Janis.

Max grinned and nodded once. "Anguillaro's our man."

"If we can get Katie," Mikhail smiled. "Anguillaro's secret place, wherever it is, would be wonderful."

As the trucks passed the tunnel that led to where Wesley met Katie, they climbed over the sides and jumped, staggering onto the concrete roadway. The guards could not be seen round the curve in the tunnel and it was not possible to know how soon they might appear. Wesley led the way by clambering up into the tunnel mouth and, pulling Janis up last, the others followed. Remembering the code, his next three birthdays, he unlocked the grid. The black Zodiac was still there. He closed the grid and clicked the lock back into place, spinning the combination wheels. They ran up the tunnel, past the old wooden door, to the pile of rubble. Pieces of metal and lumps of freshly poured concrete poked out from the base of the shaft and, with her arms rigid at her sides, Katie stood in front of it. She ran to Mikhail, clung to him and her body began to convulse with big silent sobs.

"They… blocked me… in," she managed.

"Katie," Mikhail held her tightly. "Thank God."

"Grandpa," she replied. "Can we go back now?"

"We're not going back Katie. We're going to find Laro. Remember Laro?"

"Shh.." Janis held up her finger.

The faint sound of running boots came from back down the tunnel and then a man's voice.

"Got the number here somewhere Sir," it said.

"Guards," hissed Janis. "They're at the grid. Quick, back to the wooden door."

"Hurry up," commanded another voice.

Wesley led the way into the small tunnel and began feeling his way forward with his hands. After a few steps into the darkness, a flickering light illuminated the walls beside him. He turned quickly. Janis held a lighter in front of her.

"Here," she said. "Take it."

He walked on to the end of the small tunnel holding the lighter. It blew out several times, and each time Wesley flicked it back into life. When the tunnel opened out into the cave, the small flame was just bright enough to dimly show the walls and the undulating floor. He led the way to the beach and whistled out a breath of relief when he saw that the white Zodiac was still there. They squelched through the mud to the water's edge, pushed the boat out and clambered aboard. Max and Wesley took a paddle each and propelled it out into the water. Janis held the lighter again, but the small flame showed nothing beyond the rounded rubber sides of the boat and a patch of the rock ceiling low above their heads. The mud beach was quickly swallowed up by the darkness.

Wesley and Max pulled hard on the paddles sending the black water swirling past them. Janis extinguished the lighter.

"Saves the gas," she said quietly. "Besides this thing's burning my fingers."

"Wesley?" said Max. "Any idea which direction we need to be going? Not that we can see anyway, but I mean, straight across? Or along one side?"

"The cave to Anguillaro's is over on the left side… I think.

But the lake's pretty big. Maybe if we light the lighter every now and then, find the edge and follow it. I'm sure I'd recognize…"

Torch beams flashed across the water from behind them. They licked the roof and cast long stripes across the water, dashing one way and the other. A beam lit them for a moment as it passed and then quickly fixed back on them. There were voices and a second beam swung across and on to them. Wesley shielded his eyes from the brightness. When he looked again, squinting into the dazzling light, he saw several guards carrying a black shape down to the water.

"The black Zodiac," said Max. "We should have punctured it. Paddle hard Wesley."

"Four men only," came a voice over the water. "Make sure you bring the old man back."

Wesley missed a stroke, his paddle splashing awkwardly in the water beside him. It was the voice of Spider Pearson. He dug the paddle in again and pulled hard. Pearson's voice continued. "And the boat. Get rid of the others if they're trouble. Go."

The torches lit the white Zodiac and cast long shadows across the lake. They could still hear Pearson's voice back on the beach, and the sound of dipping and splashing from the paddles of the black Zodiac. The torchlight caught the side of a black pillar of rock that rose out of the water beside them and joined the roof. Wesley could have touched it with his paddle. As he leaned forward for the next stroke there was a deafening bang and the paddle was wrenched from his hand, landing in the water, its blade splintered into several pieces by a bullet. He jumped violently with shock, rocking the boat. Katie screamed and clung to Mikhail. Max's paddle stroke, without that of Wesley's on the other side, swung the boat sideways. A second shot cracked out and the front of the boat hissed loudly. Janis scrambled into the middle and in seconds the entire front section of the boat deflated. The two sides remained full of air but the cold water flooded in around their feet. Silhouetted from the torches on the beach, the figure of one of the guards in the black Zodiac aimed a rifle for another shot.

"Jump," yelled Max. The words had barely left his mouth when cries of alarm came from the guards in the other boat. One side of the black Zodiac lifted up from the water and splashed back down. The guards fell sideways and clung to the sides. Then it lifted again, higher this time, and the guards splashed out into the water. The boat flopped down on top of them. Voices shouted from the shore. The torches fixed on the upside-down boat and the heads of the guards as they bobbed up beside it. The upturned boat began to plunge and shake, and a long black figure hauled itself out of the water and stood with a foot on each side of the hull and a hand on the ceiling.

A voice boomed out at the floundering guards. "Swim, little fishy-wishies. Quickly… or maybe I bite your heads off. Ha!"

"Laro!" Gasped Wesley. "It's Anguillaro."

Anguillaro dropped forward and dived into the water creating no more than a few ripples and the guards began to swim as fast as they could towards the shore. Voices from the beach still carried across the water. Though Wesley could no longer hear Pearson's among them. He could see that they had all moved back to the cave entrance at the top of the beach from where they continued to search across the lake surface with the beams of their torches.

Mikhail was still sitting with Katie up to his thighs in water in the boat. The others held on to the sides. There was no sign of Anguillaro.

"Are we safe," said Janis. "I mean, The Eel Catcher. He's not going to get us too is he? Don't like having my legs dangling down with something swimming down there."

"It's ok." said Mikhail. "We've nothing to fear from Anguillaro, wherever he is, but we need that black Zodiac? Max, you a strong swimmer? Could you get it? If the guards turn their torches away we'll be in darkness again."

"On my way." Max released the side of the boat and started to swim. He had only taken a few strokes when a voice came from behind them.

"Mr. Pike. I see you have bought a few friends back with you."

From behind the pillar of rock, Anguillaro's legs, walking upside-down on the ceiling, rose from his boat, which glided towards them. The hurricane lamp glowed softly on the bows and the black fabric of his trousers glistened with water. As the boat neared them, the legs folded down and Anguillaro sat up, letting the boat drift into the side of the punctured Zodiac. He craned his head forward and then reached his hands outwards with his gnarly hands open in welcome.

"Mikhail. Mikhail. My dear friend how wonderful. Such a long long time." He reached over and took the old man's hand in both of his, pulling the boats together. "And Katie. Ha! My favorite. Climb aboard, climb aboard. Wesley Pike, you did not tell me that you planned to bring so many people back for tea! Ha! Everybody, come, climb aboard."

Anguillaro helped Mikhail and Katie across while Max swam back.

"Ah!" He went on. "Is Mr. Cotton, no? Very good. Very good."

Max gripped the side of the boat, heaved himself in and then helped Wesley to climb in. Janis had pulled herself back onto the side of the white Zodiac.

"Come. Come my dear," said Anguillaro. "Do not be afraid. I am just a little tall… for my age. Ha! But I don't bite people. Come."

Janis climbed nervously into the boat. The sides were now low in the water and she took care not to rock it too much. Wesley was sitting in the bows and Max, Katie, and Mikhail in the stern. Janis sat down in the middle.

"No no no," said Anguillaro. "Not there. Here." He slapped his hand on the wooden seat by Wesley in the bows. Janis edged cautiously past him and sat down again.

The torches from the beach were still shining across the water and, one by one, the silhouettes of the swimming guards could be seen wading out of the water. Anguillaro lay back and walked the boat over to the upturned black Zodiac. Max fastened it to the back of the boat with the cord that was attached to its bows and Anguillaro set off with it in tow. As his great long legs went slowly backwards and forwards he began to quietly hum a tune.

They said little on the journey across the lake. Wesley was so cold that his teeth chattered and he held his arms around himself. He looked up at the others. Like him, they were hunched up and shivering.

"My friends," said Anguillaro. "We must get you warm. And you must eat. Tonight Anguillaro's restaurant is booked for you. Table for five. Ha!"

In answer to Anguillaro's loud 'ha', there came a deep 'woof' from the darkness, followed by another and then another. The ceiling began to lift and in the lamplight, the great black shape of Sargazzo appeared, wagging his tail, standing at the edge of the water on the stony beach. Anguillaro swung his legs down and the keel of the boat crunched onto the stones.

"Sargazzo," he called. "Good boy. Mr. Pike is back. And we have more guests for supper."

Sargazzo cocked up his ears and tilted his head to one side.

"Ah. You heard the word, eh? Supper. Cena. Eh?" He

turned to Wesley. "This dog, when it come to food. He knows two languages. He would learn ten if it meant he got more food. Ha! Mikhail. You remember Sargazzo? He will remember you… my old friend. Janis, don't you worry about this dog. You are my guest, you are all my guests. Sargazzo knows this, he will look after you too."

They clambered out of the boat, glad to be moving again after sitting damp and cold for so long. Wesley stamped his feet up and down on the stones, trying to get warm, while Anguillaro hauled both boats a little way onto the stones. He put on his turban hat and, with the three lamps lighting the way, led the way into the caves.

No light shone down from the narrow shaft above the fireplace when they arrived at Anguillaro's restaurant, for it was night outside, and Wesley soon had a fire blazing in the hearth. They warmed themselves, wrapped in blankets, discussing what best to do next, while their clothes hung and dried in the heat from the flames. Were they to have crawled through the narrow tunnel that led outside, they would have seen a canopy of glittering stars crossed with the smudgy band of the Milky Way, thick with the specks of distant suns. And were they to have looked up and waited, they would have seen, every now and again, the thin brief dashes of shooting stars cutting across the sky, granting wishes to anyone who saw them. As it was, they ate eels and nettle pancakes and then slept, with Sargazzo lying close by, awake and listening.

THE WATER OF LIGHT

Book 2

DARKWATER

13
Rebecca

In the windswept mountains to the north, cradled by a curved treeless ridge, lay the soft reedy ground of a peat bog. It was from here that the river Afen, narrow enough to leap across, bubbled into the coarse grass and bracken to begin its journey to the sea. Fed by springs and melted snow it quickly grew wider and deeper, tumbling noisily down through steep rocky valleys, cascading over falls to pause briefly in deep pools before hurrying onwards to the south. The river grew steadily broader, and when it became as wide as a stones throw, it turned east to snake through the hills of the Horse People. Here the waters slowed, looping through flat overgrown meadows and over gravel beds where salmon spawned and where, in the spring, quick brown trout gorged on the mayfly nymphs that hatched and rose from the riverbed.

A days ride along these eastern reaches, the river turned south once more and raced through the wooded Afen Valley, its waters gushing down narrow channels and foaming around jutting rocks. Then the river broadened and slowed once more as it entered the reed beds at the head of the estuary.

Here, at the fingertips of the tide, was a line of ancient crossing stones sunk deep into the riverbed. Set just a stride apart, their flat tops were smoothed by the many feet that had for centuries crossed them and there were exactly one hundred of them stretching from bank to bank. They were called The One Hundred Stones. Beside them, on the west bank, an old wooden lodge house, with a veranda facing the water, sat quietly deserted amongst the reeds. From this point on the river rose and fell with the tides then spread into the estuary and mixed with the salty water, flowing back and forth until it was lost in the sea.

At a point in the estuary where a jut of land narrowed the distance between the two shores, the old suspension bridge arced gracefully across, joining the territories of The Order in the east and the Horse People in the west. Once, the great bridge had been regularly painted, and from a distance the twin concrete pillars at each end, the cables and the slender hanging deck still appeared white. From closer however, it could be seen that the salty winds had taken their toll. The cables were rich with rust and the paint was cracked and peeling. The pillars were streaked with brown below the huge steel bolts that were fixed to them and the tarmac of the road that ran between them was pitted and cracked. In places, hardy plants had taken root and grew low and gnarled against the winds.

At one point, almost at the centre of the bridge, a section of the roadway, between the side rails, had fallen out leaving a gaping hole far above the dangerous muddy waters that, at high tide, swirled and chopped and at low tide became a flat land of mud and twisting channels where wading birds fed upon sand-worms and eels.

At the eastern end of the bridge, from their North Garrison set on a low cliff, The Order kept watch across the estuary and guards lazily manned the disused tollbooths that straddled the old road. At the western end, the lookout posts of the Horse People, wooden platforms built in the pine trees, lay abandoned, and soldiers of The Order now moved freely across the bridge.

Two gaping craters in the landscape broke the road that ran westwards from the bridge and skirted the southern hills of the Horse People territory. Streams from the hills now ran into them and in the years since the end of the meteorite storm, the holes had filled to the brim. The water that now spilled from the rocky rims had gouged new rivers into the ground, snaking through deserted farms and villages until they re-found the valleys and riverbeds in which they'd once run southwards to the sea.

The land around the River Afen had received no hits from the meteorites and on its lazy eastern flowing reaches, in the sweep of a broad bend where the river was deep and slow, there rose a small hill. On top of the hill, surrounded by a town of old stone houses, stood the ancient abbey of Saint Terresas. The roof had long since disappeared and the stone floored nave was open to the sky. The ivy-covered walls, however, still stood, and high in the gable at the western end, a great stone mullioned window still held its stained glass panels. When the evening sun reached it, coloured light flooded into the building, lighting up the stone of the far wall where a small ledge jutted out. It was said that water from the abbey well, when placed in this light, had healing properties. Though the idea had long ago been shrugged off as an old wives' tale.

It was in the tunnels and catacombs beneath the Abbey that a large group of young men, women and small children, who had moved into the area years before to take up a life of farming, took shelter from the meteorites. The town's original inhabitants had fled to seek shelter in deeply dug tunnels elsewhere. All of them had died in the virus. The newcomers took with them a stock of horses. They had remained isolated from the virus and had survived. Now they inhabited the houses of the town and worked the fields that lay in the elbows of the snaking river below. Beside the abbey, the cloisters and some of the surrounding buildings had been kept in good repair. The largest of these was the Abbot's Kitchen, a stone floored room with a high timbered ceiling, a wide inglenook fireplace and four tall arched windows set in one long side-wall. And now, the sun of a clear April evening, silvered with slowly moving particles of dust, slanted through the windows. Beneath the shafts of light, a group of the Horse People sat a long pine table.

Sarah, her grey hair braided into a single long plait, looked from one side of the table to the other, briefly making eye contact with each of the fourteen men and women present.

"Tomorrow morning then," she said. "We'll bury Joe by the yew trees."

There was silence for a while. From the open windows came the sound of a horse scraping its hooves on paving stones, and the sound of children playing in the evening sunshine. The atmosphere in the room was still and serious.

"What are we going to do?" Owen said after a time. "If we just carry on, do nothing, then we're just going to be driven out of here, or worse."

"What about getting in touch with them?" said a tall slim woman leaning forward on the table. "Negotiate. If it's food they want maybe we could trade with them. We don't have to like them."

"It's more than food they want," said Sarah. "We know from Janis that it's this place they want, the town, the land, and us to work it for them. If she's right about the slave children it shows what sort of people they are."

"How can people get like that?" said a thick set bearded man at the end of the table. His hair was tied in a pony tail and he wore a shiny copper bracelet on one of his wrists. "After everything we've been through you'd think that any of us survivors would help each other out. Not fight each other."

"When it comes down to survival Mark," said Sarah. "We're probably all capable of sinking pretty low and a powerful leader can make people think that they are doing the right thing, even if they're not. And if they use children as slaves, it shows how far they are prepared to go to meet their needs."

"It does, it really does," said Mark. "And they're not going to stroll up here for a friendly chat. I'd like to stroll down there and knock their heads together. Especially this Dove character."

"Confronting them head on is out of the question," said Owen. "It would be suicide."

"I know, I know. Just makes me angry that's all."

"Let's look at our choices," said Sarah. "We can uproot, move north and start again somewhere else."

"What and leave Saint Terresas for them to walk into, thank you very much? After the work we've put in here…"

"It's an option Mark," said Sarah. "That's all. We have to look at them all. And there aren't that many as far as I can see."

"We could make a stand, couldn't we?" said another man. "Barricade the road, let them know that they're not welcome? Maybe they'd leave us alone if they knew we'd fight."

"They're soldiers Sam. Trained," said Owen. "According to Janis, Dove gave the anti-virus vaccine that his doctor friend had developed only to those people that he saw as being useful. He searched them out. He found engineers, medics, scientists, and of course soldiers. He needed them to enforce his regime. Being given the vaccine had strings attached. Basically, your life in exchange for your allegiance. Some people objected, after having the vaccine, and he keeps them under some kind of sedation. He doesn't want to kill them because he doesn't want to lose their skills. Maybe he hopes to make them change their minds, or to force them to, I don't know, but he didn't choose anyone who could farm and their food's running low. We are an essential to them. I wish the idea of barricades would send them away, but to them, I think it would just be a joke."

"Making a stand is an option though," said Sarah. "The

only other one there is as far as I can see. But perhaps there are other ways other than barricades. Like guerrilla tactics. If we decide to resist, then we'll have to explore other ways of doing it. Let's look to our strengths."

"We're more mobile than them, on horseback," said Owen. "The roads between here and the bridge have gone. The Order can only move on foot."

"They've got that airship remember," said another man. "Besides, if we're talking resistance, we don't have the weapons." He shook his head. "Even if we did, most of us wouldn't have much of a clue how to use them."

"We've got a few rifles and shotguns," Owen replied. "If we ambushed small patrols and got their weapons, we'd start to become more of a force to be reckoned with. We may not have much skill in using them but we can learn."

"We're talking about killing here Owen," said the slim woman. "Do we want to go down that path?"

"The killing's started Elizabeth. Joe's dead."

"What about taking the fight to them?" said Mark. "To their tunnels. Block their airshafts, I assume they have them, trap them in there or something, sabotage."

"There are the children in there too remember," said Sarah. "We have to think about them too. They need to be got out of there."

"They do, they do," said the slim woman. "But we can only do so much at a time. We can't rescue anyone if we can't rescue ourselves."

"Freeing the children," observed Owen, "as part of taking the fight to the tunnels, would certainly make life more difficult for The Order. Whatever slave work they do would, I assume, have to be done by their own people."

"And we've got Janis," said Mark. "She could direct us

from the inside."

"Janis," said Sarah. "Needs to get out of there. Joe said they probably saw him crossing the estuary. And they'll be asking how come the horses were out of the corrals."

"There is something else," said Owen. "Something Joe learned from Janis. The Order is searching for something called Lightwater. Before Joe died he told us that it is some kind of powerful medicine and weapon. He said that whoever had it, the future's theirs. Have any of you ever heard of it? This Lightwater?"

"Lightwater." Mark shook his head. "Never heard of it. Can't imagine water weighing anything else but... well, what it does weigh. I can't see water being a weapon anyway. Are we to believe this?"

"If Janis passed this on to Joe," Sarah said. "Then we should treat it seriously, whatever it is. With the soldiers now roaming our side of the estuary it will be difficult to get across to meet her, if she is still at Hillside House. We may be able to learn nothing more from her. If they realize that Joseph had been crossing the estuary, they might be lying in wait for one of us to try another night crossing."

"There is one thing that the name Lightwater makes me think of." A young woman, no more than twenty years old, leaned forward from a bench. Her name was Rebecca and she worked in the abbey walled garden, growing herbs and vegetables. She wore a simple grey dress and an amethyst crystal hung from a slim leather thong around her neck. She brushed her shoulder length hair away from her eyes. There was shyness in her voice. "It's one of the panels in the abbey window, I expect it's nothing really and I'm sure you've all seen it anyway. In the left hand corner at the bottom, the chalices." She turned to Sarah who was looking at her, nodding slowly.

"It's just that it has something to do with light, I don't mean light as in the weight of something," she lifted and lowered the palm of her hand, "like you mean Mark, I mean like light and dark, you know." She folded her arms across herself. "Just thought I'd mention it."

"Show us, Rebecca," said Sarah.

The last rays of sun illuminated the coloured glass of the window from behind as they entered the roofless abbey. The window was in the shape of a pointed arch. Two thin uprights of stone separated it into three sections. Close to the top, the uprights divided and then divided again, like the branches of a tree, creating smaller areas of glass. Soft lead, joining pieces of coloured glass, shaped pictures in each of the sections. At the top, doves and cherubs with small wings looked down to the central part of the window where the figure of Christ stood looking upwards, hands held in front of him, palms open and a round halo circling his head. In the right hand section, a man knelt, a sword at his side, hands held in prayer. In the left hand section, a woman knelt, her hands in prayer also. The figures shone brilliantly in the sunlight. Beside the woman's knees, two chalices glowed deep blue against a golden background. Across each of them, a thin wavy line passed, like a simple child's drawing of water, and from them, lines of clear glass radiated in all directions. The lines from one chalice were twice as long as those on the other.

"The chalices of Saint Teresa," said Sarah. "Radiating light. If this has something to do with Lightwater, I cannot understand how it could be used as a weapon." She turned and spoke directly to Rebecca. "What are your thoughts on this my dear?"

Rebecca held her hands together as if in prayer, fingertips

against her chin, looking up at the window. She shook her head gently. "I don't know if this can have anything to do with Lightwater. I was just thinking that, well, if something has a power to do good, then it can often be used the other way too. Herbs can heal *and* poison. Water quenches our thirst but it can drown also. Lots of things are like that. If our water has special properties, if Saint Teresa used it to heal the sick, then… I just sort of wondered," she looked at the others, "if it could have something to do with it. It was just a thought."

"But we all drink water from the well and we all suffer the same ailments as anyone ever did," said Mark.

"I suspect that the truth of the abbey water is simply that it's clean," said another man who stood with his arms folded. "In the days of Saint Teresa, maybe not all water was that good to drink, just like it isn't now. Good clean water could make a big difference to someone sick. The old story about the light from the window, that's got to be an old folk story."

"It *can* cure," said Rebecca softly. "It cured me."

"Cured you of what?" said Mark.

"The virus."

All heads turned to Rebecca, some of the men and women edged slightly away.

"You had the virus?" said Sarah.

"I had all the symptoms. I had been out from the catacombs gathering food, I came across a man, an old man, slumped against a tree. It was windy and meteorite dust was blowing everywhere, even my mask couldn't keep it out. My nose and mouth were full of grit. He had no mask. I wound a strip of cloth around his face and gave him water. He was too weak to speak. I stayed with him, giving him sips of water but he died, right there while I was with him. The dust in the wind became so bad that I had to stay near the tree with the dead man, all night. When I got back to the abbey my arms were itching and when I looked I saw the rash, the little circles of red marks, and I knew I had caught the virus. I knew I had to stay outside and I thought I was going to die. I started the sneezing, and my head ached and I began to get weak. Rain came and cleared the air, everything was muddy then, you know how it used to get from the dust, and then the sun came out. I knew about the old story, so I put fresh water from the well into a bottle and stood it over there." She pointed to the ledge that jutted out from the wall behind them. "I let the light from the window shine on it until sunset. Then I drank it. I hid here and did the same thing for the next three evenings and slowly I began to feel better and the rash went away. I knew I was cured. I stayed outside for three more days and when I went back in I said that I had been lost. I thought that if I told the truth it would have been a terrible dilemma for everyone, whether to risk letting me stay down, with the fear of infection, or making me stay out, knowing I would eventually die in the dust. But I knew I was cured. Not just because the symptoms had gone but I just knew, in my heart, that the water and the light had worked." Rebecca looked from face to face. "And there was something else. A feeling. Those were terrible days, all of us underground, not knowing what the future held, but, for the first time since the meteorites, I had a feeling of hope."

"Why haven't you spoken of this before?" said Sarah. Rebecca clutched her fingers together and looked down at them. "Because I had kept it to myself and… well, I know it sounds stupid, but the longer I said nothing the harder it became to speak about it. I wasn't sure you'd believe me anyway. Perhaps you might have thought I imagined it all."

For a moment no one spoke. Mark broke the silence.

"Perhaps you did. I'm a plain honest man and to me water

is water, either good to drink or not. This *Lightwater* that Janis heard about. I can't believe that this," he pointed to the window, "and our well, can have anything to do with it. If it's a weapon, then it's going to be something scientific… technological. No disrespect to you Becci."

"Perhaps she did, perhaps she didn't, Mark," Owen replied. "Though I remember your concern when she went missing for those days and that you stayed out longer that anyone looking for her."

"I remember the old stories about the well," said Sarah.

"My grandmother used to come and fill bottles with the water and take them home. She used to say that it was good to have a bottle of Saint Terresas well water in the roof! She used to put them up there. Every so often she'd return to fill them up again. She said its good properties wore off after a while. We all believed her when we were young, but later we just though she was a bit nuts."

"Do you know anything of the history of this, Rebecca?" asked Owen.

"A bit. I looked through some of those old books in the library under the abbey. The well water is mentioned for its healing properties, and it's referred to as The Water of Light. Not so different from 'Lightwater', that's partly what got me thinking."

Owen nodded and looked back up to the window. Some of the others began talking quietly to one another. The sun beyond the window sank slowly behind the hills and shade slowly rose from the base of the glass until the chalices were dimmed with shadow. Sarah called the meeting back together and in turn, people spoke their thoughts about what could be done about The Order. That they should resist was unanimous, but how that was to be done could not be decided. It was agreed that they would bring ideas to a meeting in three days time and Sarah and Rebecca took it upon themselves to find out anything further that they could about Lightwater.

One by one they left until only Sarah and Rebecca remained. They stood looking up at the window. The colours were darker now as the twilight began to set in, but the outlines of the pictures could still be seen by the winding trails of lead.

"Why two chalices?" said Sarah. "And why more lines of light on one than the other?"

"I've often wondered but can't think what that is supposed to mean. I've read about the hospital that used to be here with the abbey, but there really isn't that much information about the window, other than that it was designed by the nuns. The few references to the well seem link it to primitive folk medicine and pagan rituals. When the abbey was built the steps down into it were made. One book refers to it as the Chinese Well, though it doesn't say why."

"Yes. I've heard that. The Chinese Well," Sarah said quietly, as if to herself. For a moment she stared at the ground ahead of her without moving. "Do you remember the Hermit, Rebecca?" she said.

"Yes, when I was young. But I only ever saw him once. Me and my friends used to make up cruel stories about him to scare kids at school. Not very kind of us I admit." She shook her head and smiled. "But we were just kids. Why?"

"Well, he might know something."

"Is he still alive?"

"Owen has seen him. How he survived I really can't imagine, but he has. I suppose he must have been safe from the virus simply because he was so isolated from everyone else. His house was never much more than a pile of stones, so I hear, up in the northern hills. Perhaps it was protection enough from the dust storms, I suppose it must have been, though quite where his food comes from I've no idea. They used to say he hardly ate anything anyway."

"And why do you think he might know something about the chalices and the well and everything?"

"He wasn't always a hermit. He was a Latin scholar, a university lecturer. He studied the Medieval Latin manuscripts, here at Saint Terresas's. Apparently he wasn't the most friendly of people. He just wanted to be left alone. He gave up his job and went to live in the hills as a recluse. My mother, like others, used to send him gifts of food, though I believe the church discouraged it."

"I didn't find any Latin manuscripts in the library."

"Nor could the church authorities after he left. Rumour has it that he had a disagreement with the Bishop, something to do with his not wanting the translations being published, and that he took them with him, the whole lot."

"Didn't someone try to, you know, get them back?"

"I believe they did, but he always denied having them. The Bishop sent search parties up into the hills around his hermitage but they were careful not to upset the old fellow. People had come to believe that he must have been an ascetic, almost a holy man, or perhaps the Bishop was still hoping he'd give them back. I don't know, but the meteorites put an end to it all of course. It was generally assumed that he must have perished. But then Owen saw him, only last autumn, while riding in the hills. Though the old man kept his distance, he and Owen exchanged a few words. Apparently, somehow, he's managing ok."

"Are you suggesting that we… pay him a visit?"

"I am," Sarah nodded. "Yes I am."

14
Road to the City

The last light in the evening sky, a streak of deep blue across the horizon, dissolved into the black of a star peppered night. Only Anguillaro and Sargazzo knew the path that led from their cave down through the valley and the others followed them as best they could, packs hitched tightly on their backs, feeling their way past the branches and brambles with their wrists. The air was cold and Anguillaro wore an old flying jacket over his black clothing. Katie and Mikhail walked behind him in the wake of the fishy smell, followed by Wesley, with Max and Janis close behind him. No-one spoke, the only sounds were their footsteps, the soft brushing of branches against their arms and legs and the sound of running water down to their left.

After about an hour, the path leveled and passed between the shadowy tall trunks of a pine wood. The water here was quieter but what little light had come from the stars was blocked out and it became harder still too see ahead. Wesley knew, from his years underground, that it was better not to look directly ahead of him. By looking a little to one side he was still able to make out the vague shapes of Mikhail, Katie and Anguillaro and he was careful not to fall behind and lose them.

He felt the ground beneath his feet change from the uneven soft earth of the woods to a hard smooth surface. The stars re-appeared above them and in the faint light, he saw that they had arrived at a narrow road. To their right, it twisted away through the trees. To their left it rose and fell over a bridge and the sound of the water could be heard, bubbling and chuckling, beneath it. Anguillaro walked onto the bridge and beckoned the others to join him. Sargazzo disappeared down to the water and the sound of his lapping tongue added to that of the water.

"Ok. You go on your own now." Anguillaro spoke quietly. "Janis, Max, if you return with the Horse People, remember – they must be very careful. The Order must be taken by surprise, caught with their pants down. Is the only way. But we have talked plenty plenty about this. Find a boat at the city docks. Crossing by the bridge?" He shook his head. "You might be seen."

The clicking pads of Sargazzo's paws sounded on the tarmac and Wesley felt the warm fur of the dog's nose nuzzle against his hand.

"Ha," Anguillaro continued. "Mr. Pike, Sargazzo knows you are leaving. He will miss you. Until we meet again, take good care of my friends here, please." He took Katie and Mikhail's hands in his. "Now I have found them I do not wish to lose them again. Good luck Mikhail. If you get the Water, I will be very happy for you and Katie but oh, having it will be so dangerous, you must take great care, do not let them get it from you. No."

"I know the risks," said Mikhail. "Don't worry Laro, we will be careful. Oh, and I almost forgot." Mikhail fished into his waistcoat pocket and held out Anguillaro's eel ring.

"Your ring."

Anguillaro took it and rolled it from side to side in his fingers. He closed his big fist over it for a moment and then opened it again, offering the ring back to Mikhail.

"You keep it for a little longer. Maybe it will bring you luck."

Mikhail took the ring and slipped it back into his pocket.

"Laro?" said Wesley. "Where will you be? I mean, if we get back here with the Horse People, will you still be at your restaurant?"

"Restaurant? I don't know. If these soldiers look hard, they might accidentally drop in for a meal. Ha! I will have to leave them to serve themselves. But don't you worry about finding me. I will find you. I will be working away here from inside. Oh yes, Sargazzo and me, we are going to make life very difficult for The Order.

"Be careful Laro," said Janis.

"Ha, yes. We must all be careful. Max, you sure that this is the road that you know?"

"Can't recognize it in the dark, but I'm pretty sure it must meet up with the old main road to the city. I will know for sure further along."

"Later you will have the moon," said Anguillaro. "But by daylight you must hide. If you are seen then we will be lost."

"Grandpa," Katie said softly. "Tired now. Can we go home Grandpa?"

"Home? You mean back to the Care Halls, Katie?"

"Yes Grandpa, back to the Care Halls. Can we go back now?"

"Katie, we're going on a journey with Wesley, Janis and Max. It's a secret journey and we're going to walk in the dark so no one knows."

"Go home now." Katie almost shouted the words. "Want to go now."

"Shhh." Janis dropped onto one knee in front of her and took her hands in hers. "Katie we need to be very quiet or people will know that we are here. There are some people around... like the soldiers, you know, we don't want them to find us."

"Want to go home," Katie wailed. "Go home *now.*"

She pulled her hands from Janis's and thrust her arms down to her sides. Wesley could see that her fingers were wiggling frantically. She stamped up and down on the spot and began to cry loudly.

"Want to go home. Want to go..."

From a tall pine tree beside the bridge came a sudden

clattering of wings beating against leaves making everyone jump. Dozens of birds burst out from the topmost braches and the stars blinked off and on as they passed them, up into the night air. Katie clung to Mikhail.

"It's just birds Katie," he said. "It's ok."

Katie sniffed. "Too dark to count Grandpa, too dark."

Anguillaro hinged his long legs and crouched down beside her.

"Ey. Little princess," he said. "We all like to go home yes, but, sometimes we need to find a new home. Just like those birds, if they want a better place to get a good night's sleep. They must move."

Katie wrinkled her nose and took a step back from him. "I watch birds," she said. "I know a place where you can see birds."

"Ha! Birds and trains eh? One day you can show me this place. I like to know where this is. But, first you must go to the city with your Grandpa and Wesley. And you know what I would like you to do? Eh?"

"No, what?"

"You can bring to me back a present, a little present."

"What present Laro, what present?"

"Oh, I don't know. Something small. A book maybe?"

Even in the dim light Wesley saw that Katie's face had brightened up. She was still wiggling her fingers, but not so frantically now.

"I will Laro." She said. "I will find you one."

"*Fantastica*. I love presents!"

"Laro." Katie took another small step away from Anguillaro. "You smell."

"Smell?"

"Smell of fish."

"Katie!" Mikhail said reproachfully.

"Fish?" Anguillaro looked around at the others. "I do?"

"Er," said Janis. "A little bit, yes."

"I smell like a little bit of fish?" He sniffed at his sleeve. "I cannot smell anything."

"I think you might have got used to it," said Janis.

"Oh." Anguillaro looked at Sargazzo. "You never mention this to me."

Sargazzo wagged his tail.

"Mmm… Maybe he likes it! Ha!"

He stood up and put his hands on his hips. "Time for you to go. Don't forget my present Katie, eh?"

"A book, Laro."

"Si, a nice book. Ok. Everyone, time to go. Oh. One more thing." Anguillaro pulled a small dark blue tube from his pocket. "This. Very handy, yes." He pulled at one end and the tube stretched out. It was a small telescope. "Mr. Pike, is for you."

"Thank you Laro." Wesley took it and looked through it into the darkness.

"Ha!" Anguillaro said softly. "It work better with the sun out."

Wesley slipped it into his pocket.

"Time really to go now. Ciao my friends, good luck. Come Sargazzo."

With that, The Eel Catcher strode back into the woods and disappeared into the darkness. Sargazzo gave Wesley's hand a last nuzzle and trotted after his master.

To begin with the tarmac was smooth and walking was easy. Tall pine trees continued to flank the sides of the road. They could see nothing beyond a few meters into them. A thick crescent moon rose ahead of them, creeping up from behind the trees like a molten silver gash in the sky and the light that it cast lit up the grey snaking road ahead of them. As they walked the tarmac became more and more scattered with stones and branches and they were glad of the moonlight to help them see. Wesley closed the gap between him and Mikhail.

"Where are all these stones and stuff from, Mikhail?"

"Debris from a meteorite hit. There's at least one crater between us and the city. Not sure if the main road is broken by it, Max knows these parts better than I do. Max?" he called back softly. Max caught them up. "Do you think we'll be able to get all the way by the main road? Or do you think the crater has broken it?"

"Not sure. We'll find out when we get there. I think we may have to avoid some of the road anyway. The Order might use it."

"How far to the main road?"

"About seven or eight miles. At the end of these woods there's a village. The main road is not far beyond it."

"Grandpa," said Katie. "Light moving in the trees."

"A light? Where?"

"Gone now."

"Gone? Where was it?"

Katie pointed towards the trees a little way ahead on the right hand side of the road.

"No-one move," whispered Max.

Mikhail drew Katie towards him and stroked her hair. Wesley peered into the trees. Nothing. The woods were silent and dark.

"I think we should leave the road," whispered Janis.

Keeping low the travelers crept beneath the trees to their left and crouched down.

"You sure you saw something Katie?" whispered Max.

Mikhail took his hand away from her hair.

"Saw light." Katie's voice was loud in the hushed quiet.

Mikhail reached for her hair again. "Not too loud Katie," he whispered. "Remember we are trying to be secret."

Wesley peered across the road to where Katie had pointed. Everything was quiet. There was no sign of any light or movement, but starring so intensely into the darkness bought dots of light, blinking on and off, to his eyes. Or were they in the trees? He rubbed his eyes and looked again. Nothing. He wondered if Katie could have imagined it.

"Let's keep to the trees for a while." Janis spoke in a low voice.

They set off again, keeping to the edge of the woods. Enough light from the moon shone in from the open sky above the road for them to be able to pick their way carefully among the brambles and fallen branches, but it was impossible for them to walk quietly. Dry twigs and pinecones snapped and crunched under their feet. They decided to return to the silvery grey band of the road. For a while they stood and listened. Nothing stirred save the feathery sound of topmost branches shifting in a light breeze that had sprung up. As they continued, more and more debris lay on the road and in places wide swathes of trees had fallen. Some blocked the way and they had to pick their way around them or climb across between the dry branches sticking upwards. The going was slow and difficult and it was not until the silhouette of a row of cottages was right beside them that they realized that they had reached the village.

Broken slates and chunks of masonry littered the road and pavement. Dark shapes of old cars lined the curb. A van sat in the middle of the road, its tyres were flat and its windscreen smashed. Wesley ran his finger along its side as they passed. It was thick with dust and grit. The pole of a streetlamp rose up from the pavement, its broken bulb hung from its electric flex and swayed gently in the breeze, scratching and knocking against the pole. The windows of the houses were, for the most part, also smashed. Some of the jagged shards of glass that remained in place caught the moonlight as they passed like the opening and closing of an eye, but the blackness of the rooms beyond was complete and even with the soft swaying of plants in the overgrown front gardens, there was a deep sense of stillness about the place. Wesley hitched at the straps of his pack and walked a little closer to Max. The whole group had, without exchanging a word, drawn together and they now walked within reach of each other.

In the centre of the village a huge tree lay on its side, blocking half of the road. A car lay crushed beneath it. Its leafless branches forked up against the glow of the moon and what had been its upper canopy lay pressed and bent back against the front of a large house. The slates on half the roof were missing and the ribs of the rafters were exposed to the sky. At the front, by the edge of the tree branches, a wide double doorway led straight from the pavement into the building. One of the doors was slightly open and while Wesley was looking, the door swung slowly closed. He tapped Max on the shoulder and with a finger to his lips, pointed to the door.

"That door just closed," he whispered close to Max's ear. Max beckoned to the others and signed to them to move quietly but quickly into the shadows at the base of the tree. Mikhail held Katie close to him with his hand gently stroking her hair. Wesley whispered again to everyone.

"That door, the one on the right, I just saw it close."

Everyone stood completely still and watched. Wesley felt his heartbeat quicken and a nervousness wash into his stomach. The door opened again half way and stayed there. Then it closed again, opened a little, then closed with a light thud against the other door and bounced back to half open.

"The wind," said Janis, relieved. "It's just the wind."

Wesley let out a long breath and dropped his shoulders, relaxing a little.

"Yeah," said Max. "It's the wind… Look, what does everyone say to having a break. It's long past midnight. Say, ten minutes?"

Everyone agreed. They slipped their packs off and sat against the tree.

Anguillaro had provided each of the group with a pack filled with provisions from his boxes, all of which had been stolen. with the help of Max, from the stores. Janis opened a packet of biscuits and passed them round. Everyone sipped at their water bottles.

"That place used to be a pub." Max cocked his head towards the building. "The Royal Oak. I vaguely remember having a drink in there once. Might just go and see if there's anything left at the bar."

"Max," Janis said, concerned. "Is that really a good idea?"

Max chuckled. "There won't be a drop in there, guaranteed. You know what it was like, when the meteorites came. Alcohol was one option for dealing with it all. Succumbed to it myself a couple of times. No, just interested to have a look inside that's all. Anyone else?"

Wesley got to his feet. "I'll come."

"Grab your lamp then," said Max, rummaging in his pack for his own.

"Don't be long," said Mikhail. "and be careful."

Wesley and Max crossed over to the door and slipped inside. It was completely dark. Wesley felt his nervousness return, but also an inquisitiveness. It had been a long time since he had been in any kind of building above ground. They fitted the straps of their lamps to their heads and scanned the room.

A bar, fitted with beer taps, ran the length of one side. Long legged bar stools lined the front of the bar and behind it, fitted to a mirrored wall, shelves ran from side to side. The beams from their lamps reflected back into the room from the mirrors. Clamped to the edges of the shelves, where a few bottles and glasses remained, were a row of optic spirit dispensers. Only one still held a bottle. Wesley guessed that it was empty.

"Looks like it's after closing time," Max chuckled softly.

"They'd chuck me out anyway," Wesley replied. "I'm too young!"

He is in a pub. In front of him his father is squeezed in between other people. He can only see his back. It smells of smoke. There are no other children. It is not a children's place. Everyone is tall and talking loudly and someone is laughing over at a table...

Tables and chairs were still laid out in the room and high on the wall in one corner, fixed to a bracket and draped in thick cobwebs was a television. Max was rummaging about behind the bar, crunching over broken glass on the floor, clanking bottles. It was clear from the sounds that they were all empty. Wesley saw a sign on a door that read 'STAFF ONLY'. He turned the handle. The door opened inwards and a shower of dust swirled in his lamp-light. Inside, a stairway led up to a landing. The wooden steps creaked under his feet. Pictures lined the walls. They looked like old maps. He ran his finger across the glass of one leaving a shiny line. The dust on his finger was thick. He rolled it into a soft dry ball and flicked it away.

Max was still clinking through the bottles downstairs. Wesley climbed the stairs and tried a door to one of the rooms off the landing. The handle turned with a squeak and, as he pushed it open, another shower of dust swirled in front of him. The small room inside was, like everything else, filled with cobwebs and dust. It smelled musty. Straight ahead of him was a double bed on which lay what looked, in the first sweep of his lamp beam, like two long heaps of cloth covered sticks. Then Wesley gasped and stepped back, his hands on his chest. What he was looking at was two corpses.

Their heads were visible on the pillow, one tipped sideways and the other face upwards. The skin on their faces was brown and dry, shrunk over the skulls. Their hollow mouths were big and round, as if the lips were missing, and long teeth showed, set in a ghastly grin. The eyes were wide empty holes and wispy strands of hair draped onto the pillow. Hands, part bone, part dried and shriveled flesh, poked from the sleeves of their clothes and between the two bodies, Wesley could see that their hands were intertwined.

He turned away, back to the door and saw that it was swinging closed. He grabbed the handle and yanked it open and was blinded by a strong light shining straight into his face. He stepped backwards two paces and the back of his ankles knocked against the foot of the bed forcing him to sit heavily. The foot of one of the corpses crunched underneath him and dust billowed up into the light.

"Wesley." It was Max's voice. "You ok? Christ, what are you sitting on?" Max's hand reached out to Wesley's and pulled him back to standing. Wesley was shaking and his breath came in small gasps.

"It's ok," said Max. "You're ok". He put his arm round Wesley's shoulders and they both looked down at the corpses.

"The virus," said Max. "Poor bastards. We're going to find this everywhere." He slipped his lamp from his head and looked at Wesley. "I guess you... You're an orphan aren't you?"

"Yes." Wesley's voice trembled. "Yes. I am. My parents…
They died in the tunnels. They…" He made a small gesture
towards the corpses. Without being able to hold back, tears
flooded into his eyes and his chest jumped with short quick
breaths.

Max nodded. "Let's get out of here," he said.

By the time they had reached the main road, the horizon to
the east had paled with the first light of dawn. Wesley still felt
wide-awake, though his legs ached. The experience in the village
had shaken him, but now the dawn had his attention. A streak
of low clouds on the horizon was beginning to glow pink with
the rising sun, and the palest blue of the sky beyond them
darkened in one smooth change of colour, up over his head and
down to the west, where the last stars still shone. Birds began
to sing. He thought of Martin, Christmas and the twins and
wished that they could be experiencing this with him.

They trudged up a long winding hill. Mikhail was tired and
the others slowed to his pace. Max walked a little to one side.
He appeared distracted, as if he were thinking something over.
The road was littered with grit and jagged stones. Some of
them were large, too large for a person to lift, and as the light
grew it was obvious that many of them had somehow been
moved to one side, to make the road passable by vehicle.

Trees large and small were down everywhere, all fallen
away from the direction in which they were heading. In
sheltered places, some still stood, but elsewhere those that
remained rooted were, for the most part, leaning at an angle or
had their tops broken off. They passed the ruins of a house set
back from the roadside. All that remained were its lower walls,
and brambles grew up through the tangle of timbers and stones
around it.

The road sloped gently up a long hill. Close to the top, a track ran off to the left and down across the rock strewn fields. The main road beyond became more and more littered with stones, completely covering the tarmac and then disappeared beneath a high ridge of earth and rocks that curved away across the landscape on each side. Bushes and grasses that had taken root in it nodded and swayed in the breeze. They reached the base of the ridge and Mikhail sat down. Katie stood beside him, her hair blowing across her face, hands at her sides, fingers wiggling softly. He eased the straps of his pack from his shoulders and sat down wearily.

"Time to rest," said Janis.

"Up there somewhere?" Max pointed up the rocky side of the ridge. "Over the other side maybe, out of sight from the road."

Janis started up the slope, scrambling on the loose earth and scree that lay between the big stones. Wesley and Max un-shouldered their packs and followed her up. Janis reached the top first. A second later she ducked down and scuffled backwards.

She turned and held out a warning hand. "Keep your heads down," she called softly.

"What is it?" said Max.

"Crawl up slowly and see for yourself. There are people."

Beside Max and Janis, Wesley crawled to the top of the ridge. Ahead of them lay an enormous crater in the ground. The other side was perhaps a mile or two away and the bottom, far below and still shadowed as if it held back a part of the night, was filled with still black water. To the left, within shouting distance, a group of people could clearly be seen making their way down a path that zigzagged down into the crater. A brief burst of men's laughter came from the group. Wesley and the others crouched low among the stones.

Above the crater's rim Wesley could see a tall telegraph pole and the corrugated roofs of several long huts in a wire-fenced compound. It was from a gate in the fence that the path descended, forking off into other paths that ran round the crater walls, up and down, leaving a web of thin trails criss-crossing the surface. In some places the steep sides were solid grey rock, rough and un-weathered, streaked with rust coloured veins. Mostly though, they appeared loose and as if the shale and rocks could only just remain at such a steep angle without sliding down. Grasses and hardy plants had begun to colonize the slopes and as Wesley looked out, the first rays of the sun, rising from behind him, lit the far edge of the crater.

The group of figures was still descending the path. Wesley reached into his pocket and drew out the telescope that Anguillaro had given him. Steadying the tube on a rock in front of him, he focused it below the compound, scanning the rock and shale until the people suddenly filled the lens. He saw a group of boys and girls, twelve of them, each carrying what looked like a canvas sack on their back and holding a small pickaxe. Their children's clothes were ragged, like the tunnel children, and they walked in single file. Behind them walked four men. Three carried sticks and the fourth had a rifle slung across his shoulder.

"What's going on Wesley?" said Janis.

"Children, like in the tunnels. Slaves. Looks like they're going down into the crater to work or something. Here, take a look."

He passed her the telescope and then turned as footsteps crunched up the rocks behind them. It was Katie and Mikhail.

Max turned to them. "Keep your heads down," he said quietly. "We're not alone."

146

Katie and Mikhail crawled in beside them. Mikhail took off his spectacles, rubbed the lenses on his shirt and put them back on.

"Phew! Some crater," he said. "What's going on over there?"

"More slave children," said Janis, still peering through the telescope. "I've heard talk about 'The Quarry', but I hadn't heard about these children. Here take a look." She passed it over to Mikhail.

"This is must be where the ore comes from," said Wesley. "Where the train goes to. They're going down to collect it, those children. I never really thought about it before."

Half of children split away onto a different path and two of the men went with them. Slowly, each group wound their way further down towards the bottom.

"Surely the meteorite's at the bottom," said Wesley. "Under the water. How could they get at it?"

"Doesn't work like that," said Mikhail. "Believe it or not, the meteorite that made this hole would have been, say, only fifteen feet wide at the most. They travel so fast that the air can't get out of the way quickly enough and the holes are made by the blast of air pressure in front of them, hard as solid rock. This meteorite would have shattered and there will be millions of little bits of it fused into the rock around this hole. Tiny blue fragments. That's what these children are being made to collect, rock with bits of meteorite in them, and yes, it'll be what you had to crush in the tunnels."

"The blue bits, yeah. They're tiny."

"It's strong stuff. More powerful than Uranium, if you know what that is. But it's safe to handle. It's a perfect fuel, but you have to crush an awful lot of rock to get enough to use."

147

"Yeah." Wesley looked back at the work gangs who had now split into four. "I know," he said.

The sound of a vehicle engine, rising and falling, made everyone turn. It came from somewhere on the track that joined the main road. A moment later a jeep carrying two soldiers came into view, lurching and bouncing on the rough surface, making its way up the track to the road.

"Quick," Janis hissed, already scrabbling back down the slope. "Find a rock, get behind it, keep low."

Wesley scrambled across the stony ground on his hands and knees and curled up as small he could behind a large stone. None of the stones within easy reach were very big but there was no time to move far. The jeep was approaching rapidly; it was only a few hundred feet from the tarmac. Mikhail and Katie had reached a rock but it wasn't big enough for them both.

"Lie here Katie." Mikhail spoke urgently. "As if you were asleep."

Wesley crawled on a little further and lay down behind a rise of small stones. Max and Janis were hunched down as low as they could behind what cover they could find. As the jeep reached the tarmac, the driver bought the vehicle to a sudden stop and switched off the engine. The soldiers climbed out and walked straight towards the slope. Both of them carried rifles. Wesley's head was sideways on the ground, not fully hidden. He could see them through a small gap between two stones. He knew that to move would almost certainly attract attention. But the soldiers were looking at something else. They stopped and one of them reached down and lifted something up. One of the packs. The other man crouched down and lifted another pack onto his knee.

"Four of 'em," he said

"Five. There's another here look," said the other.

The men were so close that Wesley could hear the straps being pulled through the buckles as one of the men opened a pack.

"Lamp. Water-bottle. Biscuits, I'll 'ave them…"

"You won't take anything." The other man clearly seemed to be in charge. "Not till we know who these belong to. Could be trackers. But why leave them here, I would like to know. Could be it isn't trackers."

"My pack that one. My pack."

It was Katie's voice. Wesley twisted his head as much to the side as he dared and looked out from the corners of his eyes. Katie was standing, arms straight at her sides, fingers flicking backwards and forwards, speaking directly to the soldiers.

15
A Good Subject for Darkwater

"The Eel Catcher eh!" Dove chuckled. He leaned back in his chair, turning the model of The Titus over and over in his fingers. "What a catch. Well done to you and your men Sergeant. Please, stand at ease. In fact, take a seat."

"Thank you Sir." The soldier stepped back from the front of Dove's desk and sat, without leaning back, in a chair. Dove, the white cat on his lap, swung his chair sideways to face Doctor Thornberry who was sitting in an armchair on the other side of the room smoking a cigarette.

"Do you know Edward, I have to admit that I never really believed he existed. But... lo and behold, we have him." He placed the model carefully onto his desk and turned back to the soldier.

"And tell me Sergeant, is it true about the dog?"

"Oh yes Sir. One of my men has lost two fingers and may lose a third. Another had a nasty bite to the leg. Huge animal. Would have shot it but it disappeared into the night. Both men are in sick bay and, er, I was wondering," the soldier looked respectfully over to Thornberry, "if you might possibly be able to take a look at them Doctor."

"Of course." Thornberry flicked a long tail of ash into an ashtray. "Straight after breakfast."

"Thank you Doctor."

"Tell me more Sergeant," Dove continued. "The whole episode sounds like a stroke of luck."

"It was just a regular night patrol Sir. We were simply in the right place at the right time. Heard the girl's voice and crept up on them through the trees. As I said, I sent three of my men to follow the party of five, and my other two men and myself followed the man. If the dog hadn't sensed us we might have found out where he was going. As it was we stopped him at gunpoint. Huge fellow he is Sir, stinks of fish or something, but with a pistol at his neck he came quietly enough, never said a word."

"Is he in the cells?" asked Thornberry.

"Yes Doctor. Wrists in the wall shackles."

"Fascinating," said Thornberry. "I look forward to meeting this… man, if that's what he is. Sounds more like a freak, eh William? Have you seen him yet?"

"Through the cell window yes, just briefly. I'll visit him later." Dove stroked the cat. It purred softly. "Now Sergeant, what about the others?"

"Haven't heard Sir. My orders to the trackers were to follow from a distance and not interfere. Not sure where they are right now."

Dove tapped his fingernails on the desktop and looked at Thornberry. His lips broadened into a brief thin smile. "The old man and his little entourage are going to collect it, wouldn't you agree Edward?"

"Indeed I do William. I knew he had it somewhere. Though I must confess that I really did believe that he'd lost his marbles. That was quite some act he kept up, even under pressure. I take my hat off to him."

"As soon as he gets it," continued Dove, "I want them back here. I'm sure there'll be lots they can tell us about their little holiday. Further more, Doctor, we shall have our prize. Sergeant!" Dove lifted the cat, cradled it to his chest and stood.

"I want a platoon from the North Garrison ready to leave. Please see to it right away."

"Yes Sir." The sergeant stood.

"Oh, and Sergeant."

"Yes Sir?"

"Well done again."

"Thank you Sir." The soldier marched from the room, closing the door quietly behind him. Thornberry lit another cigarette and inhaled deeply. Dove sat on the edge of his desk.

"Edward?" he said. "How long would it take you to manufacture a batch of Darkwater?"

"Not long at all. The actual process should take no more than a few minutes. It's setting up the lab that takes the time, focusing the Tesla Coil etcetera. But even that's no more than a couple of day's work. So long as the generators are putting out maximum power, I see no reason why it shouldn't work."

"Can you be sure that it'll have the effect that we are looking for?"

"Kuroski was convinced, though it's still an untried science. But, from what I've learned so far, for the price of a wristwatch, yes, I do believe it will. I will need to try it on someone of course."

"Indeed, yes indeed." The corner of Dove's mouth twitched with a slight smile. "Would you mind preparing the laboratory Edward? As we may have our Water in the very near future."

"Certainly William." Thornberry nodded and smiled. "Breakfast, a quick look at these dog bites then I'll get down to the lab. Might take a peep at this Eel Catcher first. Sounds quite intriguing. Does he look anything like the stories?"

"In many ways, yes." Dove stroked the cat's chin and looked towards the window. "Strange, there was something oddly familiar about him. I feel sure, sounds ridiculous I know, but I feel sure I've seen his face before, not like he is now, but as a, you know, normal person." He shook his head. "It'll come to me." He looked up and raised one eyebrow slightly. "He might make a good subject for you Edward. A good subject for Darkwater."

16
Rainwater from China Cups

"Who are you?" The soldier in charge began to walk straight up the slope towards Katie. "And what the hell are you doing here? You from the crater work gang? Eh? Well?"

This was it. Wesley knew that there was no way that they wouldn't be seen now. His instinct was to run, run back up the slope and down into the crater. But he knew that it was a crazy idea. He'd be an easy target from the top, and there were the guards on the other side with the work party. Maybe it would be best for everyone to give themselves up, look for another chance to escape. After all, it was two against five. But it was two with guns. Then he heard Mikhail's voice.

"She's with me. We were just resting up here. Come Katie, let's go down and talk to these gentlemen."

The soldier stopped and put his hands on his hips.

"And who are you?"

Mikhail talked as he walked. Wesley could see him better now as he and Katie made their way down over the stones and scree towards the soldier.

"Quite right to ask." Mikhail's voice was strong and authoritative. "I'm leading a survey team. Colonel Dove has authorized me to take some geological samples. I'm looking for traces of Nebulum Ore Crystals beyond this crater."

"Oh yes?" Said the soldier, unconvinced. He looked at Katie. "And you?"

"My granddaughter," Mikhail continued. "She always comes with me on field trips, don't you Katie?"

Wesley heard the soft click of a safety catches being released on the soldier's rifles.

"Your name?" said the soldier.

"Kerridge, Professor Kerridge."

"And how did you get here? Where's your transport?"

"We were dropped off. The driver's gone... to the compound, other side of the crater."

Mikhail had his arm on Katie's shoulder, his hand gently stroking her hair. They had reached the soldiers and had walked a few steps beyond them, Mikhail appearing to be interested for a moment in the jeep, and then turned back to face them. The soldiers now had their backs to the slope, their rifles raised.

"Gentlemen," said Mikhail. "Do we really look like a threat to you? Please, lower your guns. My granddaughter and I are hardly going to attack you... or run away for that matter."

The soldiers looked briefly at one another.

"May I ask your names?" Mikhail continued. "Colonel Dove and my colleagues are always pleased to hear of men like yourselves that we bump into. Soldiers out doing their job in a professional manner."

The soldiers slowly lowered their rifles and clicked their safety catches back on.

"I'm Lieutenant Phillips. This is Private Rudd."

Mikhail smiled, stepped towards the Lieutenant and held out his hand. "Good to meet you," he said.

The Lieutenant hesitated for a moment and then shook Mikhail's hand briefly.

"Sorry to have treated you both with suspicion," said the Lieutenant in a more relaxed tone. "We do have to be cautious, you understand."

"Quite right," said Mikhail. "Commendable. Actually Lieutenant, you may be able to assist me. My three colleagues, you see their packs here, set out over there at first light," he pointed to the rock strewn fields beyond the jeep, "and they've been gone over an hour now. I only asked them to bring me a few samples. I know I am probably just being over-concerned but, well, what with those escapees, you've probably heard about them?"

"No. What escapees?" The Lieutenant sharpened.

"Oh, just something I overheard back at the compound. If you haven't heard then it's probably just a rumour. Still, I can't help being worried. If yourself and Rudd here were able to," he waved a hand towards the fields, "see what might have become of them, I would be most grateful."

The Lieutenant looked out in the direction that Mikhail had indicated.

"I think we could do that for you Professor... Carriage was it?

"Kerridge."

"Kerridge... Rudd!"

"Sir?"

"Map and compass from the jeep."

"Sir." Rudd marched briskly to the jeep and took a flat canvas bag from the dashboard and slung its strap across his shoulder.

"Thank you Lieutenant." Mikhail smiled warmly. "For all I know they've stopped for a rest. These early morning starts you know." He shook his head, still smiling. "Some of these chaps, they'll take any opportunity to take a nap."

"Leave it to us Sir. You and your granddaughter relax. Please feel free to sit in the jeep while were gone. Rudd! Let's go."

Up on the slope, Wesley, Max and Janis remained completely still as the two men set off briskly, weaving their way between the rocks and low bushes. The sun had climbed above the horizon and Wesley felt its warmth against the skin of his face. He closed his eyes and the sunlight glowed through the skin of his eyelids. Even though the ground was hard, he felt comfortable. He yawned deeply and wanted, more than anything at that moment, to sleep.

"Wesley!"

He heard a voice calling him from somewhere far away.

"Wesley! Wake up!"

He rolled his head sideways, opened his eyes and looked up. Janis crouched beside him. She smiled

"Come on," she said. "Can't sleep yet."

Wesley took her outstretched hand and she pulled him to his feet. He rubbed his eyes and looked out over the fields. The two soldiers could not be seen. He followed Janis down the slope. Katie was helping Max carry the packs to the jeep. Mikhail leant in by the steering wheel.

"No keys," he called back to Max. "They've taken them."

"Damn!" Max arrived at the jeep and threw three of the packs into the back. "I'll see what I can do."

He lifted the bonnet and fiddled with some of the wires. Katie put the remaining two packs into the jeep.

"Right," Max spoke to himself. "Let's try that." He reached in beside the steering wheel and pushed the start button. The engine turned over two or three times and then burst into life.

"In everyone," said Max, "Let's get going. Janis, want to drive?"

Janis slipped in behind the wheel. Mikhail and Katie squashed into the passenger's seat while Max and Wesley perched among the packs in the back. They set off down the track round the edge of the crater in the direction that the soldiers had come from, bumping and lurching over the rough road. Wesley held tightly on to the seat in front of him.

"Our friends Phillips and Rudd must have been gone over twenty five minutes. If they can hear this engine," said Max, "then with luck we may have, say, up to twenty minutes before they get back?"

"Twenty-three and a half," said Katie. Her voice wobbled

with the bumping of the jeep. She was looking at her watches.

"Been gone twenty-three and a half Max."

Max leaned forward from the back. "Thanks Katie. Give them another ten minutes or so to get round the crater to those huts, where they might be a radio, that gives us…"

"Forty-three and a half minutes," said Katie.

"At the outside," said Janis.

"Right," continued Max. "Let's see how far we can get in forty-three and a half minutes before the alarm goes up."

"Three other soldiers Max," said Katie.

"What do you mean Katie?"

"Three other soldiers on the road when we left."

"You saw three other soldiers?"

"On the road. Behind us. Not Phillips. Not Rudd. Three others."

Wesley twisted round and looked back. There was no one there.

"Gone now," said Katie, "Gone."

The track skirted the edge of the crater rim and the huts, ringed by a high wire fence, loomed up ahead. The line of fencing was broken at one point by a metal-framed gate, covered in a web of barbed wire. Beneath the gate ran the same narrow gauge railway lines that carried the ore trucks in and out of the Main Tunnel beneath Hillside House. Within the enclosure, set slightly apart from the huts, a small square concrete building nestled at the base of the tall telegraph post. A single wire looped away from it to a line of poles receding along the railway track. There was no one to be seen. Close to the wire, the old main road re-emerged from beneath the rubble and rocks of the crater rim and Janis swung onto the stone-scattered tarmac. She accelerated away, steering down the pathway that had been cleared through the debris, leaving a swirling cloud of dust behind them.

Wesley relaxed his grip on the front seat and leaned back as best he could against the packs. Katie's head was sinking forward with sleep and Mikhail, squashed up beside her, held his hand up to his mouth and yawned. As if caught from Mikhail, a long deep yawn rose up out of Wesley and, a moment later, Max did the same. Only Janis, gripping the wheel tightly and staring ahead, seemed still fully alert.

As they left the crater far behind them, the road surface cleared and she drove faster. Standing trees re-appeared and they passed empty houses with overgrown gardens flowering with daffodils and primroses in the morning sun. The wind tugged at their hair, the engine droned, and Wesley felt sleepiness creeping up on him again. He closed his eyes.

He woke to the drumming sound of rain. He was still sitting in the back of the jeep, which was parked beneath the corrugated iron roof of an old hay barn. To his left, hay, grey and musty with age, was stacked to the roof. The other three sides of the barn were open and beyond its eves, rain fell steadily onto the grass of a deserted farmyard. Rusty machinery lay amongst brambles and weeds. A long low building ran the length of one side of the yard and on the other side, missing a few slates and with its white paint peeling from the door and window frames, was an old farmhouse. Mikhail still sat in the front seat with his head tipped forward and to one side. Every few breaths he gave a quiet snore. The others had gone.

Wesley tugged his coat around him, listening to the rain. He thought back to the children he'd seen in the crater and felt a nugget of anger nudge him from somewhere inside. He thought of Martin, the twins and little Christmas back in the tunnels. He wanted them to be able to hear this rain too. Once Mikhail had found his water, then they would be going on to find the Horse People. That was the plan they had discussed with Anguillaro. For a moment he imagined himself as a young fighter, riding among them, freeing the tunnel children with Pearson and the other supervisors running in fear. But the image evaporated. He was just a twelve year old boy and not brave at all and the nearest he'd got to riding a horse was a donkey at the seaside. He'd just been old enough to read its name written across the bridle in silver letters – 'Jimmy'.

Mikhail lifted his head a little, snored, and then sank down again. The rain drummed on. Wesley thought he could hear another sound, like the rain but slightly different. It came and went, and then he heard it again. It sounded like a motorcycle in the distance. He tipped his head to one side and concentrated. The sound had gone again. Then, just for a moment it returned. It sounded like the motorcycle was accelerating from a start and then it faded away, swallowed up by the drumming of the rain on the metal sheeting above him.

The door from the house opened and Katie appeared. She walked out into the rain, splashing through a puddle in the yard and came into the barn, her hair and face dripping with water. She smiled at Wesley.

"Hi Katie. Where's Max and Janis?"

"Janis is in the house Wesley. Food's ready."

She walked round to Mikhail, reached out, and put her arms around his neck, resting her head against his. Mikhail woke with a last little snore and smiled. He put an arm around her.

"Katie my lovely one… you're soaking!"

He looked out at the farmyard and turning, saw Wesley in the back seat.

"Wesley. What are we doing sitting here?"

"We've been asleep."

"For long? What's the…"

"Eleven twenty-one Grandpa," said Katie. "Asleep for four hours and six minutes. Food in the house now."

There were no remains of people in the house. What the fate of the inhabitants had been they could only guess. Janis had found some canned food in the cobweb-strewn kitchen and lunch was tuna and cold baked beans eaten off china plates, followed by some of the biscuits from their packs. They drank rainwater from china cups and refilled their water bottles. They slept then until evening, Wesley curled up in a dusty armchair in the front room and the others in any comfortable place they could find. No one chose to use the beds upstairs, although they had each taken a blanket from them. The bedrooms, with personal items still in place on shelves and in cupboards, felt as though they were still the private places of family members, now, almost certainly, dead.

Taking with them a blanket each, and a cooking pot that Janis stuffed into her pack, they set off again at dusk. They left the jeep, which was almost out of petrol, in the barn. The rain had stopped but the air was cold and the track from the farm back up to the main road was muddy and lined with long wheel-rut puddles. At the main road they listened carefully. The only sound was the wind, gusting unsteadily, rustling the spring leaves on the trees and hedges.

"It's about twenty miles to the city," said Max. "We should make it tonight if we can keep to the road. First sign of headlights though, we're into whatever cover we can find."

From the far side of the road came a loud snort. Everybody jumped. They heard something thudding on the ground. The branches of the roadside bushes waved and flicked. Something was pushing through them, coming straight towards them.

"Back, back," hissed Max. But before anyone had the

chance to move, a huge animal burst out of the bushes. It was a horse. Its hooves clattered onto the tarmac and it turned to face the way it had come, blowing out short snorts of breath, its head dipping and rising.

Katie screamed. The horse started and swung round towards them, eyes big and round with alarm, its hooves skidding on the road With its head held up and its ears turned back, it bolted away down the road, tail held high, in the direction of the city.

Wesley's heart was beating fast from the fright. In the last light of the evening, he could see that Katie was shaking. Mikhail took both her hands in his.

"It's ok Katie," he reassured her. "Just a wild horse. It probably got more of a fright than we did."

"Gave me a fright," said Janis. "You all right Wesley?"

"Think so. Didn't half make me jump. What's a horse doing here anyway?"

"There'll be farm animals that have survived, living wild, she replied. "Cows, sheep, maybe chickens if the foxes haven't had them. None of them will be much used to seeing people anymore."

"Want to go home Grandpa. Back to the Care Halls." Katie was standing, feet apart, arms rigid at her sides and her head hung forward. "Go home now Grandpa," she demanded.

"Katie." Mikhail let out a long breath. "We have to go on. We're going to where I used to work. Remember? The lab? Then it's in the boat, over the estuary. We're going to St Terresas, to the Horse People."

"You told me all this Grandpa. Told me before. Don't want to go, want to go home. Now."

"Katie." Wesley felt a slight irritation. He tried to keep it out of his voice. "We have to go to the city. I know it's... hard.

But... we have to. Look, I'll carry your pack for you if you like. Would that help?"

"My pack Wesley. I'll carry it."

Wesley looked at Mikhail. "Can't we just start walking?"

Mikhail briefly glanced at everyone and then turned back to Katie. "Remember the tunnel children Katie, who you used to listen to playing? We have to help them..."

"You told me before..."

"Yes, yes. I did. I know. I'm reminding you. They are made to work so hard that sometimes their hands bleed. We can help them so that they don't have to do that anymore. You want to do that, don't you?"

"Want to help, yes."

"Well this is the only way we can. We have to go to the city and then go over the estuary to get help."

Katie remained rigid. It was too dark to see now but Wesley imagined that her fingers would be wiggling away. Everyone stood silently by in the darkness.

"Katie," said Wesley.

"Yes?" she replied, head still down.

"Please. Let's start walking."

She lifted her head and looked at him.

"The children's hands bleed when they work?

"Yes they do."

She stared at him for a moment and then, in a cheery voice, as if nothing had happened she said, "Ok. Let's go now."

Nothing more was said. The travelers set off into the darkness towards the city. They trudged on steadily through the night using the faint dashes of the white road markings to guide them. No vehicles came along the road, though after the first mile or so they came across the horse again. It galloped away into the complete blackness of a wood. But other than the horse, the only sounds they heard were the rustlings and callings of small animals in the hedgerows and the distant barking of a dog. During the early hours it began to rain and the water soaked through Wesley's boots and into his socks. By the time it stopped, his clothes were damp and heavy and he felt cold and dispirited.

They reached the outskirts of the city by dawn. The alertness that they had set out with had drained away. Mikhail and Katie had fallen behind and the others stopped and waited for them to catch up. Ahead of them the wet road sloped down a long hill. It was once again littered with stones and rubble and the first buildings, as they became clearer in the growing light, showed signs of blast damage. On one side of the road the lifeless remains of an old factory rose four storeys high behind a car park. Sections of masonry were missing from a parapet above the uppermost windows and the stub of a broken chimney poked up from behind. Several abandoned cars were parked haphazardly among the puddles of the car park. They were covered in the grime and rain-streaked dust and some of those nearest to the building had been hit by falling bricks, their roofs stoved in and their windows smashed.

Next to the factory was a petrol station. Cars were parked in a line at the back of the forecourt with price signs still visible through their grimy windscreens. The other side of the road was lined with semi-detached houses, set back from the pavement. Patches of tiles had been ripped from their roofs and few windows remained unbroken. Television ariels, bent and twisted, pointed wildly in all directions and grasses sprouted from the gutters. Everything was in a state of decay except nature. Weeds and overgrown garden plants grew unchecked. Grass sprouted from the edges of the curb stones and birds chirped and chattered excitedly in the early light.

Wesley un-shouldered his pack and sat down, leaning against a low wall that divided the pavement from the factory car park. He took a few sips from his water flask. His legs ached and he was hungry. He thought of the house and garden of his childhood. The thought of it, empty and decaying like these houses, made him feel lost, cast adrift from his past. Seeing all the devastation from the meteorites and the great emptiness everywhere, made everything seem suddenly pointless. He wanted to wrap his blanket around him, lie down on the pavement and sleep.

Mikhail and Katie trudged up to where he sat. Mikhail looked exhausted. Katie had her blanket wrapped around her shoulders and was looking at the ground in front of her feet.

"Katie and I are too tired to walk any further," said Mikhail. "We need to rest."

Janis nodded. "We all do. How about one of these houses?"

"Anywhere," replied Mikhail. "Just as long as there isn't…"

"I'll check first," said Max.

They followed Max through the overgrown garden of the nearest house. The door was locked, so Max climbed in through a broken window. A minute later he unlocked the door from the inside, came out and closed the door behind him.

"Not this one," he said quietly. "Let's try the next."

He tried the next three houses and rejected each of them. He had taken two steps into the overgrown driveway of the fourth house when he stopped and turned back to the others on the pavement. He slid his hand back over the stubble of his head. "Not sure if I can face another house if it's… the same," he said

Janis took his arm and led him back. "Don't Max." She nodded towards the other side of the road. "What about that old factory?"

"Yes," he nodded. "Let's try it."

A rusty van was parked on the road beside them, its back tyres flat and the rear doors twisted where they had been forced open. As Wesley stepped out from behind the van to cross the road, he automatically looked both ways. To his astonishment he saw, no more than a few hundred yards further along, a boy and a girl on bicycles ride across the road and disappear into a side street.

17
The Hermit

If the Hermit hadn't been cooking his breakfast, Sarah and Rebecca might never have found him.

It had taken a long day's ride to reach the hills and they'd kept a wary eye for any scouts or soldiers from The Order. They'd camped overnight beside a grove of low windswept beech trees and now they were riding northwards again, the horse's heads nodding and lifting, pulling at their reins as they climbed a grassy hillside, their hooves leaving crescents in the springy turf behind them. A small flock of sheep watched them from a distance, and crows, cawing loudly, scattered from the ground, dipping and weaving like black rags tossed against the cloudless blue morning sky.

They reached the brow of the hill and pulled the horses to a halt. Before them, horizons of the Northern Hills, one above the other, stretched away into the distance, each one paler and higher than the last until, in the far distance, they met the sky. Between the riders and the first line of hills, the ground sloped down and up through a broad bowl of grassy land strewn with weathered rocks. Leaning back in their saddles, they rode down the slope into the bowl.

A few hundred yards to the right of them, a copse of willows and mountain ash grew on the sloping ground. They had almost ridden beyond it when Sarah reined her horse to a halt and peered towards the trees. She held her hand up, signing Rebecca to stop, then lowered her arm and pointed. On the edge of the copse, behind the first few trees, was a low mound of tufty grass. From the top of the mound a thin wispy line of blue smoke threaded up into the air and dispersed in the tree-tops. As they looked a man emerged from the back of the

166

mound, as if from the ground itself, and walked away from them towards one of the trees. He stopped in front of the tree and stood for a while, feet slightly apart, looking down at the ground. Then he stepped backwards, fiddled with the front of his trousers and walked back towards the mound. His head turned in the direction of Sarah and Rebecca and he stopped. He stared at them for a moment, then looked away and continued on to the mound where he disappeared back into the ground.

"Do you think that's him?" said Rebecca.

"Not sure." said Sarah after a moment. "I don't see any house of tumbled stones, but my guess is that it is. Let's go and find out."

As they rode down towards the grass mound, Sarah turned in the saddle to Rebecca riding beside her.

"What's his name? I mean, how do we ask him if he's the Hermit? Seems a bit rude to say, 'are you the Hermit?' Doesn't it?"

"I agree. I asked quite a few people before we left but no one knew. He was just known as the Hermit. I'll ask him, as politely as I can."

They reached the mound and dismounted, tying the horses to a slender mountain ash. They saw now that the smoke came from the stub of a rusty metal chimney pipe poking up through the grass. The smell of wood smoke was mixed with the savory smell of something cooking. After their simple breakfast of barley biscuits and apples, Sarah and Rebecca found themselves swallowing.

Sarah tilted back her head and breathed in deeply. "Lamb chops?" she said.

"Mmm..." Rebecca replied. "Yes, with a little garlic and rosemary I should say."

"He must be expecting us." Sarah smiled. "I do hope he's done some new potatoes!"

"And broccoli."

"And mint sauce and, oh. Look here. Seems to be the way in."

At the back of the mound a narrow path cut down into the slope and ended in a low wooden door. They walked softly down the path and listened. From behind the door came the sizzling of frying food and the sound of what sounded like a cooking pot being stirred or moved. The delicious smell wafted strongly out from cracks in the wood.

"Here goes," whispered Sarah. She knocked on the door. The cooking pot sounds stopped but the sizzling continued. They waited. The sizzling stopped and there was silence. She knocked again a little louder. Still there was no reply. After a minute she knocked again.

"What do you want?" came a thin high voice from inside.

"We were just wondering if you could spare us a moment," Sarah replied.

"I'm eating my breakfast," came the reply. "Go away."

"Oh, sorry to disturb you," Sarah said to the door. "We don't mind waiting."

There was no reply.

"We'll just wait then," she continued.

Again there was no reply. They walked a short distance from the mound and sat on the ground. The sun climbed higher and the air grew warmer. The flock of sheep that they had passed earlier appeared on the brow of the hill and began to wander slowly downwards, stopping to graze here and there and then moving on again. The horses waited patiently in the shade of the tree, occasionally flicking their tails and shaking their heads at flies. Sarah took a watch, one half of its strap missing, from her pocket.

"Surely he's finished his breakfast by now," she said.

"We've been waiting over an hour. Let's go and try again."

They returned to the door and knocked again.

"What do you want?" came the thin, rather irritated voice from inside.

"We wondered if we might be able to speak to you now," said Sarah.

"Why?"

"We were wondering if you might be the person that people call the Hermit, if you'll excuse me asking."

"Might be. Why?"

"Well, if you are, you may be able to help us. You see, we are from Saint Terresas's. My name's Sarah and my friend with me here is Rebecca and we…"

"You from the new horse people?"

"The new horse people? Oh, yes, I suppose we are. The Horse People, that's what we call ourselves. The Horse People."

"Horse People. Stupid name."

Sarah and Rebecca looked at each other. Sarah rolled her eyes and turned back to the door. "Look. We really are sorry to bother you. We've ridden out here to talk to you, if you are the one that they call the Hermit. We're trying to find out about the Chinese Well."

There was silence from behind the door. They waited a while and then Sarah spoke again. "Hello?"

"Yes?"

"The Chinese Well? Do you…"

"Why do you want to know about the Chinese Well?"

"Because… because we are under threat from The Order and…"

"Who?"

"The Order."

"Never heard of them."

"They come from the land east of the estuary. Soldiers,

mostly. They use child slaves. They are a threat to any remaining free people, probably including you if they come up here."

"Bullshit."

Sarah drew a deep breath and linked her arm through Rebecca's.

"Look," she said. "We're not asking for much. Just some information about the well."

"What's in it for me? Eh? If I told you anything, what can you give me in return?"

"I don't know. What do you want?"

From behind the door came the sound of footsteps, the drawing of a bolt and the door swung inwards. Sarah and Rebecca had been standing so close to the door that they stepped backwards quickly. Framed in the doorway stood a short wiry old man. He was almost bald and had a curly grey beard. He wore a roughly made sheepskin waistcoat over a stained white shirt, baggy black trousers and sandals. His feet were leathery and his toenails were long. He pushed his hands deep into his trouser pockets and stared straight at them.

"Horse," he said, looking past them to where the horses were tethered. "Give me one of your horses, and its saddle. Then I'll tell you about the well."

"A horse!" Rebecca spoke for the first time. "We can't give you one of our horses. They're incredibly precious, besides, how would we get back?"

"Your problem," said the man. "That's my price."

"Surely," said Sarah, "for a small bit of information that's rather a high price to ask? What about some information back from us? We could tell you about The Order if you don't know about them."

"Not interested," he said impatiently. "Yes, I am who you

call the Hermit. Yes, I do know something about the Chinese Well, quite a lot actually. And I also know that you wouldn't have ridden up here just because you had a passing interest in the history of it." The Hermit sniffed and wiped the back of his hand across his nose. "If you want information, it's going to cost you. Simple as that. Otherwise kindly leave me in peace."

He stepped back inside and swung the door closed with a bang.

Sarah and Rebecca walked back to the horses.

"What do we do now?" asked Rebecca anxiously. "That's a bit of a high price isn't it?"

"A high price yes," said Sarah thoughtfully. "For something that we don't know the value of. What he might tell us may be of no help at all, and we don't actually know if we can trust him. On the other hand it could be vital. If the well does have anything to do with Lightwater, then I think we need to know about it." She paused and watched Rebecca stroking the neck of one of the horses. "What do you think Rebecca?"

"Logic says to me," she put her arm affectionately over the horse's neck, "that one of our horses is too valuable to risk in such an uncertain bargain. But my gut feeling is different. We have chalices of liquid radiating light and a well with healing properties. I believe, though I can't justify it, that if Lightwater exists then it may have something to do with it and that we should agree to the Hermit's bargain. So long as we have one horse in case of danger, I don't mind walking back."

"If it comes to that we'll share the travelling, Rebecca, walking and riding." Sarah put her hands together and rested her chin on her fingertips. For a while she stood quite still and then began to gently nod her head. "Ok," she said quietly. "Let's give him his bargain."

In the soft grey light from a small window, set in the side

of the Hermit's mound, Sarah and Rebecca found the inside of the place larger and far more comfortable than they had expected. It was sunk down below the outside ground level and the sides, where they could be seen between the shelving and furniture, were lined with well-laid stonework. The floor was made of wooden boards and the whole place smelt of dry earth, wood smoke and the remains of the Hermit's meal.

From the top of a wooden pillar that rose from the centre of the floor to the centre of the ceiling, long beams radiated out and rested on the top of the stone wall that lined the room. Resting on top of the beams, and filling the fan shaped gaps in between, planks held up the turf roof above, giving the impression of being below a giant spider's web. In places, where there were a few gaps between the boards, black polythene could be seen.

To one side of the room, next to a stack of logs, was a black pot bellied stove with a kettle on its flat top, gently steaming from the spout. Beside this, a small kitchen area was laid out with shelves and a work surface covered with an assortment of pots and pans. Tins of food and rows of glass jars, containing pickles, jams and dried mushrooms, lined the shelves. Bunches of dried plants hung from the beams. To the side of this area was a large black water container with a tap at its base. On the other side of the room was an unmade single brass bed, a small washstand complete with china jug and bowl, and a large wooden chest with its lid open, revealing a jumbled mass of blankets and sheepskins.

The remaining wall space was largely taken up with shelves and it was these that caught Sarah and Rebecca's attention more than anything. All but the top shelves were lined with hundreds of books of all sizes. Some, too big to fit upright, were stacked on their sides squeezed in between the others. Many of the books, especially the larger ones, were clearly very old, their bindings worn and blotchy where pale brown leather showed through the dark pigment of dye. Some of the bindings shone with patches of gold leaf, other books had straps and buckles to hold them closed. The top shelves of the cases were lined with precious objects packed close together. A silver jug and a set of bowls, gilt framed pictures, a pair of golden candelabras, a stack of fine porcelain dishes, a bronze sculpture of an angel. Side by side around the shelves they rested, one valuable object after another. Among them, behind a throng of small silver boxes and lockets, were two cut crystal chalices.

The Hermit placed two stacks of books on the floor and beckoned Sarah and Rebecca to on them. He sat on the only chair beside a table in the centre of the room on which stood a pair of ornate silver candle sticks topped with half burned candles.

"So," said the Hermit. "We're agreed. The bay mare and saddle for information about the well. Yes?"

"As long as what you tell us isn't common knowledge," replied Sarah. "You have to make it worthwhile for us."

"It'll be worth it." The Hermit rested his elbows on the table and clasped his hands in front of his face, his small dark eyes showing above his knuckles. A large shiny watch showed on one wrist. It read half past four, though it was still before midday.

"Why do you want to know about the well anyway?"

"That's not part of the bargain," said Sarah cautiously.

"Very well, very well," replied the Hermit irritably. "I'm not interested anyway. What do you want to know?"

"Firstly," said Sarah. "Why is the well at Saint Terresas's called the Chinese Well?"

"You heard of The Water of Light?" said the Hermit.

Rebecca glanced at Sarah. "Yes," she said. "We have."

"Know where it comes from?"

"No."

"China. Came from a well in China. Bought to Jerusalem by traders in the twelfth century, in glass bottles, over six thousand miles along the silk route. Had to be glass, lead glass crystal. The water won't keep long in anything else. Was supposed to heal any sickness. The Crusaders got hold of some, sent a bit to the Pope and bought the rest back here. They called it Chinese Water."

"Why," said Rebecca, "was it called The Water of…"

"Don't interrupt," snapped the hermit. "If you want to know, just listen." He sniffed loudly. "It's called The Water of Light because under certain conditions it glows. The Crusaders, those that got back that is, gave their Water to the monks, and the monks tried making more. The way it was supposed to work is that you put the Chinese Water next to water from a holy well and it affects the holy water, turns it into Chinese Water, Water of Light. Well, most holy wells are just ordinary wells, clean water, good and healthy, but no more than that, not in my opinion anyway. The monks tried dozens of them. None of them worked, until they tried Saint Terresas's and, hey presto it worked. So they left a bottle of it down there in the water. The waters don't have to actually mix, the reaction can happen through glass. Takes just a few minutes I believe. So, that's how it got to be called the Chinese Well. Satisfied?"

"No," said Sarah, leaning forward on her book seat. "We need to know a bit more than that."

"You asked me why the well is called the Chinese Well, and I've told you," the Hermit said, clenching his fists on the table. "The horse now please."

"I said 'firstly' tell me why it is called the Chinese Well." Sarah sat, back straight, hands in her lap, looking directly at the Hermit. There was an edge of authority in her voice. "If you want your horse you need to tell us more."

The Hermit sniffed deeply and shifted restlessly on his chair.

"All right, all right. What else?"

"What about Darkwater," said Sarah. "What do you know about that?

"Water of Darkness? Something else that the Crusaders got their hands on. The exact opposite of the Water of Light. Looked just the same, just like ordinary water, but made you sick instead. Ringing in the ears, fearfulness, made the drinker docile so they wouldn't resist, do whatever anyone told them – The Devil's Water they nicknamed it. Crusaders used to pour a bit into their enemy's wells, just a few drops. Turned the whole lot into Darkwater. And if they themselves needed to use the wells that they'd poisoned, they just had to pour in a bit of Lightwater and it would clean it up; very handy. Although Lightwater can only be made from holy water, Darkwater, see, can be made out of any water."

"And where does Darkwater come from?"

"Lightwater."

"It comes from Lightwater?"

"Made from it. Chinese used lightning. Used to stick copper rods in the ground on a hilltop. Rings of them round a copper barrel of Lightwater. Then they waited. When lightning struck." He smacked his fist into the palm of his hand. "Zap. Darkwater. There was a Russian fellow researching it before the meteorites. Didn't publish much. It's something to do with the way the molecules lay next to one another as I remember. Neither of The Waters last for ever, they slowly lose their potency. He was looking for some way to freshen up Lightwater, something to do with coloured light, I don't know. Can't remember now."

The Hermit pushed his chair back, got up and poured himself a cup of water from the plastic barrel. He drank it and wiped his mouth on his sleeve.

"That it then?"

"What happened to the bottle in the well?"

"Don't know. Anything else?"

"Yes. Before the meteorites, were there supplies of Light or Darkwater around?"

"Don't know," said the Hermit. "Maybe in China. Maybe the Russian had some. I don't know."

"What about the chalices?"

""What chalices?" The Hermit shifted his feet and scratched the side of his nose.

"The ones in the stained glass at Saint Terresas's Abbey."

"Never seen 'em."

"And what about those two?" said Sarah looking at the chalices on the bookshelves.

"Those? The Hermit looked over to them. "I'm looking after them for someone. Same as all this stuff. It's none of your business. Now then, that enough?"

"What about the books?" said Sarah.

"Leaving present. They're mine, and unless there's anything else..." he added sarcastically. "We have a deal to complete." He made a mocking gesture towards the door. "Shall we?"

The Hermit examined the teeth and flanks of the bay mare and then stood with his arms folded. Rebecca transferred the saddle-bags to the other horse while Sarah held the mare's bridle and spoke softly into its ear. When the bags were secure she led the animal the few steps to the Hermit.

"One last thing," she said. "Can you tell me the time?"

The Hermit pulled back his sleeve and looked at his watch.

"Don't know. Watch keeps stopping. It's a dud."

"And are you looking after that for someone too?" There

was a controlled anger in her voice. The Hermit looked up at her and sneered.

"Willingly bargained for thank you. You're not the only one who wants to know about the Water."

"What?" said Sarah. "Who else has been asking?"

The Hermit took the reins. "None of your business. Don't ask me again."

The horse tossed and dipped its head and then allowed itself to be led away a few paces. The Hermit lifted the flaps of the saddle and shortened the stirrups, tugging the straps down tight. He swung confidently into the saddle and began to ride up through the trees.

"What's the price for telling us who's been asking," Sarah called after him.

The Hermit turned in the saddle and laughed.

"Your other horse," he called back.

18
Stones like Hornets

Still dozy with sleep, Wesley opened his eyes and focused on a grimy whitewashed wall a few inches from his face. He couldn't remember where he was. His body ached. He was lying on faded green canvas. He rolled over. The factory, of course. How long had he been sleeping? The others were still asleep beneath their blankets, each lying on one of the folded tarpaulins they had found stacked against a wall. He got up and stretched.

Apart from what looked like some offices at one end, the room they were in occupied the whole ground floor of the building and, at intervals, square brick pillars supported the high concrete ceiling. Heavy machinery occupied areas of the floor, chains hung from gantries suspended above them, and between the machines there were several long metal tables. Some of them were bare. Others had on them boxes and metal tubes, paper and pieces of equipment, all of which were covered in a thick layer of dust that merged the colours into little more than shades of grey. Sun slanted in through the broken windows at the back of the room and apart from the soft snores of Mikhail, everything was quiet.

His arms and legs were stiff. He walked across the factory floor to the door and stepped out into the car park. A pair of swallows darted above the abandoned cars, chattering loudly, weaving in and out of each other and were gone again, as quickly as they had appeared. He kicked a stone, sending it skitting across the car park, and wandered out to the road. The sun was warm and he turned towards it, eyes closed, feeling it on his face. He opened his eyes and looked up and down the road. He imagined how it used to be, busy with vehicles and people. Now there was no one but himself.

He walked along the pavement to the garage. Paper and plastic bags littered the forecourt, shifting and stopping in the light breeze. Grass grew at the base of the pumps, only one of which had its nozzle in its holder; the others had their pipes trailing onto the ground, nozzles lying among the grit and rubbish of the tarmac. Beyond the pumps was an abandoned shop and office. A sign hung crookedly above the window that read 'THOMPSONS QUALITY USED CARS'. He crossed the forecourt and peered through the broken glass of the door. Cans and empty bottles littered the floor. A cash register on the counter was open and empty. An ice cream fridge lay on its side, a congealed mass of wrappers and dried brown sludge spilled from the open top. On the shelves stood dusty plastic bottles of oil and car cleaning products. Nothing edible remained.

Wesley stepped inside and picked his way across the shop to a door behind the counter. It led into an office. Paper lay everywhere, drawers hung open from a desk and one lay up-side-down on the floor. Car keys attached to brown labels with numbers on them were scattered around it on the floor. He shuffled them around in the dust with his foot then pushed open a door that led outside and walked back onto the forecourt. The row of cars, as with the cars in front of the factory, all had their filler cap lids wrenched open. But one, an estate car that was parked close to the office wall, remained closed. Out of curiosity, Wesley read the number plate and returned to the office. He dusted off each of the key labels in turn until he found the right number and returned to the car. He unlocked the door, tugged it open and slipped into the driver's seat. Although the outside of the vehicle was so dusty that he could hardly see out, the inside was perfectly clean. He put the key into the ignition and gently turned it. A red light glowed faintly among the dials on the dashboard. He got out of the car, wandered back to the factory and went in.

"Wesley." Janis sounded relieved. "Where were you? We were about to start looking for you."

"Just outside. Looking at the cars and stuff."

"Best if we keep in sight of each other," said Max. "Or say where we're going. Those kids on the bikes that you saw, we don't know who they are, and we can't be sure that there aren't any soldiers in the city either. We have to be careful."

"Sorry," said Wesley.

"No, no. It's ok." Max replied. "It's just something I think we all need to be aware of. Any nice cars for sale?"

"Well." Wesley brightened up. "I tried the keys in one."

"Take her for a spin?" Max chuckled. "Mikhail and I were just wondering if we could find a car."

"A red light came on, very faintly."

"Did it?" Max became serious again. "You try starting it?"

"Well, just the light came on."

Max looked at Mikhail. "It'll probably be empty but maybe we should take a look at this car of Wesley's. It's already gone three o'clock and it's quite a way through the city to Mikhail's old lab. If we could drive, keeping to the back streets, we could get the Water, if it's there, and get down to the docks before dark."

"I want to go in Wesley's car," said Katie brightly.

"If it has an ignition light," said Janis, "then perhaps we could bump start it down the hill."

"Exactly," said Max.

"Except it probably hasn't got any fuel."

"It could have fuel," said Wesley. "The place where you put the petrol in, you know, on the side, that's still closed."

"Let's go and see this car of yours," said Mikhail.

He and Wesley walked out to the car with their packs and blankets while the others got ready to go.

"Know how to drive?" Mikhail asked.

"No," Wesley replied. "My Mum and Dad had a car but I was too young."

"Sit inside and I'll show you while we wait for the others."

Wesley slid into the driver's seat and Mikhail leant on the roof, looking in through the door beside him.

"That's the gear stick," he said. "See, it's got the numbers on it. 'R' means reverse. You have to have the stick in the middle to start her up."

Wesley wiggled the gear stick around, pushing it to each of the numbers and back.

"The three pedals down there," Mikhail pointed to his feet.

"That's the accelerator. The middle one's the brake and the other's the clutch. You push on the clutch, try it, that's it. Then into gear, first, to start off. You've got it, and then a little bit on the accelerator as you ease your foot slowly off the clutch and you're away. There, if the engine was running you'd be moving now." He chuckled. "If this car goes I'll teach you to drive one day."

"Nice car!" said Max arriving with the others. " Where's the key Wesley?"

"In it."

"You driving?" he winked and nodded for Wesley to move over.

Wesley slid across and Max got in. He turned the key. A faint click came from the engine. He released the handbrake, stepped out and held the steering wheel through the open door.

"Let's try her. Push everyone. Out on to the road."

Wesley leaped out and pushed with the others. The car slowly began to move, its tyres crunching on the grit. Bit by bit they pushed it across the forecourt and out onto the road. Max pulled the brake on.

"May as well put our packs in." He walked to the back and opened the boot. "Even if we just roll down the hill, we don't want to walk back. First though I need to clean these windows. Can't see a thing in there."

He fished into the boot and pulled out an old rag. He rubbed at a window with it. The grime just smeared. It was too stuck to the glass to wipe off. He rummaged in his pack and pulled out his water bottle. Sprinkling small amounts on the windscreen, he wiped away the grime until the glass was clear enough to see through. He gave each of the other windows the same treatment and closed the boot.

They pushed the car along the road to the top of the hill that sloped down into the city and climbed in, Mikhail in the front passenger's seat and Katie, Wesley and Janis in the back. Max let off the brake and the car began to roll, picking up speed as the hill steepened. He jammed it into gear and released the clutch. The engine turned, slowing the car until it almost stopped. It didn't fire. He let the car gather speed once more and tried again. This time the engine began to fire on one cylinder, bucking everyone forward and backwards. Black smoke belched in gusts from the exhaust. A second cylinder caught, there was more smoke and then suddenly it was running smoothly. The smoke cleared and the petrol gauge sprang into life. It showed nearly half a tank. Max patted the dashboard.

"Nice car you have here Wesley."

"And it looks like I'll be giving you driving lessons," Mikhail spoke over his shoulder. "You all right there Katie?"

"I like Wesley's car Grandpa. Better than walking."

"I agree," said Janis. "My legs are stiff as wood."

Wesley leant back into the soft seat, his shoulder against

Katie's. Her hands lay flat on her legs and her fingers tapped up and down with tiny rhythmical movements. In the front, Mikhail and Max were discussing a route through the city, Mikhail gesturing left and right turns with his hands. Wesley saw the dull silver band of Anguillaro's eel ring on his finger.

Though the window beside him was smeared from where Max had cleaned it, it was clear enough for him to see the streets outside. Stones, and bits of brick and slate, lay everywhere. Although some of the buildings had no serious damage showing, others had roofs with patches of slates ripped away, gutters broken, and pots and bits of masonry missing from their chimneys. Some houses were boarded up but most had shattered windows and sat, one after the other, like a parade of skulls with empty eye sockets lining the roads.

They passed a cinema. A car had smashed through the plate glass windows of the foyer, leaving its boot sticking out onto the pavement. A large shard of glass lay on its roof and the doors hung open. A peeling giant poster from a billboard outside hung limply forward and everywhere there were abandoned cars, stones and rubbish. A scrawny dog watched them warily from the pavement and slunk beneath a fence as they passed. One street that they turned into had several of its houses burned to a shell. Thick dark soot stains rose above each window. The front of one house had collapsed and a heap of charred bricks and rubble blocked the way, forcing them to find another route.

Far from getting used to the deserted word outside, Wesley found the sense of emptiness greater here than in the country-side. The place had once been filled with the hubbub of daily life but now it was silent and eerie and even though being in the car had at first given him a feeling of safety, he now felt uneasy.

Max turned into a wide driveway and drove up to a weed

covered gravel car park in front of a large three story stone building. The building was surrounded by trees and overgrown lawns. From the centre of its roof rose a tall bell tower capped with a conical lead roof, topped with a weather vane. Above the main entrance to the building, letters were cut into the stone lintel. They read 'CITY UNIVERSITY'. He drove round to the back and stopped the car. The building had fared better than most that they had seen. Some of the windows were broken but many remained in tact. Ivy flourished at one end, reaching up above the first floor windows and all but completely blocking some of those on ground level. Weeds grew through the gravel outside and a row of wheely-bins against the wall were tipped onto their sides, their contents of bottles, boxes and paper scattered on the ground.

"It's in the basement," said Mikhail, "I hope. If the back door's locked it'll be easy enough to get through a window. Won't be a minute. Wait here Katie." He opened the door and got stiffly out.

"I'm coming with you." Janis followed him out. "Hoot if there's trouble Max."

Mikhail and Janis disappeared through a door into the building. From a tree in the overgrown gardens, several pigeons flew up with a flurry of wings and wheeled away. The sky had begun to cloud over. Wesley, Katie and Max waited quietly in the car. Katie was leaning forward on the back of Max's seat. She moved her head down, looking into the rearview mirror.

"Bicycle children," she said suddenly and turned to look out of the rear window.

Max and Wesley looked round but the driveway and the overgrown gardens beyond were deserted.

"Where?" said Max.

"Gone now," said Katie. "Round the side."

"Wait here," said Max. He got quickly out of the car and ran back to the corner of the building. Wesley stepped out onto the gravel and scanned the gardens. Katie got out and stood beside him.

"How many were they Katie?"

"Seven boys and girls Wesley."

"Just... riding?"

"Just riding Wesley. Like the others."

Max came running back.

"No sign of anyone," he said. "How many did you see Katie."

"Seven."

"Seven! You sure?"

"Seven," said Katie again a bit louder.

"Sorry Katie," said Max. "Didn't mean to doubt you. I don't suppose kids on bikes, whoever they are, are too much of a threat. But what are they doing here? And who are they?" He shook his head sharply. "I don't like it. I wish they'd hurry up in there. It seems to be extra quiet round here."

Wesley felt uneasy. He looked back at the door. Something in a first floor window caught the corner of his eye. By the time he looked at it directly the window was blank. He had the distinct impression that there had been a movement there. He blinked, shook his head and stared at the window. Nothing.

"Into the car," said Max suddenly. "Quickly. Don't slam the door."

Wesley took Katie's arm and together they slid back into the rear seat. Max got back behind the wheel, pulled his door gently closed with a soft click and turned to look out of the rear window.

"I'm sure I heard voices," he said.

Wesley and Katie turned and as they did, several soldiers walked round the corner of the building, rifles slung over their shoulders, the black eagle emblem of The Order emblazoned on their jackets.

"Heads down," said Max.

Wesley sunk down in the seat and Katie copied him. His door was still open and very slowly he peered round the side. The soldiers had stopped and were looking down past the car. They seemed unaware that there was anyone in it. Two of them were lighting a cigarette from one match, one cupping the flame for the other.

"I can see them," whispered Wesley.

"What are they doing?" replied Max.

"Nothing. Now they're walking over to the grass."

Another soldier walked briskly from behind the building towards the others. The two men who were smoking stubbed their cigarettes out on the ground. All of them became attentive. The new soldier appeared to be in command. He pointed at the car and the entire group started walking briskly towards it, their boots crunching noisily on the gravel.

Max hit the horn and the soldiers broke into a run. He took a deep breath.

"We're in trouble now."

As he spoke a second group of soldiers rounded the other end of the building. There were shouts and they also began running towards the car.

"Inside," said Max quickly, already half way out of the car. "Quick, run."

Wesley jumped out. Katie stayed sitting in the back seat.

"Katie, come on."

"Scared Wesley." Katie sat with her hands trembling against her cheeks, staring straight ahead through the windscreen. The first group of soldiers was already half way between the end of the building and the car. Wesley reached in, grabbed one of her hands and tried to pull her out. She tore her hand away.

"Katie!" It was Mikhail's voice. He was standing just inside the doorway with Janis. Each of them held a wooden box. "Run, quickly."

Katie slid across the seat, jumped out of the car and ran with Wesley towards the door,

"Stop!" the soldier in charge of the first group shouted. "You can't get away. Give yourselves up."

Wesley and Katie reached the door and dived in. Max swung the door closed behind them with a crash. He slid a bolt across at the base of the door, found another at the top and slid it across too. The door thumped loudly as a soldier crashed against it. They were in a dark corridor leading along to what looked like a room that was bright with natural light. The corridor walls were lined with dusty glass frames. Light spilled from the open door of a room on one side. The sound of smashing glass and soldiers voices came from inside.

They ran to the end of the passage, Janis and Mikhail clutching the boxes. The room at the end was a broad entrance hall. Ahead was a large double door.

"That's the main door," said Mikhail. "If…"

He was cut short by the thudding of boots as soldiers ran into the passage behind them from the side room. Max ran ahead to the main door and turned the handle. It was unlocked. He swung the door open and they ran out onto a sweep of stone steps that led down to the main driveway.

Dozens of soldiers stood looking up at them with pistols and rifles in their hands. Accompanied by the metallic clicks of safety catches being released, they took a few paces towards the bottom of the steps. Katie moved next to Mikhail and held his arm. The soldiers from the passageway blocked the doorway behind.

"Down the steps please." The voice of a soldier in charge came from behind them. "No nonsense."

They walked slowly down. The soldier followed them and then stood in front of Mikhail.

"Mr. Kuroski I assume," he said evenly. "The box please." Mikhail didn't reply. He simply stood, clutching the box tightly to him. Wesley could see that he was shaking.

"Mr. Kuroski. The box. Give it to me," the soldier demanded. "Now."

Mikhail looked down at Katie beside him and then, with trembling hands, lifted the box to head height and dropped it. The sound of breaking glass came from inside and a damp patch spread out on the gravel.

"Damn you!" The soldier shouted. He quickly turned his attention to Janis, shouting an order to his men. "Grab that other box."

Four soldiers marched briskly towards Janis. She turned to Mikhail. He gave a tiny nod and, before the soldiers reached her, she dropped the box. It landed heavily on the gravel, but there was no sound of glass, no leaking water. One of the soldiers scooped it up.

"Got it Sergeant," he said.

There was a look of relief on the Sergeant's face. He turned back to Mikhail.

"Any more of these boxes in there Mr. Kuroski?"

Mikhail was breathing hard. Katie put her arms tightly around him and looked up to him. The Sergeant grabbed her by the arm and pulled her roughly away. She screamed, holding her hands over her head.

"Any more?" he shouted at Mikhail. "We'll find…" The Sergeant's head jolted violently. He dropped his pistol, staggered sideways and fell heavily, holding the side of his face in his hands. He pulled one hand away and looked at it through half closed eyes. Blood was streaked across his fingers. A small pebble flashed through the air from the direction of the overgrown gardens and a second man yelped, spinning sideways as it hit him on the shoulder. More pebbles shot in. They seemed to be coming from all directions. The soldiers leapt and shouted as if they were being attacked by a swarm of hornets. Three of them dropped to the ground clutching their heads. Another lay on the gravel, unmoving, blood gushing from his forehead. Mikhail grabbed Katie's hand and led her quickly down the side of the steps and crouched with her against a small door set in a recess in the wall. Wesley and the others followed, covering their heads with their arms. The soldiers were looking in all directions, desperately trying to see where the stones were coming from. One put his rifle to his shoulder and fired several shots at one of the upstairs windows, sending shards of glass smashing down onto the ground. Then he fell to the side clutching his knee. More soldiers started firing, aiming into a patch of rhododendron bushes beneath the trees. The men who had been standing in the main doorway backed into the entrance hall and all that could be seen of them was their rifle barrels poking out through the doorway.

"Cover the prisoners," the sergeant shouted, holding the side of his head with one hand, waving his pistol in the direction of Wesley and the others. "You two, Smith, Bream. Keep them covered."

Two soldiers hurried half way down the steps, crouched down and pointed their rifles at them. Katie screamed and cowered in the doorway. Several stones hit the masonry behind

the soldiers and one of the men yelped. He dropped his rifle
and clutched at his hand. Wesley reached over Katie's head and
tried the door latch. It was locked. Seconds after he had
withdrawn his hand, he heard a bolt being drawn on the other
side of the door. It opened half way and a boy, about Wesley's
age slipped through the door and crouched down between him
and Katie. He wore a red hooded sweatshirt, dirty jeans and
trainers. The guards hadn't noticed and seemed quite unaware
that there was an extra person in the group. The other soldiers
had regained some order and taken to the long grass, lying in
groups, firing sporadically into the trees and bushes.

The guard who had been hit picked up his rifle again; blood
ran from his hand. Stones still flew in, though none were landing
around Wesley and the others. The other guard was crouching
low on the steps. He looked over his shoulder towards the trees
and as he did so, the boy beside Wesley stood, pulled back the
elastic on a large wooden handled catapult and fired. The guard
fell backwards clutching his neck and landed heavily on the
other guard.

"This way," said the boy, pushing open the door.

19
The Well

The Abbey well was ten feet wide and over seventy feet deep. It had been hacked, perfectly round, straight through the bedrock that was the foundation of the Abbey beside it. A spiral stairway had been cut into the sides, each step perfectly flat and straight, and the wall beside them, herringboned with chisel marks, held a pitted iron hand rail that ran from the top to the bottom. So skilled had been the stonemasons that a balustrade, carved out of the rock itself, had been left on the outer edge of the stairway. At the bottom, a stone platform edged the dark still water that had remained, year in, year out, at exactly the same level since the well was dug.

Wearing trousers and a thick sweatshirt, Rebecca lowered herself into the water at the bottom. The light from a lantern hanging from the well-rope reflected the ripples, throwing dancing lines of light onto the walls. Sarah and Owen knelt on the platform beside her.

"It's... freezing!" she gasped. "Still can't touch the bottom."

She was waist deep and lowering herself slowly in.

"Should be just under five foot," said Owen. "Afraid it's going to be a little further."

"There." Rebecca was blowing out in short sharp breaths. "I'm standing. Feels like... gravel. God this is cold." Only her head and shoulders remained above the water. "I'm mad!" She laughed, stretching out a hand to Owen. "Give me the goggles."

Owen handed her a pair of swimming goggles.

"They're rather old," he said. "But they should work."

She pulled them over her head and worked them into place around her eyes.

"Ok, here goes." She took a deep breath and, dipping her

head under, she twisted beneath the surface and swan down to
the bottom. The chill quickly pushed into her skin. Her feet
were already numb with cold. Kicking to keep herself down
she dug into the gravel with her fingers causing a mist of silt
to rise into the water. Only a few inches down she felt solid
rock. She worked quickly but thoroughly across the bottom,
trying to disturb the silt as little as possible. Shards of broken
pottery lay half buried. A corroded metal bowl rested against
the stone side. A leather boot, half disintegrated, showed lines
of rusty nails in its sole and there were coins, dozens of them,
scattered on the gravel, wishes from days when the world had
been different. Rebecca closed her hand on a curved piece of
broken pottery. She turned in the water and stood, breaking
through the surface and refilling her lungs with a gasp.
Shivering she handed the pottery to Owen.

"Earthenware," he said examining it. "Could be the remains
of anything. Possibly a broken water vessel, someone collecting
water, dropped it on the stone perhaps."

Rebecca's teeth were chartering. "Lots of it. Can't see…
any bottle, or anything… not broken. I'll look again."

"Sure you can dive again?" said Sarah concerned.

"Just once more." Rebecca took a breath and plunged back
down into the water.

She bought up a more pottery and pushed it onto the ledge.
Sarah and Owen took one of her arms each and hauled her up.
Water streamed off her shaking body. Sarah wrapped a towel
over her hair and a coat across her shoulders and the three of
them climbed the stairs back to the daylight above.

Rebecca cupped her hands round a steaming mug of soup on
the Abbot's Kitchen table. She wore dry clothes, though her
hair was still damp and hung in a straggle over her shoulders.

Sarah sat beside her and Owen, sitting opposite, turned the pieces of pottery over in his hands. Mark strode across the room and slid onto the bench beside him.

"Cold down there, eh Becci?" He smiled at Rebecca. "Rather you than me! No bottle though I hear." He pushed the copper bracelet back up his wrist and reached for a shard of the pottery. "You think this could have been the container?"

"Had to be glass," said Sarah, "according to the Hermit. Lead glass crystal."

Mark shrugged. "Maybe it is just good clean water then. By the sounds of him, I'd not trust anything the Hermit said anyway."

"Mark." Rebecca focused on her mug of soup. "My story about the virus… I didn't make it up you know."

"No disrespect Becci," said Mark. "Suppose I find the whole idea a bit far fetched. That's all. Did they even have glass back then anyway?"

"Chinese had glass," Owen was trying to fit two pieces of pottery together. "And the Romans. They found the remains of glass windows in the ruins of Pompeii. That's about two thousand years ago, long before the crusades." He looked up at the others. "If a bottle was ever in the well, then it's gone now. Pottery and glass can easily smash on the stone above the water level, but once it's down there, under the water, I would have thought it was unlikely to get broken. But there was no glass down there, unless you think you could have missed it Becci?"

"If there was a bottle I'd have found it," she replied. "If there was broken glass, I'd have cut my hands." She paused and then went on. "I guess that's it. The end of our investigations. But I still believe there's something special about the well water."

"Me too," said Sarah. "You know, it's occurred to me that

the fact that none of us got the virus might be more remarkable that we think."

"Isolation," said Mark. "That's why we lived. It's because we cut ourselves off."

"But so did others. And like them, we did sometimes have contact with people from beyond Saint Terresas. I don't know. You may be right Mark, and I'm still of an open mind. There is quite a bit of written evidence that the well is special, and maybe we shouldn't be too quick to dismiss the old wives' tales. I do believe what the Hermit told us. Something about the details and the way he told us. Sounds a bit odd I suppose, given the sort of character that he appears to be. It's just my gut feeling."

Owen swept the shards of pottery together with his hands. "Well. We've drawn a blank. We'll tell the others at the meeting this afternoon and then we must get on with more pressing things. Any fresh news Mark?"

"Nothing that you don't already know. The Order getting closer and still no news from Janis. I'm worried about her."

"Me too." Owen nodded. "Me too."

20
The City Children

The gunshots, muffled now, continued outside. Janis was the last through the door and turning back, Wesley saw her hesitate, her hand on the bolt.

"Where's Max?" she said urgently.

The voice of one of the soldiers came from outside.

"They're in here," he shouted.

Janis slid the bolt into place. Seconds later someone tried to open the door from the other side. "They've locked it," came the soldier's voice. The door shuddered from a blow. Janis turned back and caught up with Wesley. The door began to thud and shake from boots kicking it.

"They've got him," Janis moaned. "Oh Max." She held Wesley's eyes for a second. "On," she said. "We have to go on. Hurry."

They followed the boy down a dimly lit basement passageway. Neat rows of pipes, encased in dusty silver insulation, ran along the ceiling above them. Other passageways branched off to the left and right and there were arched doorways leading to basement rooms. Katie clung to Mikhail. Wesley followed behind them, his heart thumping against his ribs. The boy led the way into a room at the end of the passage. To one side, a mass of pipes converged on an old central heating boiler. At the far end, a heap of coal, lit with natural light from a hatch above it, sloped up against the wall. At the top of the coal, crouched in the light beside the opening, was a girl of about fourteen. Her hair was wild and curly; she wore a denim jacket, tracksuit trousers and trainers. The boy scrambled up the coal to her, sending lumps tumbling to the floor. Together they looked through the opening. The girl crawled through the hole and the boy turned, beckoned everyone to follow and then disappeared after the girl. Janis led the way up the coal behind them and Wesley clambered after her and out through the hatch into the bright daylight.

They were at the back of the building again. The car was there, to the right, its doors still open. To the left, only a short distance away, was the corner of the building. The girl ran to the corner, looked cautiously round it and ran back, nodding her head and jabbing a finger urgently towards the trees and bushes beyond the tufty overgrown grass that edged the gravel. Mikhail crawled out of the hole, hands and knees, like everyone else's, black with coal dust.

"You the last?" the boy demanded.

"No," Mikhail replied. "There's one more."

He looked back through the hole.

"He didn't come through the door," Janis pulled at his sleeve. "They've got him. There's nothing we can do."

"Can't wait," said the boy sharply. "Run, and don't stop. To the trees. Go!"

He set off as he finished, the girl with him, sprinting over the grass. The gunfire had stopped and orders were being shouted from the other side of the building.

They ran, Janis holding Katie's hand and Mikhail running beside them, struggling to keep up. Wesley was ahead of them. The long grass flicked past his boots. The trees were only a short way ahead. He glanced back at the others and as he did, he saw two soldiers step out of the door at the back of the building. Janis caught his look, turned and urged Katie and Mikhail to run faster. The soldiers shouted and seconds later came the loud 'crack' of a rifle. Wesley punched at the air in front of him, willing his legs forward as fast as they would go. He reached the trees, rounded a bush and ran straight into the boy in the red sweatshirt, knocking him back a pace.

Both of them were breathing hard. The boy still had his catapult in one hand. For a split second he stared straight at Wesley. His hood had fallen back, revealing roughly cropped untidy black hair. His dark eyes were fierce and alert. A bullet thwacked into the bark of a tree above them, followed instantly by the sound of the shot. Wesley and the boy dropped down into a crouch. Janis, Katie and Mikhail, breathing hard, ran past them and on onto the trees. There was another shot, and then two more. The boy dipped his hand into a roughly made canvas bag on his belt, drew out a smooth round stone and fitted it quickly into his catapult sling.

Wesley half turned to go then looked back towards the house. There was no sign of Max. Several more guards had appeared from the door. There were shouts and a group of them set off across the grass at a run. Wesley heard the sound of someone moving behind him. He turned quickly. It was the girl and another hooded boy wearing a man's baggy grey suit. He carried a small backpack and wore a faded blue baseball cap. He had the same fierce look in his eyes as the first boy. Both him and the girl held catapults with stones pinched in the slings ready to fire. He glanced briefly at Wesley, crouched forward by the side of the bush and drew back the catapult. Wesley heard a 'thwang' from the first boy's catapult, then more in rapid succession from the boy and girl. As they fired, two other boys appeared behind the base of a tree, drew back catapults and fired.

One of the soldiers yelped and fell sideways clutching his knee.

"Faces," the first boy hissed. "Go for faces. Go for blood."

Another volley of stones whipped out from the catapults and the soldiers dived to the ground and began crawling rapidly through the grass on their elbows. The boy wearing the grey suit pulled a bottle, half filled with liquid, from his pack. A piece of oily rag was stuffed into its top. The other children went still.

"Don't move," the first boy said quickly. "They see you if you move."

With a plastic gas lighter, the boy in the suit put a flame to the rag in the bottle. It began to smolder. He blew on it and it glowed. Stepping out from behind the bush he hurled the bottle into the air towards the soldiers, turning to run the moment it left his hand.

"Now," shouted the first boy. "Run!"

The children scattered into the trees behind them and Wesley ran with them, crashing through the leaves and leaping over fallen branches. There was a loud roar of whooshing fire and a rush of hot air chased them through the bushes, shivering the leaves. Over his shoulder Wesley saw a sheet of flame swirling up from the grass and a soldier with the back of his jacket on fire, rolling over and over in the grass.

He saw Katie and the others ahead of him, weaving through the trees and between thick clumps of bushes with long shiny green leaves. Other children sprinted through the woods beside him. Rifle shots cracked from behind them. A dog barked and two small fluffy white mongrels appeared, running with them, bounding along between the children with their tongues hanging from the sides of their mouths.

The woodland came to an abrupt end at a tall stone wall. A section of the wall was broken and the teenagers leapt over the fallen stones and through the gap. Katie, Janis and Mikhail were already on the other side and Wesley clambered quickly through. They were on the pavement of a wide street. On the far side, a line of tall buildings ran shoulder to shoulder in each direction. The teenagers ran on ahead across the street and funneled through an archway into a narrow side street. Wesley and the others followed as fast as they could. Another group of teenagers appeared, speeding down the road towards them on bicycles, glancing sideways at them as they passed. They swung under the arch into the side street behind the runners, weaving in between them.

Mikhail trailed behind, breathing hard and Katie ran back to him. Wesley and Janis stopped and waited for them to catch up.

"What are we going to do about Max?" said Mikhail as he caught up.

"Nothing we can do," said Janis. "Keep going. Follow these children, whoever they are, it's…"

A shrill whistle interrupted her. One of the cyclists had re-appeared and was beckoning to them from the end of the side street. At Mikhail's speed they hurried on. Wesley looked over his shoulder. From what he could see back through the archway, there was no sign of the soldiers, but he could hear their shouted commands and it sounded like they were getting quickly closer. The cyclist waited at the corner. It was a girl. She wore a baseball cap turned backwards and a sleeveless leather jacket. A cluster of silver bracelets shone on her wrists and her long dark hair was tied into a ponytail with strips of coloured cloth.

They caught up with her and she turned on her bicycle, accelerating across another wide street that ran parallel with the one back beyond the arch. On the far side was a broad opening beneath one of the buildings. Above it was a long faded red sign. It had the symbol of the city underground railway at each end. Streaks of soot stained upwards across it from the opening below but the words, 'UNIVERSITY STATION', were still readable.

They hurried over the street and followed the girl into the entrance of the old station, ducking beneath a metal grille that was half raised across the opening. The place smelt of smoke. A group of the teenagers, with the two small dogs panting at their feet, were waiting for them, some astride their bicycles. When everyone was in, the first boy and four others pulled at the bottom of the grille. It began to grind downwards, unrolling from above. They jumped up, gripping onto the links and jamming the toes of their shoes between them. The zig-zag of metal links rolled down until it banged on the ground. They leapt off and the first boy lifted a long plank of wood from the floor. He jammed one end of it up beneath the roller mechanism over the entrance and wedged the other end on the floor, kicking it tight. They pulled quickly back from the grid.

Soldiers appeared in the road, running from the narrow street on the other side, spreading out to the left and right, keeping close to the walls of the buildings. Wesley watched, standing silently with everyone else, from the shadows at the back of the station entrance. Mikhail held Katie close to him, one hand stroking her hair.

"Not many of 'em," said the first boy quietly. "Where's the rest gone?"

"Chasin'," said the girl on the bicycle. "Dave slashed the front tire on their truck. They chased him and the others down Canal Road. Shooting they were, but they was too far back. Dave and them are goin' down at The Dog Hole." She turned fiercely to Wesley and the others. "Who're you anyway?"

"We're…" Janis began.

"Not here," interrupted the first boy. He nodded towards the back. "S'get down."

In the dim light at the rear of the station entrance, the disused ticket desks were thick with dust. The ceiling above them was darkened with soot and a door leading to the back of the desks hung open. One of the boys walked quickly through the door and re-emerged carrying two thick sticks with their ends covered with plastic carrier bags. He pulled the bags off. The ends of the sticks were bound with wads of old cloth, wet with a thick black oily liquid.

Beside the ticket office were the old escalators, twin stairways that had not moved in years, dropping away down into the darkness. The boy with the sticks pushed through the other children and led the way down one of the stairs. Wesley, Janis, Mikhail and Katie followed, holding the grimy rubber handrail and feeling their way down each step with their feet. One of dogs scurried down past them. The sooty wide arched ceiling, sloping down above them, quickly lost what little light filtered in from the entrance behind them and it became completely dark.

A yellowy flickering light sprang up ahead of them, dimly lighting the ceiling and the second stair flight beside them. It grew brighter and Wesley saw that the boy with the sticks had lit the end of one and was holding it above his head. The flame flickered as he jogged down the steps and a stream of sooty smoke trailed behind it and up to the roof. A line of pictures, too grimy to make out, sloped down the walls beside them and the smell of burning oil filled the damp air. Something brushed past Wesley's leg. He looked down and saw the white fur of the other dog scampering down between the hurrying feet.

A sound, the groan of bicycle brakes mixed with a patter of light thuds, came from the top of the second stair behind them, getting quickly nearer. Wesley turned to see the cyclists, standing on their pedals, riding down the escalator on the other side, their bikes bumping down the steps, one behind the other. Around them, conversations started in quiet but excited voices, adding to the sounds of the bikes and feet travelling downwards. Wesley picked up a few words here and there. There was talk about the fight. How many soldiers they had hit. Close shaves. Routes they had taken getting into range and running away afterwards. Two boys seemed to be having a light-hearted argument about which of them had hit a particular soldier. There were snatches of laughter and there was talk of blood and wounding. Some of the talk was mouth to ear with glances back at Wesley and the others. He felt a strange familiarity, that of being underground with children and he hurried on down, between the throng, deeper into the old underground railway of the city.

A soft chanting began from some of the children lower down in front of them.

'*Stonem, stonem, stonacrowmen*'.

More children joined in, not loudly, but the sound thickened, hissing and humming in the tunnel.

'*Stonem, stonem, stonacrowmen. Stonem, stonem, stonacrowmen. Stonem, stonem...*"

Janis, a step ahead of Wesley was craning her neck to one side, peering down amongst the bobbing heads.

"What are they saying?" said Wesley.

"Stone them," she replied, still looking. "Stone the Crowmen. The soldiers, you know, with their eagle symbols."

The leading children came to the bottom of the escalator and, led by the cyclists, flooded out onto level ground. The boy with the torch stood stationary among them, holding the flame high while the others parted around him and turned into a tunnel to the left. The chanting died down to just one group of voices that sounded younger than the others. After repeating it twice more, they too tailed off and began to talk amongst themselves again.

Wesley stepped off the bottom of the escalator behind Janis,

Mikhail and Katie. Keeping close together, they hurried past the boy with the torch who turned and followed. The children crowded them on. There seemed to be girls and boys in roughly the same numbers, Wesley guessed about twenty in all. Two of the boys had long hair, tied behind their heads with strips of cloth. Others were wore hoods or close fitting woolen hats. Some of the girls wore their hair short, roughly cut and spiky. Like the boys, they were all dressed individually in an assortment of old clothes. Among them Wesley saw the girl who had been at the top of the coal heap. She had a streak of coal dust across her cheek. She looked back at him for a moment and gave a small nod.

With Katie clinging tightly to Mikhail's hand, the four of them followed the children through the tunnel. A dim light appeared ahead, steadier than that of the burning torch, and the heads and shoulders of the children in front of them became silhouettes hurrying towards it, the sounds of their footsteps and voices echoing in the confined space. The tunnel came out onto a dimly lit railway platform. The light came from dozens of candles placed against the wall or set on crates and boxes.

On the single line track that ran between the platform and the far wall was a train. Its rear carriages were still in the tunnel beyond the far end of the platform and its nearest carriage, with the windows of the driver's compartment at the front, was half way into the station. Littered on the tracks in front of it were piles of discarded boxes and rubbish. Against the wall of the platform small compartments, little larger than a bed, had been made from crates, cardboard and pieces of material. Within them were piles of bedding and belongings. Here and there were high stacks of boxes. As he passed Wesley read the print that was repeated on some of them: PARAFFIN WAX CANDLES X 1000. Other boxes were labeled with food names

THE WATER OF LIGHT

and still more were simply dusty and unmarked, piled one on top of the other up to the curved sooty ceiling above.

The children boarded the first carriage through its open doors and when Wesley and the others reached it they were beckoned in. The seats ran along the sides and, beneath streaks of soot on the glass, candles burned on the narrow window ledges. Rolled up blankets were tied to handles that hung from the ceiling and the last of the children pressed in through the doors beneath them. The first boy was there, standing at the end of the carriage.

He pointed at Wesley and the others and waved his finger at the seats closest to him, indicating them to sit down. Katie sat beside Mikhail, still holding his hand, looking untroubled by the sea of new young faces that gathered and were looking at them. To Wesley, sitting on the other side with Janis, it seemed as though Katie was almost excited by what was happening. But he felt nervous and alert. In spite of the rescue, there had been no friendly words or looks, other than the brief nod from the girl.

"What you doing in the city?" the boy addressed Wesley and Katie directly. "And how come you're with Growners?" Without waiting for a reply he looked at Janis and Mikhail.

"And you. You 'aint with the Crowmen." he looked uncertain for a moment. "Are you?"

"No," said Janis. "We're not with the Crowmen."

"Then where you from?" called a young voice from the tightly packed children sitting and standing in the rest of the carriage.

"What was in them boxes?" asked another excitedly.

"Yeah, what was in 'em?" came another.

Several more questions came at once and other children began talking to each other. It became impossible to tell what

204

anyone was saying. The first boy banged the wall behind him, hard, four times, with the flat of his hand and the voices quickly died down to silence.

"First you two," he said, pointing to Janis and Mikhail. "You fallen out with 'em or something? Why they wanna get you?"

"You mean The Order?" said Mikhail, getting his breath back. "The Crowmen? We were never with them, if that's what you mean. We've been their prisoners."

"You? Growners?" said the boy. "Not Crowmen? Never known Growners who 'aint Crowmen. Not since…"

"Cept for the Talkers," a young girl piped up. "But they don't do no runnin' around, like you."

There was a titter of laughter from some of the younger children.

"The Talkers?" said Mikhail.

"I'm doing the askin'," the boy replied sharply. He looked at Mikhail and was silent for a moment before continuing with his head cocked slightly to one side.

"Well?"

"We're on the run from the… the Crowmen," said Mikhail. "And… whoever you all are… for what you've just done. Thank you." He looked back at the other children. "All of you."

Some of the children murmured softly. The first boy continued loudly.

"We seen you come into the city. We seen you in the car and we followed you to the 'Versty. S'where we live, here, 'Versty Station. We saw the Crowmen following you. We rescued you because of them." He pointed at Katie and Wesley. "What was in them boxes?"

"Bottles of water," said Mikhail. "Believe it or not."

"Water!" exclaimed the boy. "What's such a big deal about

two bottles of water? S'bin raining. There's lots of water. And there's lots of bottles."

Mikhail bent forward and was seized with sudden racking cough. Janis leaned towards him, concerned. "You all right Mikhail?" she asked softly.

He recovered, holding his hand to his chest.

"I'm ok... Thanks." He turned back to the boy.

"It wasn't ordinary water," he continued. "It was medicine."

The word 'medicine' whispered like an echo among the children.

"Med'cin," said the boy. "We'd have had that. That why you came here? To get that med'cin?"

"To get that medicine." Mikhail nodded slowly.

"What yer names?" The boy looked at Wesley and Katie.

"I'm..."

"Katie," Katie interrupted. "My name's Katie."

"Katie, Katie," repeated some of the children quietly.

"We live in tunnels too," she said. "And we got trains."

"What tunnels?" asked the boy.

"Tunnels where the soldiers live."

The boy tensed. "Were they prisoners?" He nodded towards Mikhail and Janis.

"Me and Grandpa live in the Care Halls. What's your name?"

The boy seemed taken aback for a moment.

"My name? he said. "Red. Red's my name."

He looked from Katie to Mikhail and back.

"He your Dad?"

"Dad... dad," came whispers from the children.

Katie smiled. "Grandpa. He's my Grandpa."

"Grandpa", came more whispers.

"She your Grandma?" Red pointed to Janis.

Katie snorted a laugh. "Janis." She smiled. "That's Janis." She pulled herself closer to Mikhail. "Only got a Grandpa."

There was a moment's silence before she continued. "I got Wesley and Janis, and Max. Got Wesley and Janis and Max."

"You Wesley?" Red pointed at Mikhail.

"No, I'm Mikhail. This is Wesley."

"Wesley?"

"Yeah, I'm Wesley."

"Were they prisoners? Wesley?"

"We were all prisoners. There are lots more of us. Our age. Slaves."

The group of children shifted and whispered.

"Are there kids there from the city?" asked Red.

"No, not that I know of," said Wesley.

There was a pause before Red continued.

"Slaves doing what?" he asked.

"Unloading rocks and breaking them. With heavy hammers, you know, smashing them up."

"Smashing, smashing," whispered some of the children.

"Red?" Wesley straightened his back. "That man. The…"

"I 'aint finished askin'," snapped Red. "That water, the med'cin. What was you gonna do with it?"

"The Water's not our only reason for coming here," said Janis. "We want to organize a rescue, for the children Wesley's talking about. Our plan is to cross the estuary. There are people living over there who…"

"Why you goin' there then," said Red.

"We're going to ask for their help."

"Who are they?"

"The Horse People, that's what they're called. It's where I come from. We're going to ask for their help."

"And how was you planning to cross the estuary?"

"By boat."

"If you can find one," said Red. "And if we let you."

"Red?" said Wesley.

Red swung back to Wesley. "What?"

"That man…"

"What man?"

"Our friend Max. There was another one of us, remember?"

"Yeah, I saw him."

"They got 'im," a girl spoke out from the group. "I saw from the bushes."

"Might be they shot 'im," said a boy. "Might be he's layin' on the grass."

It felt to Wesley as if the train had given a small lurch. Janis stood. "What do you mean? Did you see him? If you know where he is, tell us."

"Not our fault!" Red spoke angrily back. "We risked it, coming to get you."

"Yes, yes. You did." Janis lowered her head a little and held up one hand. "We're indebted to you, not defying you."

"We could have 'bin hit, same as him."

"Yes," said Janis. "I know, I know."

"Probly 'es in the grass. A deadunn." said one of the children. "S'what they done with Billy. Just left him."

"Billy?" said Janis. "Was he… shot?"

"Yeah," said another child. "They done and shot 'im."

"Red!" said Janis urgently. "We need to get back to look for him, if he's there, in the grass…"

"No," said Red loudly. "Not yet. Not while the Crowmen are there. We gotta wait, and anyway we don't know what happened to 'im, and," He looked at Janis and Mikhail. "We don't know if you might be trickin' us. You might lead 'em to us."

"A trick," gasped Janis. "Max our friend might have been

shot. Does that seem like part of a trick?"

"Maybe. Maybe you tricked Wesley and Katie."

Wesley took a deep breath.

"No." He took a step towards Red. "Janis and Mikhail are not Crowmen. If it wasn't for them I'd still be a prisoner."

"Prove it," snapped Red.

"Prove it... prove it." The words rippled quietly through the others.

"If you don't believe what I say, then how can I prove it?" Wesley said angrily.

The girl who they had first seen at the top of the coal heap pushed forward. She was rolling a catapult stone between her palms.

"We'll ask the Silent Talkers," she said

21
Lightwater into Darkwater

Dove's shoe heels clacked across the flagstones of the cellar where a guard sat slumped on a bench outside one of the cell doors. Beside the door, Anguillaro's bag hung from a peg. As Dove neared, the man lifted his head with a start, quickly stood and straightened his hat.

"Evening Colonel, Sir."

"Jarvis isn't it?" said Dove as he arrived.

"Yes Sir."

"Sleepy Jarvis?"

"Couldn't help myself sir. Just nodded for a few seconds there. Sorry Sir."

"Stay awake man," said Dove angrily. He sniffed and grimaced. "Surprised anyone could sleep with this smell."

He peered through the bars of the small cell door window, his lower eyelid twitching.

The Eel Catcher sat against the far wall, head down as if sleeping. His matted oily hair hung down in front of his face and his long legs spread out onto the damp stone floor. His wrists were shackled by chains that hung from the wall above, holding his arms suspended on either side of his head. His hands flopped loosely forward. He looked like a giant spidery black puppet. Dove put his fingers under his nose and stepped back.

"Open up Jarvis," he said quietly.

Jarvis unlocked the door and Dove took a step into the cell. He tipped his head to one side, trying to see more of the shackled man's face. Then in one swift movement the Eel Catcher drew his knees up and pushed himself up against the wall to standing. He lifted his head and looked straight at the Dove.

210

"Scum!" The Eel Catcher spat. "I remember you."

Dove stepped sharply back into the doorway.

"You all right Colonel?" said Jarvis.

Dove nodded slowly, as if to himself. "Fine. Thank you Jarvis."

He stepped forward again.

"Ferrarazi," he said quietly. "Who ever would have guessed. Eh? Engineer turned Eel Catcher. A secret survivor. Anguillaro Ferrarazi. I must admit," he continued, his eyelid twitching more violently, "I thought you had passed away with dear Mrs. Ferrarazi. I do regret that we were not able to spare her any of the vaccine."

Anguillaro lunged forward, tugging at the chains. "Murderer," he shouted. "You had plenty vaccine. You had it in your hand."

Dove's wiped a bead of sweat from his temple then held his fingers to the skin below his eye to control the twitching.

"Ferrarazi." He shrugged. "The virus got her, not me. If she'd been sensible enough to join us I'd have been able to justify giving her some. And you. Not, it seems, that you needed any!"

"You had plenty vaccine, Dove. You let people die. You would only give them life if they would give it back to you."

Dove shook his head sadly. "And what, Ferrarazi, would you have done? Given it to every person you came across until it ran out? Eh? Where would that have got you? Or anyone? What good would be a rag-taggle bunch without the skills needed to re-build and survive?" He stepped back into the doorway. "You think I was ruthless?" He nodded. "Yes. I was. Someone needed to be. Without The Order we would have chaos and anarchy. Instead, we are able to bring stability, health, the rule of law and hope for the future."

"And what about your slaves?" Anguillaro glared at Dove.

"The children of the tunnels. What hope do you give to them? Eh?"

"They're lucky to be alive." There was irritation in Dove's voice. "Without us, they'd starve."

"That does not give you the right," Anguillaro shouted, "to make them slaves!" He stretched forward, his arms held fast behind him, and spat, hitting Dove's sleeve with a gob of spittle. Dove raised his arm and looked at it in disgust. With a last angry glance he turned and stepped out of the cell.

"Lock the door Jarvis," he commanded.

"Yes Sir." Jarvis obeyed.

Dove scooped the cat up and pushed it into the basket.

"And wash him."

"Pardon Sir?"

"I said wash him. The Eel Catcher. I want him washed down. He stinks."

"You mean like a bath Sir?"

"No you idiot. Hose him down."

"Yes Sir."

"And cut his revolting hair."

"Yes Sir."

"And that." Dove tipped his head towards Anguillaro's bag. "Is it his?"

"Yes Sir."

"Have you looked in it?"

"Yes Sir."

"And?"

"Slimy Sir."

"And?"

"Knife, spectacles and a torch in the front pocket Sir, and inside, some strips of something black and rubbery. Smells like fish or something."

"Everything around here stinks of fish Jarvis. Anything else?"

"No Sir." Jarvis pulled at the cuff of his sleeve, covering his wrist. "Nothing."

Dove returned back up the stairs. In the outer room of his office, a plump girl in her late teens sat at Janis' old desk. She had the same thick red hair as the Matron from the Care Halls.

"Elizabeth." Dove approached the desk. "Got the hang of the telephones yet?"

The girl sat straight and put a podgy hand on the receiver beside her.

"Yes Mr. Dove," she replied importantly. "I spoke to my mother."

"You spoke to your mother. How is she?"

"Fine Mr. Dove. Thank you. She…"

"Good. Elizabeth, now that you're working up here you will need to call me Colonel." He smiled thinly. "All right?"

"Yes Mr. Dove."

Dove, looking at her, raised his eyebrows a little.

"Colonel, Mr. Dove," the girl said.

"Just Colonel will do Elizabeth thank you." Dove turned and walked towards his office door.

"Colonel?"

Dove stopped. "Yes Elizabeth?" he replied without looking round.

"Doctor Thornberry rang."

Dove turned his head.

"And?"

"Said something about he's got some water."

Dove turned fully and faced the girl.

"When did he call?"

"Just a short while ago."

"Did he say where he was?"

"Said he was going to the laboratory."

Dove clasped his hands together and twisted them against each other.

"Call him please Elizabeth, at the laboratory. Zero two three."

The girl lifted the receiver eagerly.

"Tell him I'm on my way."

"On your way. Yes Mr… Colonel."

Dove retraced his steps across the hallway of Hillside House and back down the stairs. He strode across the cellar towards the entrance of the connector tunnel where a bicycle leant against the wall. As he passed, Jarvis called out respectfully from beside the cell door.

"Colonel Sir?"

"Yes." Dove continued walking.

"About this washing sir. Don't think I can manage alone sir."

"Of course you can't Jarvis. You'll need at least two of you. Organize it when you're shift is relieved." Dove reached the bike and sat astride it. "Get an electric pump from stores. And enough hose to reach the bottom of the well." He pushed off and pedaled away down the Connector Tunnel.

"Don't take his shackles off," he shouted back to Jarvis. "And report back to me when you're done."

The Order's laboratory had been set up in a room beside the Generator Hall. The steel door, ginger with rust from the damp atmosphere underground, was beneath the steel walkway. Dove caught the faint smell of cigarette smoke as he leant the bicycle against the wall outside and pulled the door open. The long low room was lit with strip lights that glared off the white tiled walls. Around the walls, steel shelving held an array of equipment. Bottles of liquid, conical flasks, glass and rubber tubes, electrical components and boxes were squeezed side by side. One section was given over entirely to books and manuscripts while another was lined with masks and breathing equipment. Mixed with the stale smell of cigarette smoke was the soft acidic smell of chemicals.

Doctor Thornberry, wearing a white lab coat, was busy connecting some thick wires together that ran across the floor from a metal box on the wall to a long table in the centre of the room. On the table, taking up its entire surface apart from a small area at one end, was a long rounded glass canopy clamped onto a metal frame. The space beneath the table was filled with a mass of cables and heavy electrical terminals. Attached to the side was a control panel of switches and dials. Inside the glass, set one at each end, stood two stubby rods, rising from the centre of dishes, the size of dinner plates, made from coils of thick copper wire. On top of each rod, was a thick metal disk.

Thornberry looked up as Dove closed the door behind him.

"William," he said with a smile. "Look what we have here."

He reached down to a wooden box and carefully lifted from it a wide glass bottle.

"The old man led us straight to it," he said.

Dove strode over.

"How do you know it's the real thing?" he said.

The Doctor smiled.

"Watch," he said.

The Doctor replaced the bottle into the box. Reaching up to a shelf, he lifted down another bottle, empty, of similar size. From a tall curved brass tap at an enamel sink, he filled the bottle with water, then walked to the table and placed it by the end of the glass-domed apparatus.

"Stand here William," he indicated to the floor beside him. "I shall be turning the lights off."

The Doctor slid a long wax taper from a jar and walked to the light switches beside the door. He drew a box of matches from his pocket, lit the taper and turned off the lights, leaving only the flickering glow of the taper lighting his face and the wall beside him. He walked slowly back to the table, drew the first bottle back out of the box and placed it beside the other one with just a finger's width between them. With a sharp breath, he blew the taper out and the laboratory fell instantly in complete darkness.

After a few seconds, the bottles became visible in a soft silvery glow that came from the water inside them. They glowed strongest at the sides where they faced each other, faintly illuminating the table surface and the end of the glass canopy. The light grew brighter, softly lighting up the whole room and the faces of the two men as they stood watching. Then it faded and disappeared, leaving the room once again in total darkness.

A match flared in the Doctor's hand and he relit the taper. His eyes glittered in the flame light. "Quite simple really," he said quietly. "Now we have two bottles of Lightwater. They won't be strong, I'm afraid, because the old man's bottle had been left for so long, needs freshening, and the water in the new bottle's only from the tap."

"What's wrong with tap water," said Dove.

"Doesn't work so well. Needs to be from another source. Only Kuroski knows where from. We can freshen up the original though, quite simply according to our hermit friend, by exposing it to light shone through a prism. Or, we can turn it into Darkwater with the Tesla Coils."

For a moment neither of the men spoke. Their breathing was the only sound in the room. Dove broke the silence.

"Is everything ready?"

The Doctor nodded. "I've spoken to Generators. They just need the nod."

"Now?"

The doctor smiled. "Why not."

He returned to the door and switched the lights back on. Dove plucked a telephone from its cradle on the wall.

"Elizabeth? Put me through to the Generator Halls please… What?… Numbers are all on the wall… Oh never mind. Zero seven one. Zero… Seven… One."

Dove held the telephone to his ear with his shoulder and slipped his arms into a white lab coat that the Doctor held open for him.

"Generators?" he spoke suddenly again. "Colonel Dove here. I believe that Doctor Thornberry has put you on standby for a temporary increase in power… Yes we are. Please go ahead now… How long?" He glanced at his watch. "That's fine, thank you."

Dove hung up and pulled the coat properly over his shoulders.

"Five minutes Edward."

The Doctor lit a cigarette, inhaled deeply and put it to rest on the table edge.

"Right." He clapped his hands and rubbed them together. "Canopy off first. If you'd take one end William."

Between them, they unclipped the catches that held it down and lifted the glass canopy from its rubber seal, placing it down gently on the floor. The Doctor poured some of the original Lightwater into a spare bottle and put it to one side. He placed the remaining water, in its bottle, onto a rubber pad mid way between the two metal discs. The strip lights in the ceiling of the laboratory brightened and began to hum. The Doctor picked up his cigarette and continued to work with it in his mouth. With a steel tape measure he calculated the distance between the sides of the bottle and the rods, adjusting the bottle several times until he was satisfied that it was exactly central. The lights brightened a little more. The Doctor stubbed his cigarette out under his shoe.

"How long to go William?" he said.

"Bit less than two minutes."

"Right. Canopy back on."

The men replaced the canopy, snapping closed the fastening clips around the rim. The lights brightened noticeably once more and the humming from them increased. Dove was looking at his watch.

"Five minutes is up," he reported.

The doctor nodded. He flicked a switch on the control panel and the apparatus began to hum. A row of small red lights glowed and a needle on one of the dials bounced into life, quivering against the printed numbers on its white face. The Doctor tapped another dial. It too sprang into life. He flicked a second switch and the sound of a small electric motor whirred.

"That's the vacuum pump," he spoke without looking away from the control panel. "Shouldn't take more than half a minute."

The ceiling lights brightened further and with a soft popping sound, one of the fluorescent tubes blew. Seconds later two others popped and went out, leaving the room lit by one remaining tube. The Doctor remained focused on the dials of the control panel. He instructed Dove to light the stub of a candle that was melted to a small glass specimen dish on the shelves behind him.

"And William," he added. "Bring over one of those spare fluorescent tubes from the corner."

Dove bought over a tube, still in its long cardboard box. The Doctor flicked off the pump. Slowly, he began to turn two black knobs on the control panel, one in each hand and the needles on the two dials crept upwards. Inside the canopy thin lines of quavering purple light appeared, flickering around the rims of the two metal discs. As the doctor turned the knobs, the light grew brighter, fizzing and buzzing, sending tiny shoots out into the vacuum around it.

"Nikola Tesla," said the Doctor lightly patting the canopy. "What an inventor! I think he would have been impressed with our home made model here. William, draw the tube out of its box would you."

Dove looked at the Doctor, then the ceiling and back. "You want me to replace one?"

"No, no. It's to check the electro magnetic vortex. That's what is building up here. We're standing in it now. It's quite safe."

Dove opened the end of the box and slid out the tube. The entire length of it was glowing as brightly as if it were plugged in. The bones of his hand, holding the tube in the middle, showed through the glowing red skin. The closer to the canopy he held it, the brighter the tube glowed.

The Doctor chuckled. "Working fine. It might be more comfortable, William, to stand a step back when I turn it up. It will get a bit tingly."

Dove stepped back and the tube glowed less fiercely. He slid it back into the box. The Doctor, at arm's length, turned the knobs further, ensuring that the dials rose to exactly the same settings. The coils began to buzz and crackle loudly. Shoots of light from around the discs leaped out like reaching purple tree roots, branching brilliantly and then disappearing. He turned the dials more and the light leaped out further, flexing and reaching across the inside of the canopy as if, from each disc, they were reaching for each other. Then they connected, buzzing loudly, like the fingertips finding each other, and they held together, the brilliant purple beams bucking and zig zagging between the coils. The Doctor made a final adjustment to the dials and the beams from each side latched onto the bottle between them and became two smooth bolts of dazzling light that rippled slowly from side to side, licking at the glass.

The Doctor stood back, his lab coat purple in the light and the water in the bottle glowing with the same colour. Dove narrowed his eyes from the brightness. And then, though the dazzling chords of light still played on it, the water ceased to be illuminated, as if it were blocking out the light from its core. It grew darker and darker until it became a dense black shadow into which no light entered, and from which none was reflected.

The Doctor reached forward and bought both dials back to zero. The tongues of light disappeared instantly and the room, lit once again by the one ceiling light, seemed dim after the brightness. The water in the bottle looked exactly as it had before, clear and ordinary, as if nothing had happened. The Doctor reached behind the control panel and released a valve. Air, replacing the vacuum, hissed into the canopy. He and Dove released the catches and lifted it clear. A faint fresh smell wafted out. Dove touched the bottle cautiously with his forefinger.

"It won't be hot William," said the Doctor. "Amazingly. Twenty eight thousand volts and not one bit of it converted into heat. But I have every confidence that it has made the conversion that we wished it too. And I must say," there was a note of emotion in his voice, "that although I always believed it would work, there is nothing quite like the confirmation of one's theories. The blackness is exactly what I would expect, and what old man Kuroski said would happen. I used to wonder if he hadn't perhaps even made some himself!"

"Is it safe to handle the bottles?" said Dove.

"Lightwater's fine," replied the Doctor. "Probably good for you. But the Dark, no. At least not for any length of time. Should be kept in the box. It can be handled safely that way. The Light and the Darkwater have to be kept apart, at least by a few feet, so that they don't affect each other. Preferably they should be in separate rooms."

"If they are close together, which will they turn into?" asked Dove. "Light or Dark?"

"The most recently made, or freshened up," the Doctor replied, pulling on a pair of thick gloves, "will dominate the other, turning it into the same as itself."

He lifted the bottle clear of the Tesla Coils, placed it quickly in the box and put it on a shelf on the far side of the room. He lit a cigarette and continued.

"There's only one more step in the process William."

"Trying it out?"

"Exactly. We need a guinea pig."

A half smile crept across Dove's lips.

"We have the perfect volunteer do we not? Less of a guinea pig though, more a slimy eel I would say."

"A slimy eel," the Doctor nodded, "will do fine."

THE WATER OF LIGHT

Book 3

LIGHTWATER

22
The Silent Talkers

When the first meteorites had smashed down, people every-where sought safety below the ground. Those on the coast fled inland to find caves, mines, or the underground webs of man-made tunnels beneath the cities. Many of their towns and vil-lages were all but completely destroyed by huge waves; the giant ripples of meteorites hitting the sea.

The underground railway that the City Children now lived in, had been packed with people. Down with them they bought whatever food they could find, from their homes or looted from shops, and set up camps, cramped together in any space they could find. Some bought furniture, chairs and beds. Most bought their precious possessions, items that were sold and bar-gained with when food began to get short. Candles, torches and batteries became precious objects. Oil lamps, simply made from cups and bowls with a wick, burned cooking oil or smoky diesel to provide light. Water containers big and small, refilled from rainwater above ground or from one of the many small rivers that ran in culverts below, was stored and carefully ra-tioned.

As families and friends established spaces of their own, each of the underground railway stations became small, tightly packed communities. Meals were shared and new friendships formed. At one station a choir was sprang up, and in another, a group of actors put on a play. They travelled through the tun-nels, guided by the gleam of railway lines in the occasional lamp left burning low in the darkness, and performed to lift the spirits of the sheltering citizens.

As food stocks began to dwindle, the players began asking for donations. But people chose to keep what they had, rather than be entertained, and the players stopped visiting, performing only in their own communities. Bartering systems developed between the stations, trading the most precious of possessions for food and, as the price got higher, disagreements broke out that led to fighting. A hostage was taken and exchanged for food, and the dark tunnels, where the lines snaked between the crowded platforms, became places to fear. Some were barricaded and guarded, and throughout it all, people prayed for an end to the meteorites.

But the tremors that shook the ground, showering dust and grit from the tunnel roofs, continued. The stations began to stink with people's excrement from where they relieved themselves in the tunnels. Attempts were made to dig latrines in the rocky ballast beneath the tracks but the air that filtered down through the stairways from above made little in the way of any breeze and the stench hung in the air. Rats, drawn by the precious food stores, scurried in and out of the tunnel mouths. Children made catapults and stood guard, driving the rats back with volleys of stones, and sometimes, as their aim improved, hitting and killing them.

The virus, when it came, spread swiftly through the tunnels, wiping out whole station communities within days, leaving their corpses to rot in the silence. Why the children at University Station hadn't become infected was a mystery to the adults as the symptoms spread among them. Something in their diet was suggested, or that the virus had mutated in the children's favour. Whatever it was remained unknown as the adults and younger children, one by one, died and grew cold and began to decompose. For the children the shock and loss was too great to take in. A rumour grew among them that their parents and friends, who they knew would never abandon them, remained as spirits in the tunnels and would re-inhabit their bodies when the virus passed. The idea was quickly and willingly believed and when a stray dog led them up a long narrow stairway to the cellars of the city's council buildings, they decided to haul the dead up into them to give them a place of their own. They called the stairway the Dog Hole. The cellar above they called the Talking Room.

Mikhail was not feeling well. He needed to rest. He and Katie remained in the train while Wesley and Janis, flanked by a dozen or so of the City Children, climbed down onto the tracks. Staying close, they made their way into the inky blackness of the tunnel. Three of the younger ones ran ahead, one of them turning as he ran.

"We'll go light up," he called back.

How the runners could see where they were going was impossible to tell. A torch, held by one of the boys, flared beside Wesley. The curved roof of the tunnel, carrying black dusty cables clipped to the brickwork, showed in the flickering light, and he was able to see the rails at his feet and their sleepers bedded into the rough cinders of the track-bed. The City Children started talking amongst themselves, paying little attention to Janis and Wesley. The smoke from the torch was acrid and sharp in his nostrils and Wesley moved away from it as he walked. He found himself beside the girl who had nodded to him on their way down to the station.

"Wesley," she said. "That's your name right?"

Wesley nodded. "Yeah."

"I'm Jupiter," she continued. "You got Talkers where you bin? Where you s'caped from?"

"No... I don't know. What are Talkers?"

"Talkers are the Silent Talkers. My Mum's there. She's a Talker – sometimes."

"Your Mum's alive?"

"Yeah. Well no, not like you 'n me. Not at the moment anyway."

Jupiter closed the gap slightly between them as they walked.

"You were brave standin' up to Red. He's our leader. We voted him. He's the best shot, and he ain't afraid of Crowmen. He looks after us good. But he don't like it if you talk back at him. S'just the way he is. C'ept Jess, she ain't afraid of him. She ain't afraid of no one."

"Was that Jess who said about going to the Talkers?"

"Yeah. That's Jess."

One of the boys ahead had picked up two long pieces of pale bone from beside the track and he began to clack them together in a steady rhythm. He began to chant. One by one the City Children joined in. 'Bones bones, bones on the stones, bones joined up and bones on their owns. Bones bones, bones on the stones…'

They entered another station and a faded white line was visible along the edge of the old platform. The place smelt damp and musty. The shadowy shapes of old mattresses and furniture were littered everywhere, and among them were the unmistakable remains of people. Leg bones protruded from ragged piles of cloth, some still with shoes on their feet and the pale dome of an eyeless skull lay in the shadows.

Memories of his parents nudged forward in Wesley's mind. *They are lying against the wall, side by side. His father's eyes are closed and his mother holds his thin hand. The candle is flickering. And they won't let Wesley touch them. He can only look at them, and he looks into his mother's eyes. She has said nothing for hours. She is just looking at him. She is saying goodbye with her eyes, which slowly close, and Wesley is engulfed in helplessness. His body aches with emptiness and he wants only to crumble into nothing and be nowhere.* He gasped and almost stumbled. The empty feeling returned, twisting his stomach. He drew a deep breath to steady himself.

A rat scuttled out from behind an old picture frame leaning against the wall and scurried along the platform edge ahead of them. In a moment, a boy at the front drew back his catapult and fired. The stone pinged off the ground, missing the rat by a fraction and smacked into a chair that lay on its side, sending shivers of dust from its edges drifting to the floor. The rat darted away into the shadows.

"Runaway, runaway, runaway rat," several of the City Children shouted, out of time with each other, their voices echoing off the walls. "Missed it. Billy Bird missed it." They slapped the boy on the back and laughed easily as they walked on towards the end of the platform. The white line faded away and they continued along into the next tunnel. The tracks began to slope upwards and the tunnel curved in a long bend. At intervals, alcoves had been built into the walls, each just wide and tall enough for a man to stand in if a train were passing. One of the alcoves up ahead stood out in the darkness by a faint glow from inside. When they reached it, the boy with the torch snuffed it out against the wall. The alcove had a bricked up doorway at its back. A hole, large enough to climb through, had been broken through the brickwork. Inside, a candle set on the bottom step of a narrow, well-made stairway, flickered gently.

Wesley climbed through with the others. The stairs rose steeply up. The brick walls and arched roof were flaky with old whitewash and a metal handrail ran up each side. Single candles had been lit at every twenty or so steps. With the City Children climbing above him, it was difficult to see how far up the stairs went, but what glimpses he caught showed him that the steps rose up unbroken and that the uppermost candles were hardly more than a pin-point of light far above.

In single file, Janis and Wesley, with children in front and behind them, climbed upwards. The children spoke less now, their voices giving way to the sound of feet on the steps, of hands grabbing and pulling at the railings and of hard breathing. The candles were blown out as they passed, leaving the stairs behind them in complete darkness.

One by one the candles ahead lessened and the stair ended at a wide landing roofed over with a vaulted brick ceiling. Through an arched doorway on the left, more stairs, broader that those they'd climbed, disappeared upwards. Three of the boys stood with their backs to it, watching Janis and Wesley. In the wall straight ahead was a heavy wooden door hung on long rusty strap hinges. The three younger children who had run ahead back in the train tunnel, waited in front of it, craning their necks, looking back at the last few who stepped up from the stairs. Seeming satisfied that everyone was up; they turned and pushed open the door. It scraped along the stone floor as it swung inwards.

No one spoke as the City Children, Janis and Wesley with them, walked into a candlelit room beyond. Like the stairway and landing, the windowless walls were of peeling white-washed brick. The room was long, rather like a wide tunnel with a gently curving roof. The floor was laid with slate flag-stones and along each wall, about a foot high and a foot wide, was a long continuous plinth. Though it felt dry, the place had the same musty smell as the station that they had passed through.

Wesley's first impression, which lasted no more than a moment, was that they had walked in on a meeting. On each side of the room, lines of people sat or stood on the plinths, either looking across at each other or staring at the ground. No body spoke or moved. The realization that they were all dead came a split second later.

All that showed of the bodies, for the most part, were their skulls and the long thin bones of their hands. They were dressed in what might once have been their best and smartest clothes, though the fabric was frail and faded and was, like the shoes on their feet, covered in dust. Some skeletons wore suits with cravats or ties at their necks. Others had overcoats and hats. There were those that wore once fashionable dresses with necklaces and the decaying remains of silk scarves, while others stood or sat wrapped carefully in embroidered blankets and shawls, their feet, hands and heads the only part of them showing.

The clothes hung awkwardly over the bones and some had lengths of string tied round to keep the garments in place. Skeletal hands pushed out from sleeves and cuffs. Faces stared in whatever direction the skulls pointed, eye sockets dark and empty, mouths open, showing long teeth still set in the jaw as if frozen in mid word. Traces of dry leathery skin stretched over the bones and, colourless and patchy, tufts of hair remained attached to the skulls or poked out from beneath hats. The bodies were held against the walls with crudely bent pieces of wire hooked into nails that had been driven into the mortar line between the bricks. Some of the skulls were twisted sideways, as if they were talking to their neighbors. All seemed to have an expression on their faces, some comical, some anguished and some sinister.

Among them were the smaller bodies of children, some sitting some standing, and from the candlelight, they all cast shadows on the walls behind them that moved slightly with the flickering flames and gave the impression that each body was moving, ever so slightly, in a ghoulish silent conversation.

The City Children moved out into the room, visiting chosen bodies, and some began to whisper to them, pausing sometimes as if listening. Jupiter stood in front of a tall woman. The woman's hands had been pulled together, held with a bent piece of wire. The long pale finger bones still had thin strips of dark dry skin on them and her nails showed the cracked and faded red lacquer of varnish. A ring hung loosely against the knuckle of one finger and on her wrists, where they protruded from the cuffs of a faded embroidered blouse, bracelets circled the narrow bones. Her skull was tilted slightly to one side as if listening and her jaw was open, revealing an empty hollow behind. She wore a small pale blue hat circled with a faded ribbon. Stitched to the front edge, the remains of a gauze veil hung over the dark holes of her eyes.

Jupiter stood quite still, looking up at the woman. Then she turned, quite suddenly, and wandered among the other children, pausing briefly here and there in front of other skeletons before moving on again. Wesley and Janis, staying close, walked slowly into the room amongst the quiet whispering children, looking up at the silent skeletons. There was a stir behind them. It seemed as if the visit to the room was suddenly over and the children were filing back through the door. Now they whispered to each other, glancing occasionally at Wesley and Janis. Red caught Wesley's eye and nodded towards the door.

Out on the landing once more, with the door closed behind them, the children fell silent. Red and two other boys stood with their backs to the arched doorway that led to the next flight of stairs up.

"Well?" he said quietly, looking from person to person.

"Anyone hear anything?"

"Yeah," one of the young ones piped up. "My Dad says they're mad. Especially the girl."

Some of the children sniggered.

"So what else did he say?" demanded Red sternly.

The sniggering stopped and the boy became serious again. "Nuffin'. Just that. S'all."

"Anyone else?" said Red.

No one spoke. The children looked at Wesley and Janis, and at each other.

"Yeah. My mum talked." Jupiter broke the silence.

"And?"

"Said they're all right, an' that we should help 'em."

"S'what I heard from my mum," another girl followed on quickly. "Said we should help 'em."

"So did Dad," called out one of the young ones.

"Quietly," hissed Red. "Remember where you are. Respect."

"Sorry," the boy whispered back.

"What did he say?"

"Same as her. We should help 'em."

"Mine too." "And mine," came another voices.

"Jess?" Red continued. "Yours say anything?"

"No," she replied. "They ain't talking. But I think we should help 'em anyway."

Red nodded in silent agreement, then looked at Wesley and Janis.

"Let's go up," he said, "We'll take you to the 'Versty, see if your friend's there."

Turning, he climbed the stairs behind him and Wesley and Janis followed with the others. The stair ran straight for several steps, turned sharply, and continued on up to another stone flagged landing, exactly the same as the one beneath it. On the far side, more stairs continued upwards and on the left, a door, in the same place as the one below, hung open. Through it Wesley saw dozens of bicycles leaning against the walls. For the most part their frames and wheels were rusty but their chains were dark with oil and their wheel rims shone from the rubbing of brake blocks. They passed across the landing and up the next stairs to another door at the top. Red listened for a moment and then lifted the latch and pushed at the door. It opened with a scraping sound, as if something was being pushed across the floor on the other side. The door led into a tall wide corridor, bright with natural light from windows high up in one wall. Several were broken and glass lay smashed on the floor. Large dusty portraits in elaborate frames lined the walls beneath the broken windows and wallpaper, peeling off the walls, hung over some of them in long damp folds.

Jess, at the back of the group, pushed the door closed behind them. Wesley saw that a wooden crate had been nailed onto it at floor level. When the latch clicked shut, it looked as if the crate had been pushed against the door, as if no one could have closed the door from the inside.

Red led the way down the corridor and into a large room where evening sunlight streamed in through tall windows. The walls were paneled with dark wood and the dusty floor was made of broad oak boards. Chairs, some of them toppled over, were everywhere. The high ceiling was a mass of ornate plaster patterns and in its centre, where the plasterwork formed a wide circle, hung a giant chandelier on a long chain. The hanging segments of cut glass caught the sunlight that slanted in from the windows and sparkled with tiny triangles of light. Some of its teardrop shaped glass pieces were missing and lay in the dust on a large table beneath it. Directly below the chandelier, on the table, stood a chair.

Red motioned everyone to move quietly. He walked to one of the windows and stood beside a long faded curtain looking out. Wesley walked slowly over to the table. He had never seen a room like this before. He ran his finger along the dusty table top, leaving a shiny trail of the polished wood. Jess and Jupiter moved to another of the windows and gazed out. One of the younger boys jumped nimbly up onto the table and stood on the chair. He reached up and gave the chandelier a gentle push. It jingled softly and specks of dust floated downwards, glowing in the light.

All but three other younger children had taken places by the windows, keeping to the shadows of the curtains, looking out. The young ones remained in the centre of the room with the boy on the chair, facing the wall opposite the windows. The wall was covered with small dancing patches of rainbow light reflected from the chandelier. They bobbed up and down in unison, travelling slowly across the wooden panels. They stopped moving sideways; still bouncing gently, and then began to travel back.

Snow is falling softly in big flakes onto the white contours of a park. The winter tree branches are white on top and dark and damp underneath. Wesley has thrown a snowball, hitting a tree, and snow cascades to the ground. There are children sledging and his mother is laughing. The last powdery flakes drift from the tree branches. It is as though, for a moment, the world has gone into slow motion and there is no past or future, just this one moment, nothing more, just the snow softly falling.

A chair leg scraped and Red turned back into the room to where the boy was climbing down from the table.

"Shh," he hissed at him.

The chandelier still swayed but the three young ones had tired of the bobbing rainbow lights and they moved quietly over to one of the windows. Wesley ran his finger along the edge of the table again, building up a clot of dust that he flicked to the floor. He picked up one of the cut glass teardrops, rubbed it on his jacket and held it up, turning it slowly against the light. It winked with flashes of white and blue. On the wall where the patches of light still rose and fell, he was able to add his own moving spot of light to the dancing refractions on the wood paneling and he chased and circled the others, jumping from one to another, flashing from one side to the other.

He pushed the glass teardrop deep into his jacket pocket and joined Janis. The windowsills were just a few feet above the level of a wide parking area outside, overgrown with the fresh new spring growth of weeds. Rubbish and chunks of masonry were scattered everywhere and a rusting car, its side windows smashed and its tyres flat, was parked against a stone wall that edged the car park. Two pillars, one still topped with a round stone ball, framed a gateway that led out onto a round-about from which two long straight roads ran out in an ever widening 'V' through buildings beyond. From the vantage point of the windows it was possible to see directly down both roads into the heart of the city. To the left, cranes from the docks rose above the rooftops, and beyond them lay the grey expanse of the estuary.

"See them roads," Jupiter spoke softly to Wesley. "Lots of the main roads in the city cross 'em. If the Crowmen are around there's a good chance we'd see 'em passing. You can't ever be sure though. But we always watch first before we go out."

"How long do you watch for?" asked Janis, concern in her voice.

"'Pends where we're goin'," Jupiter replied. "From here to Versty's mostly back streets but Red checks, always. They 'ent always around. We don't know where they go but sometimes they're around for days, patrolling. They know we're here and they caught some of us. Twice they done it. Took 'em away. We don't know where but we heard 'em talking about a quarry. We think they make 'em work."

"We saw kids in a quarry," said Wesley. "On our way here. Slave gangs. Maybe it was them?"

"You did?" Jupiter looked at him hard. "Bet that's them. Twelve altogether got snatched. How many you saw?"

"Twelve," said Katie, standing beside Janis.

"They slaves?"

"Yeah, slaves like the others," said Wesley. "But… they're alive."

"S'got to be them." Jupiter's eyes were widening with excitement. "You see a boy there who looked like me?"

Wesley shook his head. "Too far away. We didn't see them that clearly."

"Too far away. But he's probably there." She nodded. "I got a brother see. I'm gonna' get him out now as you've told me. Will your Horse People help? Get 'em all out of there Wesley?"

"That's what we want to do Jupiter," said Wesley. "Get all the slave children out."

"Red," Jupiter whispered over to the next window. "They seen Birdie an' the others. They're alive. They're working in a quarry. Wesley an' them are gonna get 'em out. Hey," she turned back to Wesley. "We gonna help you now. Wait till I tell the others. We gonna help you get everyone out."

23
Eel Oil and Water

There was no trace of Max. In the long shadows cast by the evening sun, they searched the ground for clues. But there was no blood, no sign in the gravel of a scuffle outside the small wooden door and there was no way of telling if he had escaped, been captured or carried away injured, or dead.

An acrid smell of burning, from the scorched patch where the petrol bomb had landed, hung in the air and, over by the car, Wesley found the spent cases of five bullets lying among the weeds. Confused and worried, he and Janis retrieved the backpacks from the boot and returned with the City Children to the carriage in University Station.

"All right then," said Red, scanning the raised hands of the City Children crowded in the carriage. "We're agreed. You come back this way with them Horse People. You take us to the quarry and help get 'em out from there and we'll help you with gettin' all them other Tunnel Children out."

"And the boat?" queried Janis.

"Yeah," said Red. "An' we'll show you the boat. We never tried it. It's a rower."

He was sitting on the floor at the end of the carriage, elbows resting on his drawn up knees, orchestrating the discussion since it had begun over three hours ago. Wesley, Janis, Katie and Mikhail sat close together on the seats to one side and the rest of the City Children were crowded into the remaining candle lit space. Some were yawning. One boy had fallen asleep, his head resting on the shoulder of another. Mikhail had curves of dark skin under his eyes. He looked drained and had said nothing. Now and again he leaned forward and coughed, holding his chest before slowly sitting back up.

"These Horse-people," continued Red. "How d'you know they'll help?"

"It's where I come from," Janis replied. "They're like my family. I know they'll help. As I said, the only reason I got to be with The Order was that I was in their area when the virus came. They had a vaccine. They gave me a shot after I told them that I used to be a nurse. I thought everyone at home must have been killed until, about a year ago now, I heard that the whole village had survived. No one else, just the village, and I found out that The Order wanted them as slaves to work the farmland there. I became a spy. I started sending them messages. They know about the Tunnel Children now but The Order are closing in on them. One of my worries is that they might have abandoned the village before we get there. That's why we're keen to press on."

"Tomorrow night then," said Red.

"Tomorrow night," some of the children whispered.

"Soon as it's dark. We'll take you down to the docks. We'll be travelin' in two groups. We got food to collect down there. One of them big containers. Half under water. Tins are ok. Just gettin' a bit rusty now. We'll give you some. Beans it is."

"Beans pudding, nice pudding, had it more than twice pudding," came a joking whispered chant. Jupiter, perched up on one of the seats opposite Wesley, shook her head and looked up at him.

"We eaten so much of that stuff." She opened her mouth and pushed a finger back at her tonsils.

Wesley reached down into to his pack between his knees and pulled out one of the long thin cans of biscuits.

"I've got some biscuits, if anyone would…" dozens of

faces leaned forward looking at the can in his hand, "...like one?"

"Biscuits, biscuits," whispered the children.

"That's a yes," said Red, looking from the can to Wesley and back. "We 'ent had biscuits since... before."

Wesley slid the packet out from the tin and offered the opened end to him. Red held his gaze for a moment, smiled, giving a small nod, and took one. Janis and Mikhail drew cans from their own packs and passed them around. There was a buzz of excitement as the City Children nibbled at each biscuit, making them last, relishing the sweet taste. The boy who had fallen asleep was woken for his share and for as long as the packets lasted the City Children became connoisseurs, savoring the simple sweetened wheat meal as if it were a rare and exotic recipe and murmuring satisfied '*mmmms*' and '*yeahs*' as they munched, bit by bit, through the feast.

Later, Jupiter bought extra blankets to Wesley and the others and left them to sleep on the seats of the carriage. The City Children took to the platform and the other carriages where some talked on quietly in candlelit groups whilst others settled down to rest. Mikhail quickly fell asleep and Janis pulled his blanket over his shoulders before bedding down herself, head to head with Wesley on one of the long side seats. Katie was wide-awake. She wandered out onto the platform. Through sleepy eyes, Wesley watched her talking with one of the groups of children around the dim light of a single candle. As he felt the welcome drift of sleep settle onto him, he saw her smile and heard a soft round of friendly laughter from the children.

Up above, nightfall had washed the city into complete darkness and a light rain dampened the dusty rubble strewn streets, in the dark houses, nothing stirred other than scavenging dogs and scurrying rats. To the east, over the silent countryside, the tunnels beneath Hillside House buzzed quietly with neon light. Most of the work exhausted orphans, oblivious to whether it was day or night outside, slept in the dormitories of their quarters. In the Care Halls, the 'Guests' dozed or sat quietly awake on their beds or in armchairs, minds blanked from sedatives, and in her room off to one side, the Matron lay in her bed on her back, mouth open, snoring lightly. Two hundred feet above her, her daughter quietly collected The Colonel's washing from outside his bedroom door in Hillside House. On the other side of the door the Colonel slept in his ironed pajamas with the cat curled up on the end of his bed. The cat, one eye half open, was listening to the girl's tiptoe steps outside.

In the cellars below, Anguillaro, faintly lit by what light filtered in through the window of his cell door, sat awake in his shackles. Outside, a guard dozed on the bench and close by, surrounded by a pile of tangled hoses, a portable electric pump rested on the flagstone floor.

In Anguillaro's cave, on the other side of the rocky hills that rose over The Order's labyrinth of tunnels, Sargazzo lay on his bed of old blankets. His big muzzle resting on his out-stretched front legs and his eyes closed. And although he slept, his ears were slightly raised, a part of him remaining alert to any sound, attuned to his master's footsteps, or the warning of those of strangers.

Between the east and west banks of the estuary, above the steady flow of the incoming tide, six soldiers crossed the old bridge on foot, their hoods pulled down against the rainy wind. They each carried a pack and a rifle. Half way across, at the collapsed section of the roadway, three of them took up watch at the edge, hunkering down for shelter beside the railings. The other three edged alongside the dark hole on a strip of metal decking that had remained in place beside the railings. With each booted step they tested the rusty sheets. Flakes of rust scattered into the windy darkness and sailed downwards to the swirling waters that slapped and chopped far below. They reached the solid roadway beyond and set off briskly into the night, talking little, following the orders that had been given to them personally by Colonel Dove.

Their route ahead lay past the cratered hillsides in the west to the small town of Saint Terresas where, hands deep in his pockets and with the rain dripping from the brim of his hat, a night watchmen sat quietly on an upturned bucket. In the houses at his back, the Horse People slept. From somewhere over the river he heard a pair of owls hooting to each other across the woods. Northwards, beyond the woodlands and far up in the treeless hills, the Hermit snored loudly.

Max is running up a long sloping tunnel. Wesley can barely keep up with him but he knows that if he falls too far behind he will become lost. Suddenly Max darts to one side and stands against the wall, which is lined on both sides with rows of Silent Talkers stretching ahead as far as Wesley can see. He looks from one to another but cannot see Max. The skeletons stare back at him and then suddenly, as one, they turn their heads and look back down the tunnel. Pearson is striding towards him with a stick in one hand. Wesley runs on but a wind is blowing against him and he can go no faster than a walk. The skeletons watch him pass. Some of them reach out their bony hands to grab at him. He swipes them away, breaking them, scattering the bones on the floor. Pearson is gaining. Wesley can see daylight up ahead but the wind makes it harder and harder to move forward. He claws at the clothes of the Silent Talkers to pull himself on but they tear away in shreds, sending dust and rags scooting back in the wind. He can see blue sky at the tunnel mouth ahead but the wind gets stronger and blows him off his feet. He shouts for Max but his voice can manage no more than a strained whisper. The wind is buffeting him on the floor and his face is rubbing against the shoe of one of the Talkers. He hears his name being called by someone at the tunnel mouth, someone he cannot see...

"Wesley," it calls again. "Wesley, wake up Wesley."

He blinked open his eyes. His face was pushed against the seat back of the carriage seat. Katie was pushing and pulling at his shoulder. She stood back as he lifted his head, pulled up her sleeves and consulted her watches.

"Fifteen hours and twenty two-minutes you've been sleeping Wesley," she said. "Thirty seven minutes longer than Grandpa."

Wesley sat up stiffly and pushed the blanket aside.

"*Fifteen hours!*" He'd never slept for that long in his life, but he knew Katie would be correct. He blew out his cheeks and shook his head to wake up properly. Katie's face suddenly dropped and she held her arms straight at her sides. Her fingers began to wiggle.

"You ok Katie?"

"Going on a boat Wesley." She looked up at him and continued quietly. "Scared. Don't want to fall into the water again."

"We'll be all right Katie. There's no one chasing us this time, no one's even going to see us." Wesley hoped that he *sounded* reassuring, but it was not quite what he felt. Even without being pursued, boat, estuary and darkness added up in his imagination to something risky.

"Grandpa's not feeling very well Wesley. Not feeling well."

Wesley followed her out onto the platform where Mikhail sat in a tatty armchair. Janis crouched beside him, his wrist in her hand, looking at her watch. The old man looked up as they reached him. Days without shaving had left Mikhail with a grey stubble. He was pale and the skin below his eyes hung loose and dark, showing thin crescents of red. He smiled thinly.

"Not feeling too good I'm afraid," his voice wavered a little. "Journey's taking it out of me a bit."

"You going to be all right?" said Wesley, waking up properly. "To carry on I mean."

Mikhail nodded. " For now, yes. But I might stay at Saint Terresas. Leave you three to carry on. Hopefully things are still safe there."

Janis put Mikhail's hand gently onto the arm of the chair and covered it with her own.

"All things considered," she said to Katie. "Your grandfather is a fit man for his age. But he needs to rest. Not here. At Saint Terresas, where there will be people to look after him properly." She turned to Wesley. "Good sleep?"

"Fifteen hours!"

"You must have needed it."

"Any news on Max?" Wesley asked.

"No nothing," she replied.

She passed Wesley a spoon; a can opener and a rusty can with no label.

"Not sure if this is breakfast lunch or tea," she said. "But it makes a change."

He wiped the top of the tin against his sleeve and opened it. Baked beans. He dipped the spoon in and ate. He could not remember when he had last tasted anything so delicious and within a couple of minutes, he was scraping the bottom of the can with the spoon.

At the same time that Wesley was wiping the last drops from the inside of the tin with his finger, Jarvis and a thin weasel faced young guard were dragging the electric pump across the cellar floor towards the door of Anguillaro's cell.

"You pulling?" Jarvis said accusingly. "Feels like I'm doing all the work around here."

"Course I am." Weasel Face defended himself in a whining voice. "I was gonna ask you the same question."

"Don't cheek your superiors."

"You're not my superior," replied Weasel Face. "You're the same as me. Bottom rank."

"Look Sonny Jim." Jarvis stopped pulling and the pump stopped dead. Both men straightened and faced each other.

"The Colonel," he continued, "has given me responsibility. You are here to help."

"You are here to help," Weasel Face mimicked.

Jarvis stamped with annoyance and stepped close to Weasel Face, pointing his finger a few inches away from his face. "I report back to the Colonel. You do as I say…Understand?"

"All right. Keep your hair on."

Jarvis clapped his hand onto his bald patch. "Another comment like that," he snapped. "And you'll be behind one of those doors." He jerked his thumb back towards the cell doors. "Now get hold of this pump and pull your weight. We have a job to do."

Without another word they dragged the pump to the cell door. Weasel Face fed its long hose down into the well while Jarvis connected the electric cable to a plug in the wall. He peered cautiously through the barred window before unlocking the door and stepping onto the threshold.

Anguillaro was standing, his dark eyes starring straight at Jarvis and then at Weasel Face who peered in around Jarvis, wincing at the strong smell.

"Blimey," he said. "Is that human?"

"That's the Eel Catcher that is," Jarvis puffed himself up with authority. "And we're going to give him a good wash."

Anguillaro glared silently at the two men.

"Pass me the hose," Jarvis commanded. "And go flick the pump on."

Weasel Face obeyed and the pump chattered into life. The hose from the well, snaking across the flagstones, twisted into life as the water was sucked along it. Jarvis held the nozzle end and braced himself against the doorframe. Dirty brown water coughed and spluttered from the end and then a powerful jet burst out, bucking the hose in Jarvis' hands. It hit Anguillaro full in the chest, knocking him back against the wall. He dropped his head to protect his face as Jarvis raised the jetting water upwards. Weasel Face edged into the doorway to watch. Jarvis aimed the jet downwards, hitting Anguillaro in the crotch, causing him to buckle downwards, twisting sideways to avoid the bruising water. A smile crept onto Jarvis' face. He sprayed up and down. Water poured across the cell floor, carrying with it a slick of oil, and disappeared into a drain in the corner. Jarvis stepped further into the cell, feeling bolder with the powerful hose in his hands. Weasel Face followed. He moved round to one side to hose down the Eel Catcher's back. The water poured off Anguillaro's eel skin suit. It ran down his arms and around the shackles that held his wrists. With it ran slippery eel oil from Anguillaro's clothes and skin, and as the water pounded into him from behind, he stepped away from the wall and leaned forward, pulling the chains tight behind him. In the spray of water, with his soaking hair flattened against his head and shoulders, and his arms held out behind him, he looked for a moment as if he were preparing to dive.

He narrowed his oily hands and pulled. He felt his bones squeezing closer and closer together with almost unbearable tightness and the metal edges of the shackles dug into his skin. For a moment he hung there, pain searing through his crushed hands, and then, with a final heave, he slipped from the shackles and lunged forward.

Anguillaro moved so fast that the guards had no chance of escape. He brushed the hose aside and it snaked wildly across the floor and out of the door like a possessed limb, spraying water everywhere. In one swift movement he grabbed both men by a wrist each and yanked them to the back of the cell.

"The keys... Now!" he shouted. Jarvis fumbled at his belt and held them out to him, trembling.

"Unlock the shackles." He towered above the terrified guards and Jarvis fumbled with the locks until they sprang open.

"Hands in," said Anguillaro menacingly. "One each."

They quickly obeyed and Anguillaro snapped the locks closed. He glared down at them, his hair and beard still dripping with water.

"Now little fishes." Anguillaro lowered his voice and looked directly at Jarvis. "What you do with my watch, eh?"

Jarvis reached his free arm forward. It shook so much that it looked as if he was waving to someone. The watch was strapped to his wrist. Anguillaro grabbed his hand, removed the watch and looked at it.

"Mmm..." he said. "Bit early for lunch."

He leaned forward, poked both men in the ribs with a finger and opened his mouth, showing his long white teeth beneath his bushy moustache.

"Maybe," he smiled menacingly, "I will come back later."

He stepped out of the door and locked it behind him. In the

cellar the hose was still spraying wildly, soaking everything. He chased it across the floor, snatched the nozzle and, returning to the cell door, wedged it between the bars, leaving it squirting the ceiling. Water rained down over everything in the small room. He took his bag from the hook and then he strode towards the connector tunnel entrance. As he passed the well he tossed the keys into it and three seconds later they plopped into the water below.

24
The Bluebird

By the time Wesley and Katie's group reached the docks, the sun was setting over the low hills in the west, beyond the mouth of the estuary. It beamed across the harbour basin, bathing the derelict brick warehouses that lined the quay in a soft warm glow. The air smelled of salt and mud. Other than small patches of ripples, chasing across the surface, the water was smooth and still and the place would have been silent were it not for the squawking of gulls from the broken rooftops.

The broad wharf spread out in each direction. Train tracks were set in the concrete surface and weeds sprouted where soil had filled the wheel grooves. By the water's edge, where bollards poked up like huge thumbs, a tall crane stood on four long rusty metal legs. The legs met beneath an operator's cab, its glass windows smashed. On the side, in faded red letters, were the words 'RANDELL & PITT. ENGINEERS. 15 TONS MAX'. Above this, the jib rose high into the air, a lattice of steel and corroded cables topped with a rusting pulley wheel.

There were more cranes up and down the quay. One had toppled onto a ship that lay tipped sideways against the dock-side with one edge of its deck heaved upwards, the other sunk beneath the dark water. The single funnel, its white paint peeling, rested huge and dented against the edge stones of the quayside and the windows of the bridge sloped drunkenly sideways.

There were a few other boats in the harbour, varying in size from large freighters down to small launches and pleasure craft. Most were barely afloat and were covered in mould and rust. One of the largest vessels had sunk in the middle of the harbor and sat on the bottom, its decks below water and its derricks and superstructure rising up uselessly above. Its twin black funnels were each topped with white gulls, preening themselves in the last rays of the setting sun.

"This is the waiting place," Jupiter nodded to the steps of an official looking building beside them. "Others'll soon be here. Takes longer their way."

Red had insisted that they travel in two parties. If one were caught, he had said, the others might have a chance to rescue them, or at least stay free. Mikhail and Janis had gone with him and two other City Children on a different route. Wesley looked back to the gap in the Port's perimeter fence that they had come through. There was no sign of them. He walked over to the steps with Katie. Jupiter and the two city children, both boys of about Wesley's age, kicked aside some of the broken glass and rubbish from one of the steps and sat down. At the top, two large wooden doors hung open. Above then, streaked with gull excrement, a faded sign read; PORT AUTHORITY OFFICES.

Katie climbed the steps, looked in through the doorway and meandered in. Wesley sat down and watched the last brilliant speck of sun shrink and disappear behind the horizon. He pulled up his collar and pushed his hands into the front of his jacket. A few weeks ago he could never have imagined all the things that had happened since he got lost in the caverns. And though he was free, there were dangers that came with his freedom that felt much more life threatening than the hardship of the underground work gangs. He thought again of his old friend Martin, and of Charlie and Bobby Withers, the twins, and wished they could just be there, on the steps, now. He imagined the Horse People riding into the Main Tunnel to their rescue, tall and proud, sweeping the guards aside. But in reality, he realized, he didn't even know what the Horse People looked like, besides, horses would be an easy target for the guns of soldiers, and riding into the tunnels would probably be suicidal.

The rescue plan seemed vague. He had relied on the confidence and know-how of Max, Janis and Mikhail. But with Max gone and Mikhail in poor health, he knew that he would have to take more responsibility now. He was nervous of the coming boat trip. Paddling the zodiac on the underground lake, he'd managed that, but the estuary was far, far bigger and, by the sounds of it, far more dangerous too, with its currents and waves coming in from the sea and its exposed rocks and mud-flats at low tide. What if the tide pushed them out to sea? How would they even know what direction they were going in the dark?

He stood up, climbed the steps and walked in through the doorway. Inside, across a wide gloomy lobby, a staircase rose to a landing where what little daylight remained outside filtered in through a cobweb-covered window. Running along the right hand side of the lobby was a counter. Katie stood at the far end, flicking through the pages of a slim book. She spoke quietly to herself as if she were chanting a poem.

"Six two two, one two four eight. Six two two, one two four eight. Six two two, one two four eight. Six two two…"

She stopped at one of the pages and ran her finger down the paper then snapped the book closed and carried it over to Wesley, as if she had been aware of his presence all the time.

"Got a book," she said. "Present for Laro. He asked me. Remember?"

She brushed the dust off the cover with her sleeve and held the book out for him to see. The title, printed yellow on a dark blue cover, read;

'HARBOUR PILOT'S ALMANAC. SUN MOON AND TIDAL CALCULATIONS'.

. "Low tide nineteen twenty-eight," said Katie looking at the book cover. "High tide two forty in the night."

"Perfect!" came Janis' voice, as she stepped through the door behind them. Wesley gave a small sigh of relief. With Max's disappearance, he felt uncomfortable being separated from any of the others.

"What time is it now Katie?" Janis went on.

"Twenty sixteen," she replied without looking at her watches. "Sixteen minutes past eight."

"Right," said Janis. "If you're ready, then let's go."

A long breakwater enclosed the harbour. The only way out to the seawater of the estuary was through a huge lock. The inner gates, made from massive baulks of timber held together with iron straps, were closed, still holding back the dock water. Jets of water leaked out from cracks between the boards. The outer gates were open and beyond them, swathes of low tide mud flanked the shipping channel that ran out to meet the choppy brown water of the estuary.

Steel ladders, fixed to the stonework, descended the walls down into the lock. Wesley held on to the top of one and peered over the edge. The mud and water below was at least twenty feet down. He spat and watched the tiny blob of spittle fall. It disappeared from sight before it landed on the mud in the fading light.

The boat, when the City Children showed it to them, was larger and heavier than he had imagined. It lay sideways on the quayside close to the lock amongst piles of old rope and rusting chains. It was half filled with rainwater. The pale blue paint on its wooden hull was peeling away, but its name, 'Bluebird', was still legible on one side of its bows. Lying on the ground among the chains were two long slim bladed oars.

It took six of them to heave the boat over onto its side to pour out the water. Once that was done, the problem of getting it down to the water was discussed, and by the time a solution had been found, the western sky was dark and the only light came from the glow of the half moon behind the clouds. Night birds called out from over the shrinking mudflats and a light breeze blew up, chilling the air and stirring the rigging of a half sunken yacht, sending the ropes softly slap slapping against its mast.

The solution was Mikhail's. The Bluebird was dragged over to two bollards beside the edge of the lock. Ropes were tied to each end of the boat and looped once around each bollard. With four people taking the strain at the end of each rope, the Bluebird was lowered, swinging and grinding, down the lock wall. The ropes, tight around the bollards, gripped and juddered as the boat descended while Mikhail, lying down with his head over the edge, called back instructions.

"Another ten feet. Keep going, gently now."

Wesley, at the back of his group, felt the frayed end of the rope reach his hands.

"We don't have ten feet," he called back quickly. "Our rope's running out!"

"Hold. Everyone," Mikhail commanded. "How much more do you have?"

"As far as us to the bollard – can you see?"

"You can all bunch up," Red spoke from the other group. "Give you a bit more."

"Go on then," said Mikhail. "Go as far as you can… together now, that's good."

Wesley's group bunched up against the bollard.

"S'it," called Jupiter from the front. "Can't go no further." Several people began talking at once. Janis hushed everyone down.

"What now Mikhail?" she said. "How much further is it?"

"About six feet." Mikhail leaned onto his side and coughed, holding his hand to his chest. His voice was weaker as he continued. "We'll have to let her drop. On the count of three, all let go together. Everybody got that?"

In the darkness, each group checked that everyone understood as they leaned back against the ropes, keeping them tight around the bollards.

"One…" Mikhail started the count. "*two…three.*"

The ropes slithered away as the Bluebird dropped downwards. The end of the shortest rope whipped round the bollard and over the side but the longer rope ran slower, still sliding round its bollard, tipping the boat nose down as it fell. The Bluebird hit the water, bows first, and elbowed into the soft mud a couple of feet below the surface. The bows hinged back up, as the stern slapped down behind it, scooping water in from the front. The water sluiced back and forth inside the boat as it settled, floating, half full, the bows covered in mud.

They took it in turns to bale the water out with an old plastic bucket and it was over an hour later when it was finally empty and the last of their packs were lowered down. Janis, Mikhail and Katie were already in the boat. Wesley was about to climb down the ladder when Jupiter and Red stopped him.

"Wesley," she said. "This is for you. Maybe you gonna need it." She handed him a catapult. "If you gonna help get my brother, an' the others, then maybe you gotta learn to shoot. We don't go nowhere without these."

It was bigger and heavier than Wesley would have expected. The handle was made of smooth wood and the thick rubber cord was wound carefully around it.

"Thanks," said Wesley. He knew that the gift was, as much as anything, a token of friendship. He didn't know what else to say so he reached out his hand and they both took it in theirs at the same time and shook it.

253

"Good luck," said Red. "We'll watch out for your friend... just in case."

Wesley swung onto the ladder and climbed down into the boat. Above him the silhouettes of the City Children, craning over the edge of the wall, were visible against the streaks of moonlit clouds. The tide had risen several rungs up the ladder.

"'Bout five, six days then?" Red called down. "We'll keep a watch out for you."

"Good luck Katie," Jupiter called down.

Mikhail and Katie hunched down in the stern of the boat with Mikhail's coat around both of them. Wesley and Janis took an oar each, pushed the Bluebird off the wall, and rowed out into the channel. The clouds thinned and the mudflats, cut with the shadows of narrow tributaries, spread out on either side of them, shining like metal in the pale moonlight. Ahead of them, the incoming tide pushed up the estuary like a shifting swirling sheet of silver, dashed with specks of white foam from the wave tops. The boat felt slow and heavy and Wesley struggled with the long heavy oar. When they reached the open water, the waves started pitching the boat into an uncomfortable corkscrew motion and he began to feel queasy. Mikhail was coughing again. Katie held on to him tightly, watching Wesley's oar as it dipped and rose from the water.

"Lights!" she exclaimed suddenly, pointing to the end of the oar.

Wesley turned sideways and looked. Tiny specks of green light trailed through the water behind the blade, like a shower of miniature stars that blinked and were gone. They rowed on, watching the lights.

"Phosphorus," said Mikhail. "Tiny phosphorescent plankton energized by oxygen in the rush of water. They're early, it's more what you'd expect to see in the summer."

Wesley, Janis and Mikhail watched, fascinated.

"Another light," said Katie. But no one noticed that she was looking not at the oar, but up the estuary to where the bridge curved across, high above the water.

Because of the breeze up on the bridge, the first soldier struck three matches before he managed to light his cigarette. He stood up from the shelter of the rail and joined the other two, leaning against it, looking down into the darkness where the tide pushed steadily inwards, churning against the retreating water of the river.

"What kind of boat are we supposed to be looking for anyway?" he said.
"Any boat," replied the second soldier. "Hardly busy down there is it!"

"Chances are that we wouldn't see it anyway," said the third. "What if they slip past? We supposed to stay here night after night, waiting for something that's already been and gone?"

"Just keep looking," said the second. "I reckon we'd see 'em tonight. So long as the clouds don't thicken up. Look," he waved his finger downwards, "you can see the water moving. See them flecks of white? That's the main current. This is where they'd pass, right under us."

"Why can't we just pick 'em off from here?" said the first.
"Save everyone a lot of trouble."

"Weren't you listening?" said the second, exasperated. "He wants to speak to one of 'em. Remember?"

"Anyway," said the third. "A moving target down there in the dark - you'd be lucky to even hit the boat. Can't even see your own…"

"Shhh," the first soldier held up his hand quickly. The

breeze whispered against the bridge and the muted rush of water came up from below. The soldiers leaned forward, listening.

"Sure I heard something down there," he went on after a while. "Sounded like coughing."

The Bluebird swayed from side to side, buffeted by the choppy waves. Mikhail coughed again, bending forward, holding one hand to his chest with the other around Katie. Wesley and Janis bought the oars in. There was little need for them now as the tide swept them up the estuary. The silhouette of the bridge, its towers and the wide arc of its deck, appeared ahead of them and within minutes they had passed rocking and swirling beneath it.

As the night wore on and they passed further inland up the estuary, the waters slowed and Wesley and Janis took to the oars once again. Though Wesley had found it hard work to begin with, after a time he mastered the dip and pull of each stroke and he and Janis fell into a rhythm, pulling the heavy boat faster than the current. The clouds thinned to a ragged veil, moving slowly beneath the brilliant half moon and, closer now, the shores revealed themselves, grey and shadowy on either side. To the east a long cliff, the height of a house at its lowest places, ran dark and uninterrupted along the water's edge. To the west the shores were flatter, flanked with reed beds, their tips swaying and jostling in the breeze. Night birds called across them while mullet splashed in the shallows. Beyond them, two days walk over the meteorite ravaged hills, or three following the river, lay St Terresas.

By midnight they reached the crossing point of The Hundred Stones. Their smooth flat tops, lit by the moon, were barely above water level. The tide had peaked and the water was, for a moment, calm and still. The stones were too close together for the Bluebird to pass between and so they rowed over to where the line of stones disappeared into the reeds on the west bank. Mikhail and Katie clambered out onto the stones. Wesley and Janis, using their oars as poles, punted the boat into the reeds as far as they could before unloading the packs and blankets. Brushing aside the reeds, they stepped carefully across the last stones and on to the shore.

Set back a little from the water, amongst the reeds and long grass, they saw the silhouette of the old lodge house, silent, grey and shadowy. Glass in the broken windows glinted in the moonlight and the end of the veranda roof sagged where a supporting wooden pillar had collapsed. They avoided the place, uncertain of what they might find inside, and walked wearily to a grassy patch in amongst the bracken on a small rise of ground. Saying little, the four travelers rolled themselves in their blankets and slept, while beside them the reeds rustled softly in the breeze and the tide turned and sucked, murmuring, back out to sea.

25
And Then There Were Three

Shouldering their packs, they set off at the first pale hint of dawn along an overgrown track that ran alongside the river. The shorter direct route over the hills, they had decided, was best avoided, even though it had been what Max had recommended. The river offered more cover and besides, they could not be sure of finding their way across the damaged landscape.

By midday they had entered the steep sided Afen Valley. Here the track ran close to the river's edge and the trees reached out over the swift flowing water that foamed and churned past large rocks and the jammed trunks of fallen trees. The sky cleared and the sun shone through the branches, casting a dappled shade over the walkers as they picked their way along the bank. The air was pungent with wild garlic and as they passed, bees buzzed from the tall white flowers of cow parsley. Above the eddies close to the bank, insects scarried back and forth just above the water surface and all of the time the sound of rushing water filled the valley.

Their spirits rose. For Wesley it was not since his first glimpse of the outside world from Anguillaro's back door that he had seen a place untouched by the ravages of the meteorites. Ahead of him, walking a step or two in front of Mikhail, Katie sang softly to herself as she walked.

By dusk they reached the end of the valley and the land gave out to overgrown meadows flanked by low hills. On the skyline, swathes of trees lay fallen but, down by the river, there was little damage. They camped beside a bend in the river where the shallow water hurried steadily over gravel and smooth rocks. Janis brewed nettle soup in the pan that she had bought from the farmhouse and each of their packs were lightened by a can of beans. The moon, a slice larger that the previous night, rose into a cloudless starry sky and the travelers slept, wrapped in their blankets, lulled by the soft chuckling of the river.

Wesley slept deeply; though he was twice woken by Mikhail's coughing. By sunrise they had set off again, keeping for the most part to the river, though where it flowed in wide loops across the broad valley, they cut across the old fields where nettles and thistles now flourished.

In places the track passed over small bridges, crossing streams that flowed down into the main river. More than one of the streams was dry, its course changed by the damaged landscape in the hills, and plants had taken root in the silty beds. In other places they had to ford new watercourses, cut by the diverted streams. Most were narrow enough to jump, though one they had to wade, hand in hand, trousers rolled high and boots, laces tied together, slung round their necks.

Towards noon, Janis and Wesley sat down against an old spreading oak to wait for Katie and Mikhail who had fallen behind. Wesley took out his catapult and flexed the thick elastic. Pulling it to its limit required a hard pull. He fitted a pebble into the sling and drew it back as far as his arm would reach. The pebble shot out over the river and thwacked into the far bank. He picked up another pebble.

"Wesley," said Janis leaning back. "None of us have talked much more about our plans have we?"

He fired off the second pebble and lowered the catapult.

"I know," he replied. "I've thought about it. Well, not *making* plans or anything, just wondering how all this is going to work out. How we can free everyone from the tunnels, and that quarry, when The Order have got guns and everything… and there's so many of them."

"I've been thinking too," said Janis. "Max thought there was no point in planning much, least not until we've talked with the Horse People, and I suppose he was right really."

"What does Mikhail think?"

Janis looked back down the track to where Katie and Mikhail were making their way slowly towards them. "Since losing the Water he seems to have sort of given up. I spoke to him yesterday but he mostly just shrugged and said he didn't know what we should do. I know he's exhausted and has, I think, a chest infection, but it's more than that, he doesn't seem to care anymore."

"What about you?" said Wesley. "I mean, have you thought of anything?"

"Not really. I agree with what Max said. We need to sit down together, at Saint Terresas, and look at what options there are. But there's one thing that I have thought of and that's this. Added together with the quarry group, The Order has got at least seventy children as slaves. If we're successful and we free everyone, there's got to be somewhere for everyone to go. Somewhere safe, if any such place exists."

"What about Saint Terresas?"

Janis shook her head. "I'm not sure about the future there for anyone. The Order wants it. As far as I could gather when I was at Hillside House, their plans are to capture it and everyone who lives there. They need farmland and people to farm it because their food stores are low. The Horse People know all this because I got the message out when I was Colonel Dove's secretary, so they'll be on their guard. Their only real choice, if The Order shows signs of attack, is to abandon the town and go north, and that brings me to my point about plans. If we manage to free everyone, Dove won't just leave everyone to run off. He wants everything under his control. He'll order a pursuit. Somehow we need to get everyone away without being seen, or at least with a good head start. That's an issue for planning at Saint Terresas. But, should anything happen to one of us, or all of us, then the children need to know that they must cross the estuary and then go north."

"To Saint Terresas?"

"No. Like I said, I don't think there's going to be safety there. I mean north from there. You see, east from the estuary, beyond The Order's tunnels, the whole area, as far as The Order scouts have been, is in a terrible state apparently. South is the coast. There's been tidal waves, too much has been destroyed to make it habitable. The far west, I don't know, The Order scouts haven't been that far yet, least not to my knowledge, but that way reaches the coast eventually too. To the north though, from Saint Terresas, there is land in the hills that is apparently still ok. There'll be villages up there. Somewhere to shelter. But in the longer term we'll have to go far further away to be safe."

Wesley sat quietly for a moment. "What if the Horse People have already left?" he said.

"Don't know," Janis replied. "I really don't know."

By the morning of the third day, Janis began to recognize the landscape. She chatted excitedly about old friends. She was sure that they would reach Saint Terresas by that afternoon. Mikhail however was faring badly. He was coughing increasingly and needed to rest after each racking fit. The others distributed what little was left in his pack between their own and Wesley snapped off a stout hazel branch for him to walk with. By the early evening, at the old man's weary pace, they reached a dense oak wood that overhung the track. The woodland grew on a steep shoulder of land that sloped down to the river and twilight was creeping in beneath the canopy of branches.

"The river meadows of Saint Terresas are at the end of the wood," Janis said. "You'll see the town then, it's just a walk up through the fields."

They passed in under the trees. The track, squelchy with half dry mud, curved gently left, following a wide bend in the river. Soon they could see ahead to where the trees ended and the track was brighter. Janis had her arm through Mikhail's and Wesley and Katie walked ahead to where the trees ended at a gate. Wesley rested his arms on the top bar and looked out. The broad bend of the river curved on round and the land on both sides of it was laid out with well-cultivated fields. Some were green with the fresh shoots of spring corn, others were pastures of lush grass for hay or held horses, idly grazing, flicking at the evening midges with their long tails.

In the shade of a grove of willows, a small wooden building was perched on the riverbank. Beside it, the upturned hull of a long canoe was visible in the long grass.

Away from the river, to Wesley's left, the fields sloped upwards. Leaning forward, he saw the slate rooftops of Saint Terresas at the top of a hill. The walls of the roofless abbey rose from among the tightly grouped houses and the old stonework shone like honey in the evening sun.

A movement down by the river caught his eye and Wesley turned to see a man's head showing over the bank. He heard a laugh and then another man's head, swigging from a bottle, bobbed up. He stood up on the bottom rung of the gate to see them better. The two men were down at the river's edge skimming stones across the water. Both wore the uniforms of The Order's soldiers.

Wesley ducked down and reached for Katie's hand. Feeling awkward, he put his arm around her, stroked her hair and whispered; "Soldiers!" He turned to Janis and Mikhail and held his finger to his lips for silence. Mikhail screwed his eyes up tightly and put his hand over his mouth. He leaned forward, dropped his stick onto the mud and held his other hand to his chest, his body convulsing with suppressed coughing. Wesley quickly led Katie back from the gate. Pointing back behind him he mouthed the word 'Soldiers' to Janis and Mikhail. Mikhail steadied himself and slowly straightened, his eyes watering and his hand still to his chest. Together, they retreated along the track and scrambled up the slope into the trees.

"How many?" whispered Janis, alarmed.

"Two," replied Wesley. "Skimming stones."

Mikhail breathed out. "Too late," he said shaking his head and looking down. "We're too late. This is the worst scenario. Your people," he looked at Janis sadly, "prisoners of The Order. Lost. And without them we're lost too. And the tunnel children."

Janis put her head in her hands and moaned softly.

"Maybe," said Wesley, trying to stay positive. "Maybe the Horse People had already left. I mean left before the soldiers arrived. They could be on their way to the Tunnels."

Janis looked up at him. "Maybe," she said unconvincingly. "It's possible. We need to get a closer look. See what's going on in the town."

"What about those two by the river?" said Wesley.

"There's another way," replied Janis. "A path up through these woods, from a bit further back. It goes up to the walled gardens." She drew herself up and nodded at Wesley. "Let's go and see."

The four of them climbed the path up through the woods. In places it was steep and slippery and they worked together to help each other up. At the top of the hill the trees ended at a high stone wall. A short way along it was a small wooden door, almost completely covered by ivy. Janis pushed it open as far as the ivy would allow. Inside was a large walled garden. Most of the ground was carefully cultivated and row after row of newly planted seeds sprouted from the rich dark soil. The smell of blossom from fruit trees, trained along wall trellises, sweetened the evening air. Against the far wall was a large greenhouse, its roof sagging with age, but with all its panes of glass in place. Beside it, an archway in the wall led out of the garden into a street.

Three women were hoeing the ground between the rows of seedlings, the sound of their hoes scritch-scratched against the stones in the soil. They worked slowly, without speaking, rhythmically scraping their hoes backwards and forwards. There was something unusual about the way that they moved. It was as if they were half asleep.

A fourth woman came out of the greenhouse carrying a hoe in one hand. Her other arm hung straight at her side, not swinging as she walked. She looked only at the ground in front of her. She joined the others and began to work.

"That's Rebecca," whispered Janis. "I swear that's Rebecca Thomas. But she isn't moving in the way that I remember her. She looks like she's in a trance. They all do."

She called out softly, "Rebecca."

The girl continued working.

"Rebecca?" Janis called out again a little louder.

Still there was no reaction. Janis walked cautiously over to the girl.

"Rebecca? It's me. Janis."

The girl lifted her head slightly, looked blankly at Janis and then continued to work.

"Rebecca, don't you remember me?"

The girl continued to gently scuff at the ground. Janis rested her hand on her arm. "Can you hear me Rebecca?" She gave her arm a little shake. "Rebecca!"

The girl stopped for a moment and looked up.

"Got to get the hoeing done," she said. "Got to hoe until the bell."

"The bell? The bell for what?"

The girl didn't reply. She had barely begun to scratch at the soil again when the single clang of a bell rang out from somewhere in the town beyond the garden wall. Without looking up, the four women stopped hoeing and walked away through the archway on the far side, leaving their hoes propped against the wall.

Janis was left standing there. She shook her head, looked back at the others and beckoned them to follow her. They hurried across the garden and gathered in the greenhouse.

Inside the air was warm and smelled of geraniums.

"Don't know what's wrong with her," said Janis puzzled. "I remember her well. She was a lively soul. Now she seems, I don't know, just completely different. I don't know if she even recognized me."

Mikhail sat down heavily on an upturned crate and held his face in his hands. "Janis?" he said. "Where does the town get its water from?"

"From the well," she replied. "Since the mains supply stopped working, all water comes from the well."

"From the well." Mikhail nodded gloomily. "Easy for them really. For The Order. All they had to do was poison the well. They've made Darkwater from the bottle that didn't break. I knew they would, and they've poisoned the well. Such a simple weapon, but so effective. Everyone who drinks the contaminated well water will become docile and loose the will to resist. And it's all my fault." He looked up at the wall in front of him and shook his head slowly. "I know the symptoms. Those women have been *darked*".

"Maybe they were just, very tired or…" Wesley couldn't think of another possibility but he wanted there to be one. Everything sounded so hopeless. "Maybe it's only them. The rest of the Horse People might be fine. Those soldiers by the river could be deserters."

"I wish that were true Wesley," Mikhail went on. "But I think not. The Order has got here before us. Everything's finished now".

"How do you know those are the symptoms of this *Darkwate*r, anyway?" said Wesley.

Mikhail drew a long breath and continued.

"Because I saw them on my own granddaughter." He looked at Katie. "On you my dear, when you were only eleven years old. And you have never recovered."

"I'm alright Grandpa." Katie smiled and sat down beside him.

Mikhail shook his head. "It was my fault then and it's my fault now. Before the meteorites and the virus I had been experimenting, as you know, with Lightwater from a well in Jerusalem."

"Mikhail," Janis interrupted. "Is this the time…"

"I want to tell you now. I want you to understand. I experimented with Darkwater too. And you became exposed to it Katie. I was foolish. I let you play in the laboratory and while my back was turned you spilled some on your hands. Exposure to the skin is enough, and you sunk like a stone into a dark world of your own. If I hadn't been experimenting with it, neither Katie or those women would have been exposed to it."

"If you had Lightwater as well," said Wesley. "Couldn't you cure her?"

"I tried. And it made some difference. It drew you out of the gloom Katie, but not back to your former self. I didn't fully understand then that Light and Darkwater has to be refreshed to keep its potency and that whichever has been refreshed most recently is the most powerful and will dominate the other. I know that now, and that's why I wanted to get what I had left from the university. When the meteorites came, my colleague Doctor Thornberry persuaded me to take refuge below Hillside House. We all went, the whole family, but there was something about the Doctor that I didn't trust and I hid the Water at the University. I could tell that he was probing for information but I was cautious and I didn't trust the organization that ran the tunnels, The Order as they named themselves." He wiped the palm of his hand across one cheek. "But I pretended to go along with them and accepted the vaccine, offered to me by the Doctor when the virus came.

"I was afraid for my own life. My daughter, Katie's mother, and Katie's father, both perished. He refused to give it to them on the grounds that there was only enough for those that would be needed to help rebuild things afterwards. But I realized that he had another motive. He wanted the Lightwater. I told him that it had been destroyed but he was suspicious. So I pretended to lose my mind, go mad with all the terrible things that were happening around us and although I think I fooled him, he never gave up trying to make me remember. I held out, but I might as well have told him everything," Mikhail gestured towards the town. "Now that they have it anyway."

"Mikhail," said Janis gently. "Without taking a look, we don't know for sure what's happening in the town."

Mikhail looked from Janis to Katie and then let his gaze fall to the dusty floor of the glasshouse. "True. We need to look. But I know I'm right. And it's all my fault."

They hid their packs beneath the plant shelves in the greenhouse and made their way cautiously through the archway in the wall. A narrow street, lined with stone terraced cottages, rose steeply to their right. Compared to the city, there was little damage to any of the houses. A few cars were parked against the pavement, though it was obvious from their dusty windscreens and soft tyres that they had not moved for a long time. The windows in many of the houses, however, were clean, as were the thresholds to their doors and the pavements beside them.

Janis led the way through a maze of small streets. The air was still. Somewhere in an adjoining street a dog was barking at its own echo, and above the rooftops, the ruined gable end of the abbey came into sight, glowing in the last rays of sun against a deepening blue sky. They cautiously turned a corner. Half way down the street, squeaking with every turn of its wheel, a wheelbarrow, half filled with potatoes, was being pushed slowly towards the main square at the other end. One man pushed the barrow and two others walked beside him. Janis hurried ahead, the others following, and fell into step with the three men. They barely acknowledged her, or Wesley, as he caught up with them.

"Cobby?" Janis spoke quietly to one of the men. "Cobby? Mike Cob, is that you?"

Without stopping the man turned and looked blankly at Janis.

"Yes, I'm Cobby," he said and turned forward again.

"Cobby," Janis persisted. "What's going on? We saw soldiers down by the river."

"Got to take these potatoes to the square," the man replied. "For the soldiers."

"What?" said Janis. They were nearing the end of the street

now. Briefly, she looked around at the others. "Cobby!" she went on. "Where is everyone?"

Cobby didn't reply for a moment and then turned slowly and looked at each of them in turn. His eyes were dull and expressionless.

"In the square," he said. "Listening. Everyone's where they're supposed to be."

At that moment four soldiers stepped into the street from the town square ahead of them.

"You got the 'tatoes there?" one of them shouted. "You been waiting for them to grow or something? Hurry up. Cook's waiting."

Mikhail spoke urgently under his breath. "Bow your heads everyone, bow your heads. Walk like these three. Act like them."

The wheelbarrow squeaked to the end of the street where the soldiers waited impatiently. Wesley and Janis shuffled along with the three men. Mikhail, so tired that he was already walking like them, rested one arm on Katie's shoulder, his hand stroking her hair.

"Gawd's sake," said one of the soldiers as they drew level. "How many of you does it take to collect a few spuds?

You..." he said to the man pushing the barrow. "Take 'em to the Abbot's Cookhouse, or Kitchen, whatever you call it. Rest of you can go. Meeting's over. Go to bed's my advice. Work starts in the morning."

With his head still bowed, Wesley scanned the wide square ahead of them. Part tarmac part cobbles, it was bordered on three sides by stone houses, many of which had shop fronts at ground level. The few items remaining in the shop windows were dusty and faded, most were stacked with sacks and crates. One was piled with bales of straw. Old buildings that had been part of the Abbey edged the third side of the square. The largest of these, long and low, was the Abbot's Kitchen. Beyond its roof rose the ruined gables of the Abbey.

In the centre of the square, with a conical tiled roof and a wide doorway in one side, sat the small round building that covered the Abbey well. Etched into the stonework above the door was a weathered Chinese symbol. From its pointed rooftop, a tall rusting weather vane, fashioned into the shape of a monk holding a chalice in each hand, stood stationary in the still evening air. Residents of the town were drifting off from the centre of the square towards the streets that led away from it. Everybody, except for the soldiers who stood around in groups watching, walked in silence with their arms hanging loosely at their sides. Wesley, Janis, Mikhail and Katie copied them, crossing the square towards a narrow lane beside the Abbot's Kitchen.

The first stars pricked the darkening sky and a group of soldiers, silhouetted against the lamplight from the open kitchen door, shared a glowing cigarette. From the open windows came the smell of frying bacon and from within came the sound of voices and bursts of laughter.

Mikhail began coughing again. He doubled forward and dropped onto his knees, each cough racking his tired body. Katie stopped beside him, her arms rigid at her sides.

"Grandpa. Grandpa," she said, loudly, as if she were lost and calling for him. The soldiers by the wall turned and watched, one of them twisting out the cigarette stub beneath his boot.

"*Grandpa, grandpa,*" he mimicked and a chuckle of laughter ran amongst the others. Katie stopped. Her lower lip trembled and she began to cry. Wesley put his arm around her and she put her head on his shoulder.

"Don't like it Wesley, don't like it," she sniffed. She lifted her head a little and looked at the soldiers. "Don't like *them* Wesley."

Janis helped Mikhail to his feet. The soldiers were still watching them. The old man was so weakened by his coughing that he walked slower than ever. They reached the corner of the kitchen and he began to cough again. He slumped down and leant against the wall. Katie began to sob again and while Wesley put a comforting arm around her, Janis crouched down by Mikhail.

Breathing heavily, he motioned Wesley and Katie to crouch beside them.

"I'm right," he whispered between breaths. "Darkwater. Everyone… they've drunk it… or come into contact with it. Must have. I…."

He coughed again. One of the soldiers approached with a bucket of water in one hand.

"Sounds bad old man," he said as he arrived. He pulled Mikhail to his feet with his free hand. "Here, have a drink of well water."

The others stood, unsure of what to do. Perhaps, Wesley wondered, the soldier was just a bit rough but meant well. Mikhail stepped away from the soldier.

"Here old man." The soldier lifted the bucket. "Drink."

He raised the bucket up, emptied the water over Mikhail's head and stepped back to avoid being splashed.

"Anyone else want another dose?" he said. He snorted a laugh and walked away. Mikhail stood motionless, his eyes closed, his hair plastered down over his forehead. A shadow, darker than the evening light, appeared around him, as if he was standing in a patch of night. For a brief moment it grew wider and deeper. Then it retreated, faded and disappeared. The soldier watched from the door. Katie tried to put her arms around her grandfather but, with outstretched arms, he held her away.

The first soldier turned back as he reached the door. "Get back to your houses," he called. "And be sure you're all back here in the morning for work."

"Grandpa," Katie pleaded, but Mikhail pushed her away weakly.

"Stay with Wesley," he said. "Don't touch me while I'm wet.

He walked unsteadily into the lane beside the Abbot's Kitchen, beckoning the others to follow with a small nod of his head. He leaned against the wall. Lamplight from an open window above his head shone onto the wall on the other side of the lane. The voices and laughter continued from inside.

"I've got a few minutes," he said quietly. "Until I become like everyone else. Simple, hopeless, *darked*. I can feel it starting... You must all leave, quickly."

"Not without you Mikhail," said Janis.

"No, you don't understand. Without Lightwater..."

"Mikhail, you're coming with us," said Janis firmly. "Back across the square." She glanced at Wesley and Katie. "Now, while there are still people leaving."

She tried to link her arm through his but Mikhail pushed her away.

"Don't," Mikhail protested weakly. "Please. I'll be better off here. I'm not being a martyr. It's better if I stay here. But get Katie out. Just do that, get Katie to somewhere safe."

The voices from through the window suddenly became quiet.

"Mikhail," Janis whispered. "We're not leaving you."

Two soldiers ran across the end of the lane and the sound

of a door slamming came from through the window. A confident man's voice then spoke from just inside. Wesley imagined that if the wall hadn't been between them he would be close enough to touch whoever was speaking.

"Everybody here now?" said the voice.

Mikhail retreated a step. Janis swung back against the wall and pulled Wesley and Katie back with her.

"Dove," she whispered. "That's Colonel Dove."

"Good. Do sit down," Dove continued from inside. "It appears that all the inhabitants are accounted for. And not a shot fired! Just two days after flavouring the well. I am sure you will agree gentlemen that we now have the most effective weapon at our command. It really has been… very simple. You will all be pleased to hear that the city urchins have been dealt with. They have arrived at the quarry where they will be kept until we have completed accommodation for them in the tunnels. We now have only our four runaways to account for. However, all of the routes into town are being observed and I imagine we shall have them safely in the fold by tomorrow.

"Today marks a new era for The Order," he went on. "This excellent home-made beer is, I am sure, a foretaste of the better times to come for us all. May I suggest that the talent for brewing is not neglected when you make an inventory of skills for the work parties here."

There were laughs and murmurs of approval from some of the men inside. Mikhail leant back against the wall, his head bowed. Katie stood beside him. Janis and Wesley exchanged glances.

"Over the coming months," Dove continued. "Our new workforce will build quarters for themselves and it is my plan to relocate most of us to this charming town as soon as possible. The tunnels beneath Hillside House will become a garrison only and there will be a clearance of our young workforce there, as they will no longer be needed. I shall be leaving tomorrow to get things underway there, and the majority of you will be leaving shortly afterwards. Those of you who have been allocated to remain will be under the temporary command of Doctor Thornberry here. As there will no longer be any problems of resistance I expect everything to be quite straight-forward.

"We can now look forward to a more secure and prosperous lifestyle. The dark days are over. I should like to thank you all for your individual contributions towards making it possible. Those of you who have made a particularly special effort in helping to bring this about will receive due reward by being able to select a dwelling of their choice here in the town. High on that list is one person to whom we owe special thanks. I would like you all to raise your glasses to this gentleman on my left, Mr. Max Cotton."

Wesley's mouth dropped open. He looked from the open window above him to Janis. She stared back, eyes wide in disbelief. From inside came the sound of chairs being scraped back on the stone floor, the chink of glasses and voices repeating the name Max Cotton. It occurred to Wesley that there might be another man with the same name, but the next person to speak left him in no doubt.

"Thank you," came Max's voice.

Katie jerked her head up to the window, smiling.

"Max," she called out loudly.

26
Fresh Eels

On the high ground behind Hillside house, amongst tumbled stones and thistles, a moss covered circular brick wall marked the top of one of the old air vents for the tunnels. The wire mesh cover had been prised from its rusty fixings and lay pushed to one side. Tied to an iron ring that was set into the brickwork, a rope fell away down into the deep shaft. The rope was taut and trembled as if it had a life of its own. Attached to the other end of the rope was Anguillaro, shimmying his way down into a blackness that was darker by far than the night outside.

Reaching the bottom, he turned on a torch. Two horizontal shafts, waist high to Anguillaro, ran off in opposite directions. He crouched down in the confined space and shone the torch down them both. The tunnels were built of brick and were completely round. After the first few feet, where stones had collected that had fallen down the shaft, they were clear. The first one, as far as Anguillaro could see, was dry and dusty. A few yards into the second tunnel, water dripped from the ceiling making the bricks dark and damp. The torch beam reflected off small puddles and lit up slimy growths of algae on the sides. Anguillaro sniffed the air from both tunnels, turned off the torch and crawled head first into the second one.

He moved fast and quietly, pulling himself along on his elbows with his body snaking behind him. He came to a fork in the tunnel and again sniffed the air before continuing. The tunnel sloped downwards for a time and then leveled off once again. After a few minutes he stopped and turned on the torch. A more recent shaft, made from concrete piping, broke into the brickwork to the right. It was narrower than the brick tunnel, but Anguillaro squeezed into it and wormed his way along. At intervals, square metal ducting joined the sides of the pipe where newer ventilation had been plumbed into the old system.

The pipe ended in a small square chamber. A dim light filtered up through a metal grille set in the floor and he could make out the shapes of dusty machinery below. He drew himself round and kicked hard at the grille with both feet. It shook but did not give way. Dust swirled up into the chamber. He kicked again, harder, and the grille swung down and open with a crash and the squeal of rusty hinges. He lowered himself down through the opening onto the top of one of the machines and jumped to the floor. He was in a long thin room. The machines were large pumps from which thick pipes led off into the walls.

At one end was a metal door and in front of it a hole had been broken through the concrete floor. It was from here that the dim light came. He hung his head down through the hole. Below was a brick lined tunnel with light bulbs set in caged holders in the ceiling. Most of the bulbs had blown long ago but those that were working shed plenty of light to see by. In one direction, right beside the hole, was a grid, secured with a combination padlock. In the other direction, the tunnel sloped upwards and curved away to the right. Anguillaro was unaware that this was where Wesley and Katie had met, but he knew where he was nonetheless. He let himself through the hole, climbed down the grid and set off up the slope. At the wooden door that led to the Dead Horse Caverns, he paused and listened before passing into the dark narrow tunnel beyond it.

Even without light, Anguillaro had the knack of walking silently, feeling forward with each footstep and brushing his hand through the air in front of him. Were someone to have stood against the walls in the pitch blackness of the Caverns, where Wesley first met Anguillaro, they would not have known he had entered until his bare feet squelched into the mud beside the river. Checking the mud in his torchlight for new footprints, Anguillaro waded though the river to the far side where a post jutted up from the mud. Setting the torch onto the mud so that the beam shone onto the water, he fished into the water beside the post, pulled up a rope and began to haul something up from the riverbed. A fine meshed metal cage broke the surface, which he set down on the mud beside the torch. He opened a hatch in the top of the cage, thrust in his hand and pulled out a long squirming eel. Its body glistened in the torchlight. He held the eel up and whispered quietly to it while he reached for the knife on his belt. With one swift movement he sliced the head from the eel and pushed its still writhing body into the bag that hung from his shoulder. He pulled a second eel from the cage and did the same, then a third and a fourth until he had seven eels in his bag. The outside of the bag moved like a living animal. He picked up one of the heads, dropped it into the cage and closed the lid. Swinging it on the end of the rope he threw the cage back into the river where it sank quickly from sight.

Bent forward, Anguillaro waded up the river into the low cave from which the river flowed. He visited more eel cages and at each one he repeated the same ritual until his bag bulged with eels. He returned the way he had come, hoisting himself, and his heavy bag, up into the square chamber above the pump room. Then, dragging the bag behind him, he crawled into the maze of ventilation shafts that fed air into The Order's underground labyrinth.

27
All About Water

"Katie," Mikhail fought against waves of darkness that washed over him. "I want you to go with Wesley. Do you understand?"

He looked at Wesley and held his gaze for a moment. Wesley knew that, without words, he was imploring him to look after his granddaughter.

"Yes Grandpa, I understand," Katie replied. "I understand."

"Hold out your hand Katie," he said weakly.

Katie held out her hand and Mikhail dropped Anguillaro's ring into her palm.

"If you see Laro," he said. "Give this back to him."

A chair scraped the floor on the other side of the kitchen wall and a second later Max's face appeared at the window above them. There was no expression on his face, he simply looked at the four of them quickly and drew back. Commands were issued inside and there followed the sound of hurrying boots on the floor.

"Run," Mikhail's voice was weak but insistent.

Wesley grabbed Katie's hand and ran with her and Janis to the top of the lane. As they turned the corner at the other end he glanced back at Mikhail standing in the light from window. The old man stood looking after them, his hands hanging limply at his sides, his eyes filled with tears.

As fast as they could run, Janis led them through the narrow streets, turning first one way and then another. They could hear the commotion of soldiers spreading out into the town to find them. They hurried under an archway and, though Wesley had not recognized the street outside, they were back in the walled garden. Grabbing their packs they raced across to the door in the far wall and out into the woods.

The moon had risen but beneath the canopy of leaves there was almost no light to see by. They pushed through the undergrowth and slithered down through the trees. Branches caught their hair and scratched their arms and faces but they hardly noticed. The sound of water grew louder and they scrambled down past the last bushes, through a patch of nettles, and onto the path by the river. Wesley's hands felt hot where he had been stung.

"Katie, you ok?" he said quietly.

"Hands stinging Wesley," she replied. "But I'm ok Wesley, I'm ok. Will Grandpa be ok too?

"I hope so Katie," was all Wesley could say.

Janis led them through the gate into the field and, under the shelter of the bank, they hurried up to the canoe house. The moon, three quarters full, shone down from above the wood. In its silvery light the dark figures of soldiers, fanning out from the town above, could be seen running down towards the river. They dragged the canoe out from the long grass and turned it over. It had three seats, one at each end and one in the middle beneath which were wedged two single bladed paddles. They slid it straight into the water, pulling it through the shallows before throwing their packs in and climbing aboard.

"Don't use the seats," Janis whispered. "Kneel. It's more stable that way."

Katie knelt down and held on to the central seat and, with Janis paddling from the front and Wesley from the back, they turned the canoe downstream and dug the blades into the water. The moonlight glittered on the swirling river as they swept down ahead of the current. They were quickly beyond the oak wood. As best they could, they tried to keep the canoe out of the shallows. But in places gravel and stones ground noisily beneath the hull when they misjudged the depth and at times they had to step out into the water and push the small boat back into deeper water.

A little after midnight they found themselves in a slower, deeper stretch of the river. Wesley's arms ached. He was tired and hungry. They pulled into the bank to stretch their cramped legs and shared their last can of beans, swilling the juice from the side of the empty can with river water and drinking it. They spoke little, each of them wrapped in their own thoughts about what had happened. With the canoe pulled up into some bushes, they wrapped their blankets around them and slept on the hard ground.

Wesley dreamed of Mikhail talking to him without his mouth opening, and of Spider Pearson, chasing him with a stick, gaining on him no matter how fast he ran. And then he was in a canoe, lying down inside while it was tipped from side to side by huge waves that threatened to pour down and drown him. Splashes of water dashed across his face and the thin wining voice of a man he could not see was speaking to him...

The voice carried on talking as Wesley awoke. He had rolled sideways in the night and found that he was under a dense bush of willow beside the canoe. Leaves tickled his face. Just beyond the bush, no more than two yards away, were the legs of a horse. The voice came from its rider who was facing away from him. He wore sandals, baggy black trousers and a sheepskin waistcoat. The back of his head was bald and he had a rifle slung across his shoulder. He was talking to Janis who stood looking up at him defiantly. Katie sat, wrapped in her blanket a few feet away, rubbing the sleep out of her eyes.

"What's it to you where I got the horse from?" said the man.

"I recognize that animal," said Janis. "And the saddle and bridle. It comes from Saint Terresas."

"What if it does?" the man sneered in reply. "I bought it if you want to know. Fair and square."

"Stole it you mean." Janis took a step nearer. "No one would have sold you that horse. Who are you anyway?"

In one swift movement, the man took the rifle from his back and pointed it at Janis. Katie screamed and shuffled backwards against a bush and began to shake, holding her blanket tight around her shoulders.

"I'm asking the questions," said the man. "I'd like to know who you are and what you're doing here and what food you've got in that pack. Well? Tell me."

Wesley was wide-awake now. As quietly as he could, he reached over into the canoe beside him and opened the straps of his pack. He pushed his hand in, felt for his catapult and drew it carefully out.

"If you're from Saint Terresas, how come you aren't there now, eh?" the man continued. "Renegades are you? Not that I'm bothered whose side you're on. And you over there." He waved the rifle at Katie. "What about you? Eh?"

Katie cowered back, pulling her blanket tightly around her, and as she did, Wesley gently slid out from beneath the bush, stood up right behind the man and pulled the empty catapult sling back as far as he could, aiming for his head. He tensed his muscles in an attempt to hide the shaking that he could feel in his body. He wasn't sure what to say.

"Drop it," the words seemed to come from nowhere.

The man swung round in surprise. He lifted his elbow to cover his face and the gun slipped from his grasp, clattering to the ground beside him. Wesley kept the catapult aimed straight at him. He could hear the voice of Red, repeating over and over in his head, 'go for the faces, go for blood', and a part of him wished he had a real stone pinched in his hand and that the power he suddenly held over the man was not a bluff.

"Don't, don't, don't," the man pleaded, his confident voice changed to a miserable whine. "Didn't mean it. No bullets anyway."

Janis leapt forward and picked up the rifle. She checked the magazine. It was full of shiny bullets. She pointed the gun at the man.

"Off the horse," she commanded.

She backed over to Katie and put her arm around her, still with the rifle pointed at the man. Wesley let the catapult flick into the air and walked around the horse. The man flinched and slid quickly from the saddle.

"Who are you?" said Wesley.

"They... they call me the Hermit," he replied shakily.

"The *Hermit*?" Janis exclaimed. "I remember you now, from when I was a kid. You had hair then."

The Hermit brushed his shaky hand over his head.

"What are you doing here?" Janis went on.

"I... I'm just travelling."

"I don't believe you." Janis kept the rifle aimed at him. "You'll have to do better than that."

"If you shoot," said the Hermit with a new edge of confidence in his voice. "And if by any chance you are on the run, then the sound will be heard for miles."

Wesley scooped a stone from the ground, and fitted it quickly into his catapult.

"This won't," he said taking aim. "Tell us what you're doing."

The Hermit cowed back, holding his arms in front of his face. "All right, I'm just taking something somewhere. That's all. Just a delivery. Nothing special."

"A delivery of what?" said Wesley.

"What? Just... just water actually. See for yourself. In the saddlebag."

Janis opened the saddlebag on the side of the horse while Wesley kept his catapult trained on the Hermit. She pulled two large old fashioned looking bottles from the saddlebag.

"This the water you mean?" she asked.

"Yes," the Hermit replied. "It's just water, you can see that."

"And why would you go to all the trouble of taking some water to someone?"

"I… just…"

"It's Lightwater isn't it?"

"Lightwater?"

"Yes Lightwater, and I think you stole it from Saint Terresas."

Wesley bought the handle of the catapult so close to the Hermit's head that it almost touched his bald scalp.

"Yes, yes. That is what it is. Lightwater. Please, don't fire that thing." The Hermit gibbered.

"Where were you taking it," said Wesley.

"To a place called Hillside House. I was going to sell it. That's all."

Janis and Wesley looked at each other.

"Well you're too late anyway," said Janis. "Over at Hillside House they have their own supply these days, so I think the best thing you can do it go home."

"Yes, yes. I will. I'll just ride back. Straight away."

"No. Walk back," said Janis.

"Walk?"

"Yes, walk. No way you're keeping this horse. Now get going."

The Hermit backed cautiously away from them, the gun and the catapult still aimed at him. Then turned and ran back up the river bank, without stopping, until he was out of sight.

The Hermit's saddlebag contained a large chunk of sheep's milk cheese and a small loaf of barley bread. Keeping a wary eye in case the Hermit came sneaking back, Wesley, Katie and Janis ate hungrily in the morning sunlight.

"How do we know this is Lightwater?" said Wesley.

"Well, he knew about it for a start," said Janis. "And I can't imagine why he would have said it was… if it wasn't. He was genuinely scared, so he just told the truth. A catapult to the head seems to work wonders!"

"If it is Lightwater," said Wesley. "And we could get back to Mikhail…"

"Or just get back to the well, reverse the Darkwater."

"Grandpa said it has to be refreshed," said Katie, holding one of the bottles in her hand. "Whichever is the freshest will dominate, that's what he said. Whichever is freshest will dominate."

Wesley and Janis both looked at Katie.

Wesley jumped up and pulled his pack from the canoe. He fished around inside and bought out the piece of cut glass from the chandelier. Holding it up to the sun he made a patch of rainbow coloured light shine onto his other hand.

"That's what you do," said Katie excitedly. "That's what you do. Makes it glow."

Steadying his hand, Wesley focused the light onto the bottle that Katie's held. The colours danced on the glass with the slight movement of his hand.

"Even if we are doing the right thing," said Janis. "How will we know if…"

She stopped in mid sentence. Even in the brightness of the early morning sunlight, the bottle began to glow with a strong clear light. It gave a pulse of extra brightness and then faded back to normal.

"It is Lightwater," said Janis. "Do the other bottle."

Katie picked up the other bottle and held it beside the first, cradling them like two babies in her arms. Before Wesley had got the light from the crystal focused onto the second bottle, both bottles began to glow together. Katie held them against her and the light shone on her face. For a brief moment, Wesley thought he saw a pulse of brightness surround her arms and shoulders. A quick burst of extra light radiated from the glass and then they returned, once again, back to two bottles of normal looking water.

"Wesley, Katie," said Janis, her voice clear and determined. "I'm going back. I'm going to reverse the well water. I'm going to find Mikhail and I'm going to cure him. But, I need to go alone. I know the town and it will be less risky if there is only one of us. I'm going to take this horse and get back there by tonight. I suggest you hide near here until I get back. Give me two days. There's still some food in the saddlebag."

Katie was looking at Wesley. She seemed to be waiting for him to speak. He drew in a deep breath and let it out slowly.

"I need go on," he said. "I need to get back to the tunnels. If The Order no longer need us, I mean them, the tunnel children, then it's obvious that they aren't just going to let everyone go free. They're going to… I don't know, get rid of them. I need to find a way to get them out, quickly. I'm going to tell the City Children what's happened, then I'm going to find Anguillaro."

"I'm going with you Wesley," said Katie. "Grandpa said so. I'm going too."

They split the remaining food from the saddlebags three ways and within the hour they had gone their separate ways. Janis rode away, upstream along the riverbank carrying one of the bottles of Water, and Wesley and Katie pushed off into the river in the canoe with the other, wrapped in a blanket. Janis took the rifle.

Wesley was surprised at how quickly Katie got the hang of paddling. She knelt in the bows, dipping and pulling rhythmically, watching for the shallows while Wesley fell into time with her in the stern, twisting his paddle at the end of each stroke to keep the canoe in line. As the sun rose higher, the banks of the river narrowed and the water picked up speed. They entered the Afen Valley with its steep forested sides and the current flowed faster still. Grey rocks jutted up, the water banking up against them and foaming round their sides. The canoe rose and fell through surging troughs and waves and the hull lifted and slapped down as they raced into the rapids.

Katie looked back at Wesley, her eyes wide with alarm. Wesley gripped his paddle hard, determined not to let his fear get the better of him, determined to do what Mikhail had asked him to do.

"Keep paddling," he shouted over the roar of the water. "We have to be going faster than the water to be able to steer."

Water splashed over the side of the canoe, soaking them both. The rocks rushed up with increasing speed and as soon as they had steered past one, yet another loomed ahead. The boat rocked and lurched onwards and they drove their paddles into the water, again and again. Katie changed her paddle from one side to the other and back to keep the bows heading in the right direction and Wesley marveled at how courageous she appeared to have suddenly become and how, like himself, she was quickly mastering the steering of the tiny boat in the rushing roaring water.

As the tiny boat lurched and sped onwards, Wesley's confidence grew and a sense of exhilaration spread through him. He dug his paddle in, time after time, quickly calculating the best route to take between the jutting rocks. He and Katie shouted to one another above the sound of the roaring water, making quick decisions, working together, never doubting each other, as if they were a practiced team.

It seemed as if it was going on forever. Their arms and legs ached from the effort of paddling and bracing themselves in the flimsy hull. And then, after what seemed like hours, they shot out into a broad pool. The banks opened out and beyond them the river wound on in a series of slow running loops. They were through the valley. Katie lifted her paddle in both hands and whooped. She turned to Wesley with a wide smile.

"We did it Wesley, we did it!"

Wesley grinned back. He felt it too, a feeling of success, elation. He slapped his paddle on the water and waved it in the air.

"We're a team Katie. We beat the rapids. We beat 'em."

"We beat 'em. We beat 'em." Katie echoed.

They paddled over to the bank, hauled the canoe out and flopped down on the grass in their wet clothes. The sun was warm on their faces and for a time they just lay there, recovering their strength, looking up at the sky.

Wesley pulled their packs and blankets out onto the bank. Everything was wet and they lay it all out to dry. Katie's book, the Pilot's Almanac, was soaked. She tried opening it but the soggy pages just fell apart between her fingers. The barley bread from the Hermit's saddlebag was wet too, but they ate it anyway with chunks of cheese and they drank river water from their cupped hands.

Wesley scooped his hands into the water again and then stopped, half way to his mouth, the water trickling out from between his fingers.

"Katie?" he said, turning sideways to where she sat on the bank. "Why don't you drink some of the water?" He nodded towards the bottle on the grass beside her.

"I already have Wesley," she replied. "Just then while you were drinking."

Wesley looked at her, expecting her to say more.

"And?" he said eventually.

Katie looked out over the river. "In the rapids," she spoke as if to herself. "When the water was splashing over me, I thought the front of the canoe would dive down and keep going down into the green water." She looked back at Wesley. "I thought we were going to drown Wesley. Drown in the green water and I didn't want to. I could feel something different inside me. Something new. Like I could see further, like I could understand more of what's going on around me. And I was thinking about lots of things while I was there, in the front of the canoe, with the rushing water so close to me. I felt like the boat was made of paper and that the river could suck us down at any moment, you and me, down and drown us. But I didn't want the river to take away my new feeling. I wanted to know it more. Wanted to know…me. So I paddled and steered as hard as I could. I wasn't going to let the river get me Wesley. I wasn't going to let it get me."

28
Faster Than Walking

By early evening they reached the One Hundred Stones. Wesley could feel the sun's warmth trapped in the skin of his face and for the first time since he could remember, his wrists, where he had had his sleeves rolled up, were turning a pale brown. They nosed the canoe into the rushes, climbed up onto the stones and stretched their stiff arms and legs. The Bluebird was where they had left it in the tall reeds, but now it sat on mud left by the outgoing tide, some distance from the water's edge. They hauled the canoe over to it, tied the two boats together and carried their packs ashore.

The old lodge was less forbidding in the daylight and they explored it. One room had a metal bed in it. Its mattress, which lay at an angle on the old frame, had been pecked and nibbled by birds and rats and chunks of stuffing lay on the floor. The only other furniture in the house was a chair that lay on its side in the kitchen by an old dusty cooking range. On the floor around it were pieces of other wooden furniture broken into lengths short enough to fit into the firebox.

They walked out to the grassy patch in the bracken where they had rested on the journey upstream. Less than a mile downstream the bridge arced gracefully over the estuary. Wesley took the telescope from his bag, steadied it on a rock and scanned the railings from one side to the other. A small group of figures were crossing from the west.

"There are soldiers on the bridge Katie, about twenty or more. Do you think they are on their way back from Saint Terresas?"

Katie appeared to be thinking.

"Katie?"

"I heard you Wesley, I heard you" she replied. "I was just working something out."

She pulled the pulpy remains of the Pilot's Almanac from her bag and tried once again to open it. It was useless, the pages disintegrated as soon as she tried to open it. She laid it carefully on a rock.

"No matter," she said. "I can remember. There's twelve hours, twenty-four minutes and thirty seconds between each tide. That means low tide tonight at twenty-one eighteen. High tide, three twenty in the morning… approximately. If we go then, the tide will take us down to the city."

"Three twenty. What's the time now?"

Katie consulted her watches. She tapped one, put it to her ear for a moment and then took it off.

"Water's got in that one," she said. "But it's eighteen fifteen… a quarter past six. She slumped her shoulders and rubbed her eyes. "I'm tired Wesley. Need to sleep."

She lay down on the grass and cradled her head on her arm.

"We've got eight hours and forty-five minutes." She yawned. "Sleep now."

With that, she closed her eyes and lay still. Wesley sat for a while, thinking of the long journey ahead. An idea came to him, a quicker way perhaps, than walking from the city to the tunnels. Then he felt his weariness begin to overtake him. He unrolled Katie's blanket and laid it gently over her. Then, pulling his own blanket around himself, he lay down beside her. His eyes closed and within a minute he was sleeping.

He awoke from a dream in which he had been in the canoe again, soaked with freezing water, rocking from side to side. Katie was gently shaking him by the shoulder. The moon was low on the horizon and it was damp and cold. He sat up. His whole body felt stiff and he ached from head to toe.

"Nearly four o'clock Wesley. Tide's already going out. Time to go."

They gathered their packs and stepped through the rushes to the boats. The water lapped the sides of the stones and, shimmering in the moonlight, the current out in the open water was already flowing smoothly down towards the bridge. Wesley was thirsty. His mouth was dry and his throat felt thick with mucus. He crouched down on one of the stones and scooped some water in his hand to drink. No sooner had it passed his lips than he spat it out. Salt! He hadn't thought to fill his water bottle further upstream and now there was nothing to drink. He climbed aboard The Bluebird after Katie and they poled out from the rushes with the canoe tied to the stern. The current took hold of the boats and, the hulls gently nudging into each other, drifted them downstream towards the bridge.

They took an oar each and forced their stiff muscles back to work. At first Katie struggled with each stroke. Her oar splashed and skittered across the surface or dug too deep, almost wrenching it from her hands. But little by little she gained control and the two of them fell into a slow even pattern, pulling The Bluebird ahead of the current with the canoe following lightly in its wake. Wesley's became more and more thirsty and his head began to ache.

"Katie," he said softly as they rowed. "I need to drink badly."

"Me too Wesley," she replied.

"Just a few sips?"

Katie pulled in her oar and slid the Lightwater out from the rolled up blanket. She pulled out the stopper and passed the bottle to him. He took a small sip. It tasted no different from ordinary water but the relief as it flowed into his mouth and down his throat caused him to moan softly. He rationed himself to ten small sips. On the last one he pulled a little extra into his mouth and savoured it there for a moment before passing the bottle to Katie and swallowing.

Katie drank and they set back to rowing. After a while, Wesley realized that almost all the stiffness in his body had vanished. He felt refreshed and alert. He was able to judge the strength of each stroke of Katie's oar, and respond to it equally, without looking, but simply by feeling the movement of the boat.

They rowed on without talking. At first the estuary was much calmer than it had been on the journey upstream. But after a while, it began to get choppy and the boat rocked and splashed into the waves.

Katie nudged him.

"Look up," she whispered.

The black shadow of the bridge was passing high above. It was soon lost behind them in the darkness and, for the first time, they realized how fast they were travelling.

When they judged themselves to be approaching the channel into the city docks, they steered The Bluebird towards the mud-banks. Close to the edge, the water was slower, but the moon was sinking fast and it became difficult to see where the water ended and the mud began. They turned the bows towards the shore and pulled hard on the oars. Almost immediately the keel scraped into the soft mud and the stern of the boat swung downstream in the current. It drifted free and then stuck again, nose upstream with the canoe trailing behind. Finding the shipping channel in The Bluebird, they realized, was going to be difficult, if not impossible. She was too big and unwieldy to nudge along the edge of the mudflats until they found the way in. Wesley pulled the canoe alongside and he and Katie loaded their things into it and climbed carefully aboard. Untying the rope they pushed away, took up the paddles, and drifted on downstream.

They could now see little more than the stars and a low band of pale sky where the moon had set. Each time the water deepened, Katie and Wesley paddled inwards again until they could feel the mud. Sometimes the current caught the stern and spun them around, and each time they paddled back into the open water and tried again. The only way they could tell in what direction they were going was by the fading light of the setting moon. They struggled on for what seemed like hours, their paddles thick and heavy with the oozing mud. It seemed more and more likely that they had missed the channel but the mud was too deep and sticky for them to get out of the canoe and walk. They were trapped inside it with no idea how far down the estuary they had been swept.

They found the channel almost by accident. They had decided that all they could do was to nose the canoe into the mud and wait until the dawn showed them where they were. They both knew that the light would reveal them to any watchers, but there was no option. It was a risk they would have to take.

They paddled towards the edge of the mud again, expecting to slide into it at any moment. But the canoe continued smoothly through the water and within minutes the stars were blocked out by the towering walls of the lock. Ahead of them, they heard the splashing water from the leaking gates and reaching out, they felt their way along the slimy stone sides with their hands. Wesley's hand closed on a cold metal bar.

"Found the ladder," he called forward to Katie. "Here, reach back." He took Katie's hand in the darkness and placed it on the bar. "You go first."

Katie clambered onto the rungs and climbed. Wesley, hoisting his pack, heavy with the blanket and bottle, followed her up to the dockside.

As soon as it was light enough, they left the docks and found their way back through the streets to the building where Wesley had found the chandelier crystal. From the car park outside, the bell tower on the University rooftop, rising above the buildings in the middle distance, caught the first rays of the rising sun. They looked through the windows into the big room with the chandelier, shielding their eyes against the glass to see better. Nothing had changed. They half expected to see one of the City Children, but everything was silent and deserted.

From the room below ground, Katie and Wesley took a bicycle each. Heading towards the bell tower they cycled through the streets until they found The University Station. The grille over the entrance had been forced open and they stepped cautiously in and peered down the escalator into the darkness.

"Hello," Wesley called. "Hello, anyone there?"

The echo of his voice faded away and there was silence.

"Red? Jupiter? Hello?" he shouted. "Are you there? Anyone?"

But all they heard was a rat, scuttling into the ticket office door and the sound of their own breathing.

They made their way across the streets, through the gap in the broken wall to the University building. The car was still there, the doors open and the keys in the ignition.

"How d'you know how to drive Wesley?" Katie asked.

"I don't. I just know what your Grandfather told me. I'm just going to do what he said... if it starts."

He checked the car wasn't in gear and turned the key. A red light came on and the fuel gauge bounced into life... but nothing else. He clicked the key off and on several times and each time the same thing happened. He snorted with irritation and banged the steering wheel. Katie appeared at the open door.

"No good Wesley?"

He folded his arms against the steering wheel and leant his head against them, feeling defeated and irritated with himself. "I thought I could do it," he said. "I thought I would be able to drive the car and I can't even start it." He shook his head, clutching his hair in his fist. "We still have miles to go, and we don't even have any food left." He looked at Katie and then stared out through the windscreen. "Sorry."

Katie reached in to the key. She tried turning it, the light came on again but she didn't see it and kept turning.

"There must be…" she began. The engine turned over twice and burst into life. Wesley jumped back, hands away from the wheel.

"Katie! What did you do? How…?" He grinned at her. "Never mind. Let's get our things in."

Katie threw their packs in the back and slid into the passenger's seat. Wesley put his foot on the clutch, put the car into gear and eased his foot slowly up as he revved the engine. The car lurched forward and slowed, lurched and slowed again, throwing him and Katie backwards and forwards in their seats. He pushed the accelerator a little harder and they raced forward straight at a wall at the end of the building. He frantically turned the wheel and swung the car round, scraping the bumper against the wall. It bounced over the curb onto the overgrown lawn and the grass swished loudly under the floor. He steered back onto the gravel. He was concentrating too hard to remember how to stop and so he drove on, round the building and down the drive. The speedometer was reading ten miles per hour but to Wesley it was all he could do to keep the car travelling in a straight line.

"Which way, Katie?" he said, half frightened, and half excited, as they neared the bottom of the drive.

"Left Wesley, left."

He swung the car out onto the road, still in first gear, and on. He began to get the hang of the steering, avoiding the debris and haphazardly parked cars on the road. Katie remembered the route they had taken exactly. At the first turn she called out at the last moment.

"Right, here Wesley."

Wesley turned sharply. The car bumped up onto the pavement, scraped loudly against another car and just missed a lamppost.

"Tell me sooner Katie, *before* we need to turn."

"Sooner, ok," she said with a grin. "I can see that now! Go left at the end of this road."

It took over an hour to reach the garage by the old factory where the car had come from. From there the road ran straight as it headed out of the city and Wesley put the car into second gear. It leaped forward at double the speed, unnerving him at first, but his confidence grew and by the time they left the last houses behind, he was driving boldly in top gear. The fuel gauge showed a quarter full, but neither of them knew how far that would take them. They were buoyant at the miles they were covering but they also were hungry, and above all, thirsty again. They allowed themselves to sip more of the Lightwater. It made them feel no less hungry but they felt refreshed and ready for whatever might lie ahead.

By early afternoon dark clouds pushed in from the west. They began to recognize some of the landscape and realized that they must have passed the turning down to the farmhouse where they had all spent the night. Rocks, large and small, appeared more frequently on the road and Wesley was forced to slow down to avoid hitting them. Grit and small stones, flicked up by the tyres, rattled under the floor and in the wheel arches. The fuel gauge crept slowly lower and a red light on the dashboard flickered on.

Katie dozed in her seat, her legs drawn up beneath her. Wesley wound down the window and stuck his head out into the rushing air as he drove to fight the sleepiness that was creeping up on him. His stomach ached with hunger making it difficult to concentrate. He didn't recognize the compound by the quarry until they were only a few hundred yards from it, where the road turned off the tarmac onto the track that skirted the crater. He reached over and shook Katie by the shoulder.

"What Wesley?" Katie sleepily shifted back to sitting.

"The quarry, look, straight ahead."

Between the low huts and the wire fence was a large group of children. They came to the fence, gripping the wire mesh, watching as Wesley steered the car towards them. Then an arm thrust out through the wire, hand in a thumbs up sign. It was Red. Wesley drew level with him where the road ran along the side of the enclosure. He put his foot on the brake to stop. He realized that as yet, he hadn't stopped the car and was not quite sure what he was supposed to do. The car slowed but was still in gear. It began to shake and judder. The engine knocked loudly as it was forced to go too slowly. It stalled and lurched to a halt in a cloud of dust. Wesley leaped out and ran back to the fence. A sea of tired young faces pressed up against the mesh. From amongst them, Red reached his arm out and gripped Wesley's hand.

"They got us," he said quickly. "All of us. You come to get us out?"

"Yes," said Katie over Wesley's shoulder. "We'll get you out, Red. We'll get you out. We're going to get Anguillaro."

"Who? said Red.

"Anguillaro, the Eel Catcher," said Wesley. "We're going to find him."

Jupiter pushed in beside Red, reached out through the mesh and clasped Wesley and Katie's hands.

"You drove that car?" she sounded impressed. "Can you drive it through this fence? Bust a hole?"

There was a commotion behind the prisoners.

"Guards," hissed Red. "Get going, escape. You ain't no match for them. Hole in the fence or no hole. They got guns. They shot Billy, didn't they Jupe."

A guard, head and shoulders taller than the children, pushed his way roughly to the fence. Katie and Wesley turned and ran back to the car.

"Eh!" the guard shouted after them. "What you...?"

They leapt into the car and Wesley turned the key. The light came on but nothing happened.

"What do you do Katie?" said Wesley urgently.

"Turn it harder Wesley, harder."

Wesley turned the key further and the starter engaged, jumping the car forward until it stalled. It was still in gear. He forced the gear lever into the middle, re-started the engine and, kangarooing forward, drove off. Clumsily changing through the gears he steered the car along the track around the crater, driving as fast as he dared. They bumped over the rough surface. Stoned pinged out from the tyres and dust swirled up behind them making it impossible to see anything through the rear window. They bounced up onto the tarmac on the other side of the crater. Wesley accelerated the car away, down the road, following the pathway that had been cleared between the rocks, the dust clearing away behind them in the breeze. Katie leant back over the seat.

"Jeep Wesley," she said loudly.

In the mirror, Wesley saw a second cloud of dust. A jeep was racing along the track. It had almost reached the road. Wesley sat forward in his seat, tense with concentration. He pushed the accelerator harder and the car began to pick up more speed. The jeep swung onto the road behind them. Wesley dared not take his eyes off the road to look in the mirror again.

"How many in the jeep?" he said.

"Four soldiers," said Katie. "They're catching up. You have to go faster."

As they left the crater further behind, there were fewer rocks on the road and Wesley edged the car still faster. Little by little the jeep began to fall behind. Katie knelt on the seat, gripping the back. When they rounded bends, the jeep disappeared from sight for a time before reappearing, each time a bit further behind. The fuel gauge was down to zero and the red light beside it glowed brightly. Twice Wesley misjudged bends and the tyres squealed as they went round with Katie hanging on to the seat.

Wesley suddenly hit the brakes hard and the car skidded sideways. This time, he kept the engine running. He looked back through the rear window. A small lane on the left ran off into the trees

"Back there," he said. "That's the turn to the village."

The jeep was out of sight. He turned the car, bumping up onto the verge, cutting through the brambles and long grass and then back onto the road. The jeep had still not appeared. He accelerated up to the lane and turned into it. Just before they disappeared into the cover of the trees, the jeep came racing into view.

The distance between the narrow lane and the edge of the woods was wide enough for any fallen trees not to block the road. Nevertheless, it was littered with windblown branches of all sizes. Wesley had no choice but to drive straight at them. They crunched into the front of the car, scraping past underneath, sending broken sticks flying up into the windscreen and over the roof. Like the car, the jeep had been going too fast to stop at the lane entrance and Katie saw them pass, braking hard. It was not long before it was on their tail again and the gap between then began to close. One of the soldiers stood up and tried to bring a rifle up over the windscreen. But the jeep was lurching as much as the car and he had to hang on tightly, unable to use his hands.

Wesley pushed on, smashing through the branches. Ahead of them the edge of the wood was closer to the road and the top of a fallen pine blocked the lane. Its brittle dry branches spread around it like a brush. He could see that the main branch, held slightly off the ground, was much thicker than anything else he had driven over. Gripping the wheel tightly he drove straight for it. Katie held tight to the back of her seat and the front of the car hit it with a loud bang. The tree top broke and caught beneath the car, scraping along for a few moments, grinding and crunching, before it passed under the rear wheels, bouncing the back of the car up and down. As it did, the engine roared like a tractor. The exhaust pipe, broken by the branch, spun like a skittle behind them. The jeep was gaining on them, steering down the pathway that the car was clearing.

Suddenly they were among the houses of the village. The exhaust noise, echoing back off the walls, was deafening, but Wesley sped down the street, driving at the limits of his control. They came to the pub where the fallen tree lay half blocking the road and Wesley swerved past it, the wheels bouncing over rubble and broken slates. Ahead of them an abandoned van was parked in the middle of the road. He swerved and the back of the car skidded into the side of it with a loud crash, jolting him and Katie sideways in their seats. He drove on, accelerating away between the last rows of houses in the village. Suddenly the engine cut out and the car began to quickly slow down. Then it roared back into life and sped forward again.

"Petrol," shouted Wesley over the noise. "It must be running out."

The road narrowed as they raced on into the forest beyond the village, the jeep close behind them. The clouds had thickened now, low and leaden, and in amongst the trees it was dark as evening. A sharp left hand bend loomed up ahead. Wesley steered into it, struggling to keep control as the tyres slid sideways across the sticks and moss that grew in from the edge of the tarmac. The road turned again, sharper this time to the right. Wesley braked but he was driving too fast. The car swung sideways and at the same time the engine cut out. It careered off the road and down a bank, crashing through bushes that smashed and scraped against the windows. At the bottom of the bank it slewed to the left and rolled up onto its side. Wesley gripped the wheel to stop himself falling sideways onto Katie who was thrown against the passenger door. For a moment the car teetered on its side and then rolled slowly over onto its roof sending Katie and Wesley falling awkwardly up against the ceiling.

After the roar of the engine it seemed suddenly quiet. They heard the jeep drive past above them and disappear on down the road.

"Katie?"

"Yes?"

"Ok?"

"Think so."

They heard the jeep stop and begin to reverse back towards the bend. Wesley's window was still open. He crawled out followed by Katie. One of the front wheels was still slowly turning. Steam was rising from the radiator. The whine of the reversing jeep was getting louder

"Run," said Wesley urgently.

"Wait," said Katie. She reached back through the window and pulled the Lightwater out, still rolled up in its blanket. Holding it tightly to her, she sprinted into the trees with Wesley.

29
Something Fishy

In spite of his long spidery legs, Pearson half walked, half ran, to keep up. Colonel Dove was marching fast up the Connector Tunnel towards the stores. Their footsteps echoed off the walls.

"I leave you in charge for four days, Pearson, and what happens?" Dove looked straight ahead. "The Eel Catcher escapes. Thornberry's lab is vandalized, completely smashed up. Two children, and we know who they are, have been seen outside the quarry compound – in a car. The soldier's quarters have the stink of rotting fish, or something, blowing through the air-shaft, and no one can find the cause. And further more, my cat hasn't been fed because Matron apparently found an eel in her bed and forgot. At least that's her excuse."

"With respect Colonel Sir," said Pearson between breaths. "The quarry was out of my jurisdiction. I couldn't…"

"I do not like loose ends Pearson," Dove cut in. "I shall have the Eel Catcher found and eliminated. The same goes for the runaways. If necessary I shall do it myself. We have the old man now. He's told us all we need to know."

Outside the entrance to the stores, Dove stopped suddenly and turned on his heel. Pearson almost walked straight into him.

"I shall give you a task Pearson," he said. " And please do it properly. Scaling down operations begin here today. The orphans are no longer needed. You know where to put them. Don't you?"

"Yes, Colonel Sir."

"Then please see to it. The ropes are to be left up. Is that clear?"

"Yes, Colonel Sir."

302

"After that please return here to the stores to oversee packing. Only essentials are to be left. Everything else will go to Saint Terresas. Clear?"

"Yes, Colonel Sir."

Dove turned and strode on into the stores, leaving Pearson standing in the tunnel.

"Get on with it then Pearson," he added over his shoulder.

The Tunnel Children had been confined to their common room for over twenty-four hours. They were glad of the break from work but were nervous. It was not a normal day off. They had not heard the ore train running past the door to the Main Tunnel and their next meal was long overdue. Something was going on. Charlie and Bobby were taking their turn listening at the door. They ran back into the common room when they heard the sound of marching approaching the door.

"Boots!" they called softly.

Everyone's attention was turned to the door. The bolt was drawn from the outside and Pearson strode in accompanied by four uniformed guards. All of them carried sticks.

"On your feet everybody," he ordered. "Shoes off."

The children flinched at the words 'shoes off'. Some began to cry. Others backed into the corner of the room. A group of girls hid beneath a table and several children fled into the sleeping quarters. Christmas crawled into the wicker clothes-basket, clutching her bear.

'Shoes off' meant only one thing, The Pit. They knew that to resist could mean a savage beating with a stick and, worse still, extra time, possibly alone, down there in the darkness. None of them dared to question Pearson about what they had done to deserve being sent to there. He was clearly angry and questions, they knew, would make him worse. The supervisors cracked their sticks down on the table and rounded the barefoot children up into a group beside a door on the far side of the common room.

Single bulbs, fixed to the wooden props that held up the roof, lighted the old mineshaft that led down to The Pit. They were so far apart that when the line of children trudged down the sloping floor, they had to hold each other's hands midway between the bulbs in the darkness. Cold water dripped from the ceiling, making the floor muddy and slippery. Talking was strictly forbidden and the children filed slowly forward in silent misery.

At the end of the shaft, the last bulb dimly illuminated a ledge beside a wide dark hole. Water seeped out from rock that sloped steeply down from the ledge into the hole. A knotted rope fastened to a rusty metal peg, hammered into the ledge, hung down the slope to the bottom, fifteen feet below. There were other pegs on which ropes had once hung but now only the one rope remained, the others had either rotted or been removed. Other than the shuffling feet and whimpering of the children, the only sound was running water.

Once, The Pit had echoed with the voices and shovels of miners, quarrying lead by lamplight. But it had been long ago abandoned. Whenever heavy rain fell outside, water flooded quickly and unexpectedly into it and all too often the miners were forced to abandon their tools and climb to the safety of the ledge and retreat up the shaft.

Now, the children were forced, one by one, to descend the rope and stand in the ankle deep water at the bottom. When the last one was down, Pearson pulled up the rope and coiled it round the peg on the ledge. Without a word, he and the other supervisors retreated back up the shaft and turned off the lights, leaving the children in the darkness waiting for a supervisor to reappear and the rope to be thrown down for them to be able to climb out.

30
The Falling Soldiers

Wesley and Katie were shivering, waist deep in water under a bridge. The soldiers searching the woods had missed them and now what sounded like all four of them stood on the roadway above them. It began to rain. Big drops pattered onto the leaves and into the water at either end of the bridge.

It was hard to hear exactly what the men above them were saying but it was clear that they were talking about finding shelter from the rain, which was quickly becoming a heavy downpour. Then the voice of one of them became clearer. He was climbing down the bank towards the river.

"Give us a chance," he shouted back up to the others.

"Come and look for yourself if you think you're quicker. Look at these brambles."

"Another minute of this rain and we'll be so soaked we won't need shelter," came a clear reply. It sounded as though the speaker was leaning over the side of the bridge, looking down.

"Just find a bit of gravel or something to stand on," he continued. "Just so's you can see underneath."

Katie and Wesley looked at each other. Wesley filled his lungs, pinched his nose and pointed frantically to the water. Katie followed his example and together they bent their knees and sunk below the water. The numbing cold in their legs now pushed into the skin of their faces and hands and seeped quickly through their clothes. Wesley reached out underwater and found Katie's arm. She gripped his wrist. Almost immediately, he was bursting to breathe again. He held on, knowing, by the grip on his wrist, that Katie was still beneath the water beside him. He opened his eyes. There was a pale light above the rippling surface where the arch of the bridge ended, but the ripples and the poor light made it impossible to tell if the soldier was there. Just for a moment he thought he saw a different light, in the water, around Katie, as if for an instant a faint ray of diffused sun had found its way beneath the bridge. Then he felt Katie stand, and, desperate to breathe, he stood up beside her and gulped a fresh lungful of air.

The soldier was gone. He could be heard climbing back up through the brambles.

"All water," he shouted up. "Nowhere to stand."

There was a muffled response and then nothing more could not be heard other the sound of the falling rain. Wesley and Katie were shivering uncontrollably. Wesley's teeth chattered together and he knew that they had to move soon just to get their limbs working again. They edged out from under the bridge and looked up. There was no sign of the soldiers. On all fours they clambered up the bank and onto the road. Wesley recognized the place immediately. It was the bridge where they had said goodbye to Anguillaro. With their soaking clothes clinging to their bodies, their shoes squelching and Katie clutching the sodden blanket holding the Lightwater, they set off up the valley with the river on their right. They knew that they were going roughly in the correct direction and Wesley hoped that Anguillaro would somehow know they were coming, that he would meet them, lead them to his cave and would know what they needed to do next.

Under the heavy clouds, evening came early and the rain continued to pour. The ground was slippery and mud stuck to their shoes making each step heavy. They spoke little. Struggling up through the trees and bushes was enough to contend with and although they were moving once again, it was impossible to get warm. The river beside them was beginning to rise, turning brown with floodwater, catching the tips of overhanging branches and setting them swaying rhythmically backwards and forwards.

Their progress became slower and slower. The rain plastered their hair flat and dripped from their noses, and they shook with cold. They came to the end of the trees, where the valley gave out to tall bracken and brambles. They stood for a moment, uncertain which direction to go in. If Anguillaro's place was near here, surely, Wesley thought, there would be a path somewhere? But there was no sign of any path, or that anyone had been there at all. The undergrowth stretched unbroken up ahead, the river on the right and the valley side to the left.

Then a movement caught his eye. Katie had seen it too. Something was shaking the bracken from underneath, travelling along beneath it, making its way quickly towards them. They were too wet and cold even to think about running. A big black head poked above the leaves and barked.

"Sargazzo!" called Wesley.

The great dog bounded towards them. His coat steamed in the wet and his tail flicked water this way and that as he wagged. He licked Wesley's hand and pushed his head against his leg in greeting, almost pushing him over. He looked up at Katie and his ears softened and lowered. She stroked his wet head and he nuzzled against her.

"Show us the way Sargazzo," said Wesley.

It was a huge relief to them both to scramble through the tunnel into the dry of Anguillaro's cave. Everything was as Wesley remembered it. It was as if no one had been there except Sargazzo who, judging by the remains of dead rabbits by the entrance, had been looking after himself. They lit a fire when it became fully dark and turning their backs to each other, stripped off their wet clothes and wrapped themselves in blankets from one of the trunks. On a makeshift frame of sticks, their clothes steamed in the firelight and little by little the warmth seeped back into their bodies. They ate hungrily from Anguillaro's supply of biscuits, having no stomach for the smelly strips of eel meat that still hung on the rack at the far end of the cave. For a while they forgot about the world outside and talked about themselves.

To Wesley, Katie seemed almost a different person from the girl he had met at the grid who had helped him with his calculations. He understood why Mikhail had so much wanted to find the Lightwater, for now she was more outward looking and confident. They were able to talk in the same way that Wesley would have done with his old friends in the tunnels, and there was a new feeling of companionship between them. Where Anguillaro was they had no way of telling but they decided that they would set out into the tunnels to search for him the next day.

They slept soundly and awoke to the pale light of morning seeping into the cave from the chimney. There was no sign of Sargazzo. Outside the rain continued and Wesley and Katie looked through the trunk and boxes for anything that would be useful in their search for Anguillaro. They found a worn old canvas backpack that had one of its straps broken, a water bottle that they filled with rainwater, and a packet of plastic gas lighters. They took six of the lighters, two candles from Anguillaro's table, and stuffed them into the backpack along with four tubes of biscuits, the water bottle and the Lightwater. Katie found a small box containing faded photographs of people, she guessed, from Anguillaro's past. He was in two of the pictures. In one he stood standing among others, the tallest by far, posing for the camera, wearing what looked like a pilot's flying suit. In another he sat with a woman at a restaurant table, smiling, his hand intertwined with hers on a chequered table-cloth.

They were looking at the pictures when the sound of barking came faintly through the narrow entrance from outside. They put them hurriedly back into the trunk, ran to the entrance and crawled through. Sheets of rain still swept down the valley on the breeze. The barking came again, deep and loud, from somewhere further down the valley. There was a gunshot followed instantly by a yelping cry. Katie and Wesley looked at one another in alarm. Men's voices, shouting to each other, came up from the trees. There was another shot and then silence except for the rain, pattering onto leaves and dripping from branches at the cave entrance.

Wesley and Katie waited, hidden under the foliage, dreading what might have happened to Sargazzo. There was no sign of movement down amongst the trees. Then a rustling sound came from the bushes below them and suddenly Sargazzo bounded up to the cave entrance. His black fur was soaking. The end of his right ear was shredded in a bloody mass, bleeding freely. Drips of dark blood fell onto the mud. He shook his head as if to free himself of the wound, wining pathetically.

"Oh Sargazzo!" Katie put her arm around the dog's neck. He lowered his head while she examined his ear. "What have they..?" She stopped.

"Up here," came a man's voice, nearer now. "The blood leads up here."

Wesley put his head cautiously through the leaves. The same four soldiers from the jeep were making their way up through the bracken towards the cave entrance.

"Back in," hissed Wesley. "They're almost here."

They hurried back into the cave, Sargazzo on their heels. Wesley grabbed the canvas pack and they ran to the narrow opening on the far side that led to the lake. Leading the way, he slung the pack over his shoulder and felt his way into the darkness, arms outstretched to feel the rock on each side with Katie holding the back of his jacket. Sargazzo panted behind them, whining softly every few breaths. They heard the soldiers enter the cave behind them. Wesley fumbled in the pack until his fingers closed on one of the lighters. Cupping his hand in front of its small flame he walked as fast as he could without it blowing out. The faint flicker of a torch beam reflected onto the walls behind them and they heard the voices of the soldiers making their way into the tunnel. The flame from the lighter suddenly showed nothing. The rock beside them was gone. Wesley took his hand from the front of the flame and there, dimly lit in front of them, was the end of the bridge.

"Go first Katie," he whispered. "Keep a hold on the rail. The whole thing tips sideways when you're in the middle, remember? Just keep holding on and walking. Here…" He took another lighter from the pack. "Take this."

Holding the lighter flame in front of her, she made her way carefully forward, sliding one hand along the metal handrail. She reached the centre and the bridge lurched, tipping sideways with a creak. She gasped, dropped the lighter and grabbed the rail with both hands. Torchlight reflected off the rock behind Wesley.

"Keep going," he called. "Quickly. It's ok. It'll tip back. Just keep going."

She reached the other side and the bridge tipped back. Wesley started out. He needed both hands. He let the lighter out, stuffed it into his jacket pocket and walked quickly forward. Sargazzo waited behind him. The torchlight flashed brighter as the soldiers got nearer. The drop below him was in total darkness. He held tight to the rail as the bridge shook and then dropped sickeningly to the side. It righted itself and, turning as he covered the last few feet, he saw Sargazzo, silhouetted by a torch beam behind him, dash onto the bridge from the far side. He bounded across, leaping over the central section. A flash and the deafening crack of a gunshot filled the cave. Wesley stumbled back onto Katie, his ears ringing, and Sargazzo ran into them both. They half scuttled, half fell, backwards into cave entrance beyond. The soldiers rushed onto the bridge one behind the other and all at once the bridge tipped sideways and broke. The men's shouts turned to screams as they disappeared downwards. The flashlight beam dashed across the rock and was gone. Then added to the echoes of the screams there came four distant splashes.

Then there was silence. Katie reached out and held Wesley's arm in the darkness. His heart was thumping and he could feel that Katie, like himself, was shaking. For a moment they said nothing. The only sound was that of Sargazzo panting and their own breathing. Wesley re-lit the lighter and he and Katie looked at each other. With her hand trembling, she wiped a thumb under one eye and took a deep breath.

"Come on," she said unsteadily. "You lead Wesley."

Using the lighters, they made their way slowly through the cave to the lake. Anguillaro's rowing boat and both of the Zodiacs were there, where they had left them, pulled up on the stony beach. They melted one of the candles onto the front of the rowing boat and while Wesley rowed out onto the dark water, Katie bathed Sargazzo's ear with Lightwater.

31
Riding the train

It took them over an hour to find the muddy beach on the other
side of the lake and by the time they reached the tunnel that
led down to the grid, the second candle was little more than a
stub. At the grid, Katie whispered the numbers under her breath
as she undid the combination lock. As she turned the dials,
Wesley briefly thought back to when he had first met her, here,
and realized how much more he now knew and how different
he had become. He felt more afraid and yet bolder at the same
time. He had set himself a task that seemed impossible, and
yet they had got this far, and he felt a determination glowing
like an ember inside him.

They relocked the grid behind them, crept to the end of the
tunnel and looked out. The Main Tunnel was quiet. The lights
hummed in the ceiling and the narrow train tracks shone in the
roadway. They lowered themselves down and Sargazzo slithered
down behind them. At a run, they set off for the children's quarters
further up the tunnel.

As they entered a bend, they quickly pulled back against
the wall. A line of stationary ore trucks curved round on the
tracks ahead of them, all of them empty. They crept past the
trucks until they reached the engine at the front. There was no
one in sight. The cab of the engine was hinged open, resting on
the pack of batteries behind it. Wesley leaned in through the
door. Quite a few of the tunnel children, including Wesley, had
a rough idea of how the train worked. They had often sneaked
into the driver's seat while the batteries were on charge in the
Generator Hall and pretended to drive. Most of the Supervisors turned a blind eye to it. It kept the children from being a
nuisance, if for some reason work was bought temporarily to a

halt. There was simply a lever marked 'forwards' and 'backwards' and another marked 'brake'. Wesley scanned the dials. The battery indicator showed that it was fully charged. Katie leaned in beside him.

"The line goes to the quarry, doesn't it?" she said.

"Yeah."

They looked at each other, knowing that they were sharing the same thought.

"Think you can drive this one too?" asked Katie.

"Yeah. This is easy."

"The trucks." Katie nodded back along the track. "Room for everyone?"

"Room for everyone." Wesley nodded and drew a deep breath. "So long as we can get out past the entrance grid".

Wesley pulled out the engine's key and stuffed it into his pocket.

They ran on cautiously, Sargazzo at their heels, past the children's quarters to the last bend in the tunnel before the entrance grid. They edged round until they could see its metal framework. The heavy door across the tracks lay open. A single guard sat on a wooden box beside it in his socks, polishing his boots. Doubling back, they returned to the door of the quarters. It was unbolted. They tiptoed to the end of the passage and looked into the common room. The lights were off. Wesley pushed the switch on the wall and they flickered into life. The place was deserted, but he knew immediately where the children were by the boots and shoes that lay on the floor and tables. Christmas's bear lay face down on the floor.

"They're in the Pit'" he said.

He looked up at the ceiling, imagining the outside world above them. "When it's raining outside, the guards don't put us down there. They say it floods." He spun round to Katie.

"Quickly," he said urgently. "Follow me."

He threw open the door to the old mineshaft and fumbled around on the dark wall until he found the light switch. In the sparse light from the bulbs, water sparkled as it dripped fast from the ceiling. It seeped from the walls and ran in rivulets along the floor. As they splashed down the shaft, the water grew deeper and noisier, rushing down the slope towards The Pit. By the time the last bulb came into sight it was shin deep. The ledge streamed with water that poured from the rock walls and the shaft and swept over the edge, down into the pit, tugging at the loops of rope wound round the peg at the top.

Sargazzo, who was used to underground water, stood by the back wall and watched as Wesley got down onto his hands and knees and crawled through the tugging current to the edge. The pack, with its single strap, was difficult to keep on his back. He flicked it round behind him with his shoulders and looked down. A mass of pale faces looked back up at him. Water lapped around their necks and shoulders. The twins stared up, they were short and the water was up to their chins. The fear on their faces turned to wonder and relief when they recognized who it was above them. A young girl sat on Martin's shoulders. She reached her arms upwards.

"Wesley," she cried. "Look everyone, it's Wesley."

"Christmas! Martin!" Wesley uncoiled the rope, letting it slither down the slope in the water. "We're getting you all out."

Martin bought Christmas to the bottom of the rope and she began climbing. She pulled herself up with her strong arms, hand over hand, but her feet, walking the slope in front of her through the cascading water, kept slipping, leaving her dangling, struggling to regain a footing. Another girl had already started up below her but Christmas's feet knocked her from the rope and she fell back with a splash sending a wave of water into other people's eyes and mouths. Wesley and Katie, on their hands and knees, took the rope between them and hauled as hard as they could, but it was impossible to pull Christmas up through the cascade and she slithered back into the water below.

At the far end of the ledge, much less water was flowing over the edge and down the slope.

"We need to move the rope," Wesley called down. "Tie it to a peg down at the end." He tried to undo the knot but it was soaked and swollen tight. The water in The Pit was rising rapidly and some of the children were already having to tip their heads back to breathe. Three were swimming and Martin, who was the tallest, held Christmas to him, her arms clinging around his neck. A boy was clinging to the end of the rope, trying to keep up, coughing and spluttering beneath the downpour.

"Katie," Wesley shouted, flicking the backpack once again onto his back. "Help me pull the rope over to the end. We can loop it around the last peg, leave this end tied."

They tried between them to pull the rope along but the boy on the end, shaking and crying, anchored it down. Wesley shouted down to him to let go, but the boy was too frightened to release his grip. Martin hoisted Christmas up so that she sat on his right shoulder. He waded forward and positioned his left shoulder between the boy's legs, reached up to the boy's hands and yanked them from the rope. The boy instantly clung to Martin's head, covering his eyes with his arms. Martin stood where he was, concentrating on keeping his balance with the two children on his shoulders.

Between them, Katie and Wesley crawled along the edge of the ledge and hooked the rope over the last peg. It was shorter now and only the tail end of it dangled in the rising water. The twins were the closest to it. They tiptoed to the rope and, one after the other, quickly climbed up the slope. Bobby reached the top first and Katie and Wesley pulled him onto the ledge. But instead of moving away from the edge, he froze, holding on to Wesley's shoulders.

"Wesley," he managed. "There's a giant dog. Behind you, look. We're trapped."

For a split second, Wesley didn't register that he was talking about Sargazzo and spun round alarmed. He lost his balance and for a moment was poised between recovering and falling. Katie grabbed his arm and pulled him and Bobbie back from the edge.

"It's ok, it's ok," she reassured Bobby. "That's Sargazzo."

Wesley was about to add that Sargazzo was the Eel Catcher's dog, but realized that it would probably have made things far worse.

"He won't hurt us," he said instead. "He's our friend."

One by one the children reached the ledge and staggered back up through the shaft to the common room. Martin was the last up.

"Pearson put us here," he explained. "And he wasn't coming back I reckon."

"We're getting out," said Wesley as they started back up the shaft. "Outside's fine. It's all a trick. That's what the grids are for, so no one escapes and finds out. We've all just been slaves."

The children were soaked, cold and frightened. Martin helped Wesley and Katie get the message across that everyone needed to leave their shoes where they were, in case Pearson or any other Supervisors came in. Even Christmas had to leave her teddy bear where it lay.

They filed into the dormitories and dried themselves on their blankets. Martin emptied the wicker baskets of spare clothes onto the floor. Each child picked something out that roughly fitted them and gradually they settled, sitting close to one another for comfort and reassurance. They were astonished when Wesley told them what had happened to him and where he'd been. Some of them would not have believed what he said about The Order were it not so obvious that Pearson had had no intention of returning to The Pit. Many of them were nervous of Sargazzo, but the great dog was all the convincing that they needed that Wesley's story was true.

Wesley and Katie's plans were far from complete and doubt gnawed away at Wesley's confidence. He was careful not to let it show. He wanted the children to have hope, to believe that it was possible to escape. He explained to them about the quarry children and that for his plan to work they all had to stay quietly where they were until it would be dark outside. Only then would they have a chance of getting away without being seen, although there was still the problem of the guard at the Grid.

Wesley and Martin dried the wet footprints on the Common Room floor. Then, leaving the dormitory door slightly ajar, they turned off the lights and waited. The Tunnel Children whispered among themselves, sharing the biscuits that Wesley passed round. Katie checked her watches. She estimated that they had another hour before darkness above ground.

The hour passed. Wesley was about to suggest that everyone should get ready to go when the door handle from the Main Tunnel into the common room rattled and the lights came on. Wesley and Martin, crouched down just inside the dormitory door and watched. Pearson, wearing wellingtons, passed through the room and into the shaft to The Pit. They gave him time to get a little way ahead and then walked softly over and followed him down. As they neared the end they heard Pearson swear. They peered down to the end of the shaft and saw him standing on the side of the ledge, leaning forward, examining the far peg with the rope looped over it.

Wesley nodded and the boys ran, splashing over the ledge towards him. Though their intention had been to push him in, there was no need. In one movement he straightened in surprise, turned and slipped. For a second he hung in the air with an astonished look on his face, balancing on one thin leg, his other leg and thin arms groping wildly in mid air like the waving limbs of a spider. Then he slid down the slope and landed in the water with huge splash. He surfaced and spluttered water from his mouth, looking up at the boys. The water was much deeper than it had been an hour ago and Pearson swam to the edge, groping for a handhold. Wesley pulled the rope up and held it coiled in one hand.

"Boys," Pearson shouted, his coat floating up around him.

"Come on now. I was coming in to…" He stopped short.

"Pike!" He exclaimed. "Where did you…? What are you…? Pike… Look… Throw me that rope. There's a good chap… No need for this."

Wesley and Martin's decision to follow him down and push him in had not included whether to leave the rope down or not. Now they were faced with the decision of whether to save him, or let him drown. Pearson continued to plead with them, making promises that the boys knew were bluffs. An image of the four soldiers falling from the bridge flashed through Wesley's mind. He was aware that they had probably died and that, in a way, he had been the cause. He heard Red's voice in his head, 'go for blood'. He felt too young to be making a decision that could kill someone. And yet he couldn't avoid it. They had to decide. Right now. Him and Martin.

"Martin? What'll we do?"

Martin shook his head. "Don't want to kill anyone," he

spoke close to Wesley's ear.

"Give him a chance then?"

"A chance. But he needs to stay here for a bit," Martin looked back down and spat. "Rope from the middle peg. No light. And he can count himself very lucky," he added.

They unhooked the rope from the far peg, let it hang down in the main rush of water from the ledge and splashed their way back to the shaft. As he passed under the first light bulb, Wesley pulled his sleeve over his hand, reached up and smashed it. They worked their way up, smashing each bulb as they passed and closed the door at the top, pushing a table from the common room against it.

According to Katie it would now be dark outside. The children put on their shoes and filed through the passageway into the Main Tunnel and on Wesley's whispered orders, clambered into the trucks. Their instructions were to keep their heads well below the sides and when Wesley climbed into the engine and looked back, the trucks looked as empty as they had been before. He pulled the hinged cab roof forward over his head. The windows were so dusty that he could see little more than the lights and the shiny rails ahead. He inserted the key and turned it. Nothing happened. He turned it backwards and forwards again and again, but it made no difference. Katie was in the first truck behind him with Sargazzo and Christmas. He pushed the roof back and called quietly back to her.

"Won't go Katie. I turn the key and nothing happens."

"Turn it again and try pushing the lever," she called back. "It's electric. The key probably just unlocks it. Try."

Wesley did as she suggested. He pushed the lever and a deep buzzing started. The engine began to move. He pulled the roof back down. The trucks behind him clanked as their couplings tightened and slowly, with the engine whining loudly, the whole train began to move up the tunnel.

32
Frank

After the rain, the ground around the huts in the quarry compound was muddy and pocked with bootprints from where the prisoners had assembled before being locked in for the night. The only lights were those that shone from the windows of the two huts that housed the guards. Everything else was in darkness. It was quiet and a light breeze chilled the damp air. A hungry fox barked from the stony hillside of the crater.

Two guards walked, one behind the other, along a line of planks laid over the mud, checking that all was quiet in the locked huts where the children were squeezed, two to a bed, in the homemade wooden bunks.

"I'll be glad to be leaving," said one. "Saint Terresas sounds like a breath of fresh air after this place. Decent houses there, so they say."

"Decent food too," said the other. "And no more kids. I heard that the new workers there are easy. Had some kind of drug or something. Makes them do whatever you tell 'em without any bother."

"What, *anything*?"

"So I heard."

"Are we all going there, or what?"

"Just a few'll stay at the tunnels apparently, as a garrison. Same as the one by the bridge. Drummer reckons that it'll be shifts like. A few weeks at the garrison and then back to Saint Terresas."

"'Bout time I say. I'm fed up with kids. Especially now with all these new ones from the city. Where they all going to go anyway?"

"Tunnels, Drummer thinks. Don't know what they're going

to do with 'em. Get rid of them I say. I don't want to sound cruel but there's no room for sentiment, not these days. We wouldn't have survived any other way."

They approached the guard huts and reached a point where the pathway of planks forked and led off to the doorways of each. The two men were billeted one in each hut and they stepped onto their separate boards. One of them yawned, and as if it were catching the other yawned too.

"Night then Frank."

"Night Vic. See you in the…" The guard cut himself short and cocked his head to one side. "You hear that?"

"Yeah. Sounds like the train."

"What's it doing this time of night?"

"Dunno."

They listened again. The distinctive wine of the engine, and the dull clap of the truck wheels crossing the joins in the tracks, came and went on the breeze.

"Parking it here? Maybe to take the kids in the morning?"

"Could be. Can't think what else. Not supposed to be any more ore going."

Vic snorted with annoyance. "Better go and open the gate."

"I'll do it. I got the keys," replied Frank. "No point in the two of us."

"Sure?"

"Yeah. See you tomorrow."

Wesley's hand on the driving lever glowed green from the light of the dials. He peered forward through the dusty windscreen of the cab. Since the end of the tunnel, where the guard had waved him through with hardly a glance, he had been driving through almost complete darkness. Thick clouds veiled the moon. Occasionally they thinned enough to reveal a misty round glow, which illuminated no more than the horizon of the hills to his left and the grey edges of the trucks that rattled along behind him. He wondered how the tunnel children would be reacting to their first experience of being outside for so many years. He imagined, from his own experience, that they would be excited and frightened at the same time. Some of them had been badly shaken by their experience in The Pit. He hoped that they would all be able to stick to the plan; that whatever happened, they were to stay quiet, down in the bottom of the trucks.

By the time he noticed the lights from the guard's huts in the compound, the train was almost there. He squinted through the windscreen. A guard was approaching the gate. Stopping now, outside the compound as he had planned, would arouse suspicion. The man would surely come out to talk to him. His decision was so instantaneous that he hardly realized what he was doing. It was almost as if somebody else had made it for him. He pushed the horn twice and two loud hoots blared above the sound of the engine. The guard broke into a trot, quickly opened the gate, and Wesley drove through into the compound. He saw heads appear at one of the lighted windows, watch for a while, and then draw back inside. He had no idea of how far the track ran on and it was too dark to see on past the huts. Peering back through the dusty rear window to see that all the trucks had passed through the gate, he bought the train squealing and clanking to a halt.

The guard walked past the trucks and up to the engine. Wesley had no idea what to do. He sat still with the cab roof closed.

"You alright in there?" said the guard after a while.

"Fine," Wesley replied, trying to keep his voice low.

"This for the kids tomorrow?"

"Yes," said Wesley, not fully understanding the question.

"You coming in or what then?"

"In a while." Wesley knew his voice was unconvincing.

"Who are you?"

"Drummer." The name sprang to Wesley's mind.

There was a pause and then the guard lifted back the cab roof.

"What're you doing?" he said, puzzled.

"I'm... I'm one of them who... who's allowed to drive the train now."

"Come 'ere." The guard reached in and grabbed Wesley's arm. "I think you've got a bit of explaining to do, you have."

The guard pulled at his arm and then suddenly let go and fell backwards to the ground. Sargazzo held him down with one paw, his muzzle inches from the man's face, the sides of his mouth pulled up showing his white teeth.

"Don't say a word," Christmas leaped down from the truck. "Or he'll bite. It's what he does. Bites if you speak... if he doesn't like you."

The guard lay trembling beneath Sargazzo's paw, eyes wide open and mouth tightly closed."

Wesley quickly stepped down and Katie climbed out of the truck behind him.

"Where are the children?" Wesley crouched down beside the guard.

A dribble of saliva drooled from Sargazzo's mouth onto the man's cheek. His eyeballs looked sideways at one of the long huts.

"Is it locked?"

The man gave a tiny nod of his head.

"You got the key?"

He nodded again.

"Then give it to me."

"But don't move too fast," added Christmas. "The dog might, you know…"

"Bite your face," Katie finished for her. "And once he starts it's impossible to stop him."

The guard reached carefully down to his belt and unclipped a ring of keys. Wesley took them slowly, acting out the bluff that the dog was jumpy and unpredictable.

"Stay Sargazzo," he ordered. "Keep him down." He glanced at Christmas, her shoulders were little higher than the great dog's back but she showed no fear. "Do you think you could stop him biting?" he said to her. "Until we get back?"

"Think so," she replied. "So long as… what's your name?" she said to the guard.

The man just gave a small shake of the head.

"Well so long as you don't move… at all."

Wesley and Katie gave the huts with the lighted windows a wide berth. They squelched across the mud to the long hut, unlocked the door and tip toed in. The light from the guard's huts shone weakly through the barred windows. All the children were awake. They had heard the train hoot and had watched everything from the windows. Now they were ready and eager to go. Red gave Wesley a friendly punch on the arm.

"You're a goodun," he whispered.

Without a word, the children from the hut moved as quietly as they could over the muddy ground to the train. Dozens of heads poked above the rims of the trucks, watching. Wesley and Katie waved everyone out of the trucks.

"Out of the gate and up the line. Keep together. Pass it on," they whispered to the children nearest to them. The message spread fast and Katie stood by the gate, waving children through and away up the line.

"Seventy-two," she said to herself under her breath.

Christmas, Sargazzo and the guard were where Wesley had left them. Martin had joined them.

"What we going to do with him," Wesley whispered to him. "We can't, you know, kill him. And we can't leave him."

"Tie him up?"

"No rope or anything."

"'Cos we kindly left it for Spider."

"Then he'll have to come with us," said Wesley. "Least some of the way."

Wesley turned to Christmas. "The man's coming with us. Would you be able to keep Sargazzo from attacking him? So long as he doesn't talk or run?"

"No problem," said Christmas. "Up man," she ordered the guard. "And put your hands on your head. Be warned, this dog'll tear your throat out if you don't do exactly as I tell you."

With no sound other than their feet sucking in the mud, all of the children made their way out of the compound and along the railway track. Sargazzo and Christmas walked among them with the guard. Wesley, Katie and Martin caught up with Red and Jupiter.

"Where's your others?" Jupiter asked Katie. "The Janis woman and your Grandad."

"Grandpa's caught," Katie replied. "Janis has gone to help him."

"Crowmen got 'im?"

"Yes, the Crowmen," said Katie.

"You get to the Terresas place?" asked Red.

"That's where he got caught," replied Katie, and added looking at Wesley. "I want to go back there to get him."

"You talking different Katie." chuckled Jupiter. "You talking different."

"Well… I am different," said Katie. "I'm the same, but different too."

"What we all gonna do?" said Red. "Us 'Versty kids can t go back now, Crowmen know our places. We led 'em away from the Talkers though. We ain't never gonna let 'em find the Talkers. Where you gonna go now?"

"The bridge," said Wesley. "We need to cross it and go north. It's safer up there. And I'm going with Katie." He looked aside to her. "To see what's happening at St Terresas."

"Why go on the bridge?" said Red. "They'll see you."

"Because north of here, on this side of the river, is an Order garrison, the Crowmen that is, and even if we got past that, the next place up, where there's some crossing stones, you can't get down to because there's a cliff... it goes all the way along that side of the estuary. You'd have to go miles further up to cross."

"You just gonna walk over?"

"Yeah," said Wesley. "We're going to walk over. In the dark." he paused and then continued. "Red? Why don't you come? All of you."

After they'd walked for an hour, the message was sent out to stop and gather together for a meeting. The wind had risen and the clouds, like a ragged black petticoat, passed quickly across the moon. The guard had been walking in dread of Sargazzo. The great dog seemed to completely understand what was required of him and never left the man's side. Christmas, Martin and Sargazzo took him to one side where he would be out of earshot.

It was quickly agreed that everyone should stay together, at least until they were on the west side of the estuary. They would keep walking and try to cross the bridge before dawn, before the alarm was raised in the compound. The problem was how to know what direction to walk in. It was Katie who had the answer. She could roughly tell, by the time, and where the moon was, in what direction the estuary lay. When they reached it, it would be possible to see the bridge upstream and they could walk up to it.

" Bridge might be guarded. We won't know in the dark," said Red.

"We've been under it," said Wesley. "Twice. No one shot at us or anything... it was night, each time."

"Ask the guard," said Jupiter.

"How would we know what he says is true?" said Red. "Could be he'd lie, just to get us trapped. We wouldn't know, nor would the dog."

"Well least let's try it," said Jupiter. "See if we think he's lying or not."

The guard was bought back, Sargazzo at his side, into the middle of the children.

"What's your name?" asked Wesley.

"You can talk now," said Christmas to the guard. "Sargazzo knows when he can and when he can't attack."

The guard looked nervously at the dog. "Frank," he replied quietly.

"Frank," echoed Red, standing with his arms folded. "We want to know, Frank, if the bridge is guarded at night."

"And if you lie," Christmas added. "The dog'll know straight away."

"I..." The guard cleared his throat. "Er, I don't think so. Well, not as far as I know. Please, could the dog just... back off a little."

"No," said Red sharply. There was a murmur of pleasure from amongst the tunnel children. They'd never seen anyone talk to a guard like that.

"How do we know that you're tellin' the truth?" Red continued.

Christmas leaned on Sargazzo, pushing him against the guard's leg.

"I am," he said shakily.

"Then why you shakin'?" said Red.

"Because I'm scared of dogs," said the man.

"Katie?" said Wesley. "How long have we got till sunrise?"

She crouched down out of the wind and looked at her watches in the flame of a lighter. "Seven hours Wesley."

"So let's walk for three and a half hours and then let Frank go," suggested Wesley. "By the time he gets back it'll be light anyway, the alarm will have been raised."

"But now he knows where we're going," said Martin. "Can't we, I don't know, tie him up so'as it takes a long time for him to get loose?"

"He could get loose really quickly or he might never get the knots undone," said Katie. "Then he'd just die."

"Tie 'em tight then," said Red.

"No rope anyway," said Katie.

"Then he'll have to come with us then," said Wesley. "For three and a half hours. What else can we do?"

Red reluctantly agreed and there were no more objections. The children set off in single file, led by Katie, away from the railway track and down through the fields in the moonlight that came and went with the scudding clouds.

At three o'clock, Frank was released. He ran back the way they had come, soon slowing to a walk, out of breath, when he was sure that there was a safe distance between him and the dog. The children filed on into the night, like a stealthy centipede, winding beside hedges and along overgrown tracks and lanes. So astonished and excited were they at all that had happened to them, they hardy noticed their empty bellies and tired legs. But by the time they reached the estuary and saw the bridge at least five miles upstream, it was light and they grew nervous. They knew that they would have to cross it by day.

33
"Good, very good…"

Dove walked briskly into the outer office, buttoning up his freshly laundered military jacket.

"Major Phillips from the quarry has phoned you four times already this morning Mr. Dove," said Elizabeth immediately, sitting importantly in Janis's old chair. "Said it was very urgent."

"Phillips? Get him on the line for me then, Elizabeth."

He walked on through into his office and sat down at his desk. The white cat lay curled in the leather armchair. It opened one green eye and slowly closed it again. The phone rang.

"Dove… Ah yes, Phillips, what can I do for you?"

For a while he just listened, fiddling with the model airship with his free hand.

"I see," he said. "And who actually opened the gates?… No, can't put a face to the name. No doubt I will when I see him. And you say he went with them?… As a hostage? Of children?… What? A dog? Phillips, bring all your men back here, straight away. I shall want to speak to you all. Goodbye."

He replaced the phone and sat looking directly at the wall in front of him. There was no expression on his face, until presently, the corners of his mouth twitched into a slight smile. He pushed the intercom button.

"Elizabeth?" he said calmly. "Get Commander Morton from the North Garrison on the line please."

He replaced the handset and walked over to the window where he straightened his cuffs and ran his finger round the inside of his starched collar. It was a blustery morning with a ceiling of high monotonous flat cloud. The long wild grasses in the fields at the bottom of the hill rippled like a silky sea. But Dove was looking beyond them. He picked up the silver binoculars from the windowsill and focused them on the skyline north of the city. The towers of the suspension bridge were just visible, four stubby white columns against the grey smudge of the horizon, the mountains in the north. He scanned the landscape in front of the bridge. It was too far away to see anything but the green mass of treetops. The phone rang again. He turned, leaned forward over the back of his chair and picked it up.

"Morton? "Good. Have you been in contact with the men returning from Saint Terresas?... Where are they now?... Good, very good. Who's in charge?... Blackmoor. Contact him please. I want him and his men to wait on the western approach to the bridge until further orders. As for yourself, assemble your men and have them ready to cross from the east within the hour. They must not be visible. Understand?... Good. I shall be joining you there shortly and you will receive further orders then. That is all."

He put down the phone and pushed the intercom again.

"Elizabeth? Please contact the Airship Port immediately and tell someone to bring the car up here. Thank you. Oh and find Pearson, he's supposed to have been here by now."

Dove clutched his fingers together and cracked his knuckles. He walked over to the armchair, crouched down and stroked the cat's head with one finger. The cat began to purr.

"Shall I tell you what I'm going to do?" he said softly. "I'm going to trap our little birds, in a cage. And because there's no floor in the cage they're going to go out through the bottom. And because they can't fly they're going to fall, all the way," he ran his finger down the cat's spine, "down into the water."

330

34
Dove's Trap

The children climbed up an embankment and onto the old road. The bridge reached out before them, cradled between the long curving cables that hung from the towers. It was deserted. At the far end, over half a mile distant, the road snaked away westwards, up into the cover of pinewoods. The children set off, walking in groups, talking excitedly.

It was some distance to the first pair of pillars and by the time they had reached them, they felt the keenness of the wind that blew down the river. It whistled in the thick wires that held the roadway to the cables above. Fifty yards ahead was the missing section of roadway where the only ways across were the narrow strips of tarmac that remained at the edge alongside the railings. Wesley heard a drone, coming and going in the wind. The Titus, half a mile or so downstream and angled into the wind, was flying west across the estuary. The children all turned to watch. Wesley, Sargazzo at his heels, ran over to Red and Jupiter.

"They must have seen us," he said.

"Yeah, we seen that thing before," said Jupiter. "The Crow Balloon. Over the city. Looking for us they were."

"We should run," said Wesley. "Least, once we've got past the hole."

At a shout from one of the children at the back, everyone turned. Behind them, at the start of the bridge, a line of soldiers blocked the road. Between them, in the middle, was a car. To the south, the airship droned on over the water. The children began to run, Katie ahead of them. She turned at the edge of the hole and shouted back.

"Along the sides. Go in single file. Hold tight to the railings."

But the front children stopped running before they reached her, looking beyond to the far end of the bridge. The children behind slowed and gathered up behind them. Katie walked back from the edge of the hole. Coming over the bridge from the other side, another line of soldiers walked towards them. The children looked one way and then the other. There were cries of alarm, they grouped together, shuffling inwards toward one another until they all stood, not knowing what to do, close to one of the concrete pillars. The twins stood at the edge of the group beside the railings.

"Wesley," Charlie called out and waved his arm in the air. "Here."

Wesley pushed his way through the children. Charlie was leaning out over the railings, looking down.

"Look," he said.

The side of the huge pillar fell vertically away down onto a narrow platform of exposed rock. The muddy waters of the incoming tide flowed swiftly past the rock edge, flecked with spray that the wind tore back from the tops of the waves. Fixed to the pillar, facing away from the soldiers with the car, was a rusty metal ladder that ran down to the rocks below.

"What do you think?" said Charlie.

Wesley held the rail tightly. He felt slightly dizzy with the thought of climbing down from such a height.

"Would you go down?" he said.

"Not if I had a choice."

"We don't have one."

Charlie took a deep breath and blew his cheeks out. "I'll help people on to the rungs then," he said.

"Wesley," Red called out to him. "What we gonna do?"

Inside Wesley a horrible feeling was growing. This was his fault. Going down the ladder was going to be terrifying. He had no idea how many children would be able to do it. He didn't want to be in charge. He'd risk climbing, but those who wouldn't would be captured. Was it better that a few of them, including himself, got away? Or should he stay with those who couldn't make it? It was him, after all, who bought them here. And besides, what about Sargazzo?

"Everybody," Wesley called, trying to sound confident.

"There's a ladder here. It's a long way down but... You can make it. It you stick to the rocks below the cliffs, there's a crossing a few miles up from here. Katie?"

"Here Wesley." Katie waved her arm up.

"What time's high tide?"

"Three forty-seven."

"How long's that?"

"Four hours and three minutes. But the rocks will be covered in two hours."

Back at the eastern end of the bridge Dove stood by the car, watching the group of children who had assembled beside the pillar. He watched with satisfaction as the soldiers advanced from the other end. He watched the Titus, admiring the way the ship turned gracefully beyond the far shore of the estuary and flew towards the other end of the bridge.

"Who ordered the ship up Morton?" he asked the commander at his side.

"Thought you would have done Sir," the man replied.

"No. I didn't. But it's a good initiative. I will, however, have to speak to whoever is responsible." He pulled some leather gloves on, swung in to the passenger's seat of the car and reached for the short wave radio set on the dashboard. Before his fingers had reached it, it crackled into life.

"*Calling Colonel Dove. Blackmoor to Colonel Dove.*"

"Dove here Blackmoor. Everything all right on your side of the bridge?"

"Sir, they're climbing down the side of the tower."

"What? How?"

"On the ladder Sir"

"On the double then Blackmoor. Get your men up to the edge."

"Yes Sir."

Dove leaned out of the car window. "Order your men forward Morton," he commanded. "Time to close the cage, quickly."

"Hold tight and don't look down," said Charlie as he helped a girl over the railings onto the ladder. Six other children climbed slowly down beneath her. The wind tugged at their hair and clothes. The next to go, one of the youngest, a boy of no more than ten years old, leaned over the railings and looked down.

"Charlie," he whimpered. "Couldn't you come down with me… Please?"

"You're going to be ok Micky. Come on," Charlie helped the trembling boy over the railings. "You can do it Micky. Go on, down you go."

The boy clung to the ladder without moving. There was a stir from the children behind Charlie.

"They're coming," someone said.

"Micky," said Charlie. "Just imagine it's a short ladder that keeps on going. Look straight at the wall. That's it, and another step."

The boy began to descend. Christmas was next. She climbed onto the ladder with her teddy bear tucked into the back of her trousers. She began whistling. The wind pulled the notes from her mouth as she followed the boy beneath her.

Dove's car proceeded at the running pace of the soldiers. The soldiers from the other side were nearing the edge of the hole. Behind them, the drone of the airship engines got louder. More children mounted the ladder. The first had reached the bottom and had begun running northwards, along the rocks, under the shadow of the cliffs. Another identical ladder was found on the pillar on the other side and some of the children dashed over to it. Life underground had been tough and risky and now, with the dread of being caught, the children found the courage and determination they needed. They climbed faster and with more confidence than Wesley had thought possible, but the distance between the soldiers and the remaining children was closing fast. Jupiter climbed onto the ladder, leaving only Wesley, Red and eight others on his side. The pitch of the Titus's engines rose suddenly, and the drone became a roar, drowning out the tramping feet of the soldiers.

"What's going on?" shouted Dove to the driver. "Stop the car." He shouted out of the window to Morton. "Wait. Stop the advance." He opened the door and jumped out. "What the hell is going on?"

The Titus had turned towards them from the other side of the bridge. It had flown between the pillars and with its engines at full throttle, was flying at road level, its gondola only inches above the tarmac. Two bombs hung beneath each engine. The wind buffeted it from the side, sending it bouncing against the wires, but it kept coming, its long mooring ropes trailing along behind it. The soldiers in front of it began to run but they were no match for the airship's speed. They reached the edge of the hole. Some clawed at the wires on the wind-ward side, hoping not to be hit. Others leapt off, down into the salty tide that churned up the estuary. The gondola scraped along the ground sending up a shower of sparks. When it reached the hole, the engines slowed and it rose briefly up, its black nose cone rearing above the remaining children. The gondola passed over the hole and landed on the road with a crash. All the children had scrambled onto the ladders, as closely as they could, except for Wesley. He stood cowering against the rail with Sargazzo. A rifle shot rang out, followed by a fierce command.

"Do. Not. Shoot!" It was Dove. "Not the Titus. She's filled with hydrogen."

The airship blew sideways against the wires on the side of the road. It rocked and bucked in the wind. The engines were burbling at their slowest speed, but the propellers were still a blur. The door of the gondola opened and Sargazzo bounded forward. Anguillaro leaned out and waved.

"Mr. Pike," he shouted. "Get over here."

Wesley ran across, his pack bouncing against his shoulder. Anguillaro half helped, half dragged him through the door, slammed it shut and sat quickly back in the pilot's seat. He pulled back the throttles and the engines roared. Wesley gripped the back of the co-pilot's seat and swung himself round into it. Sargazzo was wagging his tail so hard it seemed as if his whole long body was wagging. He slurped Anguillaro's face with his great tongue.

"Eh! Can't you see I'm driving?" Anguillaro shouted above the engines. "Ha! My dog. Yes. And my good friend Wesley Pike. Welcome aboard. Hold tight. Bridges are very tricky. Ha!"

He pulled on the controls and the ship accelerated forwards between the pillars and lifted slightly. The soldiers dropped to the ground or scattered. Dove dived back into the car. Seconds later the floor of the gondola crunched into its windscreen and scraped across the roof, shattering the side windows. The airship nosed upwards and Anguillaro turned it north, into the wind, with the engines on full power.

Far below, the tide was licking at the bottom of the ladders. Wesley saw the last of the children run through the water and follow the rest along the rocks beneath the cliffs. The water pushed relentlessly in from the sea. The mud flats had all but disappeared and there were places where the rocky edge beneath the cliff was no more than a few feet wide. On the other side of the water, some of the soldiers from the western side who had stayed on the bridge, were now running north-wards along the far bank towards the other end of The One Hundred Stones crossing. The airship was making slow progress against the wind. Anguillaro swayed sharply forward and backwards in his seat, rocking the gondola.

"Come on, come on. You big old gas bag," he urged the craft forward, shouting above the din of the engines. "This as fast as you can go for me? Eh? Just overtake them." He looked down to the left at the running soldiers. "We can drop them a present."

Sargazzo sat between him and Wesley, panting hard with his jaw open and his huge tongue lolling out of the side. Wesley looked back. They had not come very far. He saw Dove run out onto the bridge. He had a box in his hand. He reached the broken section and edged along the side until he reached a point above the fastest moving current below. He took a bottle from the box, leaned over the rail and emptied the contents over the side. Wisps of liquid, scattered by the wind, fell to the water below.

The soldiers on the west bank were ahead of the children, and the first of them had arrived at the One Hundred Stones and taken up positions in the reeds. Anguillaro took the airship lower where the wind was not so strong. It made things little better. The first three children had arrived at the stones and were beginning to make their way across.

Wesley looked down at the water, now less than thirty feet below them and saw a band of dense shadow, moving rapidly up the estuary from the bridge. It sought out the creeks and rivulets along the banks and swept into them, swallowing them in its blackness. The main band of darkness pushed up towards The One Hundred Stones like a crooked rainbow of night, overtaking the airship, leaving all the water that was in its wake dull and dark.

More children were on the crossing now, jumping from one stone to another. All of the soldiers had arrived and had hidden in the wildly swaying reeds. The wind strengthened still more, whipping up spray from the water behind the children who were struggling to keep their balance, sometimes two on a stone, in some places three. The airship was making no headway at all now and one of the overheated engines, its exhaust pipes glowing red, spluttered and seized. The ship lurched round immediately, catching the wind in its side, sending Sargazzo and Wesley tumbling to the floor. It began to travel backwards, rocking and swaying out of control.

"Out!" shouted Anguillaro. He reached over with one hand and lifted Wesley by the arm back over his seat and pushed him towards the door. Wesley slid across the floor. He reached back and grabbed the strap of his bag, dragged it towards him and unfastened the flap. He pulled out the Lightwater. Anguillaro slithered over to him and kicked the door open.

"Wait!" screamed Wesley. He opened the bottle and held it out of the door. The Water cascaded down from the spinning gondola and disappeared onto the darkened seawater. Before the bottle had emptied, the floor tipped violently again. Sargazzo slid into Wesley, his paws scrabbling for grip, and they both fell from the door.

The water flew up to meet him and then he was under, struggling not to breathe. It was completely dark. He didn't know which way up he was. He felt himself being swirled around by the current. He was bursting to breathe and he knew that in a few more seconds he would have to. He felt a hand touch his neck and suddenly he was being pulled through the water by his collar. Then he was up. It was Anguillaro. He gasped, gulping at the air, floundering and spitting water. Anguillaro let go of him. The water around them felt thick and heavy and Wesley felt himself begin to sink again. He resisted feebly, not quite sure anymore what he was doing or where he was. He felt Anguillaro's hand pull him up once more, but it was not the strong pull of before, rather just a tug, just enough to bring Wesley's face to the surface. He breathed in another lungful of air and then sank again into the dark water.

He hadn't realized that his eyes were open until he saw speckles of bright light in the water in front of him. They rushed forward and engulfed him. Bubbles of light, brilliantly shiny, washed over him. He kicked hard and broke the surface again. Anguillaro burst up beside him. They were swimming in a slowly expanding area of lighter coloured water. The edges glowed and sparkled fiercely against a rim of darkness. Other areas of light were spreading, joining up, seeking out patches of darkness and soaking them up.

Wesley and Anguillaro were being swept upstream towards The One Hundred Stones while the Titus was blowing wildly back towards the bridge where Dove still stood gripping the rails. He began edging back along the side towards where the roadway was complete, then broke into a desperate run. The Titus, heading straight for him, turned and turned until it hit the wires of the bridge. For a brief second it wobbled and then erupted in a fireball that burst out in all directions. It grew from within itself with swirling gouts of dark flame, getting bigger and bigger. The noise thundered across the water and a rush of hot air followed, flattening the waves and scalding Wesley's face.

A huge plume of dark smoke replaced the fireball and the wind rushed into it sending it streaming downstream towards the sea. Wesley was struggling to stay afloat. Anguillaro grabbed his collar again and in one movement Wesley was pulled onto the man's long back. His huge hands scooped at the water like paddles and his body snaked from side to side as he swam with the tide towards the stones. At least half of the children had fallen into the water. Some clung to the stones while others floundered in the current upstream. Some of the children had made it across. What the others could not see, and Wesley and Anguillaro could, was that those who had crossed were lying face down on the ground with their hands over their heads, being held at gunpoint. Wesley shouted into the wind but neither the children or the soldiers heard him. Anguillaro struck out harder and Wesley clung on. They were approaching the stones fast. There was a gunshot, and then several more. The children on the stones crouched down, looking to see where the shots had come from. The soldiers were also looking. When they realized what was happening, they broke into confusion. Horse riders galloped down the west bank towards them, rifles in their hands, firing warning shots into the air. They thundered across the springy turf and wheeled round in amongst the soldiers. Clods of grass and earth flicked up into the air from the horses hooves and the soldiers scrambled away in fear and confusion, trying to avoid being trampled. High in their saddles, the riders trained their guns on them and within seconds, it was over, the soldiers too taken by surprise to do anything but drop their weapons and surrender.

By the time Anguillaro reached the stones, the soldiers were sitting, hands on their heads, under the watchful eye of some of the mounted riders. Others had dismounted and were helping the children out of the water and over the stones. Anguillaro grabbed one of the stepping-stones and Wesley climbed onto it. The great man heaved himself up beside him and stood, water pouring off his hair and clothes. He scanned the river upstream for children who had fallen in. They seemed to have all reached the side and were now pushing their way through the rushes.

He turned back and looked down the estuary towards the bridge. There was a faint shout on the wind and he spun back. Leaning forward he narrowed his eyes, searching for the source of the voice. Then he scissored down on to his heels, leaned forward and dived. The brown water, rushing up between the stones, closed over him. Wesley heard the voice cry out again. This time the wind carried it clearly to him and he knew it was Christmas, somewhere, being swept along by the current. Far upstream he caught sight of her head. She disappeared again and then Anguillaro broke the surface not twenty feet from her. He pushed through the water with astonishing speed and grabbed her, hoisting her onto his back as he had done with Wesley and swam to the shore.

Wesley sat down on the stone and drew his knees up. He was cold but not shivering. Inside, in the core of himself, he felt warm. He looked down the estuary. The entire centre of the bridge was missing. All that remained of the roadway and cables, hung from the towers at each end in a twisted mass of metal and slabs of concrete. Small streams of smoke blew away downwind from the wreckage, and the water of the tide stretched from one side of it to the other. Of the Titus, there was nothing to be seen.

He felt the smooth wet surface of the stone with his hand.

*He is on the beach. He has a child's spade and he is holding it across his lap as he sits, knees drawn up, on a rock beside the sand. His father is finishing the sandcastle they have made and his mother is walking up from the sea, flicking her wet hair from her face, laughing. And he feels saf*e. And all he can hear is water, rushing.

35
The leaving Day

Anguillaro could find no trace of Sargazzo. He spent days wandering the shoreline of the estuary alone, spending little time at the camp that had been set up by the old lodge. It was Christmas who persuaded him to stop looking. He held a quiet ceremony down by the water's edge, attended by Wesley and Katie. Katie had made a wreath of wild roses that Anguillaro threw far out onto the surface of the outgoing tide. Long after it had drifted from sight, Anguillaro remained, standing silently, looking out across the water. Only after the sun had set did he rejoin his companions around the camp fire.

Janis, who had been among the riders who had swept down on the soldiers, rode back to St Terresas the next day and returned with Mikhail. The old man sought out Katie immediately and wept with joy to find that the Lightwater had unlocked the part of her that had lain inaccessible for so many years. He was in good spirits but tired. The one remaining chair from the lodge house was bought out for him and he spent the following days resting, sitting looking out over the estuary from the campsite.

The weather brightened and the warm sun seeped into the pale skin of the tunnel children. Wesley, Katie and Janis spent time walking together. They pressed each other for every detail of what had happened after they had separated on the river-bank. Janis had successfully placed the bottle of Lightwater into the well. She had then risked delivering vegetables to the Abbot's Kitchen where she had poured a portion of the old tainted well water into the water supply kept strictly for the soldiers. It had not taken long for the tables to turn and the captors turned to captives.

The soldiers who had surrendered at the crossing were sent back over The One Hundred Stones to the eastern side of the estuary. The others, from Saint Terresas, including Doctor Thornberry and Max, arrived the following day at the camp. They needed no guarding. Under the influence of the Darkwater they did whatever was asked of them and they sat quietly in groups, docile and aimless. Janis had kept a portion of Lightwater and from it Mikhail had made more, using the water from the well at Saint Terresas and the light from the Abbey window. She gave each of the prisoners a sip of the new Lightwater before they too were sent over the stones. Wesley and Mikhail helped, organizing the prisoners into lines, moving them forward and showing them the path through the reeds. Some even waved back from the far side before setting off beneath the cliffs. When it came to the turn of Max and the Doctor, Janis hesitated.

"After all they've done," she said to Mikhail. "Is it right to give these two back their former selves. Is it wise even?"

"To deny them the Lightwater," he replied. "Means releasing a couple of empty headed hopeless cases to wander off aimlessly. Without anyone to look after them they'd probably starve to death." He sighed. "I have no wish to kill anyone, and that's what we would be doing. I think I know you well enough now Janis. You have no wish to either."

Janis looked hard at the Doctor standing in front of her. It was hard to believe that he was cruel and ruthless. He stood quietly, hands hanging limply at his sides, looking dolefully at her, seemingly unaware that Janis held his future in the glass of water in her hand.

"Drink this," she said, thrusting the glass at him and turning her attention to Max.

"Why, Max?" she said.

"Why what," he replied in a dull voice.

"Why?…" Janis tensed with barely held anger. "Why did you betray us? How could you be so friendly when all the time you… you were on the other side? We trusted you. Didn't you feel anything?"

"Janis," he replied, "I remember you from somewhere." He shook his head and then seemed to lose the thread of his thought. He gazed blankly out over the estuary and said nothing.

"Just give it to him," said Mikhail gently. "Send him on his way."

Janis looked at the ground for a minute and then back up at Max. She held the glass out to him, her hand trembling. He took it and drank.

Max shuffled off behind the Doctor through the reeds to the stones. When he reached the first stone he stopped for a moment and then turned and walked slowly back.

"I remember you," he said to Wesley. "In that house, upstairs, the skeletons on the bed… and the car." He shook his head sharply, as if trying to dislodge something in his mind.

"You found that car. It's coming back to me now. Lightwater, of course, I remember."

"We trusted you Max," said Wesley. "We believed you were our friend. We went back to try to find you, at the University. But you were faking it, all the time, weren't you."

"Faking it." Max sighed. "Yes, I was. I liked you though, I wasn't faking that." He glanced at Mikhail and Janis and then looked at the ground. "I liked you all. S'just that… I wanted to be on the winning side. Dove offered me a reward, a house, promotion, security. It was too good to turn down, and I couldn't see how you could possibly win. Simple as that. Stupid of me, stupid."

He turned and walked away, back through the reeds and over the stones.

"I'll try to forgive him," said Janis. "Even just for my own sake. I don't want to be living with anger and resentment inside myself." She brightened and turned to Mikhail and Wesley. "I suppose I was a spy myself once. Faking it, just like Max did. Though I was never sure if we were going to be the winning side or not."

"I liked Max," said Wesley, watching him go. "Part of me still sort of does. S'funny, liking and disliking someone at the same time. I wonder if we'll ever see him again?"

"Who knows," said Mikhail. "Chances are though, with so few people left, one day we will."

On a sunny day in May the camp was packed up and everyone prepared to leave. Wesley found Anguillaro inspecting the old range in the lodge house.

"Ah. Mr. Pike. How are you today? Ready to go?"

"Yeah, pretty much," said Wesley.

"And *where* have you decided to go, eh?"

"I'm going with Mikhail and Katie. We're going to find a house in Saint Terresas."

"Very good, very good. Janis will be there, no?"

"Yes, and the tunnel children. They've all been adopted by families there."

"Mmm. Good."

"What about you Laro?"

"Me?" Anguillaro looked around the old dusty old kitchen. "I think I will stay… right here. What you think? This house. Is a good place, no? I like it. Close to the river. Plenty of nice mud for those tasty little eels." He sighed. "Besides, my friend, this place, is where Sargazzo is. I will not leave him. And anyway, it will be good for someone to be here. Keep an eye open on the stones. See who cross over. If I don't like them, I will push them in the river! Ha!"

Wesley brightened. "I'll come and visit. Me and Katie."

"Visit? Yes! And you can bring Christmas with you. I can take you out in my new boat."

"You've got a new boat?"

"Oh yes. I found it on the mud. Very nice wooden boat, just right for me. Blue. Is called Bluebird."

Wesley heard Jupiter calling him. He ran down to the edge of the rushes where the City Children were gathered, preparing to cross the stones. Katie and Mikhail were among them saying their farewells.

Jupiter and Red broke away and walked towards him.

"We going now," said Red.

"Back to the city? You decided?" asked Wesley.

"Yeah, we going back. Talkers are there. Can't leave them. And the dogs too. We gotta find 'em. 'Member them?"

"Yeah," said Wesley. "The little white dogs, I remember."

"We gonna live upstairs now. Move into some of them big houses."

"What about food?"

"We still got plenty," said Jupiter. "And we're gonna start tradin'. Janis and them are gonna send stuff down. And we're gonna send stuff back. Stuff we got stored away. Where you going then?"

"Saint Terresas."

"Then we'll see you," said Red. "On tradin' trips."

"Yeah." Wesley replied. He wasn't comfortable saying goodbye and it made it easier to think that he might see Red and Jupiter again soon.

"See you then," he said simply to them both.

Jupiter just smiled, nodded and walked away.

"Yeah, see you," said Red. "And… you know… thanks." The City Children filed over The One Hundred Stones. Wesley, Katie and Mikhail climbed a grassy bank above where the camp had been and watched them, small figures on the rocks beneath the far cliffs, slowly moving southwards, back towards the city. The tide followed them down, sucking the river water away to the sea.

"Mikhail?" said Wesley. "How come the whole sea isn't all Lightwater now? And all the rain and everything? It took over the estuary, where does it stop?"

"It's powerful stuff Wesley, but I suppose the seas and oceans are a power of their own too. Far greater than Light or Darkwater, thank goodness. Imagine if they were not. Lightwater, released anywhere, would affect all water, everywhere, because all water mixes together at some time or other on the planet. Sounds wonderful. But suppose the same were to happen with Darkwater. I think it's best that Mother Earth has final control over these things." He swept his arm out at the distance. "Planet earth looks after herself. Even after all of this destruction, she'll recover, nature will find a new balance, even if it's not the same as it was before."

Anguillaro and Janis climbed the bank and joined them. For a while the five of them sat, comfortably silent, looking out over the estuary. A flock of black-headed gulls landed on the newly exposed mud below the One Hundred Stones. Wild bees buzzed zig-zag paths through the clover on the bank, and the long grasses, already forming heads of seed, waved gently in the breeze.

"Do you think," said Wesley after a time. "That there are other people alive, I mean in other places around the world?"

"Of course," replied Anguillaro. "There will be others. Somewhere."

"Could even be nearer than we think," said Janis. "People asking the exact same question. People just like us. I think we'll find them, in time."

"Laro?" said Katie. "I've got your ring here."

She held out her hand to him, the eel ring on her palm.

"Ha!" said Anguillaro. "My ring. Thank you for looking after it. Now I know you are all safe, I will take it back." He picked the ring from her hand and rolled it between his long fingers. "It reminds me of someone from long ago. Now, we must all look to the future, make new lives. But is good that we keep a little place." He tapped his chest. "Somewhere in here. For those special ones. Ones that once we did love. Oh yes."